VICIOUS KARMA

To Terri Ruffin
Thanks for your support.

VICIOUS KARMA

A Mosee Love Mystery

Asa Allen- Showell

To order additional copies of this book, contact:
Image Press Publishers
P. O. Box 162 Somerdale, NJ 08330
856-783-9820
www.viciouskarma.com
asashowell@juno.com

Printed in the United States by
Morris Publishing
3212 E. Hwy 30
Kearney, NE 68847
1-800-650-7888

This book is dedicated to my sons:
Elias and Bryce Showell.

I want to thank my editors,
Cece Whitaker and Ms. Fordham; artist,
Keita Joynes for the cover design.

For my husband, Craig

1

I got an instant headache from the blazing sun's rays beating on my forehead. It felt like someone had taken a sharp knife and cut through my temples. I grabbed my head, feeling the throbbing sensations as I stepped inside the building. The security guard sat at the podium waving to me.

"Hello," he said with a smile.

I gave him a semi-wave, continuing to hold my tormented head.

I couldn't walk the flight of stairs as I usually do because of the pain in my head. I took the elevator instead. Riding the ancient elevator to the third floor felt like an eternity.

I opened the door with a disgusted expression on my face, looking at the twenty-five empty seats. Students have no respect for education, I thought.

I stood at the chalkboard, contemplating ending class early. No sense in lecturing to a classroom of half empty seats. I reviewed my criminal law notes for next week's final and dismissed class half an hour early. The students were happy and so was I.

I loosened my tie outside the John Jay building. Hearing the sound of my stomach growling, I imagined savoring the taste of fresh salami, ham and cappicalo with provolone cheese and a cold Pepsi to wash it down.

Despite the heat, I made the four-block hike to Jameson's deli. They're known for having the best deli meats in Manhattan. I made the hike during lunch hour traffic, walking bumper to bumper.

After I made the three block hike, I got into my black Volvo attempting to start the engine for the fifth time. Beads of sweat dripped from my forehead. My muscles were getting tight. I closed my eyes and said a prayer. Bingo! It started on the sixth try. There is a God after all.

Vicious Karma

The black Volvo was becoming an embarrassment to drive and the noise was drawing too much attention to me. Even the passengers and motorists had started giving me snarling looks as I passed them. I knew the muffler and catalytic converter needed fixing. Aside from car repairs, I was nearly three weeks behind in child support payments. Taxes, car repairs, and child support is half the battle. My head was pained from the thought of all those bills.

I turned around to the sound of a horn blowing behind me. A man in a red pick-up truck was yelling and giving me the finger.

"Move it asshole—some of us have places to go!" other motorists were cursing me with their looks. By two-thirty in the afternoon, when I arrived at the doorstep of my best friend, I was famished and exhausted from the heat. I hated to see what the remainder of summer had in store for us. It was only May and I was ready to pack my bags and head to a cooler climate.

Cedric lives in the exclusive section of Brooklyn, where crime is a hush word. Cedric answered the door, dressed in a Tommy Hilfiger sweat suit. He gave me a puzzling look when he saw me standing there.

"You glad to see me?" I asked.

"Yes . . . Mosee, I wasn't expecting any visitors today." He glanced at his watch. "I thought you had classes on Fridays."

"I do, but I let class out early, since my finals are next week." I became irritated, standing outside in the heat, debating over why I showed up at my friend's house unexpected. "Are you gonna let me in or what?"

I followed Cedric into the kitchen, placing the hoagies on the counter. Cedric had a half semicircle kitchen counter that covered seventy percent of his kitchen. The pot and pan hanging rack from the ceiling gave the kitchen a professional culinary look. His stove was black lacquer with a matching refrigerator, where a light fixture hung. "I brought you a sub for lunch."

"A sub?" Cedric looked surprised. "To what do I owe this special treat? Did I do something to deserve this?"

"No. I'm in a good mood; the weather is nice, and I'm off the entire summer. Besides, I haven't seen you in three weeks."

Cedric smiled. "I never turn down a free meal, brother."

"I have some beer in the refrigerator."

I went into the living room and sat on the Italian brown leather sofa. Cedric kept a meticulous apartment, right down to the shine on his hardwood floors. I always admired his fastidious persona.

"What's been up, Mosee?" he yelled from the kitchen.

"Nothing new—same old problems," I said, sighing before taking a bite of my sub. "Joyce wants more money. Be glad you're single, man."

Cedric shook his head in disgust as he walked into the living room.

"I wish you and Joyce would learn to get along. All those wasted years for what? Nothing," he said, pouring the beer into his favorite mug.

Cedric placed the mug on a coaster atop of his glass, granas lacquered steel table top. He returned to the kitchen and brought out two black serving trays. Everything Cedric did, he did with style. He believed in putting one hundred percent into whatever he did.

I always felt as if I were walking on eggshells when I came to my best friend's house despite our twenty year friendship.

Cedric's tidiness shows not only in his home, but also in how he dresses. His wardrobe and shoes were all color coordinated. His bedroom is large enough to fit two Queen bedroom sets, is always neat with it's matching gold and black tone comforter, sheets, and drapes and there is a large bathroom and a cozy little fireplace. It makes me want to vomit.

Cedric's house contains many classic paintings of Romare Bearden, and artwork from many of the places he has visited—

Kenya, Brazil, and Puerto Rico. Collecting art is a hobby he picked up while traveling.

"I've been thinking about starting my own business on the side."

"Let me guess. Private investigations, right?"

"Yeah, I think it's about time. I've been out of the loop for five years, now."

"Sounds good to me. You are good at what you do, why let your talents go to waste? You've been talking about this since you left the Bureau. Now five years have gone by."

I ate my hoagie with ease, sitting in the recliner. "You meet any women lately?" I asked changing the subject.

"No. The women I meet are so plastic:—hair, nails, makeup, and attitude. You name it, black women have it," he declared, taking another bite of his hoagie.

"You need to settle down and have a family."

Cedric shrugged his shoulders. "No rush. Men don't have a biological clock."

"Yeah, but who wants a baby at sixty? You'd be dead by the time the child's in high school," I said, taking a gulp of beer. "I'm serious, man. Your problem is you place too much emphasis on your career. That's why your relationships don't work. You're a workaholic."

Cedric's motivation and drive evoked feelings of admiration and jealousy. He was tenacious and resourceful. Important qualities I lacked. I'm what you call a slacker.

In between biting his hoagie, Cedric paused to swallow." You have a point, but women want men who got big bucks and when they find one, they complain. That's a black woman for you. I'm thinking about crossing over," he chuckles.

"I'm surprised I caught you at home on a Friday afternoon."

"Friday is the only day I work from my home—you know, catching up on paper work." Cedric smiled, a sly grin creeping across his face. "What about you; have you met anyone?"

"No. Just a few dates here and there," I said, nonchalantly scratching my eyebrows.

Cedric yelled excitement in his voice. "I know when you're lyin' because you always scratch your eyebrow. You've been doing that since we were kids."

I laughed. "All right I confess. I was dating this NYU professor. We met at an African Women's Writers seminar. I was impressed by her poise and intelligence."

"No bull shitting. Mosee, was she fine?" Cedric asked.

"Yeah, she put the "F" in the word fine; and she had a body too. After dating for five months, she became too possessive. She'd call me everyday, questioning me about my whereabouts, who I'm with, and what I'm doin'. I eventually changed my telephone number."

Cedric laughed aloud hysterically. "You must've put some moves on her to cause that type of reaction."

"We slept together a few times, but nothing serious. She was a true psychotic. After I changed my number, she would sit in her car in front of my house waiting for me to come home. I had to go to the police and put a restraining order on her. Man, after that incident, I'm thinking about taking a vow of celibacy."

Cedric frowned giving me a puzzling look. "Are you crazy man? I would never get that desperate."

"Just joking, I'm not crazy."

We sat around talking about politics and life and whatever subjects came to mind. One thing about Cedric, he could talk endlessly and you would never know it.

He looked at his watch and jumped up, mumbling. "It's five o'clock. I didn't notice the time. I hate to throw you out, but I have a date with this honey I met at a party two weeks ago."

"That's okay; I have to go, anyway. Call me later and fill me in on the details of your hot date."

Pulling into my driveway, the only thing I could think about is bed and watching a good HBO movie.

Once inside, I could see the flashing light from my answer machine. I pushed the play button. "Hello, Mo, this is Dee, give me a call when you get in? (Next message) "Mosee, it's me Joyce, I'm trying to be patient with you, but I haven't gotten a payment in three weeks. You're gonna force me to take you to court. I can't live on one payment this week and none the next. Also I need to know if you're going to take the girls for the summer."

After hearing that last message, I thought how wonderful it would be for people to go back in time and be able to erase all the errors in their life. The first day I laid eyes on Joyce, my ex-wife, was the start of my downfall, a wrong decision I had made that I have to contend with for the rest of my life.

After listening to the answering machine, I went to my bedroom down the hall. When I am not in the mood to hang up my clothes, my Lazy boy recliner comes in handy. I lay in bed pondering the endless possibilities of going into business for myself. The thoughts scared me about stepping out on my own, putting myself on a limb. The more I came up with negative excuses, the more I chose to run. Maybe Cedric was right: I was nothing but talk and no action. Every time I procrastinated, those words made me quiver.

The phone rang five times, jarring me back into reality. I was reluctant to answer the telephone—I wasn't in the mood for a shouting match with my ex-wife.

"Hello," I answered with reservations, on the sixth ring.

I exhaled, when I heard my sister's voice on the other end. "Hello, Mo. I'm calling to invite you to Sunday dinner. I know you haven't eaten a descent meal lately."

"Dee, I hope this isn't another one of your family reunions

with our father. You know my position on the subject. The last time you invited me, I was left with an uneasy feeling. I was angry with you for months."

"I only did it because I love you. You're too damn stubborn, Mo. You have to learn that we all make mistakes in life. He's old now and he needs us."

"He wasn't there for us for over twenty years, and now he wants to play Daddy. No thanks!"

"You're his only son, Mosee, have a heart," said Dee.

There was silence on the other end of the telephone. I had grown tired of my sister's harassing me about making up with our father. I found it difficult to forgive my father. I continued to harbor hatred and anger about my father's decision to walk out on his family and the subsequent death of my mother. I continued to blame him today.

"Mosee, are you still there?" said Dee.

"Yeah, I'm here. I was just thinking ...", still simmering.

"No, he won't be here, so relax," Dee said, wanting to change the conversation. "How's your teaching coming along?"

"Okay."

"Just, okay? Stop fooling me; I know you're bored with teaching. I can hear it in your voice. There's no excitement when you talk about teaching. You've been in a slump lately, that's why I'm inviting you to dinner."

"Alright, I'll be there, providing that you don't pull any tricks," I said.

"No tricks, little brother."

2

I slowly lifted my head off the pillow, looking at the alarm clock on the nightstand. I jumped up out of bed, knocking over the clock, when I realized it was twelve noon on a Saturday. The thought of sleeping until noon gave me a repulsive feeling— only lazy people stayed in bed.

I sat up in bed, my face contorting in different shapes, when a stale musty odor made me nauseous. I happened to look over at a pile of dirty clothes that lay in the corner of my bedroom. I tripped over a pair of shoes on my way to open the window. I figured a little fresh air was just what the doctor would order.

Teaching full-time left little time to attend to my personal duties. Saturday is what I call catch up day: cleaning the house and doing laundry.

The grayish beige curtains hanging over the window; the green and white bedspread covered with fur balls, and the dull, sky blue rug created a depressing atmosphere in my bedroom.

My pockets dictated that I keep my aunt's original bedroom furniture. I knew it was time for new furniture. Money had always been an issue with me ever since I left my government job. People thought I was crazy or on drugs the day I announced my resignation. 'Are you crazy, man?' 'You know how hard jobs are to find. Most people would love to get a good government job, with benefits and stay there until retirement age. That's the American dream for most people.'

Dee, my sister, always told me what I wanted to hear "Do what makes you happy, that's what's most important." My other sister, Shelby, was next to the oldest, under Dee. "Mosee, really now you have to be realistic. You don't have a clue as to what you wanna do with the rest of your life. You're not some college graduate who's out to explore the world." I hated telling Shelby my business. She never held back her tongue. She was too critical of me.

Money is one thing I don't have. Sometimes I wondered if leaving my FBI job had been such a good idea, after all. Leaving a job after ten or more years is like learning to walk for the second time.

I had to make major adjustments in curtailing my luxuries, including dining out and once-a-year trips. The summer months were the most difficult times. There were no classes to teach and that meant no income. I had my ten-year pension, but that's earmarked for my retirement. Two alternatives to bring in extra cash are to do surveillance and investigative consulting work. People who work for large corporations are always under the watchful eye of a camera.

I looked around my room, trying to come up with a color scheme. An interior decorator is something that I was not. Being raised in a household full of women had not given me time to focus on household duties, that task was left up to my two sisters and aunt.

The lumps in my mattress made it difficult for me to sleep, most nights. The bed has no head board only a frame holding up the mattress and box spring. I made a promise to give my bedroom a face-lift whenever I got some extra money.

I walked down a long hallway to the kitchen, which wasn't very big except for a small glass oval table. The three black vinyl chairs exposed white foam from the seat cushion where the seams were splitting. A cup of coffee is just what I needed to get my adrenaline flowing. I sat at the kitchen table sipping my black coffee when the telephone rang. I decided to let the answer machine pick up.

"Hello, Mosee this is Joyce calling for the second time. You haven't been returning my calls. I need to know if you're picking up the girls for the weekend."

Vicious Karma

Hearing her voice gave me a throbbing pain in my head. But after twenty-minutes of contemplating, I decided to return Joyce's call. The longer I avoided her, the harder it is for me to return her call. It's inevitable that Joyce wins every argument. She was loud and boisterous. She rambles on until the opponent gives in. Joyce's mouth was like being shot by a Smith & Wesson.

I slowly dialed Joyce's telephone number, taking a deep breath each time I punched in a number.

"Hello. Who's calling? Hello, somebody say something," Joyce said with frustration in her voice.

I took a half-minute to speak. "Hello Joyce, it's me calling."

"About time you called. I've been trying to reach you for the past two days. I figured you were ignoring me, cause you're behind in child support." Joyce talked on without taking a breath between sentences. I wondered how anybody like her could function. She managed to make a speech without taking a moment to breathe. By the time most people would finish a sentence, Joyce would be into her second paragraph of thoughts. She often sounded like everything was a single thought.

I imagined pushing my ex-wife off a cliff or maybe she would disappear. "I'll be looking for another job soon; maybe some private investigation work on the side."

"I don't care what you do, just have my money on time!" she yelled through the telephone.

I placed the telephone on the couch as Joyce continued to ramble on. She was so loud I could hear every word she said.

"Mosee, answer me. I hate when you ignore me."

"Joyce, I'll be over to pick up the girls around two today and I'll return them on Monday."

11

Asa Allen-Showell

I could not figure out why I had stayed married to my wife for ten years. The only intelligent reason I could come up with was that she'd been good looking and great in bed. Every time I thought about leaving her, sex always made me forget about her imperfections—for a couple of days. I also had my two daughters to think about. I wanted them to have a stable environment, but my sanity and peace of mind were more important.

I spent the remainder of the afternoon doing laundry and house cleaning. I have a bad habit of putting those things off until the last minute and that is something I'm not proud of. I went to the kitchen and washed two days' worth of dishes. Getting a female companion to do the house duties wouldn't be that bad. Housing cleaning was one of my few worries growing up. When I fell in love with Joyce, she picked up where my sisters and aunt left off.

I pulled out of my driveway of my row home in Queens around 5 p.m. that Saturday to pick up my daughters in Jersey City. Not a good start. I looked out the car window and noticed the grass on the lawn was over three inches tall. I shook my head with a disgusted look on my face. Moving to a condominium complex sounded more appealing; at least they kept up the landscape. I had a lawn mower but it needed repairs and that cost money. My neighbors probably thought I made the value of the neighborhood go down.

The drive took nearly one hour. Saturday traffic added an extra half-hour on my driving time to Jersey City.

Joyce is one of three children, who lived close enough to be caregiver for her mother following her mother's stroke, after her father had sustained a massive heart attack and died two years before. I frowned on her decision, not relishing the thought of having my children raised in the city. Once upon a time, living in New York was a beautiful experience, especially in Brooklyn, where I grew up. The neighbors all looked out for each other. People weren't afraid to walk the streets. Today the city has taken on a different look. Now people are colder and unfriendly.

12

Vicious Karma

I never did take well to Joyce's older sister. She was one of those liberated women who believed women should not depend on a man to take care of them. She always gave Joyce advice about our marriage. It's funny how someone can give advice on marriage, when they themselves cannot maintain a relationship for more than three months at best. Joyce's sister thought she was too financially dependent on me. She filled Joyce's head with ideas that a career came first and marriage second. I thought that Joyce's sister needed a good lay to loosen up.

Joyce's older sister's persona was like her physique--stiff and rigid. Joyce confided in her sisters and mother about every detail of our marriage. I felt that I had no control over my marriage. My ex-wife was weak, when it came to her family.

My ex-wife's mother was a strong-willed, independent woman. After her stroke, she continued to volunteer her time between church and school. Joyce's mother taught third and fifth graders for over thirty years.

When Joyce moved back home, she started taking classes at NYU. She had two years to complete her BSN degree. She chose pediatric nursing, because she loved children. She also worked part-time as a bank teller at Chase Manhattan to supplement her child support and alimony payments.

After our separation, she announced to her family that I was leaving my job with the Bureau after ten years of service. Joyce's mother thought I was a lazy bum.

I approached my ex's house with caution. I prepared myself for meeting the Grinch—Joyce's mother. I was about to knock on the door, when I felt something akin to a gush of wind that almost knocked me off my feet. There she was, blocking the entrance of the door, with arms folded across her chest. She had a row of wrinkles on her forehead for every evil thought she ever thought of me. Joyce's mother always has a frown on her face, even when she tries to smile. I never met anyone that it pained to smile. She had a smooth coca complexion which complimented her grayish blue hair. She looked as though she rarely missed a hairdresser's appointment. She didn't look half-bad for a woman who'd had a stroke.

"Hello, Mo," Joyce's mother said, looking at her watch. She only called me that when she had an attitude.

I bent over kissing her cheek. "Hello, Rebecca how are you? You don't look a day over forty."

"You're still a charmer, Mo," she said walking into the living room.

"Where're my daughters?"

Joyce's mother yelled to her daughter, telling her that I was here.

Joyce came into the living room, wearing a skimpy, laced, black camisole top and denim shorts. Her hair hung in black spiral curls.

Watching my ex-wife made the blood rush to my loins. I fantasized about snatching her in the back room and licking every inch of her body. Reality hit me when she opened her mouth.

"Mosee I thought you weren't coming," she said standing by the kitchen door.

"I'm single now, and I had a few things to do around the house."

"Mosee, what do you plan on doing about my child support payments? I need my money on a regular basis, not whenever you feel like it," she said sarcastically.

I suddenly felt a coldness come upon me. I no longer saw her beauty, but only a nagging beast.

"I plan on getting a second job," I said.

Joyce's mother folded her arms, staring at me with a disgusted look on her face.

"Joyce give me time," I pleaded, avoiding eye contact, with the Grinch.

Vicious Karma

"Time—what about your daughter's?" she echoed. Her voice started getting harsh and coarse.

3

Every fourth Sunday of the month is the ritual family gathering at my sister Dee's house. The family get-togethers were held in the suburbs of the Bronx. Driving to Dee's this particular day made me remember the first time I met Dee's second husband, after their first year of marriage. I thought it was strange that Dee kept it from the family. Meeting him two years ago today, crystallized in my mind why she decided to keep her marriage a secret from the family.

Dee was a registered nurse at St. John's hospital in New York. That was where she first met her second husband, Chip Preston, who was a patient. He was tall and his skin had a smooth caramel complexion. He was a meticulous dresser and a rambunctious talker. When Chip was in the hospital, he bragged about his business ventures whenever he found a willing victim that would listen. One day, I got a call from my sister, Dee, announcing her plans to remarry. And this time it would be for keeps. Unfortunately it turned out to be a little less than two years.

Chip could never keep a job; his excuses were his business deals kept him too busy. A regular nine to five would be too confining. Dee found herself investing in his ventures, which always turned out to be failures. Within the first year of their marriage, Dee found herself getting more deeply into debt. When I first met my brother-in-law, I didn't sustain a conversation with him for more than twenty-minutes before he fled the house rushing off to some business meeting. After Chip found out that I was a former agent with the FBI; he made a conscious effort to be out of the house whenever I came to visit.

I recall our brief encounter vividly—an encounter in which he revealed his true character.

Chip was preoccupied during my visit at my sister's house. I attempted to drill my brother-in-law about his latest business venture, but Chip literally ran out of the house in order to avoid answering any questions. When Chip managed to spare a few moments alone with me, he never looked me in the eye when talking, as though he had too many pressing issues on his mind. He could never give me a straight answer about what his business entailed. He always changed the subject. My first character summation of my sister's husband's could be described in one word—imposter. I hated to disrupt her fantasy, but the truth had to be told.

Dee thought that we were finally getting along. I told her that I had an uneasy feeling about her husband. I wanted to run a check on him. 'No, Mo leave your investigation work where it belongs!' 'I appreciate your concern, but I'm a big girl and I don't need my little brother giving me advice on my love life.'

Chip returned a half-hour later, looking flushed. 'See you guys still talkin'. I forgot something.' he said going into one of the back rooms. 'Chip will you be back in time for dinner?' Dee asked. Chip came back carrying a brown Coach, leather brief case. 'I'm not sure what time I'll be back. You guys better start dinner without me.' I interrupted Chip before he headed out the door. 'Chip, I like to invest in one of your businesses. I'm looking to expand my portfolio investments.' Chip shrugged his shoulders. 'We'll talk later, man," he said slamming the door.'

Dealing with crime and criminals in my career gave me the instinct to size up the Chip Preston's of the world. Chip was one of those pretty boys, who used their looks to manipulate people, especially women. He was a smooth talker, who knew how to charm women. I figured Chip made his living being a parasite on lonely women.

After taking a stroll down memory lane, I parked my Volvo in Dee's driveway. I enjoyed spending Sunday's and special occasions at Dee's house.

My next to oldest sister, Shelby, is stuffy and reserved. Dee is more down to earth and easy to talk to. If I ever needed to tell my problems to anyone of my sisters, it would be Dee rather than Shelby. Dee always gave me her sympathetic ear.

Shelby is more critical. She is so fast to give her opinion about everything, trying to push her views on people. Sometimes I'd call Shelby to get a different perspective. She never lied to me, that's one thing I can say about Shelby, she spoke her mind. Dee is the nurturing mother type. This personality type comes in handy when I need to be pampered.

I snapped out of my trance, when I heard my daughters, Jewell and Tiffany in the back seat giggling. "Okay girls, you can get outta the car now, we're at your Aunt Dee's house."

"Oh goody, we're here," Jewell said, racing Tiffany to the door.

I walked up to the front door and saw my niece standing in the entrance.

"Well, who is this pretty woman?" I said, giving her a hug.

"Hello, Uncle Mo," she said, kissing my cheek.

Jewell and Tiffany ran up the stairs with their cousin, while I made myself at home stretching out on the lounge chair, watching basketball—Knicks vs. Bulls.

Dee made the best ham, collard greens and candied sweet potatoes I had tasted in a long time. After finishing a Sunday dinner, I could always feel the food settling in my stomach the following day.

After taking my daughters home, I spent the rest of the evening preparing for final exams in my Criminal Justice courses, at John Jay College in Manhattan.

It took me nearly five hours to make up the test from scratch. When I finally finished, it was close to twelve midnight.

Vicious Karma

It was, Tuesday, May 16, '98, the last day of classes for the summer. Casual wear was my attire. I chose a pair of jeans and a cream color short sleeve shirt. I wanted to be comfortable, since I planned on being in class for two hours for the exam and another two hours grading papers. In the middle of giving finals, I felt a vibrating sensation on my left side. I looked down at my pager, quickly recognizing her telephone number. Joyce knew it was payday. I promised her three weeks of child support payments. Joyce would leave me broke, but somehow I felt a sense of relief. I only had myself at home, which gave me little to worry about except the notices I received from the city, threatening to take my property for unpaid taxes and shut off notices from the Sewer and Water Company. The thought of falling further behind in my bills made me realize a summer job was pertinent to my survival. Freelance investigation was an option, but that required finding businesses that are willing to hire me which could take months to find.

I had always dreamed of working for myself. The idea had become more attractive since my resignation from the Bureau five years before. I had more time to seriously think about what I wanted to do with the next twenty years of my life. Sometimes fear and frustration about what laid ahead would overwhelm me. Now the ball was in my court, and that was a scary thought.

4

Trying to find an empty parking space on Friday evenings the busiest time at O'torios—is a serious challenge. The usual after work crowd makes its regular Friday visits. That included single women who came out specifically on the weekends filling the void in their lives, and husbands stopping in for quick cocktails before facing the nagging wife and kids after a stressful day at the office.

O'torios Sports Bar is a cross between an expensive chocolate mousse and cheap vanilla pound cake. The black marble bar stretches fifteen feet long. A sports betting lounge is located in the back; where regulars participate in illegal gambling activity, no one ever comes to investigate. The wide screen television located behind the bar is visible to everyone.

O'torios is a frequent hangout for sports agents and athletes. There are oval and rectangular tables and a few black leather booths along the side of the walls. The place has an aura of sophistication. When you enter, you know you're in an A-class place; the nuts tasted expensive, not like your supermarket brands, but imported nuts from exotic countries—like Brazil.

The waitresses and bartenders are dressed in satin black pants and white tuxedo shirts. The sports bar doesn't cater to your average drinker whose pockets can only afford a two-dollar beer. The owner is always up front greeting customers. Regular customers, he greets by name. "Hello, Mosee," Salvatore smiled from behind the bar.

No wonder Salvatore was grinning. The place was packed with people. You could barely find a place to sit. There were yuppies dressed in suits, standing around the bar discussing politics and world events. I looked at the pompous crowd and yawned, shaking my head. What a bunch of overdressed suits. Half of the corporate yuppies looked overly stressed. I wouldn't want that world if they paid me a million dollars, I thought to myself. Cedric would fit in perfectly with this crowd. He sometimes can be pompous and boisterous. He's what you would call the "perfect corporate image." He is always dressed in expensive suits, and he adhered to the principle of spending money extravagantly.

"Hello, Sal, how's it going?"

"Can't complain. Business is great these days." Sal placed his hand to his mouth and blew a kiss. "Magnifico," he said in Italian.

"Glad to hear it."

"How's teaching these days, Mosee?"

"It's okay I had my last final so I'm free this entire summer."

"Lucky, you, must be nice to have three months off."

I shrugged my shoulders. "I'm trying to pick up some private investigative work on the side this summer. I've been thinking about starting my own business. I might try my hand at some corporate surveillance and take a few cases on the side."

Sal nodded his head. "Sounds good, Mosee, I'll pass the word around."

"Thanks, Sal."

"Cedric is in the back waiting for you. He has the last booth on the right."

Salvatore's hair and mustache is the color of coal with a gray streak down the middle. He wears his hair slicked back with a greasy look. His skin looks like he has a tan year round. I figured he was probably from Sicily. That would explain his olive skin tone. Give him a little tan and a new hair cut and he could pass for a brother. He's a handsome man and well built. He doesn't look a day over sixty.

"Thanks, Sal. I think I see a hand waving at me."

Cedric wore yellow linen shorts a black printed silk shirt, and a linen vest.

"I'll send someone over to take you guys' order."

21

I casually strolled toward Cedric, giving him a fake smile. "What's up Cedric?"

"Hello, Mosee. You can have a seat," he said smiling and sipping on a vodka and cranberry drink. "I wasn't sure if you were going to show up. I promise you won't be disappointed. I believe this will help your morale. How about a beer and cognac from the bar?"

Cedric knew just what I wanted to help me relax before I began badgering him about my blind date. When the questions started, Cedric's concentration was focused on the door and his watch.

"Is she fine, Cedric? Come on don't bull shit me, man."

"Be patient, Mosee, you'll get to meet her in a few minutes."

"Here comes the waitress."

She had a wide grin on her face as she walked toward the table.

"Hello, gentlemen today must be my lucky day," she said looking at Cedric "How can I help you?"

"My friend here needs a drink to relax his nerves." Cedric pointed in my direction. "Get him a beer and cognac, please." Her eyes stayed focused on Cedric as she took the order.

Cedric's six feet two frame fits perfectly with his thin body type. His caramel color complexion matches his brown hair. He has what black folks would call "good hair." His curly brown hair doesn't need processing to lie down. His impeccable dressing always carries over well with the ladies. He knows how to put clothing together from his shoes down to his handkerchief. He was never one who believed in buying cheap clothing. His immaculate dressing also transcends itself in how he lives.

His brownstone in Brooklyn is a place where you can find everything in exact order. There's never a dish in the sink or a pillow fluffed out of place. I find it repulsive to go inside his house; I have never felt one hundred percent comfortable in his home, even though we've been friends for over twenty years. In my house, you can always find some evidence of habitation. My bedroom is always messy and dishes stay in the sink from the night before.

Cedric had looks and style. He has a successful job as an entertainment lawyer. He has a wide base of clients, from the music industry to movies and the sports field. At thirty-six years of age, Cedric was already making six figures. Graduating top in his law school from Columbia helped to give his career an extra boost.

The waitress came back to the table to ask if we wanted anything else from the bar.

"No, thank you that'll be all for now, but we are expecting someone to join us later, so if you can check back with us in about fifteen-minutes, that'll be fine."

She walked away, swaying her hips from side to side. She looked backed to see if we were watching her.

"She's a fine sister, huh?"

I agreed. "I guess so."

Cedric frowned. "Man, I hope you ain't turning gay on me." He took a sip of his drink. "You've been actin strange since you divorced Joyce. You should have filed for divorce five years ago."

"You know me. I drag my feet when it comes to important matters."

"I began to think that you wanted her back."

"I don't want her back. I got a lot of pressing issues on my mind," I said, shaking my head in disbelief that Cedric would insinuate such a thing. "I'm trying to make a career change; I have money problems, and Joyce is on my back about child support," I told him, my voice rising. "You have the gall to say that I want Joyce back.

"And what do you mean my money troubles will be over soon?" I asked. "You always have something up your sleeve. I don't know why I let you talk me into coming out here tonight on some blind date. You must really think I'm hard up for a woman."

Cedric didn't care to respond; he kept looking toward the door. I didn't wanna get into a heated confrontation with Cedric. I hate it when he ignores me. He knew it infuriated me; yet he still continued to push my button.

Cedric avoided eye contact. "So you're desperate for a woman," he commented.

I was in rage now. I wanted to get up and leave, regardless of my commitment to him. "I'm leaving, Cedric, I don't feel right. You know how I feel about blind dates." I stood up, and I was about to leave when Cedric stood up waving to the woman who was standing by the entrance. I immediately sat back in my seat. "Well, I guess I can manage to stay for a few more minutes. The night is still young."

Cedric looked at me with a sly grin on his face.

The closer she approached the table, my sweat glands increased, causing beads of sweat to drip from my forehead. I reached for a napkin from the table to wipe away any indication of nervousness. I said innocently, "I hope you didn't fix me up on a blind date."

It was my first blind date when my college buddies set me up with a hideous looking girl as a joke. Her body would make any man take notice, but her face told a different tale. I took her out on several occasions after our first date. I find it hard to disrespect any woman regardless of what she looks like. I'm what you call a bleeding heart.

"I don't need your help in the romance dept," I said nonchalantly.

"Who's gonna look after your well being except me?"

We both laughed. We had a bond since sixth grade. Cedric lived down the street from my family in Brooklyn. He was the only child in the neighborhood raised by his father. Cedric became attached to my family, thanks to my Aunt's cooking and her famous peach cobbler. We filled in the gaps that were missing in each other's lives. Cedric yearned for a mother and siblings. And I envied Cedric for getting anything he wanted and having a father.

She walked with a sway that sounded like one of John Coltrane's tunes. My mouth gapped open, watching her walk toward the table. Cedric stood up extending his greetings with a friendly hug.

"It's good to see you again, Cedric."

I stood quietly in the background, waiting my introduction.

"Mosee Love meet Zoe Owens, Zoe Owens meet Mosee Love."

Everyone said their formal hello's and took their seats.

"Cedric tells me you're good at what you do," she said flirtatiously.

I paused and smiled shaking my head. "Yes that's true," I laughed.

I felt myself melt like butter each time I looked into her soft hazel brown eyes.

Her nails and feet were neatly manicured. Her perfume awakened my hormones that lay dormant for so long. I looked down and notice a pear-shaped diamond. But I quickly relaxed when I noticed the diamond was on her right hand.

"I've come here tonight to ask you to help me find my father."

My lower lip almost dropped to the floor. Help locate her father? It wasn't exactly what I was expecting. I was waiting for more like a when can we get together for dinner kind of question.

I shot Cedric a piercing look. He quickly turned away, focusing on the bar. Then he stood up. "I'll leave you two alone to discuss your business," he said. "I'll be at the bar if you need anything."

As I watched him walk away, I felt betrayed, allowing Cedric to tempt me into taking on an investigative job. He knows I'm vulnerable, when it comes to investigation matters. I have three simple passions in life: my daughter's, investigative work and pretty women in distress.

"Cedric told me you were once one of the top FBI agents. Why did you leave such a good job?"

I went into a long narration, explaining one of many episodes that led to my resignation. "As a rookie, me and another new recruit were assigned to infiltrate a black organization called the Black United Front. Our superiors told us that the organization had a conspiracy going on against the government. Through my seven months of investigation, I discovered compassionate men and women working to better the lives of black folks. When I went into the office of the head of the organization, I discovered the body of Omar Mohammed. His limp body was hanging over the desk with a rope around his neck." I paused to take a deep breath, closing my eyes as I continued the story.

"I'll never forget his face. It was a dark shade of gray and his eyes were blood shot staring down at me. He looked like he was cursing me for betraying his organization. Blood flowed from the side of his mouth. Here I am a black man who was sent by the government to bring down a black organization, which was trying to do good things for the community. Jeffery and I were pawns used in a set up."

"After that incident, which followed a string of other actions over the years, followed by bullshit and lies, I finally conceded and handed in my resignation. It was five years ago today. The other agent was transferred to another office in the Midwest. I never saw him again."

Zoe sat in awe with tears in her eyes. "I don't know what to say. I . . . I'm really sorry, Mosee, that's a tragic story."

"That's okay. I still have flashbacks from time to time, but life goes on." I was exhausted, telling my story. "That's why I got outta the business, too many painful memories for me. I still love the field of investigations. It's in my blood."

Zoe had a look of guilt written all over her face about asking me to help find her father after hearing my story. She was stunned and at a lost for words. "I don't feel right asking you to help me find my father."

"Please don't feel that way. Besides, I haven't made up my mind whether I'll take your case. I like to analyze the facts before I make a decision."

"What happened to your father?" I asked getting back to business.

She paused before speaking. "I don't know. The only piece of evidence I have is a letter postmarked from Denver twenty-five years ago."

"What does the letter say?"

"The letter states that he's sorry for running around with women. And he wants to come home and be a family."

"Did you question your mother about the letter?"

"I tried, but she refused to talk about him. She's strongly against this investigation, you know."

"You think she's hiding something?"

"Hiding what?" she snapped, moving her head in a circular motion. This is a popular nonverbal form of communication, often exhibited by black women.

I felt I'd better learn to phrase my questions differently. "Does your mother have any knowledge of your father's whereabouts?"

Her persona changed from a vulnerable woman to a home girl with an attitude. She shrugged her shoulders. "My mother said he'd disappeared." She started shaking as she took a cigarette and lighter from her purse.

"You smoke?" she asked gratuitously

"No."

"Mind if I smoke? It 's my nerves."

"I don't mind, if it makes you happy. Your mother's reactions should give you an indication she's hiding something. She could be withholding information. There are times when a woman is wounded from her relationship when the man ends it abruptly. This leaves the woman vulnerable, and she breaks off any communication from the man. This sometimes puts the children in the middle."

"You sound as though you're speaking from experience."

"Sort of, you could say I've had my share of missing fathers and failed marriages."

"We have something in common. Tell me what happened to your father?"

"I'd rather not comment. You're here about your problems, not mine."

"What you're trying to say is that my mother is the reason why I haven't seen my father. That's something I don't buy," she said. "My mother's a Christian woman."

"What does God have to do with this, Zoe?"

"Nothing. My mother wouldn't lie to me. People in church don't lie."

"People react and do things out of desperation, Ms. Owens. Even Christians lie."

Zoe looked down at the table, as if she were searching for the right answer. She turned to face me, looking into my eyes. "Give me your honest opinion," she said in a low voice. "You think I have a good chance of finding him?"

She waited for my response, watching me sip my cognac. I didn't wanna sound too pessimistic, but the odds were stacked against her. For one, she didn't have any current information on her father. "I can't take on a case when I have no background information. It makes my job twice as difficult."

"So you're telling me, I don't have a chance in hell of finding him!"

"I didn't say that. I'm saying don't get your hopes up. Sometimes missing persons aren't solved." I didn't wanna give Zoe the statistics on missing persons. If she found out the true facts, she would probably change her mind and call off the investigation. Fifty percent of missing persons are dead; and thirty percent are homeless and living on the streets, and the other twenty percent do not want to be found; those are the ones who have changed their identities.

"Please, Please, Mosee," she begged, with tears in her eyes.

"Cedric told me you're the best and you can solve anything," she said wiping her eyes with a napkin.

I'm what you call a bleeding heart for women, especially pretty ones. But taking the case would take me away from my daughters. I knew it could last months. I also knew I needed the money.

"I need time to think this over. I won't give you a yes or no, but if you give me your number, I'll promise to call you in a few days." I drank the last of my Millers Lite.

"You know, Zoe, there are social dynamic's that come into play with black men deserting their families. For one, economics makes it difficult for the black men to stay in the home. Black men are discriminated against in the workplace. This makes it difficult for him to support his family and comply with the pressure put on by society to obtain material possessions. In addition, this makes black men feel less of a man. This affects black men today. Twenty years ago, jobs weren't plentiful. Many that lived in the south were forced to migrate north to find employment. Many black men sent money to their families while others chose to disappear and start new families."

"You're telling me every black man who doesn't support his family should be excused?" she said angrily. "I call it lazy."

"There are no easy answers, Zoe. Life has no guarantees."

The sad thing about this scenario: this woman sitting in front of me is in her mid thirties and she is still yearning to be loved by a father she never knew. I, too, had the same need as Zoe once, but that was shattered when my father deserted my mother with three children. Since my mother's death, I never fully came to terms with forgiving my own father for my mother's death. I felt empathy for Zoe, because I, too, share the same emptiness.

Her hands were shaking as she took a second cigarette from her purse.

"You smoke a lot."

"I know, I keep promising myself I'll quit, but I'm addicted to the damn things. Besides, smoking helps calm my nerves, like alcohol."

"There are other alternatives, besides smoking, you know." "Really, Like what?" she said sarcastically. "Exercise, reading a good book is better than smoking." "Sounds easy for you, if you've never smoked. I'm sure you indulge in something if you're under stress." "I drink a lot of coffee." "Look, I did not come here to debate the plight of black men or my smoking habit. I came here because I need your help," she said, taking a drag on her second cigarette. "Would you care for a drink from the bar?" "No, thanks I'll be leaving in a few minutes." She jotted down her number on a napkin. "Call me anytime with your decision, but don't wait, too long because I'll be leaving town in a few days," she said handing me the paper. I folded the paper and put it in my wallet. "I'll call you before you leave town." "I'll pay you whatever your fee is." She had desperation in her eyes.

My heart pounded when she mentioned money. I began thinking about all the possibilities extra money could do for me: pay my back child support payments, get repairs done on my Volvo, fix up the house. I tried to have a logical head when making my final decision. I didn't want greed to be a deciding factor, but money talks.

"Call me anytime with your answer, day or night." she said getting up from the table. I stood up from the table, being the perfect gentleman, giving her a firm handshake. "I'm glad I had the opportunity to meet you, Mosee. Cedric says you come highly recommended." My chest automatically extended forward. "Well, Cedric exaggerates at times. Other people are just as qualified as I am." "Nice meeting you, Mosee. I hope we can do business together," she said shaking my hand. "Me, too," I said.

My eyes stayed focused on Zoe, watching her walk toward the bar to say good bye to Cedric. I continued to drink my beer, when Cedric returned to the booth. I gave him a long hard stare.

Cedric looked at me, like he was trying to interrupt my thoughts. "Are you gonna take her case?" he said in a demanding tone.

"I don't know Cedric; I need time to think this thing over."

"What's there to think about? You need money don't you?"

"Don't force me into making a decision. I'll decide when I get ready!"

"You only have one option—money."

"What you think about Zoe, is she a number or what?"

"She's okay."

"Just okay?" he said with a smirk. "I saw the way you perspired when you first noticed her. I know you better than anybody."

"I confess she resembles a red ripe apple ready to be eaten. Is that what you wanna hear? That's all you think about sex and women."

"Now, that's the home boy I remember. I thought your hormones were asleep," he said taking a sip of his cranberry and vodka drink.

"Don't harass me, man."

"Okay, okay, I wont push, but she needs your help," he said.

After Cedric finished his drink, he signaled for the waitress to return to our table.

"Seconds, huh gentlemen?" she said smiling.

"Drinks are on me tonight," Cedric offered. I ordered a Cognac

31

with a twist of lime.

Sitting there drinking with Cedric reminded me of when we were at the pinnacle of adolescent manhood. The neighborhood park was our place of refugee, where we shared beers and stories about girls, life and our aspirations. Cedric always tried to outdo me in story telling, boasting about what girls he had. But he later confided in me that he was a virgin until he finished his second year in college.

"Cedric, how's your private practice comin' along?" I asked.

"Couldn't be better."

"I hear you, man, and the positive thing about running your own business is no clock to punch. Your time is yours."

"I couldn't agree with you more."

"I feel the same way about private investigations. The idea of going into business for myself becomes more appealing each day," I said. "My daughters are getting older. Before I realize it, they'll be going off to college, and I'll need extra money, too."

Cedric and I sat at the sports bar, drinking, and reminiscing about old times.

5

After leaving Otorio's, the drive home gave me time to come up with excuses not to take Zoe's case. This is my way of saying no, without putting the burden on myself. So far, I came up with: The need to spend time with my daughters, Tiffany and Jewell, and teaching is safer than investigation work. For one, I didn't have to look over my shoulder and worry about dodging bullets or doing late night stake-outs. The positive side of taking Zoe's case was that it would give me extra cash in my pocket. That's one solid, motivating factor.

Summer felt like it arrived early that year. It was becoming a little unbearable to drive my car. I thought about getting an air conditioner system installed. One thing I couldn't endure was another summer, driving in an uncomfortable car. My house also needed central air, but that cost money. I smiled to myself thinking about how I would spend the money if I were to accept Zoe's missing person's case. Air conditioning would take top priority.

The people on the streets of New York were enjoying an evening stroll. Some looked to have traded in their jackets and sweaters for short sleeves shirts and shorts. Traffic was finally easing up, after the nine to five'ers made it to their destinations.

I happened to glance out the window to my left side. There was a homeless man sitting outside a store, huddled in a corner. He was a white man dressed in an oversized wool coat. He was partly slumped over. I thought he might be drunk, asleep, or maybe even dead. No one cared about anybody. The pedestrians walked past the homeless man as if he were invisible. I shook my head in disgust at the way society has become so heartless.

A young black man came up to my car, carrying a bucket and a window blade. He started cleaning my windows without permission. Just as the light was about to turn green, the man ran up to me, with his hand extended forward in my face. I could smell a foul odor that emanated from his body. I quickly reached in my pocket and pulled a five dollar bill, handing it to the man. Why not? It was Friday and I had a little money to spare.

I got a tingling sensation, whenever I thought about returning to investigative work. It's like experiencing my first love.

I stumbled into the door headfirst with my feet not lingering too far behind. Entering my box-shaped living room, I gave my walls a rub down, tryin to locate the nearest light switch on the wall. After being blinded by the bright lights, I walked in a swaying motion holding on to the wall until I found my bedroom. Along the way I left a trail of clothing behind me. I lay in bed trying to convince myself once again why I should take Zoe's case.

For starters, my daughters' college education is something to start planning for, and my continuous child support payments needed to be made in advance to get me through the slow periods when I had little income. Those are just a few pressuring issues that raised a red flag. I had to face it; I was flat broke and close to forty. Not a pretty sight. This stage in my life is when you're supposed to have investments a nice pension, house and money in the bank. But here I am heading towards my forties with no job security and no money. I had images of myself sitting in a one bedroom apartment over top of a seven-eleven store, with no retirement saving and only a six hundred dollars a month social security income. Just enough to get me by and a monthly food stamp allotment. That is one image that is real to many older Americans—facing poverty. This is not what I envision for myself.

Now at thirty-eight I feel that I have one last chance to make it right in my life. My only passion is the investigative field.

Vicious Karma

No matter how hard I try to ignore it, I keep thinking about reentering my old career choice, but this time working for myself.

A half past midnight, I dialed Zoe's telephone number. After I completed the task, I kept my eyes focused on a fixed spot on the ceiling, in order to contain the spinning feeling that emanated from my stomach. I managed to muster up enough strength to sit up in bed. It took five rings before someone answered.

I heard a man's voice and immediately hung up the telephone. I didn't know if Zoe had a boyfriend. I knew whoever it was thought I was insane for calling so late.

I checked my shirt pocket, making sure I had dialed the right number.

When I dialed Zoe's number a second time, a woman answered in a horse voice which sounded like someone awakened from a deep slumber

"Who the hell is calling at this hour?" she snapped. "Do you have any idea what time it is?"

"It's me, Mosee," I said in a low whisper." I'm calling to tell you that I'll take your case."

There was a moment of silence on the other end of the telephone.

"I'm glad you're taking the case. It means so much to me to find my father," she said.

I sat at my computer in one of my spare bedrooms that I converted to an office. I became overwhelmed with a mixture of apprehension and bad nerves that caused my stomach to cramp up. I figured a cocktail would help me relax. I went to the kitchen and found two beers, so I settled for a Milwaukee Lite, since that was my only choice.

So far, I had Zoe's mother name—Emma Daniels—who had an intimate relationship with the missing party—Foster Owens, and a faded letter written from Foster postmarked from Denver,

Colorado, over twenty years ago.

I gulped down the two beers staring at the file I had created, taking a deep breath and letting my head tilt back on the pillow.

I was suddenly overwhelmed with anxiety. I did not know if I still possessed my savvy investigative skills. It suddenly occurred to me that it was only me and the three pieces of evidence.

One thing I disliked about being an investigator was that you're on own your own; no one has your back. There was a time when I wouldn't hesitant to take a criminal case, no matter what it entailed, but that was in 1993--five years before.

Zoe informed me that she would be staying with a relative for a couple of months. She was skeptical when I told her fees are one hundred dollars an hour, cash only, plus traveling expenses. I had my reasons for taking cash only: Reason being, it would be hard for the IRS and my ex-wife Joyce to trace the money.

I had a restless sleep the night before, both from excitement and apprehension about accepting Zoe's missing person's case. During the highlight of my career, ninety-nine percent of the time, I experienced what you call—sleep anxiety on any new assignment.

The following morning, I showered and sprayed Men's Fahrenheit over my body. It's best to apply your cologne when you first get out of the shower, when your body is practically damp. This enables the scent to linger longer on your body. After I freshened up, I fixed myself: egg whites, beef sausage and a fresh brewed cup of coffee. An hour later my tummy was full. Now I was ready to take on the world.

Zoe arrived promptly at 12 noon Sunday, to discuss the details of her case and my fees. She was a little uptight when I answered the door. "Hello, Zoe, how you doin'?"

"Alright, I guess. I just wanna get this over with before I change my mind and call the whole thing off."

She arched her back sitting at the edge of the chair, squinting her eyes at me. "How do I know you won't run off with my money and call a week later, telling me you couldn't find him," she said, darting her eyes at me.

"Cedric is my best friend. He knows what I'm capable of handling."

She looked at me with such intensity; I felt a chill go through my body.

"What if you don't find my father?"

"There's always that possibility. Your chances are fifty-fifty. Either he'll be found dead or alive. You haven't physically seen your father in over twenty years. That's the chance you take."

"How can you find someone whose been missing for over thirty years?" Zoe asked.

"That's easy," I said leaning back in my chair feeling in control. "Most people who do not wanna be found can be. They leave something behind—family, friends, job, birth records, driver's license, etc. It could be a number of things. Finding someone who is missing today, is easier than it was twenty years ago.

"If you think I'm ripping you off, then find somebody else. I don't play games, Ms. Owens. I have a reputation with the FBI and over ten years of experience. I don't need your money that bad," I said angrily. "You can stop wasting my time and yours."

What an idiot I was for making such a statement. I needed her money, but my pride got in the way. I felt a lump in my throat after I uttered those words. I hope she didn't take me seriously, I thought.

"I just wanna warn you there're many scam artists who will take your money and run. Ten years of experience, working in investigations with the FBI should be good enough."

Finally, after a half-hour of deliberation with her, she agreed to pay me my asking price. "I'll pay you twelve thousand dollars, but nothing more."

"If you want the best, you have to pay. At least you know I'm a close friend of Cedric's."

She agreed to give me half the money up front and the rest payable upon completion, whether her father was found dead or alive.

"I'm a cash and carry guy."

She gave me a cautious look.

"If you don't feel right, don't do it. I'm not hurtin for money."

When she handed me half the cash, I had the biggest inner smile you ever saw. I hadn't smiled that much since my father took me to my first baseball game. That was the happiest time in my life.

Zoe left the house at two in the afternoon. I called the JFK airport to make reservations for the first available flight to Westfield, South Carolina. I made reservations for a Sunday flight at 8P.M. I had seven hours to pack. The only things I needed were my two suits, one black and the other brown, a pair of jeans and two neckties and causal shirts and any hygiene essentials.

I made it just in time for my flight. The last passenger was boarding as I rushed toward the boarding gate. I grabbed the first available seat in the third row, closest to the aisle.

The plane landed at the Westfield International airport at nine forty-five. I stood in front of the Hertz's rental car section. I noticed Hertz's changed their advertisement since the O.J. trial. Instead I used my Sears credit card to rent a sky blue Lincoln Town car for two weeks. I followed the sales person's directions to the nearest Holiday Inn. The hotel had come highly recommended. It was located on airport property on a loop road which is about fifteen minutes from the airport. I made my choice the Holiday Inn, a widely recognized name. I wasn't in the mood to travel any great distances to get to a hotel, besides I was experiencing fatigue and jet lag. I parked my rental car and checked in at the front desk.

My room was on the sixth floor. Traveling extensively throughout my career had heightened my awareness of the workings inside a hotel room. The bathrooms are usually by the door and the closets are either by the bed or next to the bathroom.

Most hotels have twin or king beds. Next to the beds are the windows. If you're lucky, you can find a balcony overlooking the city skyline. I unpacked my clothes, hanging my shirts suits together in the closet. I took out my hygiene essentials, lining each one in order along the dresser. I lined my shoes neatly in a row in the closet. I placed my underwear, socks, and tee shirts in the top dresser drawer. I showered and changed into a short sleeved, white silk tee shirt that clung to my muscular upper torso. I looked into the mirror, inspecting my creased denim jeans. Being on a new case for the first time in five years called for a celebration.

Soft fluorescent lighting surrounded the lounge. The bar area was located by the entrance, just off the right from the hotel lobby. Behind the bar were octagon mirrors on the back wall. I ordered a Miller's Lite and a cognac. I was on my second drink, when I heard a woman's voice.

"Hello, my name's Everee, how you doin? I seen you sittin by yourself for the last hour. I figure you must be alone."

I extended my hand, giving the proper greeting. "Hello, my names Mosee Love. "How are you?"

"Fine, "I ain't seen you around here before. I know all the familiar faces that come through here."

"I'm down here on business from New York City."

"New York City?" she said excitedly, "I always wanted to visit the "Big Apple." There's so much goin' on. Living in this small town can get routine at times."

I took a sip of cognac. "A big city has its positive and negative aspects, small or large town. I happen to live in the suburbs of Queens New York. I have the best of both worlds."

"What is it you said you do again?"

"I didn't tell you the first time." I took another sip of beer.

"I'm a private investigator."

"Ain't that somethin', you like a cop, huh?"

"Yeah, I have the same privileges, except I work for myself. I don't have to answer to anybody."

She moved her seat closer to me. Her perfume engulfed my nostrils, making it difficult breath. I picked up a napkin from the bar, wiping my forehead. "What do you do for a living, Everee?"

"I'm into freelancing. Whatever you need done, I can do it," she said stroking my inner thigh. "You need a secretary, sugar?" she asked taking a piece of paper and pen from her purse. "Here's my number, Sugar, in case you needs my help. I'm willing to relocate any time," she smiled.

I took the number placing it in my wallet. "Thanks, Everee, if I ever expand my business, I'll look you up." I knew I was playin' with this girl's head. I knew she never stepped foot in an office environment in her life. "You want a drink?"

"Sure. I'll take a sex on the beach," she winked.

"You have any children, Everee?"

She put her head down, pausing. "I was pregnant when I was fourteen years old. My mama didn't want me to keep it, cause I was too young. I gave my child away to a preacher and his wife. I have nightmares about what I done. Sometimes I wish I could go back and change the past," she said looking into my eyes.

"I'm—I'm sorry, Everee."

"That's okay, how you suppose to know? You just met me," she said quietly.

I saw tears roll down her cheek. I pulled out a handkerchief from my shirt pocket, and wiped her eyes. She turned to me and smiled. "You got any children?"

"Yes, I have two beautiful girls."

"What are their names?"

"Tiffany and Jewell."

"They have pretty names. I bet they look like their names sound." "These are the only women in my life. Tiffany is my oldest, she's seven and Jewell's five." I pulled a picture of each from my wallet.

"My they are pretty girls, Mosee. They sure do look like their daddy."

I smiled proudly. "You think so?"

"I wish I had someone to love me like that."

"Well, you're a nice lookin' lady; I can't see why a man wouldn't want a pretty woman like yourself."

"You need some company tonight?" she said moving in closer.

"I have a busy schedule tomorrow, maybe some other time. I'll be in town for a couple of weeks. Maybe we can get together, before I leave."

She got up, stepping away from the bar, finishing her drink. "Well I guess its best I get goin' then. It's been nice talking with you, Mosee," she said extending her hand for me to shake.

I watched her walk out the door. A part of me wanted to run after her, but as I stood up my head began to spin. I quickly sat back down and finished my drink.

I tried to get some equilibrium. The bartender came over, asking me if I was driving home.

"No, I . . . I have a room up stairs. Thank you." I said staggering outta the lounge.

6

I'm speaking into my tape recorder now. Today is the first official day of my investigation in Westfield, South Carolina, and I have a headache from too many drinks last night. Anyway, it's ten o'clock, Monday morning. The weather feels like ninety degrees and I'm dressed in a light brown suit and tie. My first witness is the former girlfriend/lover of Foster Owens—Emma Daniels. Ms. Emma Daniels, Zoe's mother, has a ranch style house with a porch and two green fold up chairs on each side. The house is partially surrounded by a fence. It looks like someone didn't finish the job. The house is a dark brown faded color with missing and loose shingles on the left and right of the house. The miniature yard looks like it needs a good lawn mower to go through it.

She came to the door in a beige house coat. Her hair was pulled backed in a single braid. She was a stocky woman about five feet tall, golden brown complexion.

"Who are you?" Emma demanded, looking me up and down.

"My names is Mosee Love, I'm a private investigator."

"A private what?" she frowned, standing in doorway, with both hands on her hips.

"A private investigator; I help people solve criminal cases, you know, missing persons, murder cases, what ever your problem is providing that you have a legitimate problem."

"I ain't done nothin, so you might as well be on your way." She partially closed the door. I pushed the door open before she had a chance to close it.

"No, wait," I said pushing the door back open.

She screamed, "Go on get away before I call the police!"

I pulled out my identification, showing her my credentials. "Please wait! Here's proof of who I am. Your daughter hired me to find her father, Foster Owens."

"Is she in some kind of trouble with the law?"

"No."

She stood there in silence for few seconds.

"Are you alright Ms. Daniels?"

"Yes, I'm fine it's strange to hear that name after forty years," she whispered.

"I just wanna ask you a few questions about Foster." She finally invited me into her home with reservations written all over her face.

I walked into her house taking a seat on a brown recliner chair, in the far corner of the room by a large window. The house had a fresh pine scent. The couch was covered in plastic seat covers. There was blue-eyed picture of Jesus hanging over a gold toned beaded wall shelf.

"You want some coffee, Mr. Love?" she yelled from the kitchen.

"Yes, please," I said. "I take mine black with three sugars."

"You people sure work early," she yelled from the kitchen. Her voice carried an echo that rang through my ear. "You should've called before coming over. I ain't have time to dress."

She brought my coffee from the kitchen on a brown serving tray. "I haven't seen the man in years. How can I help you?" she said, placing the coffee on the end table with a napkin underneath.

Her skin was smooth, no wrinkles. "I think it's a waste of time for Zoe to go off and find a man who didn't care nothin' bout' her, no way."

"Well you can start by answering my questions, Ms. Daniels."

"How long did you date?"

"A very short time," she said sinking into the love seat. She folded her arms across her chest. That told me there was anger and bad feelings from the relationship.

"Does he have a family?"

"The only person he ever talked about was a sister named

43

Jessie."

I could tell Zoe's mother was uncomfortable with answering my questions. She was fidgety in her chair and she couldn't keep her eyes focused on one thing at a time.

"Do you know anything about her?" I asked. "If she has kids, is she married? Does she like sports? Where does she work?"

"Yeah, now I remember. Foster talked about being proud of his sister graduating from nursing college."

"Do you remember which college?"

"No, can't say that I do," she said. "Foster was a private person when it came to his personal life."

"Can you remember any close friends he may have had?" I said taking out my notebook.

"Now that you mention it, he did have a friend he spoke about. His name is Ellis Worthington. My memory ain't that good, but I can recalls a few things."

"Was Foster ever enlisted in the Army, Navy or Marines?"

"Yeah, he was in the Army with, Ellis Worthington."

"Did you ever meet this Ellis Worthington?"

"No sir, I ain't never laid eyes on the man."

"Where did you meet Foster?"

"At a dance hall called the Peacock. The Peacock was a place black folks called their own after working for white folks all week. The place didn't have much, but the atmosphere was full of energy that caught you by surprise, yes Lawd. The place was an abandoned warehouse turned into a dance hall. There were round tables throughout the place, and there was a homemade bar that one of the fellows built. We didn't have a floor either, nothin but dirt under our feet. We sure ain't needed no floor cause we danced holes through that dirt. A band played Friday through Sunday. Sunday was blues night," she said smiling. "Folks came out mostly on Saturday night. Sunday was a day Zoe and me went to church."

"When I met Foster he was a looker. He knew how to work a crowd. The women loved him and the men hated him.

"I first saw him sitting across the room. He must've saw me watching him, because he comes over strutting like a Peacock, introducing himself to Margo and me. He asked our permission to join us for a drink."

"Is this dance hall still around?"

"No. The place burned down to the ground. A supermarket is there now."

"Who was the owner of the club?"

"Mr. Shep Anderson was one of the few blacks who owned a business. That was rare back then. I think his family was into boot legging and running numbers. You name it, they was into it."

"Is this Shep Anderson still alive?"

"Yeah, he lives on Chestnut Hill estates. That's where the rich black folks live."

"Were Foster and Shep Anderson friends?"

"Far as I know they became business partners," she said.

"Were you and Foster married?"

She had a blank look on her face. I felt the tension fill the room. She was stiff and rigid in her seat.

I cleared my throat, to break the silence. "Ms. Daniels, were you and Foster married? Ms. Daniels ... Ms. Daniels."

"Oh, forgive me, Mr. Love, I must've drifted off. What were you sayin? You want somethin to eat?"

"No thank you, I'm fine. Can we get back to the question about you and Foster being married."

"I believe I answered all your questions, Mr. Love."

"That means no."

"I'm an upstanding Christian woman; I belong to the women's club, and I cooks for all the special events, and I pay my tithes every Sunday," she said folding her arms.

"Ms. Daniels, I've come down here to help your daughter find her father. I'm not here to judge you on your past." Judging from

45

the look on Ms. Emma Daniels face, I concluded that the

Interview was over. I had to accept the information she gave me and move on.

I thanked Ms. Daniels for her time and continued on my way to my next interview. I assured her that I'm only looking out for her daughter's best interest.

The next person on my list to interview was Mr. Shep Anderson.

After thirty-five minutes of driving, I drove up to a gas station where a young boy in his early twenties was sitting by the gas pumps reading a fishing magazine. Behind him was a brown wooden store front with wood falling off the building frame. It looked ready to be bull dozed to the ground.

"Excuse me. I need some gas," I said, trying to sound polite.

The boy looked up with a frightened expression on his face, when he saw my height and physical appearance.

"How can I help you, sir," he said in a squeamish voice, standing up.

"I need some gas. Fill her up."

"We have self-service, sir, you can go inside and pay first and bring your receipt, too. Nice car you got there," he said, looking at me. "I bet you from up north, huh? You don't look like you're from around these parts."

I nodded showing no emotion. The last thing I needed was trouble with this white boy. I know how southern cops can be. "I am from New York," I answered.

He smiled showing his missing teeth. His skin was full of blotches and holes. He looked liked one who proudly displayed his confederate flag in his truck.

I walked toward the musty store that resembled a breadbox. The inside had poor lighting. A man wearing torn faded blue jeans with a cut off white tank top stood behind a counter His age was hidden behind his life experiences. He had greasy hair that was slicked back away from his forehead. His skin had a dehydrated look. He looked as though his diet consisted of too much starch. One thing that struck me about him was the tattoo

of a snake on his upper right arm with black jade eyes. I approached the counter, giving him a cold stare, pulling my jacket open, and exposing the gun that sat in my holster rubbing against my side.

How can I help you, sir?" When he smiled, he exposed his brownish teeth that were filled with gaps and holes. "We's aim to please," he said looking down at my holster.

"I'll take Pepsi," I said, handing him a crisp fifty dollar bill.

He looked at me and then at the bill and back at me.

"We don't change this kind of money too often," he said with a fiendish grin. "I can change this here bill," he said spitting tobacco in a rusty black can that sat on the counter.

"You have a phone book on the premises?"

"Yeah," he said bending down behind the counter. He threw the phone book on top of the counter. I had to restrain myself from taking this guy out. The last thing I needed was trouble with southern cops—a black man's worst nightmare. I experienced racist cops in all parts, but the ones down south have no problems displaying their animosity against blacks.

"You some kind of cop?"

"A private investigator" I said.

"You here on business?"

"You're more intelligent than you look," I said.

"You don't talk much," he said.

I took the phone book and proceeded to look up Shep Anderson. I was lucky there was only one Shep Anderson in the phone book, but a dozen or so people with the last name Anderson. The address is eleven-fifteen Chestnut Hill estates. My search was on.

"Do you know where Chestnut Hill Estates is?"

Asa Allen-Showell

He looked me up and down before answering. "Yeah, that ain't but seven miles from here. You make a right once you leave here and go about seven miles north until you see a winding road off to your left. Stay on your left-hand side and go up the hill. That's Chestnut Hills Estate. That's where the rich folks live." I thanked the young fellow for my gas and drove off, to my next interview.

7

The three car garage, with a circular brick drive way, has a reddish brown oak finished door with a gold plated door knocker. Peaking through a fence in the back of the house, I saw an in ground pool that could be compared to an Olympic size pool. The windows in the front of the house have an octagon shape. The outside of the house is done in red brick. To the left of the door was an intercom system. I pushed the white button and waited for a response. A female voice came through on the intercom. "Who is it?"

"My name is Mosee Love. I'm a private investigator hired by Ms. Zoe Owens's," I said speaking into the tiny box. "I am here to speak with Mr. Shep Anderson."

The intercom spoke back at me. "I'll be there in a few minutes," The female voice said back to me.

A dark skinned woman with a close box cut, who looked to be in her mid thirties, came to the door. She wore a cream color baby doll dress. Her gold toned sandals exposed her neatly pedicure toes in a cream color nail polish. Looking at her toes gave me an immediate sensation. Her calf muscles were the shapes of bowling pins. I looked her over with the word lust written all over my face. She wore very little makeup, except for gold color lipstick. "Hello," she said smiling. "My name's Ursula," she said extending her hand for me to shake.

"My name's Mosee Love. I'm here to see Mr. Shep Anderson about a personal matter. I reached into my suit jacket, handing her my identification. Her eyes shifted from me to my identification and back to me. I waited for a response, trying not to over exert my authority. Sometimes people in law enforcement with a badge tend to have a god-like complex.

"A private investigator?" You're from New York?" she said,

handing me back my badge and giving me a seductive smile.

"Yes, to both your questions."

"You don't look like a cop. I know a cop when I see one."

I smiled back trying to be patient, but the blazing summer heat wasn't helping my condition. "I do similar work that cops do, except I work for myself."

She had a perplexed look on his face. "My father's not in any kind of trouble, is he?"

"No, I just wanna ask him a couple of questions about an old friend of his." She drilled me for fifteen minutes, before agreeing to let me in the house.

I followed her down a long corridor. As we came to the end there was a living room to my right. The decor of the room was done in old colonial style furniture, from what I could see. There was a set of spiral stairs in the hallway. Finally, I was lead into a back room. I assumed this was the family room. There was a cream color book shelf that covered the entire length of the back wall. The hunter green and cream colors put me in a relaxed mood. Also, there was a 50 inch screen color television screen that made me feel like I had a front seat at a movie theatre. The oak wood floors had a brilliant shine that reflected the sky light in the ceiling. There was an oak wood desk to the far right side of the room.

"Dad, this is Mosee Love, he's a private investigator who wants to ask you some questions. I'll be going out. Do you want anything?" He made a grunting sound, keeping his eyes focused on a newspaper. She turned around apologizing for her father's behavior. "I'm sorry he can be so rude at times. I think he takes advantage of people because of his age. You can take a seat over there," she said pointing to the hunter green sofa. "He should come around in a few minutes, nice meeting you, Mr. Love. Ok, I'll see you tomorrow dad," she said, bending over to kiss his forehead. As she walked out the door, she put an extra stride in her walk.

I tried clearing my throat to get his attention. Maybe he was sleeping or pretending to read the paper. Some older people tend to forget easily. Maybe he forgot I was in the same room. Sitting in silence seemed like an eternity, waiting for him to respond to my presence. I didn't know if I should shake the old man to see if he's still breathing, or reading the newspaper. I'm not in the mood for another rude episode, after the gas station incident. A simply please to meet you, or do you care for something to drink would be nice. For the second time clearing my throat," Hello, Mr. Anderson," I said speaking loudly." I'm Mosee Love a private investigator, I ..."

"I heard your name the first time my daughter brought you in here, I ain't deaf." I tried to remember what my mother taught me. 'You can catch more flies with honey, than you can with vinegar.' He sat in a black recliner chair, wearing white Bermuda shorts and a tan and white sleeve shirt. "Well, boy, speak up I ain't no mind interpreter. What you come here fore?" he said looking over his spectacles.

"Mr. Anderson sir..."

"Don't call me that, most people calls me Shep." I figured we must've broken some ground, since he allowed me to refer to him on a first name basis.

"Shep, I'm here to ask you a few questions about Foster Owens." He immediately sat erected in his chair, looking at me with intensity. "Did you say Foster?"

"Yes."

"Foster Owens, I ain't heard that bastard's name in over forty years. Is he still alive?" Cause if he is, he owes some money; he done ran of with fifty grand," he said breathing heavy. "I may be senile, but I never forgets when someone owes me money."

"I don't know Mr. Anderson, I mean Shep. I 'm here to help Foster."

"I can't tell you much son, cause I ain't seen him in over forty years."

51

"For starters you can tell me about your relationship with Foster." He was silent for a brief moment, as if he was searching his data bank for information.

"He started working for me in my club, called the Peacock. He kept people in line, you know when folks drinks too much booze," he said coughing uncontrollably. I got nervous when Shep continued coughing nonstop. He stopped talking briefly to catch his breath.

"Are you okay, Mr. Anderson.?"

"Yeah, son," he coughed. "I'm getting a little excited that's all. What was we talking about?" he asked with his face flushed from excitement.

"You were telling me about Foster working for you."

He inhaled taking a deep breath. "He talked folks outta fights at my club. He had a way with words; he could charm the pants off your mama," he said laughing to himself.

"I wouldn't call that a business partner."

"Later on I took him on in my number's business," he said sitting relaxed in his chair.

"He collected my monies from people who bet on street numbers. Back then, son, black folks had five kinds of entertainment: booze, dancing, women, numbers and church. This helped us to keep our sanity," he said shaking his head, smiling. "Lawdy you taken me back some years."

"You want somethin' to drink?"

"Yes, I'll take some juice, please."

He called a woman who came into the den smiling. She bent over kissing him on the cheek. "You want somethin, sugar?" she smiled.

"Essie, this is Mosee Love, he's a private investigator." She smiled nodding her head. "Please to meet you, Mr. Love." This Essie, he called her is a medium built woman about twenty years his junior. I figure she had to be sixty-something. She kept her eyes focused on me smiling. "Essie get the boy somethin' to drink," he grunted. "Ain't she a looker? I see her eyes are on you. She ain't bad for a fifty-five year old woman," he smiled fiendishly. She's my companion. Been with me for quite sometime." He was lying back in his recliner chair.

"Mr. Shep, sir I would like to know what you remember about Foster." "Did he have friends? Did he have any hobbies?" Where was he from?" Did he have any girlfriends?" Did he have enemies?"

"It takes a while for someone my age to remember things," He paused.

"He always kept enemies. Foster was always trying to steal somebody's woman. He never could turn down a piece. I remember one time he tried to hit on my woman at the club. He knew she was my woman, but that ain't never stop Foster from getting want he wanted," he said taking a deep breath. I tried to kill the bastard for tryin to make a pass at my old lady. That's when I fired his black ass."

"Two things you don't mess with: a man's woman and his money. Those two things got many a men killed in my time. One thing he sure could cook a mean meal. He usd'a talks about opening up a soul food restaurant. He could cook anything from scratch. Sometimes folks come in just to get some of Fosters cooking."

"Any enemies?" I asked a second time.

"He always kept a list full. Men's was jealous of him because the women wanted him."

"Do you remember the names of Foster's enemies?"

"I ain't got much more to say about the man."

Essie came back into the room carrying a black and gold serving tray, with two large sodas sitting on top. She gave Shep his drink, placing it on the end table next to his chair. She made her way towards my direction greeting me with a friendly smile. "I hope your stay in Westfield is a pleasant one," she said placing the drink and coaster in front of me on the black coffee table.

I smiled nodding my head. "Me, too," I said, looking at her exit the room, I quickly darted my eyes back to Shep. "Mr. Anderson, do you know if Foster Owens had any relatives? Mother, father or sister?"

I picked up my glass swallowing a big gulp of soda; it was refreshing going down my throat. The summer heat down here made it unbearable for me. The only thing I could think about was a cold shower and changing into a pair of shorts and a tee shirt.

"Now that you mention it, I do remember him taking about his sister."

"What's her name?"

He squinted his eyes at me. "Well now let me think. Her name is Jessie. I don't know much about her."

I had to rephrase my question differently, hoping that he remembered something in that old brain of his. "He have any friends?"

"Foster?" He ain't have no friends." He paused, shaking his head, "but lord he sure had plenty of enemies, that's for sure."

"Do you remember any names?"

"Can't say that I do."

I handed him one of my business cards, concluding our interview. "Mr. Anderson if you remember anything, please feel free to call me anytime." I wrote the name and room number of the hotel where I was staying on the back of my business card along with the telephone number. "Mr. Anderson thanks you for seeing me."

He smiled and nodded his head. "Essie will see you out."

"It's been nice meeting you," I said walking over to shake his hand.

"If you find him, you come back and let me know. I'd like to collect the money he owes me."

"Will do, Mr. Anderson." I wasn't out to collect old debts, just find my client's father and return back to New York.

I returned to my hotel room mentally exhausted from the two interviews. Before getting too relaxed, I telephoned Zoe to check in. I was feeling good about my accomplishments today. "Hello Zoe, it's me, Mosee Love."

"I'm glad you called, I was wondering how your investigation is going, any progress?"

"Some. I've spoken to your mother, and she gave me the name of two people: Shep Anderson, a former business Associate and Ellis Worthington, your father's army buddy."

"So, what's next?"

"Well, I made my first initial contact with Shep Anderson. Next I'll try to locate Ellis Worthington. Hopefully, his military personnel files will tell me something. I forgot to mention; he has a sister named Jessie."

"You need my help down there?"

"What kinda help, Zoe?"

"I can be a part of the investigation." I was silent for a few seconds.

"Are you there?" she said.

"Yes."

"Like, I said I, need to come down there and help."

I tried to choose the correct words not to offend her. "Zoe, I feel that it would be inappropriate if you come down here and make initial contact with your father. As your investigator, I should be the one to make the initial contact. I have to question him to make sure everything is legitimate. I wouldn't want to put you in jeopardy."

The last thing I needed is a female sidekick. A liberated woman was not mentally or physically inept to handle any type of job. The white women's liberation movement is nothing but a bunch of lesbians trying to push their agenda. I thought the liberation movement put outlandish ideas in black women's minds.

The idea of having Zoe come down here to work along beside me, made me remember being assigned to my first kidnapping case with a female agent. She complained about everything: Cramps, hungry, exhaustion. I refused to answer her, avoiding the inevitable.

"Mosee, are you alright? Say something, anything. Do you think I need to come down and join you?"

I was silent for a moment, trying to come up with another valid reason to discourage her. "Zoe, I really don't think it's a good idea for you to come to Westfield. You have no idea what dangers may lie ahead. I wouldn't want you getting hurt."

"Okay, I get the message," she said in a whisper.

After I ended our conversation, I took a Tylenol, stretching on the bed in my underwear. Sleep was becoming impossible these days, so an HBO movie was becoming appealing. The growling of my stomach made me realize I hadn't eaten since yesterday. My taste buds put me in the mood for a triple Decker turkey sandwich with cheese and bacon and a side order of fries. Everyone deserved a treat in life. I sat up in bed and reached for my wallet on the nightstand. I took out a napkin with Everee's name and telephone number, and stared at the telephone for five minutes.

After I ate my turkey sandwich, I attempted to get some sleep, but the jarring ring of the telephone, interrupted me. It rang five times, nonstop. I rolled over on my left side, trying to go back to sleep. Finally, I drifted into a deep slumber. When I heard the phone ring again, I answered it with reservations in a low voice. "Hello who's calling?"

"I'm sorry. I must have the wrong room; I'm looking for Mosee Love's room."

"Zoe?"

"Mosee, is that you? Why you actin so secretive?" Mosee, I

been thinking, I need to come down there and help you with my case.

"Help me. I thought we discussed this earlier."

"Yeah, but it's my father you're looking for. I feel that I should be included."

I rolled over on my left side, reaching for my watch. "I didn't know it was ten o'clock at night. I must've been really tried. I'm working the case as I chose and I say no. That's final."

"Have it your way", she said slamming the telephone in my ear.

The following morning, Tuesday, May 20, 1998, I awakened with empathy on my mind for Zoe, wondering if I was a little too hard on her. Maybe Zoe would be a help to me, but on the opposite side of the spectrum having her down here would only complicate things. I showered and put on a pair of jeans and a white tank top exposing my muscular biceps. The white cotton top hugged my upper torso, exposing the curvatures in my chest.

Seeing the line in the dining area crowded with parents and kids on their summer vacation made me remember the pleasant times I spent with Joyce and our children on our summer trips. Those rare moments are the only pleasant memories I have from my ten years of marriage. I looked over the crowd with embarrassment written all over my face, when I heard my uncontrollable stomach muscles growling. A white woman in her early twenties, wearing stone washed jeans and a rolling stones tee shirt turned around smiling. "Hungry aren't we?" she smiled.

"Yes, I laughed."

The brunch spread looked appetizing, as I surveyed the food choices. I filled every inch of my plate with scrambled eggs, sausages, French toast and grits. My eyes are bigger than my stomach, but I managed to clean my plate and get seconds.

I was on my second plate when I felt the presence of someone standing over my table. "Hello, Mr. Love, My name's Margo Watson. May I join you?

She caught me in between chewing. I moved my head in an up and down motion. "Have a seat."

She wore a green print dress that came to her ankles. She wore open toe leather sandals that exposed her neatly trimmed toes, which were polished in an off white color. She carried a small black leather hand bag with matching sandals. After taking a brief survey of her body, I concluded that she was a member of some health club. Her body was that of a forty-year-old. Her face and hands told her true age. I figured she had to be in her mid sixties. She smiled showing her pearly whites. "I'm not disturbing you are I, Mr. Love?"

I nodded my head in between swallowing a mouth full of grits. I extended my hand to introduce myself, even though she knew who I was. I hate when someone knows about me, without ever meeting me. It puts me on edge. Like someone is stalking me.

"Please, Mr. Mosee, don't rush on my account, she said.

"I'm a close friend of Zoe and her mother."

"How do you know who I am?"

"Well, Westfield is a small town, and words travel fast. Besides, you went to visit Zoe's mother yesterday. She and I were friends before Zoe was even born." I finished my scrambled eggs and sausages before they became too cold to eat. Margo Watson rambled on about Foster being a smart man who never wanted to work for anyone. He was always out for a quick buck.

"You from around here, Ms. Watson?"

"Please, call me Margo", she smiled. "All my friends do.

"I know nothin' else but Westfield, South Carolina. I live in Oak Meadows, which is thirty minutes outside of Westfield. I'm a true southern gal, Mr. Love."

The waitress came over to the table. She asked me if I wanted any more drinks.

"You want something to drink, Margo?"

"Yes. I'll have an ice tea."

"What stake do you have in The Foster case?"

"My best friend Emma's daughter, is looking for her father, and I wanna help anyway I can. A child deserves to know who her daddy is. I never did know mine; she said looking down at the table. I took my last bite of maple syrup pancakes trying to finish the last two, but my stomach wouldn't stretch any further. The waitress came back with Margo's ice tea. She asked me if I was finished with my plate. She cleared the table and left my unfinished orange juice.

I reached into my wallet taking out one of my business cards. "Here's my card, Margo; you can call me any time you come across any pertinent information that may help me locate Zoe's father." After she took my card, she placed it in her small hand bag and rose from the table. I stood up giving her my hand to shake. "It's been a pleasure meeting you, Margo."

"The pleasure is all mine," she smiled. "Oh, by the way don't tell Zoe or Emma that I came to see you. I don't want her to think I'm being nosey. You know how folks can be."

I smiled acknowledging her statement. After finishing my last gulp of cold orange juice, I staggered off to my room sleeping off the sluggish feeling I always experience after eating a hearty meal.

I was dreaming when I was awakened by loud excessive banging on my hotel door. I tried to place myself back in the dream where I left off, but a distressful voice kept interrupting me. "Mosee, open up, you in there?" a voice cried out. "It's me, Zoe." I rolled over on my left side putting the pillow over my head. Nothing worked. The annoying voice became louder and persistent "Mosee Love, I know you're in there. I'm not leaving until you open this door. It won't help ignoring me, you know."

I was hoping all this was a nightmare, and I would wake up. The knocking became louder and persistent. Hesitantly, I reached for my black biker shorts that lay on the lounge chair by the window. I took my time getting dressed before answering the door.

"Oh, it's you," I whispered opening the door slowly trying to sound surprised.

"I came anyway, even if you don't want me." She forced her way into my room without any regard for my privacy.

"Zoe . . . I . . . Before I had a chance to respond, she was sitting on the lounge chair in the far right corner of my hotel room. She took out a black cigarette case and lighter from her purse. She took a few puffs before speaking. "I'm stayin on the tenth floor, room ten fifty-two. I don't know why you picked this hotel to stay in, when they have so many nice bed and breakfast inns. These hotels along the strip can be so congested. Coming from the city you're probably used to this."

She rambled on for the past fifteen minutes about nothing.

I opened the window to let the fresh air in. I despised cigarette smoke. "I'm sorry I didn't know you weren't a smoker," she said continuing to puff on her cigarette.

I sat on the edge of the bed, not uttering a word. I was trying to contain my anger, when I realized Zoe had no respect for me. "Mosee, I want you to know I'm here to help any way I can."

I looked at her with intensity, showing no outward signs of emotions. I wasn't here to play games. "No problem," I said in a low voice.

"So when can we get started? I figure we can meet for dinner. I know a soul food restaurant that specializes in southern cuisine."

"Sounds alright. You're the boss," I said sarcastically.

We sat in a booth in the far corner of the restaurant. The place has oval tables in the middle of the floors and booths along side the walls. There's black art work hanging on the walls. One particular painting I was drawn to was a painting of three black men surrounding a newborn baby. The painting showed the human side of the black male. It captured the true essence of the black male in his most vulnerable state.

Vicious Karma

The people at the restaurant went that "extra mile" that made you feel special.

I ordered southern fried chicken and yams with collard greens and corn bread and Zoe ordered fried pork chops smothered in gravy with a side dish of rice and macaroni and cheese.

"Mosee, you'll find the food appetizing. Everything is made fresh."

"I shouldn't have any problem with cleaning my plate."

She sized me up smiling. "A man of your size should have no problem eating a healthy meal."

"True, I do like to eat."

"What made you choose detective work?"

"There was a time I was considered the neighborhood detective. Everyone came to me to find out who was doing what. I always came up with answers to everyone's questions. Sometimes the adults came to me to find out if their spouses were cheating. You can say I had a nose for other peoples business."

"Cedric told me you were an FBI agent."

The waitress brought over the food. I smiled when she placed the food on the table.

"You can say I got tired of airing out the governments dirty laundry."

"What's our next move?" She started irritating me, as if she was in charge. She rambled on like I was her assistant. I allowed her to hear herself talk.

I tried to come up with an excuse to ditch her. My first instinct was to get up extra early at "the crack of dawn." Zoe looked liked she enjoyed her beauty rest. I shouldn't have a problem avoiding her in the morning

I picked up a fried chicken thigh, sinking my teeth into the chicken, watching the juices squirt forward. "My first step is to contact an old friend of mine at the bureau. I'm sure he can get information on Ellis Worthington and your father." I drank my ice tea drink, gulping down half the glass.

"Whose Ellis Worthington?" she said looking at me with intensity.

"He was your father's closest friend in the army."

Her expression took on a different shape, like a pretzel twisting itself into different directions. "I didn't know he had a friend. Actually I don't know anything about him." At that moment, I no longer saw a woman sitting in front of me, but a scared little girl.

I picked up my fork diving headfirst into my yams covered in thick maple syrup. I can taste the cinnamon and brown sugar juices. "Oh I forgot to mention that a woman came by to see me named, Margo Watson. She claims to be a friend of your family."

"She's a friend of my mother's. I call her Aunt Margo. My mother's been friends with her before I was born."

We finished eating dinner in silence, enjoying the southern food and hospitality.

Wednesday morning, I heard someone knocking on my hotel door at seven o'clock in the morning. "Open up!" she yelled, pounding on the door. "I need to come in and talk to you."

I buried my head between the two pillows. The voice was still persistent. After fifteen minutes of interrupted noise, everything was quiet. I was hoping to get an early start and avoid Zoe. After the knocking ceased, I dialed Rex Thomas's telephone at the Bureau in Washington. "Hello, Federal Bureau of Investigations, how may I help you, the operator said in a smug voice?"

"I like to speak with agent Rex Thomas." I stayed on the line until I was connected to Rex Thomas.

"Hello, this is agent Rex Thomas," how can I help you?"

"Red hair Rex."

"Mosee?" Mosee Love."

"That's right I'm the only black friend you got. I'm the one who introduced you to Luther Vandross." Rex and I laughed and reminiscence about old times for over half an hour.

"So you wanna come back and join us?"

The painful memories crept back into my consciousness reminding me why I resigned from the Bureau. When I made the announcement to my sister, Shelby had thought I was going through a mid life crisis. Her answer to my brief insanity--see a psychologist.

Shelby is a woman, who believes in job security. She would rather build up years on the job, instead of taking a risk to start over again in another career. She always preached 'why leave a job when you don't know what your getting.

My older sister, Dee has a reputation for quitting the so called good jobs with different hospitals because she's independent and outspoken. This makes it hard for people to adjust to her personality. Some people tend to misjudge being independent and outspoken for being too pushy and overbearing. Confiding in Dee gave me a sense of security. For one, we are so much alike. After my resignation, I began to doubt my actions, but after talking to Dee I felt confident about my decision to resign from my job and move forward. "Thanks, but no thanks. I've had my full of government bureaucracy to last me a life time."

"What's been up, Rex?"

"Same old shit, man, nothings changed since you left."

"How are your daughters, Mosee?"

"Getting bigger, Jewel's five and Tiffany's seven. Soon I'll be paying for college and wedding's.

"I remember when they were born," Rex said reflecting on his thoughts.

"What else is new? Doing any investigative work since you left? I cannot believe five years have gone by. Boy do I feel old. I admire you, Mosee, you chose to take a stand and start over again. That takes courage, something I wish I had."

"Recently I took my first missing persons assignment in five years."

"I've been hired by a woman, who's a close friend of my best friend. She wants me to find her father, whom she hasn't seen in over twenty years."

"That's great, Mosee, I hate to see your talents go to waste. You were one helluva agent. Anything you need, just say the word."

"I need some information on Foster Owens. He's the man I'm looking for and his army buddy Ellis Worthington who served in The Korean War with Foster."

"You think he's one of those fathers who went to the store for a loaf of bread and never came home?"

I could see my chest rise and fall, when I thought about my father leaving home. I felt myself reliving the nightmare. I came home early from school and found my mother crying hysterically. Her only words were, "How am I going to care for three children and pay a mortgage." I didn't fully comprehend the words my mother spoke. My mother tried to explain to us that Daddy wasn't coming back, the words cut through me like a thick blade. I was numb for months. I couldn't eat and I barley got through Jr. high school. My oldest sister, Dee, adjusted well and pulled everyone together, but she held her silent rage in for years. Later her anger was displaced by her inability to choose decent men. Shelby developed a hard exterior towards men. She never could sustain a relationship for more than a year at a time.

"I'll see what I can dig up on these two men. You can call me back in an hour; hopefully I can come up with something for you."

"Thanks, Rex, I really appreciate this."

I sat in my room watching television, trying to make the last half hour go by quickly. I looked over my notes to see what connections I made thus far. I had nothing but a blank page to show my progress, besides interviewing Zoe's mother and Shep Anderson. I repeatedly looked at my watch counting down to the last second. Just as I was about to call Rex back, the knocking on the door started again. "Mosee, it's me Zoe. Are you busy?" she said yelling from the outside of the door.

"Yeah, I'm kinda busy."

She continues to yell from the outside of the door. "I promise not to talk too much please let me in!"

I hesitantly walked to the door to let her in. "Hello, Zoe come on in," I mumbled, sitting on the edge of the bed.

"What kinda' business were you conducting?" she said flopping down on the twin bed.

"I was going to call a friend of mine, who might have some information on your father and Ellis Worthington."

"That's good I was getting worried, I thought I was paying you for nothing," she said sarcastically. She took a cigarette from her pocketbook. "Who's this friend you keep talking about? she said puffing on her cigarette. "What do you think he'll tell you?"

I hated playing the question and answer game. I was beginning to regret her being here even more. "Please, Zoe don't asked so many questions. I'll tell you what you need to know." I picked up the telephone. "May I speak to agent Rex Thomas? Please."

"Whom should I say is calling," the woman asked.

"Mosee Love."

Zoe sat motionless like someone waiting to be saluted, as I proceeded with my telephone conversation. I jotted down the information Rex gave me. And I responded to him with yes and no's, in order to keep Zoe from knowing too much.

After I ended my phone conversion, Zoe was ready with her 101 questions. "What did he say?" she asked taking a puff of her cigarettes.

I opened the window to air out the cigarette smoke. "I found out that Ellis Worthington is the owner of a construction and demolition business in Denver, Colorado," I said leaning by the window.

"What about my father?"

"Nothing on him except his military papers have him listed as a resident of Denver over thirty years ago."

Zoe looked like she aged ten years in the past half hour sitting in my hotel room. She had distinct lines on her forehead along with heavy bags. The dark circles under her eyes were more visible. It showed all over Zoe's face; she was experiencing a lot of stress about seeing her father for the first time in thirty years. Who could blame her for the way she felt. "Are we going to Denver?" she whispered.

"Yeah, that's what we'll have to do. I'll make our reservations for the next flight. You go pack a few things, nothing heavy. I'll let you know what time our flight leaves."

"Okay." She held her head down low walking out the door.

Zoe's face was full of stress, the last few days. The tedious task of investigation can be a stressful job. I wanted to tell her to stay with her mother, but she had a mind of her own.

After I made plane reservations to Denver, I telephoned Zoe to inform her what time our flight left from Westfield International airport. It's impossible for the opposite sex to pack light clothing; they need two to three outfits per day with matching shoes. I grabbed what little clothing I thought would be appropriate, and stuffed my suitcase along with my trusty Smith and Wesson. Packing a gun is just as important as having a driver's license.

I quickened my pace to the elevator, pushing the up button five times before the elevator stopped on the fifth floor. I continued my pace down the long hallway. Zoe had a corner room at the end of the hallway. I knocked on the door shouting. "Zoe, open up I hope your ready, our plane leaves in an hour and forty-five minutes."

She opened the door in a jovial mood, smiling. "I'll have a few more things to pack," she said.

"I told you to pack light; we're not taking up residence. We're going there to question Worthington and check on any other possible leads. Hopefully we'll be there only a few days. This is not a vacation,"

Zoe sighs, continuing to pack her bags. "I know, but I've never been to Denver; it'll be nice to take in some sights. Essence did an article on some of the popular places for blacks to visit. I was …"

"Don't even think about it. You can visit Denver on your own time, not mine. I have a job to do, remember?"

"Learn to relax. I'm the one who should be nervous, not you," she said.

"I'm not nervous. I take my work serious, that's all."

Zoe struggles to carry her two bags to the elevator. "Do you mind giving a woman some help," she said with attitude in her voice.

"I didn't tell you to bring your wardrobe."

The airport was busy with people arriving and departing to and from their destinations. I went to the ticket window to register for our flight to Denver, Colorado. There was at least a forty-five minute wait until our flight departed. Passing the variety of restaurants on my way to gate 3B made my stomach rumble, reminding me that I hadn't eaten since lunch time. I decided to stop at Burger King and order a Whopper, large fries and a coke, and Zoe ordered a Chicken Caesar's salad and a glass of water. I said, "Watching' our figure, are we?"

"I try to avoid those fatty fast food restaurants."

I looked her over taking a mental survey of her body. "You look good to me."

"Thanks, but we women have to keep our figure, so you men don't run off with younger women."

"Me, I like my women mature and ripe. I don't have time for a woman who's just going into puberty."

"I'm so excited about going to Denver. I've never been there.

I took a bite of my Whopper sandwich, looking up at Zoe with a stern look on my face. "This isn't a vacation, Zoe, we're going on business, remember?"

She nodded her head in agreement. "I was hoping we had time to sight-see, after we finish our business there."

"I doubt it," I said in between chewing my food.

"You're too serious, relax sometimes."

"You're paying me for my services, and I intend on giving you one hundred percent," I paused to swallow my food. "If you choose to sight see, while I work that's your business." "Have you ever been to Denver, Mosee?"

"Yeah a few times on business, why?"

"Did you travel a lot when you worked for the FBI?"

"Yeah, I did my share of traveling. Once you get tenure with the bureau, they tend to station you in a permanent city. They might transfer you if you were assigned to a special case."

"You must'va had a pretty exciting job."

"At first every new job is exciting, until you learn the ropes, but I learned the true faces behind the mask of the people I was working for," I said. "I didn't like what I saw."

"Yeah, I know what you mean. You think our government is protecting us, but in reality they're our enemy," she said shaking her head.

We finished our food and checked our tickets at the desk, where a female ticket agent was checking the passenger's tickets upon boarding.

8

The stewardesses dressed in blue skirts with matching blazers and white shirts walk down the aisle, giving a brief lecture on plane safety. I yawned on this part; I could recite the presentation with my eyes closed. My job assignments took me all over the world. Sometimes the stewardess called me by my first name. After the lecture was over, the stewardess went to the rear of the plane; she returned pushing a tray full of beverages and snacks. She approached the aisle where we sat. "Hello, my names, Tammy," she said smiling. "Do you care for anything to drink?"

"Yes, I'll take a diet Pepsi" Zoe said

"And you, sir?"

"I'll take a glass of white wine."

"There's a five dollar charge, sir"

"That's no problem." The stewardess went to the back of the airplane and returned with a wine glass. After three glasses of white wine, I began feeling the effects when the plane landed.

We retrieved our luggage and went outside where many taxis awaited their victims. One taxi driver stood out amongst the others, by going one step further—he introduced himself to the

Prospective customers, looking for a taxi. "Hello, names Louis," he said smiling. "My names, Mosee and this is Zoe."

I liked the way he introduced himself. "Yes, we need a taxi to take us to the downtown area. We're looking for a reasonable hotel to stay in the city."

He quickly grabbed the bags, putting them inside the trunk. Louis was a dark skinned man average height. His curly hair was a mixture of white and a hint of black. "You folks here on your honeymoon? It's nice seeing young people in love," he said, glancing in the rearview mirror.

Zoe looked at me and smiled moving in closer grabbing my arm. "Yes we're honeymooners," she giggled like a schoolgirl.

"That's great; it's good to see young people in love. I've been married to the same woman for over forty years. Yes sir it's been a wonderful forty years. "I got two boys and one girl, and I'm a grandfather of five," he said shifting his eyes from the road to the rearview mirror.

Zoe started getting nervous watching him drive. She wished he did less talking and driving. Louis looked liked he was a mixture of an Italian and an Afro-American, but his strong African features: nose, lips told his true heritage.

"Where you folks from?"

"New York, Westfield South Carolina," we echoed in harmony sounding like a choir.

I spoke up trying to gain control of the conversation. "Can you recommend any nice hotels in the area, Louis?"

"The Hyatt is a nice hotel for honeymooners," Louis said. "We'll be heading towards the downtown area in twenty minutes. When you see the traffic getting heavy that's a sign."

The taxi pulled up to the Marriott, where other taxis lined up assisting people with their luggage entering and exiting the hotel. "If you need someone to show y'all around just ask for Louis," he said taking out his yellow business card, handing it to me.

"Thanks, Louis I'll look you up if we need you," I said

Louis got the bags from the trunk placing them on the sidewalk in front of the hotel.

We thanked Louis for his hospitality. "Nice meeting you, Louis," Zoe said waving goodbye.

I cringed when I stepped inside the eloquent hotel. I knew the price of the rooms were over my budget. Zoe's mouth flung open when she saw the lobby. "Look at this place, it's simply elegant. I'm glad we're staying here. I bet the rooms are pretty, too."

I mumbled to myself. "I bet the prices here are over rated. I know it cost a minimum of two hundred dollars a night. This is not in my budget, Zoe."

"Calm down. I'll compensate for the difference. I refuse to stay in a cheap motel on my first night in Denver." I did not want to argue with a woman. A skilled I acquired being raised in a household full of women. I learned early that arguing with a woman was useless energy. A woman always gets the last word.

"All right, Zoe, we're staying here," I said giving in to her wishes. I wanted to avoid a confrontation with Zoe, besides I was physically exhausted from the plane ride, and having Zoe as my side kick didn't help matters.

Inside the lobby, there was a waterfall in the sitting area. The lobby floors had black and white marble diamonds shaped tile. I sat in the soft Italian, leather sofa, while the automatic piano played tunes. I hoped she had brains to get separate rooms. I didn't want a woman in my presence twenty four hours. There was a lounge located to the right of the waiting area. I fell asleep on the sofa, waiting for Zoe to return with our hotel keys.

"Mosee wake up," she said shaking my shoulders. "Their all booked up. I got the last room. Someone canceled at the last minute. The room has twin beds.

"Zoe I need my own space."

"You can go someone else, but I'm staying here," she said folding her arms, hovering over me as if she was trying to intimidate me. "The woman at the front desk said nearly every hotel is sold out, because of some music convention."

"I'm comfortable with the arrangements if you are, "she said bending down to pick up her bags.

"You're not the first woman I've slept with."

"You have a sense of humor, too. Well you're not the first man, I slept with," Zoe chuckled.

While Zoe was showering, I called the operator to find out if Ellis Worthington's telephone was listed. Bingo. Ellis Worthington's telephone number was listed under Worthington's construction and Demolition Company, in Lowery Colorado. "I

Yelled to Zoe, who was in the shower, I got something for you, I yelled." I was so excited that I was making some progress. Life didn't seem so bad after all.

"What," she said coming outta the bathroom, in her red terry cloth robe.

"I got your father's army buddy's address. He owns a construction and demolition business here in Denver."

9

Louis was dressed in Khaki shorts and a white cotton short sleeve shirt, standing by his taxi smiling. "I'm glad you'd decided to call me, I promise to show you guys a good time. There's plenty to see here. When I get finish showing you around, you'll gonna fall in love with place and wanna settle down," he said opening the car door. "Nice day we have. I hear there's gonna be plenty of sunshine all day," he said getting into the driver's seat. "Any place you folks have in mind you wanna go?" he said turning around in his seat. "I know popular tourists . . ."

I interpreted him mid sentence. "You can take us to 123 Sycamore drive in Lowery," I said abruptly. I Wasn't in the mood for a sight seeing tour. I had work to do, and I wanted to get what information I needed and head on back, if that was possible.

"That's no problem it's just thirty minutes from here. You got folks out there?"

We looked at each other exchanging glances. "You can say that," I spoke up.

He pulls his taxi into the parking lot where a beige building stood alone. On the right side of the building there were cranes and forklift machinery. There was a sign that read—Worthington's Demolition and Construction Business. This was getting easier than I thought.

Demolition and construction business, Louis mumbles to himself.

"We shouldn't be too long, Louis you don't mind waiting, do you?"

"No, I got nothin but time."

"See you in about half an hour."

Zoe felt a mixture of apprehension and excitement, as she stepped inside the office. A part of her wanted to turn back around and go back home to her mother in Westfield South Carolina. She began thinking about taking her mothers advice and calling off the investigation. Her mother told her searching for her father will bring her nothing but bad luck. She could hear her mother's words as if she were standing next to hear. "Leave the man alone. You think he wanna be bothered with you after thirty years. The man is nothing but trouble. Zoe felt beads of perspiration drip down from her face. A part of her wanted to tell me to keep the money and call off the investigation, but she had an emptiness of not knowing where she came from. She had so many questions that gnawed at her causing her to ignore her insecurities.

As we entered front door of the office, a small frame woman, about ninety pounds with grayish blue and white hair, was sitting behind a desk buried in paper work and answering telephones, too busy to notice us. I stood hovering over her desk, trying to get her attention. It's hard not to notice a six feet man standing in front of your desk. "Hello we're here to see Mr. Ellis Worthington about a personal matter."

She looked up frowning, peeking over her wire frame glasses, "Do you two have an appointment with Mr. Worthington?" she asked in a frail voice.

"No, Ma'am we just flew in from Westfield, South Carolina, to see Mr. Worthington. The matter is very urgent."

She looked over Zoe and me before giving her approval. "Wait a minute, must be mighty important. "Your names please."

"My name's Mosee Love, I'm a private investigator and this is Zoe Owens." I took out my identification card from my wallet, handing her my credentials. She examined the picture thoroughly, like she was reading a novel. She spoke into the telephone ringing his office. "Mr. Worthington you have visitors. Mosee Love and Zoe Owens are here to see you. Send them in." he chimed.

"You can go through the second door on the right."

A man was sitting behind a dusty desk covered to his neck in blue prints, wearing a yellow hard hat. Behind him was a small window over looking a huge dirt field, with construction equipment. "Hello, Mr. Worthington, I'm Mosee Love and this is Zoe Owens. I extended my hand to greet Mr. Ellis Worthington. He extended his hand to shake mine.

"Hello, Mr. Love and Ms. Owens, please pull up a chair. There two in the corner. Do excuse my office, it's a bit untidy. You know how we construction guys are, always carrying dust around."

"What can I help you with?"

"I'm a private investigator, hired by Zoe Owens to find her father."

Ellis Worthington had a bewildered look on his face, sitting up right in his chair. "What do I have to do with her missing father?"

"The man was a friend of yours. His name is Foster Owens."

He sank back in his chair laughing loudly to himself. "Foster Owens, I ain't heard that name in forty plus years. He was somethin. Always tryin to pick up somebody's woman. He had an over worked libido," he said laughing.

"Can you tell us anything about him besides his sex drive?" For example, what his hobbies were, what his favorite foods were, any unusual birth marks."

Ellis stretched his arm, and cleared his throat. "Well, Foster loved to cook; he always dreamed of opening up his own restaurant some day."

"Did he serve in the army with you?"

"Army? He laughed. "That's a joke. He got out of the war, just as fast as they took him in. Foster refused to fight for this country. He said 'why fight for a country that doesn't have respect for the black man.' "He used some lame excuse about arthritis in his leg, so they transferred him to the kitchen for two years. After that he got an honorable discharge from the army."

Zoe sat quietly in her seat, soaking up the information, while I took notes. Ellis Worthington spoke freely about his former friend. "Did you two stay in touch with each other after the Korean War?"

"Yeah, for a while, but the bastard tried to make a move on my old lady," he said with anger. "Can you believe that, after all we been through. He'll sell his mother's soul for a woman," he said snickering to himself.

"After you left the army, what did you do?"

"Foster and I were going in half to open up a soul food restaurant. I had confidence in his cooking abilities. In the army he turned the worst slop into a gourmet meal. He was known for his cooking antics. Everything was in motion. We had the perfect location and our GI loans to open the restaurant, but ..."

"But what?"

"He tried to make a play for my old lady, like I told you. He accused her of hitting on him. This brought on friction in our relationship. I was never able to trust him again. After that we stopped talking," he said sitting erect in his chair.

"Are you still married to the same woman Foster tired to take from you?"

"Yes. I later found out that he was lying. My old lady never tired to come on to Foster. He tried everything to break us up. Because he never found a woman he loved, he felt he could justify seeing other people miserable in their relationships."

"Is that why you left Westfield, South Carolina?"

"No . . . huh, he was hesitant. My uncle left me this construction business. Been here ever since."

"Do you know where Foster sister lives?"

"I ain't seen her in ages, but I do remember she was married to some black doctor she met in the hospital where she worked as a nurse."

"Can you remember anything else?"

"No, but if something jogs my memory, I'll give you a call. How long you gonna be in town?"

"For three days, depending how the investigation goes."

I got up signaling the end of the interview. Mr. Worthington rose from his desk and walked over to say his good-byes. We exchanged business cards with each other. I wrote my room number and the name of the hotel on the back of my card, before handing it to Mr. Worthington. "Please feel free to call me anytime, day or night." I gave Ellis Worthington a firm hand shake. Zoe stood beside me, smiling extending her hand to shake with Mr. Worthington. "We thank you for taking the time to speak with us. This means so much to me to find my father."

"No, problem. I wish y'all luck in your search."

Louis was reading the newspaper when we approached the taxi. "Well, I see you guys are finished."

"So how was your visit?"

"Fine, just fine," I said.

Louis turns around in the front seat to face us. "Where you love birds wanna go next in the Rocky Mountain state?"

"You can take us to the county court house."

"Court house?" he repeated in a puzzling tone. "What kinda honeymoon are you on? Going to a government building."

"We have a friends to visit."

"You sure do know plenty of folks here," he said in a suspicious voice.

"I'll take you where ever you like, as long as you payin' me. I'm your personal chauffeur," he said backing out of the driveway. We'll go back downtown; I'll have you there in no time."

"Thanks, Louis, we really appreciate this."

"No problem at all."

"How long you plan on staying here? Cause I like to show you more of Denver."

"Were staying two to three days tops. It depends on how things go."

"What kind of honeymoon is this? You didn't get the chance to enjoy yourself.

I wanted this guy to keep his mouth shut. I wasn't in the mood for a nosey cab driver.

"You awful quiet, Zoe." She leaned closer to me, whispering into my ear.

"I'm thinking about calling off this investigation."

Calling off the investigation is the last thing I needed to hear, after I made plans to spend my money. I didn't want to think about the consequences. I had to think of something to convince Zoe to keep her case open. "Zoe you need patience, after all you waited over twenty years to see your father, I'm sure you can wait a few more months. "Were closer than you think."

"Yeah. I guess your right. It's my nerves. I can use a cigarette about now."

I put my arm around Zoe's shoulder, comforting her.

"Mosee, I like to go with you if you find my aunt.

"Huh. I'm sorry can you repeat what you said?"

She hesitated for a moment. "I said I would like to go with you when you find my father's sister.

We're going to the court house to look at some public records."

"Public records. What's that gonna tell us?"

"Hopefully something."

"You heard the man, Fosters sister was married. Well' look up public records on Foster and his sister.

We entered the court house, where a guard sat behind a desk, in front of a metal detector. I inquired about the location of the public records Dept. The guard told me the office is the last door on the right, down the hall. We walked down the hall, until we came upon a door marked public records. Behind the counter, a group of women huddled around a desk, chattering and drinking coffee. Zoe and I waited patiently for assistance. "We must be invisible," I said speaking loudly. I cleared my throat. "Excuse us for disturbing your social hour, but we're here to look at your public divorce documents, if it's alright with you?"

The group of women remained silent for a moment. A tall woman walked towards the counter with a smirk on her face. "What year, sir?" she said with irritation in her voice.

I think we'll start with the year 1950's and working our way up to ... 1960's.

I can't guarantee that our records are current.

"That's fine, Miss." We sat at table in the middle of the room. Zoe was fidgeting in her seat, looking restless. "We haven't had time to take a tour of Denver. Do you think we'll have time to take in some sights?"

I shrugged my shoulders not uttering a sound. The woman came back pushing a rolling cart stacked to the sky with binders. "Here are the books you requested, they're arranged by year and last name."

"We'll be here for ever tryin to find her name."

"This is the boring side of investigations: Countless research."

I handed Zoe one book that started with the year 1950 and I started with the year 1960. Zoe stopped at the year 1965. She looked distant, like something was bothering her. "Zoe, are you okay?" You don't look well."

"Oh I was thinking—is this worth the effort? My father could be dead, or he might be one of those fathers who just didn't give a shit," Zoe said with streams of tears running down her face.

I took a deep breath, reaching over to embrace her. "Now you understand why I didn't want you coming with me. Things can get very sensitive." Zoe didn't say anything. She reached inside her bag and pulled out her cigarette purse, and walked out the door. I returned to my seat, consumed in the books, until I felt a light tap on my right shoulder.

"Excuse me, sir, but we'll be closing in a half hour."

"Thank you." I believed in using every minute of my time to the fullest. I have the tendency to work myself to death, when I get excited about my work. I haven't had this feeling in a long time.

Vicious Karma

Zoe exhibited a wide range of emotions in one person. I have empathy for Zoe's brief encounters with confusion. I went through a period of confusion when I was contemplating rekindling my relationship with my father. Five years have come and gone and I still haven't been able to look my father in the eye. Apart of me wanted to embrace my father, but there is that lingering side of me that refuses to forgive him for deserting our family.

Endless searching through the volume of books didn't get me any closer to finding Zoe's father. I used up the last fifteen minutes doing research, until the building closed, while my partner in crime took refugee in the taxi.

Louis talked Zoe's ears off until she drifted off to sleep. Zoe had a complete mental autobiography of Louis, while she waited for me. When I came to the taxi and climbed into the back seat, she had a blank expression on her face. "Any luck in there?"

"No. I think we should make an extra trip out here tomorrow. We have to get an early start, when most of the government buildings are open.

We returned to our hotel room. I laid across the bed snoring, while Zoe showered. She smiled watching me sleep peacefully. She did not want to wake me, so she decided to venture to the hotel's twenty-four hour restaurant. She slipped on a pair of denim stone wash Guess jeans and a Howard University alumni tee shirt. Putting on the tee shirt made her feel like a college girl again. She managed to keep her girlish figure after being out of college for ten years.

Zoe ordered a turkey club with a side order of fries. Sometimes eating after a certain hour brought on nightmares, especially when her mind was plagued with stress. When the waitress returned to the table, Zoe ate half her turkey club sandwich. Her apprehension about seeing her father for the first time in thirty years brought on anxiety and stress. She imagined her story would have a happy

81

ending. Like in the movies, Zoe pictured her father embracing her with open arms, kissing her gently on the forehead and whispering in her ear that everything will be ok. She realized that's fantasy and this is reality.

Her growing anxiety and apprehension caused her to eat less, so she opted to return to her hotel room.

She opened the hotel door slowly walking in the dark. Mosee slept peacefully in the twin bed. Zoe was both too lazy and tried to take the extra time to change in the bathroom. She slipped out of her jeans, placing them on the chair. She climbed into bed wearing only her alumni tee shirt that made a great over night gown. Zoe didn't believe in night clothes, unless it called for a special occasion.

Loud banging on the door startled Zoe. She jumped outta bed, trying to wake me. She shook me a number of times, before I finally responded. The banging continued. Who ever it was certainly wasn't about to give up without a fight "Wake up, Mosee there's someone knocking at the door, please see who it might be." I refused to move outta my peaceful slumber. She tried to go back to sleep, but the rhythm of the knocks became louder. She looked over at me watching me snore. She wondered if Mosee too heard the knocking on the door. Whispering she said, "Mosee there's someone knocking at the door." I moaned rolling over on my left side burying my head between the pillows. "Mosee wake up I don't know who is at the door." She continued to shake me violently.

"Alright, I'll get up, but whose at the door Zoe?"

"I don't know, you're the detective. You answer it," she snapped, trying to get her bearings together.

I rose out of bed slowly. "Now you're giving me job descriptions," I said sarcastically. I went to the top drawer, reaching for my 9MM Semi Automatic. "Who is it?"

"It's me Ellis Worthington."

I kept my gun pointed forward, as Zoe ran in the bathroom,

peeking behind the door. I thrust the door open, standing at a distance. Ellis Worthington entered the room startled when he saw the gun pointing in his face. "Man, I ain't here to cause harm. Put that gun away; I just wanna tell you some information that may be helpful to you," he said wheezing. Zoe came out of the bathroom, after she heard Ellis Worthington's voice.

"I'm sorry Mr. Worthington, but I believe in taking precautions at all times. In my line of work you can't afford to sleep."

Mr. Worthington took a deep breath, trying to calm himself. "That's ok, Mr. Love, I know you have a dangerous job. I can't blame you for being cautious. You never know what might be waiting for you."

"Please take a seat," Zoe said.

"Mr. Worthington, you said you have some information to tell us?" said Mosee.

"Yes. That's right. I wanted to wait until tomorrow morning to see y'all, but I didn't know how long you two plan on staying in Denver," he said frantically. I got this information a little past eleven o'clock and I couldn't sleep.

"We can go to the hotel lobby and talk."

Zoe yells, "Hotel lobby. What about me?"

"I'll tell you all the pertinent information." I slammed the door behind me.

"My secretary asked me why you two were here to see me. She has ears and eyes everywhere. Anyway she knows a friend of a friend who was very close to Foster, about five years ago."

"Is this friend a female?" I asked taking out a tape recorder.

"Female, of course, he said in a surprising tone. Foster relocated to South Carolina somewhere, after his breakup. His sister went to live with him after her divorce."

"What's the woman's name?"

"I don't know, she didn't want to give her name because she didn't want to get involved in this investigation."

"Why did his sister get divorced?"

"There were many rumors. Some say Foster's sister, Jessie was physically and mentally abused by her husband.

"Oh, I forgot to mention that his sister used her divorce settlement to help her brother finance his restaurant."

I hoped to put a closure to this case soon. I anxiously wanted to return to Queens and spend the summer with my daughters. I felt guilty about being away this long. The summer months were always my time to spent with my children. Joyce could be temperamental if I didn't adhere to her rules. She could be a real bitch at times. I grew accustomed to her irrational behavior.

"I hope I was of some assistance to you and ...."

"Zoe," I said helping him out.

"Young people have odd names. They don't believe in old fashion names," he said. "I hope you find Foster."

"Everyone deserves a chance to know their father and mother."

I nodded. I found it harder to keep my eyes open. Sleep is important when you are in my line of work. "Thank you for coming to see me, Mr. Worthington, this information is the break we've been looking for."

"Any time, son. don't mind helping people. I believe in giving something back when you can. I help the young people in my neighborhood. I have an internship at my company, and I give to the needy."

I glanced down at my watch—12 30 A.M. For the past fifteen minutes, Worthington rambled on about nonsense. I cleared my throat interrupting his thought process. "Mr. Worthington, I hate to break up this conversation, but I have an early day ahead of me. I glanced at my watch, hoping he got the message.

"I'm sorry to keep you; I love to talk. If I was born a woman I would be a busy body in everyone's business. I wish you and Zoe luck." I stood up and watched Mr. Worthington walk out the hotel.

I was elated at my first accomplishment. Now I felt like an investigator again. That's one hurdle down.

10

Plaguing thoughts of the grudge I held against my father occupied my mind, since I took Zoe's missing person's case. I was twelve when my father left my mother and my two sisters. A part of me wanted to forgive him, but the painful memories of the past always manages to seep its way back into my consciousness. It's like reliving that dredged moment all over again. Now I'm thirty-six and I still haven't resolved my past.

I remember my father didn't show up for my first baseball game; my mother confronted me with the news that our father left us. It took me weeks to comprehend what that meant. I barricaded myself in the room for days. I withdrew from all sports and I went from an A—student to a C—student. Everyone in the household suffered both economically and emotionally. My mother was forced to take on two jobs. This was her first time taking employment outside the house since she married. She was an abandoned wife with no job skills. It was difficult for her to find employment; the only alternative for a black woman with no marketable skills in the sixties was domestic work.

She would come home most nights when it was close to our bed time. This left little time to spend with us. Even though my mother worked two jobs, it still was difficult for us to manage the bills. The stress of falling behind in her mortgage payments caused her to age fifteen years. This tragedy transformed her into a decrepit woman; this nearly drained her. She often complained about not having enough energy to do anything.

I was in shock the day I came home from school and found my mother sitting on the edge of the bed with a blank look in her eyes. I was shaking my mother, trying to break her trance.

She continued to laugh and cry simultaneously. I was startled when my mother didn't realize I was in the same room. 'Mom, it's me Mosee.' She looked at me as if I was a stranger. She yelled, telling me to get outta of her house, before they take me away.

I yelled frantically, trying to snap her back into reality. Mom it's me your son, Mosee, remember? I sobbed with tears running down my cheek. She looked at me like I was a stranger. I can still feel the pain and hurt of that day. Sometimes I look back trying to make sense out of all this madness.

"Boy, I don't know you. How you get in my house? Get out before I calls the cops." She shouted. I locked myself in the room crying hysterically.

Half an hour later, I hear knocking on my bedroom door. "Open up son, it's the police. We won't harm you, we're here to help you," the voice said in a soothing tone. I opened the door slowly, wiping my eyes. "What's wrong with my mother?"

The police officer took me by the hand, leading me into the living room. "We had to take your mother to a hospital that will help her." I've heard horror stories about crazy people going to hospitals, sitting in dark rooms, wrapped in strait jackets. People who go into those places never come out the same. They stuff drugs that make you hear and see crazy things. I didn't wanna picture my mother in one of those places, rocking in a chair, staring off into space. I somehow knew this was the last time I would see my mother again.

My two sisters came through the door. The oldest, Dee, came over to me to find out what was going on. "What's wrong did something happen?" The police officer sat next to me and my two sisters, Dee and Shelby, explaining that our mother had a nervous breakdown. We all started crying. I didn't know what a nervous breakdown was, but I knew it was something terrible from the expression on my sister's faces. The cop asked us if we have any family. Dee replied. "Yeah, my mother has two sisters; one lives in New York, and the other lives in Roanoke, Virginia."

One of my aunts came to stay with us for three weeks. When

my mother returned from the hospital, she was never the same person. She began to deteriorate at a rapid rate. She eventually had two strokes. The second stroke caused her death. My sisters and I went to live with our aunt in Brooklyn, New York. It was a transition from living in the south. I had a difficult time adjusting to my new surroundings. Being the youngest child took a toll on me in a house full of women.

I met Cedric and bonded with him instantly. I was lucky he lived a few doors from us. Cedric befriended me at a vulnerable time in my life, when I lost my mother and father.

Zoe was on her second cigarette, when I came through the door. She sat in a chair with her back towards the door, waiting anxiously for me to return with good news about her father. She jumped up when she heard the door open. "Mosee, what happened? Did Mr. Worthington have any information? What did he tell you?" she said anxiously.

"Zoe slow down, please I'll tell you everything, don't worry, Worthington stated his secretary called him tonight and confessed that she knew of a friend who had an intimate relationship with Foster ten years ago. She said after their breakup he went to live in Westfield South Carolina. I don't know exactly where. And his sister went to live with him after divorcing her husband. Foster's sister was mentally and physically abused by her husband. She used her divorce settlement to help finance her brother's restaurant."

"That's great now we have something concrete to go on," she smiled with sparkling eyes. "I had it with this investigation," she said taking a puff of her cigarette. When we get back to Westfield, you can take over. I'm drained from this trip. I need plenty of R&R." Hearing those words made me feel energized, knowing she will not be glaring over my shoulder questioning me every five minutes. "That's good, Zoe, I really think being on this case is too much pressure for you."

"You are absolutely right it has put a strain on me. I think its best that you work alone."

"Yes, I agree."

"Are you sure you don't need my help?"

What help I thought. "Zoe, you've been a big help, but I'm going solo from here."

She exhaled, showing a sign of relief on her face.

"Ok, fine with me, but you can reach me at my mother's if you need me." "Okay, I'll keep that in mind," I buried my head between the pillows, trying to block out Zoe's presence.

Once again, I'm seated inside the home of my first witness, Ms. Daniels, but under different circumstances. This gave me an opportunity to learn more about her, without pressuring her.

I have a television set to entertain myself in the living room, while Zoe unpacks her bags. I listened attentively, as yelling in the back rooms increased. "What you bringing him back here fore? I don't want any parts of this investigation." And ... the door slams shut. I get up to turn the volume down on the television set, but the only thing I can decipher is muffling sounds.

Zoe came into the living room taking a seat on the sofa, across from me. "I'm sorry, Mosee I hope you didn't hear us," she said with a distressful look on her face. "My mother still doesn't approve of this investigation. She doesn't want me to get hurt. She thinks my father won't accept me as his daughter. I'm not expectin' him to welcome me with open arms. I know it's going to take time to build a relationship. I'm not tryin' to relive the past, or anything. I'll take one day at a time." Her eyes looked at me, as if she was waiting for me to give her the answer to make the transition smoother. I didn't know what to say to her. I didn't wanna lie to her either. It wasn't going to be easy for her.

This is the last thing I needed in my life; Zoe canceling her investigation, after all the plans I made to spend the money. I don't need her to get fickle on me now.

"Zoe you have to do what makes you happy. If finding your father will help put your life in perspective, than I suggest you continue with this investigation. It's only a matter of weeks before I find him."

"You're right, Mosee this is something I have to do for myself. Anyway, enough of this moping lets celebrate your first victory. My mother can cook a mean meal, I hope you're hungry."

"Mama always has something cookin on the stove. I didn't

gained weight until I moved on my own.

"Oh no!" Zoe yells from the kitchen.

I jump outta my seat, running to Zoe's aide.

"You're ok?"

"Yeah, I'm fine. I just discovered my favorite dish—pork chops smothered in brown gravy with fried cabbage and homemade buttermilk biscuits."

"That sure sounds like a southern dish."

"I hope you have a healthy appetite, cause mama hates when folks don't finish your meal. She thinks it shows disrespect to the cook."

"What if you don't like the food?"

She laughs. "There's no such thing as not liking southern cooking. Mama's cousin came to stay with us for a spell when her husband died. She came to us weighing only 120lbs, but when she left she weighed one eighty-five. So there's proof for you."

"Your mother has strong southern values, huh?"

Zoe smiles nodding her head. We return to the living room until diner was served. I needed to take this opportunity to question Zoe about her father. "Was your mother always a Christian woman?"

"As long as I can remember. She always lived right."

"How can you say what's right and want isn't. Your mother didn't marry your father?"

"Well . . . I didn't say she was perfect. I'm sure she did her dirt. "Do you always work, even when you're not?"

"In my line of work you have to stay alert and ready. Old habits are hard to break."

This makes the fourth court house; I've been to in the past three days, but whose counting. One thing I found out through my observation of most court house employees is that they share one commonality—frustrated workers who hate their jobs.

Asa Allen-Showell

I emptied the contents of my inside pockets: coins key and placed them beside my gun on a tray, before going through the metal detector. I knew the inner workings inside most law enforcement agencies.

The sheriff sat on the opposite side lumped over in his chair, looking half asleep. He wore a grayish uniform. "Excuse me, sir, but We's don't allow guns in this here building," he said in a southern accent. "Why are you carrying that gun anyway? You have a license for that? Cause we don't allow civilians to carry firearms without a permit.

This is probably the only time the sheriff got up to do any work. I nonchalantly flashed my FBI badge quick enough to allow the sheriff to see the initials—Federal Bureau of Investigations. The sheriff immediately stood up, as if he was getting ready to salute the red, white and blue. "Excuse me; I didn't know who you were. You guys always doin' something undercover. If I can help you in any way don't hesitant to ask. I believes in helping my country, yes sir," he said proudly. I felt myself getting impatient with this patriot bull shit. I wanted to get in and out as fast as possible. "Thank you for your time."

"What you workin' on? I bet it's some high tech stuff."

I picked up my belongings, putting them back into my wallet. "I'm working on a missing person's case.

His eyes became wide with excitement, like a kid getting his presents on Christmas day. "Is it drugs, murder?"

"No. I'm trying to locate a woman's father, whose been missing for over twenty years."

"What happened to him? Kidnapped? He said answering his own question.

"No. One day he decided to abandon his family. The daughter wants to reunite with him."

"That's nice. I wish you all the luck."

"Thanks."

"What I need to get started is to look up some civil records, to

92

see if he's ever been taken to court by anyone in this area."

"Sure thing. You take the elevator up to the fifth floor and make a sharp right. It's the fifth door on your left. You can't miss it, cause it's the last door on your left."

"How is it working for a big place like that. I bet you never have a dull moment. We barely get any excitement in this town. I wouldn't mind getting' a little action ever now and then."

"Don't wish cause you never know what you might get."

The sheriff gets up and follows me to the elevator. "Well, I must say you boys do get around," the sheriff said putting his hands in his pockets. He continues to make small talk, causing my head to pound. "So how long you been workin' for the FBI?" he says with a Southern Drawl. I focused my concentration on the lights as the elevator stopped on each designated floor. "Have you ever been shot?"

I look over at him forcing a smile on my face. "Well, I've been shot at more times than I can count, but no I've never gotten shot, if that's what you're asking."

"Well, I ain't never been shot, but I had a shot gun pointed in my face once. I was a patrol officer ten years ago, when I got a domestic dispute call that changed my life. I knocked on the door and the husband points a loaded twelve gage shot gun in my face. I thought I was gonna die for sure. The only thing I could think about was my wife and three kids being without a husband and father. This guy was beatin' up on his wife somethin' terrible, almost killed her. I talked him out of taking a shot at her. After that incident I transferred to the sheriff's office. That was over ten years ago, been here ever since," he said proudly.

My eyes shift towards the sheriff, who nods his head, smiling. "That's some story, huh?"

"Where you from?"

I continued pushing the up button on the elevator several

times. "New York City."

The sheriff smiles ,I ain't never been there."

The only thing I can think of is taking a Tylenol for my headache. "You should visit sometime; there's something for everyone to do," I replied.

The sheriff has a perplex look on his face, as if he is in deep thought. "Yeah, I might do that."

Small talk is not one of my strong points, but I'm a good listener. Letting a person talk, is a valuable skill I learned in my field. You can get a mini documentary on a person's life by allowing them to talk.

I stepped inside the elevator, smiling as the door closes, waving to the sheriff. Civil records, Room 552. "How can I help you sir?" she smiled.

"I'm here to look up public records on business that registered with you in the past five years and civil law suite records."

"You can have a seat over there. I'll bring you the binders."

Three hours of searching through five volumes of binders. Nothing. I began to see double from too many names and dates.

Everything was running into one line. My beeper goes off, setting my equilibrium off balance. Maybe someone had some information for me. My adrenaline started racing. I suddenly got a spark of energy, but when I looked at the number my energy rush left.

"Excuse me, Miss where are your public telephones?"

"The phones are located down the hall to your left."

"Hello, Joyce what's up? I got your page."

"You're late picking up the girls again," she says in a monotone voice.

"I'm sorry Joyce, what date is it? I've lost track of time since I've been in South Carolina for the past week."

"South Carolina?" she said, in a puzzling voice. "What the hell you doin' down there?"

"I'm workin' on a missing person's case; I took as a favor for

Vicious Karma

Cedric."

"I thought you were through with that kind of work. Are you back with the Bureau and you didn't tell me? Are you holding back on your financial obligations?"

"No, I didn't take my old job back. I took this case as a favor for Cedric. His friend needed someone to help her find her father."

"How much you getting' paid for that case?"

I tried to hold back the anger in my voice. "Remember we're not married, I'm not obligated to discuss how much money I make. As long as you get your child support payments on time you don't have to concern yourself with what I make." I felt myself hyperventilating. I took a deep breath and counted to ten.

"It's my concern to know how much you make. You never know when I might need an increase."

"I'm payin' you child support, plus the girls' tuition for school. What else do you want outta me? I snapped. "I didn't call to argue, Joyce. I'm sorry about the girls, but I needed the money. My classes aren't offered in the summer, so I had to make up the difference."

Silence on the other end. "Mosee, how long do you plan on being in South Carolina?"

I paused before speaking. "Well, I'll be wrapping this case up in two weeks. I'll be home the second week in June."

"Do you remember how many times I've heard that in our ten years of marriage. You always called saying you'll be home in a week. Well, one week turned into three months."

The long hours and years of dedicating my life to the bureau wasn't recognized. I felt my hard work and commitment were in vain, looking back in hindsight. The effects took a toll on my children. My daughters never made friends because they were afraid of moving. Just when my family was settling in Seattle Washington, after three years we were asked to relocate; my

95

superiors said it was good for my career. They told me relocating

is normal in the beginning for new agents, but the beginning turned out to stretch throughout my entire career. I realized my career lead to the break up of my marriage, along with a list of other problems.

"Kiss the girls for me, Joyce and tell them Daddy loves them."

I continued searching through three-fourths of the binders, starting with the year 1992. I didn't come to a name that even sounded similar to Fosters. Maybe going through the civil records was a waste of time. Everyone doesn't have a record from the courts, unless you're being sued or someone has a complaint against you. My instincts told me to try another mode of research. I thought about something everyone did that's common for most people everywhere—voting. Everyone votes if you're a concern citizen. Even if you don't vote your name can be registered with the county clerk's office. I ended my search in Oak Meadows and returned to the town where I started—Westfield.

I decided to drive thirty minutes back to Westfield to the county government building. I rode the elevator to voter's registration dept. room six twelve. "I need to see your voters registration books from nineteen ninety five to the present."

"Here are the binders you requested, sir. Is they're anything else?"

"No. I'm fine, thank you."

"Don't hesitate to ask. It's no trouble. I'm here if you need me." She stood next to the table, looking at me. I kept looking up at her, wondering when she was going to leave.

"Ok, sir, I'll be going back to my desk." She looked back at me, smiling."

The idea of running my own business is becoming more appealing. Taking on Zoe as a client, put a spark in my decision to open a private investigation firm. Being back in the business made my adrenaline flow. I forgot how much I missed being in the trenches. When I get back to New York, the first thing on my agenda is to open a PI office. After all, I have over ten years of criminal investigations experience. Two problems I foresee, building up clientele. This is something that could take up to a year, before I get any steady work. The second problem is sometimes you eat filet mignon and other times you eat tuna fish. Me myself I prefer filet mignon and prime rib steak.

My old FBI badge gave me influence; people were automatically more cooperative.

She came back, again carrying another stack of binders. My shoulders felt numb, watching her place the binders on the table. I took a deep breath, before plunging into my work. Twelve noon was fast approaching. I was famished and needed to fill my stomach, before finishing the day.

I walked ten blocks from the courthouse, with the sun's rays meeting every step of the way. Finally, I came upon a restaurant on the corner, where a mixed crowd stood in line half way around the block. I stood behind a dark skinned woman, with silver and black hair. I politely tapped her on the shoulder, smiling. "Excuse me, miss I'm trying to find a descent restaurant in town."

She turned around smiling." This restaurant has the best food in Westfield, she said, smiling," folks will wait in line for hours, just to get some southern cooking."

"Thanks."

My thoughts were focused on what my next move would be. I didn't have a plan, but something would come about eventually. The half an hour wait didn't seem very long. I was moving ahead inch by inch. That made me feel like I was making progress. I took a seat in the waiting area. A girl approached me, wearing a short black skirt, with silver high top sneakers. She wore three earrings in each ear, plus a mini stud in the right nostril. Her hair has a frizzy look that appears to need combing. Her skin was like dark smooth chocolate. "Hello, sir," she said smiling. "Do you prefer smoking or nonsmoking?"

"I'm starving, so I'll take what ever you have." The hostess escorted me to a booth near the back of the restaurant. There was a crowd of ten people who sat at a large rectangular table. Everyone cheered happy birthday, Minnie. A tall gentlemen carried a cake to the table. The crowd cheered and clapped. I was drawn into the excitement of the people, that made me deaf when the waitress returned to my table.

"Sir, excuse me, are you ready to order now?" "Yes, I'll have the fried Whiting special." "What kind of vegetables would you like with that?" "Everything sounds so appetizing." I continued looking down at the menu, "I'll have the yams and a bake potato." "Do you care for something to drink with your meal?" "I'll have a glass of Lemonade and some water, too." "That will be all, thank you." I nearly jumped outta my seat when the waitress said Foster. I thought to myself, no this can't be the same Foster I've been looking for. I took a deep breath inhaling slowly. I reached into my wallet and examined the photo of Zoe's father, trying to imagine what he looks like today. I waited anxiously for the waitress to return. "Miss what is the gentleman's name you just called?"

"Oh, that's my boss, Foster he's the owner of the restaurant," she said placing the food on my table. My mouth watered when I smelled the food.

"What's his last name?" "Owens." I sat in a comatose state, when she told me the owner's name.

I couldn't fathom what I just heard. "Did you say Foster Owens?" "Yes, he's the owner of this place." she said smiling. "The Under Ground cafe is known throughout South Carolina.

"I see that I found the right place. My cousin told me that Foster's restaurant has the best southern dinning, I commented reconfirming my suspensions. "I had to make sure I had the right place."

"You found the right place, Sir," she said placing the drink on the table. "How long as this place been open?" "I'd say a little over eight years."

"That's excellent for a black business. I feel we should patronize each other."

"Is he from this area?"

"No, "she said looking impatient. "Is there anything else you need?"

"No. thanks you."

I took out my note book pad and jotted down the information on Foster, when the waitress walked away.

I ate my food in a hurry, savoring every morsel, trying to contain myself. The waitress returned to clear my table. When I went to pay the check, there was a long line outside the door. I took out my note pad, writing down the address. What a coincidence, I thought. I wasn't looking for the guy, and he shows up right under my nose. If that ain't luck, I don't know what is?

12

The Oasis Jazz coffeehouse served specialty coffees like, Raspberry Chocolate and Mocha Cappuccino, along with calorie rich desserts, like Chocolate Moose and Cherry Cheese cakes. The place was located in Westfield in the downtown business district. Westfield was a mixed place, but you still had your dividing lines of black and white entertainment. When you step inside there's a bar located near the front entrance. The end of the bar around the right corner leads to a room where the band played. There's a small rectangular stage up front, where the band is preparing to set up for the first set. A waitress comes over to the table smiling. "Hello, my name is, Delphine, I'm your waitress for this evening. Welcome to Oasis Jazz Coffee House, how may I help you," she said with a southern accent. Her eyes focused on me as she continued to talk.

"They certainly have the most beautiful women down south," I said flirtatiously. Yes, I'll take a pumpkin mocha coffee and a cranberry orange muffin." I turned to Zoe. "You want something?"

"I'll have the chocolate mousse and a White Russian."

"Will that be all?"

"Yes."

She walks away putting emphasis on her walk. Zoe looked at me smiling. "You have a secret admirer."

"Women can't seem to keep their eyes off me for some reason."

"Conceited are we?"

"So why are we here? You got some good news for me, I hope." She squirmed in her seat, like a child waiting for ice cream at the candy store.

"Be patient, Zoe."

She folded her arms, pouting her lips like a spoiled child. "Alright, I hate to be kept waiting. I hope you're not wasting my time, Mosee."

A saxophone player began to prep his instrument. He wore a shoulder length Jeri curl. Another member of the band took her trumpet out of a brown leather case. A man in his early twenties wearing a green stripped suit and a wide brim black hat brings his drum set to the back of the stage.

The waitress sashays back to the table grinning with a gold tooth reflecting from the dim lightning. "Here y'all drinks and desserts," she says placing them on the table. Mosee looked at the gold tooth sparkling in the light. He felt remorseful when he noticed her mouth. He didn't realize people still wore metallic jewelry in their mouths.

"Thank you very much, Delphine, that'll be all for now."

She stands there in a daze with a glaze over her eyes, looking at me. "If there's anything else you need don't hesitant to ask for Delphine," she said looking at me.

Zoe cut her eyes at her as she walks away from the table. "She doesn't know if I'm your wife or girlfriend. Some women have no respect." She picked up her drink taking a sip.

"Today I went to the court house to check out some voter registration records and registered business in the past five years. I took a lunch break from my investigation to grab a bite to eat."

Zoe interrupts me mid sentence. "I hope this isn't going to be a long story."

"No. I decided to walk down the street and check out a few restaurants. I go into this one restaurant, I'm sitting at the table waiting for someone to take my order, and I over heard someone say the name Foster. I jumped outta my seat, when I heard the name. I wanted to confirm my suspicions, so I questioned the waitress, and she tells me exactly what I needed to put the missing pieces together."

"Oh my God!" Zoe shouts. The couple sitting at the next table turns around giving us a nasty look. Zoe jumps out of her seat shouting. "You've found him, I can't believe it! She reached across the table, hugging and kissing me. "Tell me everything. What does he look like? How old is he?"

I smiled at her. "Ok one question at a time." I gloated over my accomplishments, but the hard part about finding a missing person is hoping they are willing to accept the other party. I was in awe that I still possessed my skills. Now it's time to move on to bigger and better challenges.

"When can I meet him?" I was so ecstatic for Zoe; she was finally going to reunite with her father after thirty years. My one concern was that he would not accept his daughter. It's nice when cases have happy endings. When you can go home and sleep peacefully. One thing I admired in Zoe was her strength and determination.

"First I have to pay him a surprise visit to feel him out. This is done for your protection."

"Wait until my mother gets the news. She didn't think you could find him. My mother still has animosity towards him, because he abandoned us."

Zoe lifts her drink. "A toast to your brilliant investigative work," I said picking up my coffee.

"To you, Zoe, may you get everything you're searching for. Once I give you the information, the rest is up to you. I'll give you the address once I visit with him and set a date for you two to meet."

Thursday, May twenty first, is my first unannounced meeting with the missing party—Foster Owens. In the car, I rehearsed what I was going to say to Foster for fifteen minutes. I could start out with a Hello, please to meet you. I'm Mosee Love a private investigator By the way your daughter, Zoe, hired me to find you. Or I could make small talk and tell him I enjoyed the food here. I'm not one for small talk. I believe in getting down to business. A firm introduction of who I am, show my identification and give him the facts. This should make my life and his easier. My hand slipped, as I tried to lock the car door. There was a woman taking names of the people who waited in line. I walked up past the crowd. "I'm here to see Mr. Foster Owens about a personal matter."

"Your name sir?"

"Mosee Love."

"You can have a seat in the waiting area. I'll let him know you're here to see him."

"Thanks." I was scared as shit, sitting, waiting. I pondered in my mind a dozen times how I was going to present my case. I didn't want to scare him off. I prayed that he would be receptive to what I was about to say.—" 'Hello, sir, you have a daughter whom you haven't seen in over thirty years. Not a good opener to say to a stranger, whom I'm about to drop a bomb on.

A five feet nine, stocky man walked towards me. He wore an ear ring in his left ear and his hair was tapered on the sides with a low box look cut on top. Now the time was here. I stood up to greet him, with a big smile one my face, extending my hand. "Hello, Mr. Owens, my name is Mosee Love, I'm a private investigator. How are you, sir?" I had to be submissive to get on his good side, if he had one.

"Private investigator," he repeated. "What is this matter about?" Foster asked. "I like to know." I tried to choose my words carefully, so I wouldn't aggravate him. I took one step back, when Foster stood in my face. I wanted to give him enough space in case things got physical. I estimated Foster to be in his early sixties, but he looked strong enough to take me on, I thought. If things did get physical, I carried my Colt 9"mm" semi automatic, something I learned—"never leave home without it."

"I've been hired to find you."

Foster moved in closer again. "Find me? For what?" I don't

know whose lookin' for me, but you better leave before I get ugly."

I tired to think of something to appease the man, before things got out of hand. "Please Mr. Owens, I think it's best that we talk in private." Foster paused for a brief moment, as if he was searching for the right response. I stepped back, giving myself room to talk. "Please, Mr. Owens, just give me ten minutes of your time, that's all I'm asking, please. I pleaded with Foster for fifteen minutes, before I convinced him to allow me to speak with him in private.

I followed Foster to the back of the restaurant, where a black door, with the words private office inscribed in gold plated letters. "Excuse my office, I been tryin' to do my books," he said nervously. You can have a seat in that chair."

"Thank you, Mr. Owens, my client and I really appreciate you talking to me." One thing I learned that being humble always work, when I want to get information. I took out my license and handed it over to Foster to examine. "You can call me Mosee, Mr. Owens.

Foster looked over my identification, examining the contents for thirty seconds, before he spoke. Thirty seconds seemed like three hours waiting for him to open his mouth. He handed me back my PI license, when I cleared my throat.

Whose lookin' for, me? I like t to know cause I have a list of enemies a mile long, people I owe money to, women whose hearts I broken, but those things are behind me now. I'm a redeemed man. I even go to church now," he said leaning back in his brown cloth swivel chair, feeling at ease and more comfortable like he was ready to expose his soul. "So you're a private investigator, huh?"

"Yes. That's correct. I was hired by, Zoe Owens, to find you. Does the name sound familiar?" I watched his reaction closely. Foster was immobilized, as if he was going into shock. His mouth hung open, but no words came outta his mouth.

He sat up in the chair, more alert. That's my daughter's name.

Is this some kind of a sick joke somebody's playing on me," he said frowning. I have only one daughter named Zoe. I haven't seen her in over thirty years."

Dollar signs were calculating in my head. All was going as planned.

Foster looked at me with his pupils dilated. "How do I know you ain't lyin?"

"You have to trust me, Mr. Owens. I'm here to find you and report to my client. I get paid for my services."

"Where is she? What does she look like? She got any children?"

"Slow down Mr. Owens, I'm sure your daughter can share that information with you. She's staying with her mother temporarily, until I make contact with you."

"She lives that close, I can't believe it. "Ain't' that a bitch," Foster said shaking his head n disgust. "She's been here all this time, ain't that something."

"When can I meet her?"

"I can arrange to have her meet you at your earliest convince."

Foster looks down at the desk. "I bet'cha her mother still hates me. I loved her you know, but my weakness for women caused us to break up. That's in the past now."

"Mr. Owens, I am not here to judge you. I'm just doin' my job."

"How about the two of you coming here for dinner." he said in an excited tone.

"No thanks, I don't wanna intrude on your family gathering, after all, this is you and your daughter's family reunion."

"By the way, how did you find me?"

"I went to visit two of your old friends: Shep Anderson and Ellis Worthington. I ..."

"Shep Anderson," he interrupted. I didn't know he was still

alive. I know he told you I took off with some of his money," Foster shakes his head in disbelief; when you young, you do all kinds of crazy things." He was silent for a moment, like he wanted to repent his sins. "It's funny when you try to block out certain things, but somehow they find a way of creeping back into your life."

"Shep Anderson did mention that you owe him some money." Speaking of money the only thing on my mind was collecting my four grand and going home.

"Ellis and I were in the army together, during the Korean War. I haven't seen him since I left Denver. I still don't understand how you found me."

"After I went to visit Worthington, he told me you went to Westfield, South Carolina to live. I flew from Denver back to Westfield, South Carolina, where I went to the courthouse to research voter's registration records. I was exhausted after looking through three volumes of books, so I went out for lunch. I just happen to pick this restaurant by chance. When I was sitting down, I overheard someone call your name. That's when I compared your old photo with how you look now. However, that wasn't the determining factor. Your friends told me you loved to cook and wanted to open a restaurant. I asked one of your employees some questions and what I gathered from talking to your friend, I put two and two together."

"My sister loaned me the money to open up the restaurant, after her divorce was final."

"Where is your sister?"

Foster bowed his head down. "My sister died of breast cancer two years ago."

"I'm sorry to hear that, I didn't know."

"It's ok. When can I meet Zoe?"

"You pick the time and day."

"How about two days from today—Thursday around 4pm. That's when we close two hours before supper time."

Vicious Karma

I reached into my pocket, handing him a recent photo of Zoe. He looked at the picture in awe, with tears rolling down his cheek. "Thank you very much, Mr. Love."

I stood up reaching across the desk to shake his hand. "It's been nice talking to you." I was glad this meeting turned out to be a success; now the easy part a waited—collecting my money. It took approximately one month and a half to find someone who's been missing over thirty years. Before driving off, I jotted a list of things that needed my immediate attention: car repairs, Joyce, house taxes and repaying Cedric his money. I phoned Zoe on my cellular phone, asking her to meet me at the hotel.

Zoe sat in a silver Mercedes' Benz 500SL convertible, waving as I parked my rental car. "Hello, Zoe I got some good news," I said walking towards her car. She stepped out of the Benz, wearing linen, lime short set, with matching open toe sandals. She jumped out of the car hugging me tightly around the neck and kissing my lips.

"You better be careful I don't reciprocate your generosity."

Once we went into the hotel room, Zoe started smoking a cigarette.

"Please don't smoke in here, Zoe"

"Oh, I'm sorry smoking cigarettes is a force of habit, whenever I get uptight or nervous. My mother's been nagging me to quit. She doesn't allow me t smoke in her house; I usually go on the front porch. She reached into her straw bag, and handed me a vanilla envelope. "All of your money is there—four thousand in cash. Your services are worth the money. I'm glad I hired you; you're one helluva of an investigator.

I slowly opened the envelope, trying to conceal my enthusiasm. "Thank you, Zoe; it's been a pleasure doing business with you." I wrote down the name and address of the restaurant and the time she was to meet her father. With her face looking flushed, her appearance quickly changed to an elegant woman to that of a little scared girl. I felt guilty abandoning her at this crucial time. Within a few seconds after everything had sunk in, her facial expression seemed more relaxed now. "Thanks, Mosee, this really means a lot to me. Now I feel I can begin to feel like a whole person."

"I hope everything turns out for the best. Long awaited reunions can be very emotional," I looked out the window admiring the view of the lake. It gave me a sense of peace. Being in the country gave me the idea of retiring down South. City living was becoming difficult with the increase of crime and raising children in the city was not appropriate. I turned around to face Zoe, who sat on the bed. "How is your mother going to handle the news?"

"I don't know, hopefully she can deal with it. Frankly, I don't care what she thinks, it's my business. I'm the one who wants to see him. Whatever happened between her and my father is her business. I don't care to know why they broke up, it's so long ago."

"Yeah, you're right."

"When do you plan on returning home?"

"I'll probably hang around for a day or two, until I know everything is ok with you."

I walked Zoe to her car, where we exchanged our good byes, hugging one another. "Call me before you leave town."

She stood at the door, looking confused. "What's wrong, Zoe?"

"I didn't think this day would ever come, but now that it's here I don't know what to feel about seeing my father: anger, joy or love."

"Take your time, don't rush things between you and your old man, give him and yourself time to adjust." Her eyes averted away from mine looking down at the floor.

"You're right. I'm a little apprehensive about seeing my

108

father."

"Why don't you give me a call and let me know how things went."

"Thanks for everything, Mosee. Stay in touch."

I jumped on top of the bed like a kid, counting candy, after she left. The money is arranged neatly in an envelope from the smallest to the largest in denomination—exactly four thousand dollars, not bad for a month and a half worth of work. My money problems are over. I felt like I was born again. Now I can pay my over due bills and still have enough to live on until the end of summer.

I made my plane reservations for Thursday, two days from today. I couldn't leave my client, not knowing how things turned out for her. I felt good, knowing I had extra money in my pocket. Life was looking great for a change; a few extra dollars is the boost I needed.

13

On the second day back in New York, the first thing on my agenda is to start advertising my private investigation business. Today is a good day as any. The weather is eighty degrees, my bills are paid, the Volvo had major repairs done and I had money to spend. After I printed business cards on my PC, I drove around the remainder of the day distributing business cards to friends and associates. The third day, which is Saturday, is what I call my relaxation day. This is the last day I had to myself for two months. Tomorrow I promised to pick up my daughters to spend the last two months of summer with me. After eating left over bake chicken, yellow squash and broccoli, I settled into bed with a good mystery book, before drifting off to sleep.

Just as I was about to go into a deep slumber, the telephone started ringing; I rolled over looking at the clock on the nightstand—2A.M. I procrastinated over answering the phone this late. For one, my bad nerves told me, whoever was on the other end had bad news to deliver. No one calls at two in the morning for small talk. I hoped my daughters were safe. Maybe Cedric was sick or hurt in the hospital. I laughed to myself. Not Mr. Meticulous. The last person on my list I thought about was my sisters, Dee and Shelby. Maybe they had a car accident. I went through the names of people who might be calling, exhausting every possible name in my immediate family.

I put the pillow over my head, hoping to drown out the sound of the ringing telephone.

Twenty minutes later the phone started ringing again. I reached over to turn the ringer off. I tried numerous attempts to return back to sleep, but my curiosity kept gnawing at me, causing me to toss and turn most of the night. I pushed the play button on the answer machine; after I retrieved my messages, it would be easier to return to sleep. First message. "Mr. Love, please call me Zoe's in jail.

Vicious Karma

You can call me anytime at (336) 718-2196. I was in a daze, after I heard the message. I sat up in bed replaying the message a second time. The only thing that registered in my brain—Zoe's in jail. How could something like this transpire? It's been only four days since I last saw Zoe. The last words Zoe said to me were. "Mosee, everything is working out fine with my father, thanks for everything. Don't forget to keep in touch." I felt like a Vietnam Vet going through shell shock. I replayed the message a fifth time, making sure my mind wasn't playing tricks on me. "Mr. Love, Zoe's in jail for murder. Please call me as soon as you get this message." Apparently this was the second message Zoe's mother left on my machine. Zoe's in jail for murder, I mumbled to myself. I dialed the telephone number, getting a distraught, Ms. Daniels on the other end. "Ms. Daniels, this is Mosee, I …"

"Oh, I'm glad you done called," she said sobbing. "My baby's in jail, please help her. You have to come down here." It's your fault she's in this mess, tryin' to find her no good father."

I let her vent her anger and frustration towards me. She continued for another fifteen minutes. She paused in between sentences, catching her breath. "Ms. Daniels, I'm sorry about your daughter, but you have to calm down and explain what happened."

"He's dead, someone killed him. Zoe couldn't have done it; she was so happy when you found her father," she sobbed.

"Foster's dead?" I asked. I couldn't believe what I just heard. The man I helped to reunite with his daughter just four days ago is now a corpse. I repeated the same answer again, to myself out loud. "Foster's dead?"

"Boy, ain't you been listening to what I been sayin'?" she said in an angry voice. "He's dead and they wanna charge my baby for his death. They don't care nothin' 'bout no black folks. They snatches the first available person they can put blame on."

I repeated for the second time, "Please tell me what

111

happened?"

"I don't know much. All I know is Zoe went to see her father again twice last night. Once in the evening and late at night, around 11:30P.M. at the restaurant. The next thing I know, I gets a phone call from Zoe about 1:00 A.M. in the morning from the Westfield County jail." There was silence on the other end.

"Ms. Daniels are you alright?"

"Yeah. I'm tryin' to stay strong.

"I'll see if I can get a flight as soon as possible."

"God Bless you, Mr. Love. I have some money put away, but it ain't much."

"Don't worry about money, we can work something out. You can worry about paying me when I find the person who murdered Zoe's father." I surprised myself at what I just said. Don't worry about money. I was just recuperating from my financial problems and now this. What else could go wrong in my life.

I hung up the telephone, amazed at what I just said, working for nothing until Zoe's out of jail; what a premature statement I just made, committing myself. I didn't know how much time I needed; one month could turn into a year. In this business, there are no guarantees on how long it takes to solve a case.

I recalled some of my cases at the bureau took me away from my family for months at a time. I began having reservations about accepting Zoe's case. I wanted to call her back and tell her to leave it in the hands of the police or hire another private investigator; my job was finished. I found her father, now the rest was up to the police, but I knew how lackadaisical the law can be when it came to black on black crime. They could care less if we killed each other. The law isn't on our side, that's for sure. I hated to admit, but I was Zoe's only hope. She was an easy and convenient target to blame for the murder. After all, she had all the right motives: A distraught woman looking for her long lost father. The police figured she has enough animosity build up over the years. The motive can be summed up in one word; Revenge.

Vicious Karma

The difference between Southern cops is their overt outspokenness to racism, and the northern cops hide their feelings. I couldn't go back to sleep after hearing the bad news. Somehow I felt responsible for Zoe's fate. Maybe if I wasn't so greedy for money, she wouldn't be in jail.

Sunday afternoon, I packed my three bags, and made a list of things to do when I get to Westfield, South Carolina. This is my second visit to Zoe's mother. I hoped she would show good faith and allow me to stay with her while I conducted my investigation. I had to watch my spending. Most of the money I spent on bills, car repairs, and paying extra in child support payments. This kept me ahead for any slow months I might encounter. I was hoping that I could receive a down payment, but I knew that was impossible with my client sitting behind bars. I didn't wanna put pressure on Ms. Daniels she had enough troubles of her own. I had to spend the remainder of my money with caution. Next, I wanted to visit the crime scene and the Westfield police station. The local police force probably consisted of no more than one hundred law enforcement agents and about fifty civilian personnel. The most excitement they probably see is passing out traffic tickets.

I suddenly got a brainstorm—driving down South. That would save me money on plane fare and car rental expenses. My car was in good shape after the tune up and other repairs that were long over due. I went to my computer, researching traveling time and directions. It would take eight to ten hours, in addition to any stops I had to make along the way. I wanted to get as much daylight driving as possible. Finally, I finished loading my bags into the Volvo and headed for I-95 South.

I forgot that I needed to call Joyce and Cedric. One thing I could count on was my ex-wife having a pleasant attitude, once she heard I was on another assignment, which translated into dollars. She wouldn't be as argumentative when she knew her

113

pockets would be full, once again. Cedric had to be told about Zoe's murder charges. I would make all my necessary calls once I settled.

The mixture of heat and humidity made me regret, not having my air conditioner fixed. I stopped at a few rest stops, loading up on water and fruit. It's three o'clock, Sunday afternoon, when I pulled my black Volvo in front of the ranch style home of Ms. Daniels in Westfield. Driving made my body feel limp and weak. The only thing on my mind is a cold shower and a home cooked meal.

I stood at the front door of Zoe's mother's house, bracing myself for the uncharted waters ahead. Before I knocked a second time, the door flew open. There stood a teary eyed Ms. Daniels, with blood shot eyes. She grabbed me, hugging me tightly. "The Lawd has answered my prayers, Mr. Love."

"Hello, Miss Daniels, I'm sorry to hear about your daughter." My humanistic quality made me embrace her.

"I'm glad you came. I had no one else to turn to."

I sat on a red velvet chair; sitting on the chair made my skin feel sticky against the plastic seat cover. Zoe's mother sat on a matching velvet love seat "I fixed a room up for you. Ain't no sense in you going to a motel when there's plenty of room here. "I cooked meat loaf, collard greens with home made biscuits and sweet potato pie for dessert," she said going into the kitchen.

"You didn't have to go through the trouble of fixing all that food." She came from the kitchen, placing the remainder bowls and serving dishes on the table. The table is covered in a cream tablecloth. There are fresh flowers sitting in a red vase. The cream color china with its black trim complemented the table arrangement.

I freshened up before settling in for dinner. After I freshened up, I took a seat at the end of the large wooden rectangular table. "Everything looks appetizing," I smiled "Did you get a chance to speak to the investigating officer assigned to the case?"

"I spoke to so many folks. I can't remember names." She sits down at the opposite end of the table. Ms. Daniels looked like she aged ten years, since I last saw.

"Did you get a chance to see Zoe?"

"Yeah. She doesn't look well. She told me she didn't kill her father. I believe her, too."

"What else did she say?"

"She told me she went to see him after they had an argument at his house. Later that night, she went to the restaurant to apologize. Zoe was in the kitchen helping clean up, when she heard a loud banging sound. When she went to see what was wrong, he was layin' there dead in a pool of blood," she bowed her head down. "Lawd knows I can't have my only child in some jail, Mr. Love. I know my daughter. I ain't raise no murderer."

The juices from the meatloaf, dripped from the corner of my mouth. "Where was he shot?"

"They say in the chest."

"Do you know of anyone who would want to see him dead?"

"I knows nothin' 'bout that man. He was bad luck ever since I laid eyes on him."

"Does Zoe own a gun, Miss Daniels?"

"Gun?" She repeated with streams of tears rolling down her cheeks. "No is you crazy, fool?"

"I'm sorry, Miss Daniels, but I have to cover every angle in case you mention something that can lead me to other clues."

"Miss Daniels what time did Zoe visit her father last night?"

"She left here about eight o'clock and then again at eleven o'clock for some unfinished business."

"Was she angry when she left the second time to visit him?"

"Yeah. She was angry. She said her father was no good and she wished you never found him."

I picked up a biscuit and filled my plate with seconds. "Why did she say that?"

"Zoe and her father had a disagreement."

"Did Zoe mention to you, why they were arguing?"

She shrugged her shoulder. "I don't know she wouldn't tell me nothin."

"You haven't touched a thing on your plate."

"I haven't had much of a appetite since all this mess started."

"Do you think Zoe killed her father to get even?"

She gasped, with her mouth hanging open. "You tryin' to say she set this whole thing up?" Her face twisted like a pretzel. She had a look of rage in her eyes.

"My daughter ain't no murderer, like I said!"

"I'm just covering all bases, Miss Daniels."

After we finished dinner, Miss Daniels retired to bed early. She said that she was mentally and physically exhausted from yesterday; the stress made her want to sleep more.

I telephoned Cedric to inform him of the tragedy that struck his friend and I had to contact my children's mother to inform her about my change of plans.

Monday morning I dreaded calling the Westfield police station. I had to prepare myself for the sarcasm and prejudice that came along with the territory of confronting small town law enforcement agents. One, I'm a black man; and second, most cops hate PI agents. They consider us an annoyance. I got the name of Detective Burke, who was the chief homicide detective assigned to the murder investigation of Foster Owens. I didn't make an appointment; I figure the best way to get direct information is to catch a person off guard. They make the best interviews.

116

14

The office was small and cramped, paper cluttered the desk. A stale cigarette odor filled the office. A bald pudgy man with a receding hair line, sat behind a desk reading a newspaper. When I entered the office, Detective Burke continued to bury his head in his newspaper, pretending he did not see me standing over his desk. I had to swallow my pride and go the extra mile; be cordial, I thought.

"Hello," I said, smiling, extending my hand. "Good afternoon, my name is Mosee Love. I'm a PI hired by the Owens family to find the killer of Foster Owens."

He put his newspaper down and picked up a cigar. "You a investigator, huh?" He said leaning back in his swivel chair, sizing me up. "You come to find out who killed Foster?"

I nodded.

"Well you wastin' your time. We already done found the murderer."

"Who?"

He snarled taking a puff of his cigar, blowing the smoke in my face. "Name's Detective Burke, I'm in charge of the Owens murder investigation," he said coughing. "You got a license or something I can see?"

I reached into my wallet and handed the detective my PI license to examine.

He looked over my license carefully, before uttering a word. "New York, huh? I reckon a big city like New York would keep you fellas busy. We don't need no fast talkin' guys like you comin' down here tellin' us how to do our job," he said in a southern accent. "'The case is closed."

"Closed?"

"Ms. Owens is the one who killed her father. We got her prints all over the gun that was found at the crime scene."

"What other evidence do you have to charge her with murder?"

"I interviewed the victim's girlfriend, who was in the house when Foster and his daughter were arguing. She overheard Zoe say she wish he were dead, and she hated him."

"Your charging her with murder based on what someone heard? Did this girlfriend see Zoe in the house?"

"No, but she remembers what she sounds like."

"That's not enough to convict her on."

"We got a gun, too, and the victim's blood matches the blood we found on the girl. When I questioned the girl, she didn't show any remorse."

"Your evidence is pure speculation, Detective Burke." Remember keep your composure, I kept telling myself. I knew small town cops rarely get any excitement, except for giving out parking tickets. Making Detective Burke feel important might work. I tried an alternate approach. "I'm glad to hear you solved this case so quickly. You must be the best detective in the business."

Detective Burke's face took on a different expression. He sat up in the chair, proudly stuck out his chest, simultaneously revealing his stained teeth.

"Huh, Detective Burke, would it be possible for me to see the police report and the evidence you found at the crime scene? Oh one more thing, I would like to see Zoe, too."

He paused for a moment, as if he wanted to avoid making a mistake. "The police report isn't ready yet, but you're welcome to come back if you like. "I guess you can take a look at the evidence," he said standing up.

"We have a small crime lab; we just added right here on the premises, got about five employees workin' in there. Our crime scene technicians collected evidence at the time of death."

Vicious Karma

We walked down a long coordinator and down a set of steps that lead to the basement. The third door on the right had a sign that said "Crime Lab and Identification Section" in bright blue letters. A man sat behind a desk, also buried in paper work, and sipping coffee. The sign on his desk said "Crime Scene Supervisor."

"Williams, I have someone I'd like for you to meet. His name is Mosee Love; he's a private investigator from up north, investigating the murder of the black man, Foster Owens."

The supervisor stood up to shake my hand. "Please to meet you," he said.

"He's here to look at the evidence that was collected at the crime scene."

"No problem, come this way."

Detective Burke and supervisor Williams filled out paper work, requesting to see the evidence being held in the Foster murder case. Then I went to a private room, where Detective Burke watched me examine the contents of a gray metal box.

Exhibit A contained Zoe's bloodstained clothing found at the crime scene. I was given a pair of plastic gloves to wear, to avoid contaminating the evidence. I took out a green silk shirt and ankle-length cream color skirt. The clothing had bloodstains in disarray of patterns. It was a .38 caliber handgun that had been used to kill Foster Owens; it was included as well.

"That's what we found at the crime scene." He pointed to a second metal box. "This box contains the bullet casings found at the crime scene. Ballistics matched the bullets in the gun, with the bullet casings, found at the scene. The bloodstains on Zoe's clothing and the gun were a perfect match. So you see there is nothing more to investigate. You might as well return up North."

We walked further down a long hallway to a room with noticeably poor lighting. There, a cop opened the door and lead me to Zoe. He took off her handcuffs. She wore a bright orange jumpsuit. Her skin was a faded shade of gray and her hair was matted on her head. She sat at the far end of the table. Silence filled the room for thirty seconds, before anyone spoke.

"Zoe, I'm here to help you. Your mother called and asked me to come down here."

"Help me?" she snarled. "Everything points to me. What can you do, Mosee?"

"First, tell me what you were doing the day your father was murdered."

She paused a few seconds, trying to collect her thoughts. "There isn't much to tell. I left my father's house around nine that night."

"Why did you go to his house?" I took out my notebook to make sure I didn't miss anything. Either I'm getting too old or I needed some Ginseng for mental alertness.

"I went to his house to express how I felt about the selfish bastard. And ..." She paused reflecting on her choice of words. "We had some words. I told him I wished he turned up dead, and I hated him," she said taking a deep breath.

"Was anyone else in the house when you had your argument?"

"Yeah. One of my father's girlfriends."

"What's her name?

"Iris Hall."

I wrote her name down in my note book. "You know where she lives?"

"No. I only met her once."

"How serious was she with your father?"

"I don't know anything about his love life."

"How old is she, Zoe."

"Compared to him? I'd say he was robbing the cradle."

"Did your father have any other women?"

She shrugged her shoulders. "How am I suppose to know about his love life? I just met the man, remember?"

"Look, Zoe don't waste my time. I have more important things I rather be doing."

"There isn't much to tell. I went to his house about eight thirty. And after our confrontation ended, I went to my mother's house. About ten-thirty that night, my conscience started working on me, so I decided to go to the restaurant and apologize for my behavior."

"After you went to the restaurant, what did the two of you discuss?"

"He said I was moving too fast and he needed room to digest everything."

"After he said those words to me, I went back to my car and drove around the block to let off some steam. When I returned to the restaurant, I found him lying in blood, face down. I grabbed my father and held him against my chest. I heard the back door slam shut. I ran to the back door to see who it was, but they drove off. I grabbed the gun and sat there in silence for a few seconds."

"You didn't call the police right away?"

"No."

"Anyone other than you in the restaurant?"

"No one except me. On Fridays he usually lets his employees go home early."

"Did your father have any enemies?"

"I really don't know, Mosee. You think I've known the man all my life? I barely knew him."

"Oh, one more thing, Zoe. I need your father's address, too."

"123 Sycamore Place. He lives about forty-five minutes from the restaurant."

"You have the keys to his place?"

"No. Give me a break I just met the man and now you're asking me if I have keys to his house," she said sardonically.

121

Then unexpectedly, Zoe put her head down and began to cry as if she had lost all hope. "Mosee you have to find out who did this. I don't know how much longer I can hold up."

I got up and walked over to her and gave her a kiss on the cheek. "I'll promise to do my best."

She looked up, struggling to put on a smile. "Thanks Mosee, I really appreciate your efforts. I don't have the money to pay you now, but."

I interrupted her. "Don't worry I told your mother if I find the killer, then you pay me, but if I don't, I'll charge you the minimum fee."

"My assets are frozen. I have no money. I . . . I can sell my Mercedes Benz and pay you. And bail hasn't been posted."

"Let's concentrate on one thing—getting you out." I parked down the street from Foster's house. I made a quick surveillance of the homes, along the block. Everything was quite. That gave me a seventy-five percent change of getting in and out with no one calling 911. At least I hoped.

I searched the contents of my trunk, for a quick change clothing to disguise myself from any busy bodies that may be lurking near.

I stumbled across a cable repairman and a plumbing uniform, a pair of jeans and a white tee shirt, construction boots and a hard hat. The disguise I chose was the cable man uniform. Everyone in America owned a television set, rich or poor.

I moved with the quickness and swiftness of a rabbit. I got dresses in less than one minute, surprising myself. I even had a tool box, as an added feature.

I strolled down Sycamore Street, taking a tour of the neighborhood. The homes were mainly ranchers and a few two level homes. For the most part all the homes resembled one another. One level ranchers, that looked box shaped.

I stopped in front of Foster's house, not knowing how I was going to manage getting inside. I walked around the house, checking for any open windows.

I took out my toolbox and went to work, with my state of the art lock smith kit: Guaranteed to get results.

The rectangular shaped window leads to the kitchen. I pried open the window and squeezed my way through. I became stuck just below my waist. I knew it was time for a rigorous exercise and diet regime when I return home.

After landing headfirst on the floor, I felt a little lightheaded. The house had a musty smell, being locked up for the previous four days in the middle of summer. I put on a pair of gloves to eliminate any evidence of my presence in the house.

The kitchen was decorated in black and white prints. Everything was in place except for a few dishes in the sink. It looked as if Foster's last meal had been a cinnamon Danish and a cup of coffee. Upon opening the refrigerator, I was hit by a pungent odor that made my stomach tightened in a knot. There were a few items in the refrigerator, not much for a bachelor; string beans with some kind of white molding forming on top. The fruit salad had a slimy look to it. Besides the usual apple juice and fruit juice, there was nothing out of the ordinary.

The living room had very little furniture, which included a cream lounge chair and exotic painting and prints on the wall. A fireplace stood in the far corner of the room. In the middle of the living room was a red and black Oriental rug, covering a portion of the hard wood floors. A massive stereo system took up the entire length of the back wall. The drapes were suspended in a balloon valance formation that hung over the sheer cream color curtains.

I walked down a flight of steps to a spare room and found a desk in the corner and three gray metal filing cabinets. The olive green carpeting complemented the cream color furniture. On the desk was a notebook that had recipes scribbled on the pages. I sat at the desk, going through each page, hoping in vain to find something of importance.

I ventured back up stairs to check the bathroom medicine cabinets. You can always learn about a person by the contents of their refrigerator, medicine cabinets and the bedroom. Inside were Tylenol, aspirins, nose spray and Zantac pills. I was surprised to see pills that are used to treat depression.

The master bedroom had a deck that overlooked the back yard. There was also a fireplace in the middle of the bedroom. The yard had beautiful landscaping of chrysanthemums in reds and yellows. Everything was meticulously kept; even his closet and shoes were arranged by color. I wondered why a person would spend so much energy keeping their home neat. The waterbed had curtains around the poles and mirrors up above. A bottle of wine sat on the night stand, half full. The answering machine caught my eye. I pushed the play button.

The first message on the machine went, "Foster this is Blake Reed, in case you forgotten who I am, you son of a bitch. I want what's due me or you'll get what's comin' to you." Click.

I wrote down the message and the person who had left it.

Next, I found a telephone book and searched for Blake Reed and Iris Hall's addresses. There were sixteen Hall's listed in the phone book, but only one Iris Hall; I couldn't have asked for better luck. But Blake Reed's number wasn't listed.

Next, I checked the caller ID box next to the answering machine and wrote down the telephone numbers and names that appeared on the box. I dialed the first telephone number and name that appeared on the box.

"Yes, who's callin'?"

"My name's Mosee Love I'm a private investigator looking into the death of Foster Owens. May I speak to Ms. Channel Reyes?"

There was a long pause on the other end. "Look-a-here, the police have been harassing me, puttin' me through the third degree. I don't need you harassing me, too. I done told them cops everything I know."

I pleaded with her to let me come over and talk to her. After fifteen minutes of negotiating, she agreed to give me twenty minutes of her time.

Foster's house was thirty minutes from Channel Reyes's. I knocked at the door for about ten minutes. I gave up and walked back toward my car. But just then, I heard someone call my name. "Wait, Mr. Love, you can come on in." Channel waved, standing at the door. "I was upstairs." I went back to the door and showed her my ID. "How are you, Ms. Reyes?" "Please call me Channel." I followed her to the back of the house where a sun deck extended to the back yard. "Do you care for something to drink?

Mr. Love?" "No, I'm fine." "Foster's dead? I figured someone would do it sooner or later." "Why do you say that?" Channel sucked her teeth. "Well, he was always doin' somebody wrong. If he wasn't sleeping with someone's woman, he was steppin' on somebody's feet. Foster had the appearance of a gentlemen, but underneath he was nothin' but a snake in the grass. The trouble with him was you didn't see him coming until you felt a knife in your back."

"Karma. That's what came back to bite Foster in the ass." "Anyone in particular he treated unfairly?" I asked. "Women. And just about damn near everybody. He always dated two or three at the same time." "What was your involvement with him?" "We dated for about a year and a half." "Why did your relationship end?" "He started seeing this young thang name Iris Hall. I told him I ain't gonna play second fiddle to no one. And that ended our relationship. We never spoke to each other after that." "How long ago was this?" "We stopped seeing each other about five months ago." "Didn't you feel hurt? You sound like you accepted the outcome graciously." She looked away avoiding eye contact. "I was devastated, Mr. Love. What do you expect? I loved the man and he treated me like dirt." Channel was a refined, elegant-looking and very petite woman. She wore her hair short and curly, with the sides shaved close. Her skin is as smooth as dark chocolate. "I wanted to kill Foster when I first found out he was cheating on me. He never tried to hide his extra curricular activities. When I first heard about his death, I was happy. It was as if a burden was lifted off my shoulders, but ..."

"And?"

"I felt bad about what happened. I never wanted to see him get killed the way he did," she said shaking her head.

"You're saying that you're glad he's dead?"

"No! Mr. Love. I . . . I . . . never wanted anything to happen to the man."

The eyes tell all: sad, hurt, depressed and angered.

Suddenly she looked up with a smirk on her face. She switched on me like Dr. Jekyll and Mr. Hide. Seeing her emotions change from a grieving widow to a non-caring person sent chills through my body. In a split second, she had no remorse for the dead man.

"Can anyone vouch for your whereabouts Saturday between the hours of ten and midnight?"

"Yes. My daughter Billie can." She was becoming very fidgety in her chair.

"Did Foster have any enemies that you know?"

She lowered her eyes in silence. "Yes there is one man that stands out in my mind: Bake Reed."

I wrote down the name in my notebook, recognizing it as the name I'd heard on Foster's answering machine. "Did you ever hear Blake and Foster argue?"

"One thing about Foster, he always kept his business affairs private. He was never one to discuss his business with me."

I wanted to call her bluff, to see what angle she was coming from. "You could have a motive."

She jumped out of her seat in a rage. "Now wait a minute, Mr.

Love I ain't no killer."

"I didn't say that you were a killer, but everyone gets that feeling, to do harm to a person when we're mad and angry. We all think about killing someone who wronged us, but if the opportunity presents itself where we could get away with it, I think we would strongly consider it."

"True, but I ain't kill the man. All the dirt he done did, I believe he helped pull the trigger." She walked out from the sun deck, opening the door for me. "I think you over extended your twenty-minutes, Mr. Love."

I rose from my seat following her to the front door. I handed her a business card, before leaving. "If you find out any information that may be helpful, feel free to call any time. The number is on the back where I'll be staying until the case is finished. One more question, Channel. Have you ever seen Foster and his daughter?"

"No, I can't say that I have," she said standing at the door.

I shot one more question by Ms. Channel. "Did you know Foster had a daughter?"

"He never confided in me about his personal life. He was a very private man. Is that all?" she snapped, narrowing her eyes at me.

"Thank you for your time." I waved goodbye, climbing into my black Volvo. I phoned Ms. Daniels from my cellular phone, to let her know I'd be late for dinner. I hadn't eaten since breakfast. My imagination started working overtime, thinking about Ms. Daniels cooking. It was 6P.M. when I finally started eating my meatloaf smothered in gravy, and a side dish of collard greens and homemade biscuits.

"Ms. Daniels, everything tastes great."

She sat down on the opposite end of the table. "You get any new information today?"

"I saw Zoe, today," I said.

"How did she look?" Ms. Daniels asked

"Alright, she's holding up well, considering all she's been through." I paused between bites. "Ms. Daniels, I don't wanna be a burden. I think it might be best that I check into a hotel."

"No, Mr. Love I got plenty of room. Don't be silly, why waste your money? It's the least I can do to repay you."

"Please call me Mosee."

I felt sorry for her—her only child facing murder charges. I wanted to tell her that everything was going to turn out alright, but I didn't wanna make empty promises. Before retiring for the evening, I made a phone call to Foster's former girlfriend, Iris Hall. She agreed to meet me at Daddy O's the following day. I looked over some of the names on Foster's employee list. I made appointments to see Danny Watson and Agee Johnson, who were former cooks in Foster's restaurant.

15

Following Danny's directions were simple. I walked up to building number 131, Point Plaza Condominium Complex. The area was neatly kept with green shrubbery and Rhododendrons closely flanking the building. Danny lived on the south side of Westfield. This was considered the middle class section.

A young woman in her late twenties answered the door wearing an elegant display of cornrow braiding that wrapped around her head, with curls in the center. She greeted me with a warm smile. Whenever I think of a southern woman, I think of four burners in the kitchen operating simultaneously and the oven is set at 400 degrees.

"Hello, you must be Mr. Love. Danny is expecting you, please come in," she said. "I'm Johnny Mae, Danny's sister."

"Please have a seat, Mr. Love. My brother will be out shortly."

A tall slender brown skinned man emerged from the back room. "Hello, Danny, I'm Mosee Love. I'm a private investigator working on the Foster Owens murder case."

"How are you, Mr. Love?" He said taking a seat across from me. "Everything happened so fast, I'm still in shock over his death."

Danny was about six feet five inches tall, same height as I am. He appeared to be in his early forties. He had a warm smile, the kind that makes you feel at home.

"Danny do you know of any employees who hated Foster?"

He was silent for a moment, collecting his thoughts. "Yes," he answered pausing between thoughts. "There is one employee that sticks in my mind, Agee Johnson; He was a cook at the restaurant who was fired about two months ago."

"Do you remember why?"

"Foster tried to hit on his girlfriend, and when Agee confronted him about the issue, Foster fired him."

Ironically, I had already resolved to see Mr. Johnson. I pulled out the employees list, looking for Agee's name and address. Nothing. "You know where he lives?" I asked.

"Sure he stays in a housing complex about twenty minutes from here, on the north side."

"How was your relationship to the deceased?"

"It was tolerable. I did my job and went home. I didn't have time to dwell into every aspect of peoples lives," he said.

I handed Danny one of my business card. "If you should come across any information, please call me any time."

One down and two to go, I thought as I headed out. Next on my list was Agee Johnson. He went to the top of my list for possible suspects; his motive was strong.

When you go from the south to the north side of Westfield, you can't help but notice the change in the atmosphere. The air on the north side is thick and harsh. The people carry an attitude on their shoulders. And there's no struggle to find a bar on every other corner—with a funeral parlor not too far behind. There are a flood of government housing complexes and abandoned apartment buildings.

Agee's apartment building looked as though it should be condemned by the board of health holding onto half a banister, I walked up the rickety stairs. I came upon a group of kids playing with bottle caps in the dimly lit hallway, when I finally reached the top floor. A young man wearing a head scarf, holding a Colt 45 bottle in his right hand.

Who looked to be in his late twenties answered the door, wearing a head scarf, holding a Colt 45 bottle in his right hand.

"Who is you, man?" he greeted me. He studied my face intently.

I smiled trying to convey a non-threatening attitude. "My name's Mosee Love, I'm investigating the murder of Foster

Owens. Mind if I come in and ask you a few questions?"

"Foster's dead?" he said looking genuinely bewildered. "Well I'll be damn. Somebody done beat me to it," he chuckled. "You a cop or something? I ain't killed Foster, so you best be on your way, man."

I handed him my PI license, to examine.

"What you want with me ? I ain't killed the bastard."

"I'd like to ask you a few questions. May I come in?"

He pointed to a gray sofa with white stuffing jetting out from holes in the seams. When I sat down, I felt my body's weight shifting the sofa off balance. The walls in the room were dingy white, looking as if they hadn't been painted in years. There wasn't much furniture except for the sunken-in sofa and plastic milk cartons he apparently used as coffee tables. A dark brown kitchenette with one black and two white nylon chairs sat off from the living room next to an open window. The apartment had an emptiness and coldness that made you feel depressed the moment you walked in. You could walk through the apartment with your eyes closed and still find everything.

"So you wanna know who killed him, huh?"

I figured I'd get straight to the point, to see where it would take me. "That's why I'm here, 'cause you have a motive for killing Foster."

He looked at me, suspiciously, trying to decide what information he should tell, before he spoke. He sunk farther into the sofa, sipping his beer. "How you find me?"

"Through contacts and a series of interviews."

With a smirk on his face he asked, "How did the old bastard die?"

"From a gunshot wound."

His mouth opened, blinding me by the sight of the initials, AJ, inscribed in gold metallic on his two front teeth.

"What did you and Foster argue about?"

"He tried to take my woman and I told him I don't go for that shit," he said taking a gulp of his Colt 45. "The next day I comes to work and he tells me I don't have a job, because I dissed

him in front of everyone," he said shaking his head in disgust. He had anger in his eyes that told me he didn't have a remorseful bone in his body, for Foster. "I came to work everyday. I never messed with anybody. I did my job and went home and look at the treatment I got. And you expect me to shed a tear?"

"Was your girlfriend attracted to Foster?"

He shrugged his shoulders. "I know she talked about how much money he had. You know how women folks are, always looking for a rich man."

"Did you ever suspect your woman was having an affair with Foster?"

"I ain't have no proof, but a man knows when his old lady is cheatin'."

"If you did know, how did you feel about it?"

He avoided eye contact, and looked down at the floor. "I don't care no way."

He became fidgety moving around in his seat. "Are you with your girlfriend now?"

"No after I lost my job, she left me."

"May I have her name and address? I'd like to ask her some questions," I said, taking notes.

"I got nothin' to hide. Her name is Mimie Anderson. She lives with her sister over on Wedgewood Place condominium #45. Her phone number is 561-2193."

"Thanks a lot, Agee." I ended our conversion trying to catch him off guard. "The way Foster treated you didn't have an effect on you? I mean if that was me, I would've tried to beat the shit out of him."

"He took two things that are important to me—money and my woman."

He nodded, keeping his head down in silence.

I knew that Agee was lying, trying to conceal his true emotions from me.

"Did you love Mimie?"

He got up and walked toward the window. "Yeah, man she was the only woman I ever cared about. I could've . . ."

"You could've what?" I asked probing. I found contradictions in the guy's actions.

He hesitated before speaking again. "Naw, man don't be puttin' words in my mouth. I was gonna say I felt like kickin' his ass."

"The man is twice your size. You're a small man."

"I ain't stupid, man."

"Meaning?"

He said nothing, taking another gulp of his Colt 45 beer. This time taking his sweet time to finish what remained in the bottle. "You wanted me to say I killed him. That would've satisfied you," Agee said, turning around to face me.

"Foster took the woman you loved and money out your pocket. That's enough to wanna kill anybody."

He had anger in his voice. "Man, I couldn't find a decent job no where. A black man can be either a cook or pump gas, but them Indians are comin' over here and taking the gas station jobs. What's left for a brother to do? Unless you a professional like yourself!"

"I worked hard for what I have, Agee. Nothing comes easy unless you work at it."

"Yeah, yeah, I heard that shit before. Work hard and you'll move up. That's the American Dream, well, man as long as your face is black, like mine, you ain't gonna live that "American Dream", bull shit!

"That's what my woman wanted—money. I promised her that

I'd work two jobs if I had to, shit. That wasn't good enough for her. A Black woman puts too much pressure on a brother. Workin' hard isn't good enough anymore. Mimee said she wanted a man like Foster, somebody older who can take care of her." He walked over to the sofa, taking a seat next to me. "I was out of work, collecting unemployment for three months, before I found me a McDonald's job. It only pays $6.00 an hour. At Foster's, I was makin' eight and a quarter."

Agee had an empty look in his eyes. I had recognized that look, before in plenty of black men. A defeating look that says he's given up on life. Once you get that look, it's hard to have a positive attitude on life. This attitude can make a man turn to a life of criminal activity.

"Foster got what he deserved. He didn't care 'bout nobody except himself." He stood up signaling the end of the interview. "Is that all, man? I gots things to do."

I stood up, thanking him for his time and followed him to the door," Agee, here's my business card, if you come across anyone or anything who can help, please call at anytime."

He nodded, grabbing the card and slamming the door.

A group of teenage boys, who looked like they had missed puberty, were standing next to my Volvo "Hello, fellas how you doin?"

"Nice car you got there, mister." My height and muscular frame made the boys back away. I was in excellent shape; taking on two or three of these young boys would not have created a problem for me. Driving to meet Iris took twenty-five minutes. This gave me time to rehash my list of possible suspects. Agee couldn't be trusted as far as I could see him. He rarely gave me eye contact, during the entire interview. Agee is one of those men who will always have a chip on his shoulder; mad at the world. He was a disgruntled employee, who lost his woman and job because of Foster. And Channel, the sophisticated woman in her late fifties, broke up with Foster when he left her for Iris Hall, a young and vibrant woman. I didn't know if Iris had a motive to murder Foster. I'd find out after our meeting.

I thought about what the interviewees had in common. They all had a beef with Foster. Agee's words stuck to me. "He got what he deserves." It seems that Foster was not a popular man. He seemed to spit on people who crossed his path.

16

Daddy O's, was the Expresso and gourmet coffeehouse located on Tenth and Vine Streets. Oval tables that seat four faced a dark-skinned brother on stage, wearing a red, black and green dashiki, which complemented his dread locks flowing down his back. He recited poetry to the soothing sounds of jazz. In the far corner was a counter where you could sample a variety of coffees.

The people were a true reflection of what the atmosphere represents a yip hop Afrocentric culture. For every five females, there were three who have their hair styled in some exotic braiding style or a short Afro. Even their dress was Afrocentric. Some of the men and women wore round wire-framed glasses. The storytellers recited poetry to the sounds of classic jazzman like John Coltrane's and Ramsey Lewis.

Iris had given me a prefect description of herself. I spotted her the moment I walked through the door. She wore her hair in dread locks that resembled a bob hairstyle. Her eyes were a light shade of gray and she had flawless fair skin. She had a natural look about her. She wore very little make up except for a gold shade of lipstick. She was dressed in all black. From what I could see, she weighed about 110 lbs., and stood nearly five feet tall.

Squeezing through the crowd in the middle of the floor. I walked to a table near her.

"Hello, you must be Mosee Love? You're not what I was expecting," she smiled.

"You're not what I expected either. I can see Foster had good taste."

She smiled, looking into my eyes. "Thank you for the compliment."

I wasted no time getting to business. "Mind if I tape this conversion?"

Iris nodded. "No. I have nothing to hide."

She inhaled, deeply, holding her head down, softly sobbing. "We were lovers and best friends."

"How did he treat you?"

She didn't speak right away, as if she was choosing her words carefully. "He had a split personality. He could be the sweetest man you ever met, but he also had dark side, which was very evil. He could be a bastard, too."

"Did he have anyone who disliked him?"

"You can say he had his share. There's a man Blake who came over to the house and restaurant to air his differences with Foster. I heard him threaten Foster once, over money that Foster owed him."

"What did he exactly say?"

"He was gonna kill Foster, if he didn't give him his share of the restaurant or his money."

"Do you remember his name?"

"Blake something. I can't remember his last name." She paused trying to recall his last name. "I believe its R something.

A woman approached the stage wearing an oval stub through her nose. She dressed in all black and her hair was in a short chic style that was close to her head. Everyone became silent when she stepped on the stage. She started her show by speaking in Afrocentric lyrics. The band started playing, as she spoke about the negative direction relationships have taken among Black males and females. She spoke about the hurting Black female as the victim.

I felt like I'd better hit the trail after she ended her poetry/ storytelling entertainment. She made the Black man the problem. The real issue is taking responsibility in a relationship. After I analyzed her story, I realized that she experienced pain in her relationship, making it a black woman's issue.

The women in the audience started cheering and applauding when she ended her story. The men in the audience, looked as if, a dark cloud hung over their heads. While most of the men in the audience held their heads low, I held my head high; I had nothing to be ashamed or guilty.

"That was nice, huh?" Iris said.

"Depends if you find any truth in what she's saying."

"But the Black man needs to respect the Black woman and treat her like a queen. That's not practiced enough," Iris protested.

"It goes both ways, you know. Black women need to respect the Black man. Bad enough Black men must suffer and bear the ills of society. It's my opinion that black women need to love herself, before she can demand respect from anyone."

"Yes," Iris said, shaking her head in agreement. "However, don't you think that Black women should be treated like queens?"

"I think that black women don't respect themselves."

Iris shifted the topic of conversion. "Foster's funereal is the day after tomorrow, you going?"

"Sure I'll be there."

"The services are at Union Temple at 12 noon. I'll be over to pick you up at 11 A.M."

"That's fine, Iris."

"I'm glad you're going, I hate funerals," I said.

"We all have to go sooner or later."

"Mosee, do you think Foster is in heaven, after all the dirt he's done?" Now I understood Foster's past finally caught up to him.

I disliked discussing religious issues. I tried to avoid the topic altogether. After my mother died, I felt that God took my mother away from me. I really didn't have much faith in God after that. I responded to her question, after a few moments. "I can't answer that question."

She gave me a look of bewilderment. "You don't believe in God?"

"I didn't say that. You're putting words in my mouth. I do believe that there has to be a better place than our lives on earth. Listen, I may need your assistance, Iris, during the course of my investigation."

She frowned with a look of disgust on her face. "Help for what? I don't know nothing about no police work."

"The only thing I need you to do is give me information about some of the people at the funeral."

The waitress brought over our Mocha coffee and chocolate espresso, along with our muffins. I hoped I'd still have room for Mrs. Daniels famous cooking after I finished my muffin.

I Left Iris behind at the coffee house with some of her friends and I returned to the home of Ms. Daniels.

When I got there, I could smell the precious aroma of food cooking. Ms. Daniels yelled from the kitchen.

"Hello, Mosee how's your investigation goin'?"

I took a seat on the sofa. "I'm making a little progress. I interviewed Foster's former girlfriends, Iris, and Channel. Also, I spoke to Agee who was employed at Foster's restaurant. I'm thinking about keeping a close eye on him. He was terminated by Foster because he accused Foster of making advances toward his girlfriend."

wearing a beige housecoat, she emerged from the kitchen. She sat down at the dinning table. "I can't believe he hasn't changed in over thirty years. They always say, "a dog don't change his strips." Any other leads?"

I laughed. "You mean a leopard don't change his spots? Well, yes, also there's another suspect. I forgot to mention a man named Blake Reed who was supposedly cheated out of some money by Foster. He's next on my list to interview."

She bowed her head down and mumbled to herself, "Please Lawd, help Mr. Love find the killer, 'fore my daughter goes crazy in that jail."

I tried to comfort her. "Everything will be over soon." I put my arm around her.

"I hope so, Mr. Love," she said trying to force a smile on her face.

"What's for dinner, Ms. Daniels? I saved plenty of room for your delicious cooking."

"We havin' leftovers."

"Sounds good to me." I took a seat at the dinning room table. "You gonna join me this time. I hate eating alone, you know. I prefer to dine in the company of a pretty young woman."

She emerged from the kitchen, carrying a large dish in her hand. She was blushing when she placed the dish on the table. "Okay, you convinced me to join you."

We ate dinner in silence. After about fifteen minutes, I said, "Ms. Daniels, you the best cook I know."

"Don't be silly! Can't your mama cook?"

"She was a good cook, but ..." I said taking a deep breath.

"I'm sorry, Mosee. I ..."

"That's okay, Ms. Daniels, she died when I was twelve years old. She didn't have to die, but the stress of losing a husband and raising three children alone caused her to have a nervous breakdown and a massive stroke."

"Did your father die, too?"

I felt anger and found it impossible to keep it out of my voice. "You might as well say he's dead. I haven't spoken to him in over twenty years, since he left us."

"You should pray and ask the Lawd to help you forgive him."

"Does Zoe know her father's funereal is Wednesday at Union Temple Church?" She looked at me with disappointment written on her face.

"I didn't know. I usually keeps up on the news in this town, but I ain't had no interest, since Zoe's been in jail."

"You should attend the services. After all, he was your daughter's father."

"That man was never no father. A man that takes care of his own is a father, but someone who fathers children, then turns

140

around and leaves is called a daddy."

Shortly after dinner, I went to my room and went over my notes on what I had gathered at this point. The only possible suspects were Agee Johnson—a cook, and Blake Reed, who was allegedly a silent business partner who Foster cheated out of money.

I looked over the employee list that I had found on Foster's desk. I thought about interviewing a few more names on the list. I got hold of the phone book and looked up the last name Reed in Westfield County, South Carolina. After ten minutes of searching, I found a Blake Reed in the book. How could I ask for better luck than that.

I wanted to set up an interview with Blake, but I learned through experiences as an FBI agent that unannounced visits make the best interviews. Instead, I telephoned the police station.

"Hello Detective Burke speaking."

"Hello, this is Mosee Love, Detective Burke. I need to ask you a favor?"

"Love, I told you to back off this murder investigation." I swallowed my pride and became humble.

"I'm trying to help my client, Zoe Owens. Please Burke, you're the only one I can count on. This is the last favor."

"Go on," Burke grunted.

"I have two names I need you to do a search on Blake Reed and Agee Johnson. Blake was a former friend whom Foster owed some money to and Agee Johnson was a disgruntled employee, who was fired because Agee confronted Foster about making advances towards his girlfriend."

"Look, Mosee, I don't need you tellin' me how to do my job. Like I told you before—the Foster murder investigation is closed!"

"Wait, don't hang up, Burke. I just need this one favor from you, I pleaded. "I really would appreciate your help." There was a long pause on the other end that lasted nearly fifteen seconds. "Detective, are you still there?"

"Alright, I'll do it, but this is the last time I better hear from you. Why don't you take your butt back to New York," he said coughing.

"I hope you take care of that cough," I said trying to show concern. "Thanks, Burke." I hung up the telephone, hoping those two names would yield me something. I decided to call it an early night.

I went to my room, thinking about the funeral I had to attend. Foster's funeral was the first one I attended since the death of my mother. I made myself a promise not to attend another funeral, but, the fact was, funerals came with the job. The following day, I made it in enough time, to see the beginning of the funeral services, wearing my basic black funeral suit.

It wasn't too difficult to find a seat. Everything was wide open for the picking of my choosing. My first preference was a seat in the last pew. The back of the church gave me a clear view of everyone. Iris sat up front in the second pew, pretending to be the grieving widow, along with Foster's other women. The church was medium-sized. There were colorful flowers surrounding the casket. The pulpit was above the casket where the choir sat. There was a woman in the middle pew that resembled a woman I met on my first night in Westfield at the Holiday Inn. I tried to recall the woman's name, but nothing came to mind. I had to look through my wallet to check the name she wrote down.

The title of the services was—preparing for Brother Foster's Homecoming. The choir sang uplifting songs that moved the people to shout and stomp their feet. The funereal lasted about forty-five minutes, with a few of the church members and friends giving brief eulogies.

A woman stood out amongst the crowd. She wore a bright red dress that clung to her hips. She wore dark shades and a black brimmed hat that covered her face. I heard whispers as she made her way up front to view the body. She looked like she was headed to a party rather than of a funeral. I have to say I drooled over the woman as she passed my aisle. She exited the church in a hurray, through the back doors.

I tried to follow her to catch her license plates, but it was too late. I saw a glimpse of the car: A late model sky blue Lincoln.

After the services, the funereal procession proceeded to the burial ground. I kept my distance from the crowd, hoping to observe something out of the ordinary.

When I returned to the church, I picked up the guest list and slipped it in my pocket. I hoped some of the names would come in handy for questioning. I managed to corner Rev. Elders when the crowd died down. "Hello, Rev. Elders, my name is Mosee Love; I'm a Private Investigator looking into the murder of Foster Owens. I hope you don't mind if I ask you a few questions?"

He hesitated before responding. "No problem, Mr. Love. We can go into my office." We walked down the hall toward the back of the church, where a brown door held the word office, hanging in black letters. The inside of the office looked like a Penthouse apartment. With all the amenities, including the plush leather furniture.

I looked around and wondered how the Reverend could afford these things. He was a striking, middle-aged man whose flawless dark skin looked as soft as butter along with his keen features. He had a thick black mustache. The man was dressed in an expensive black tailored suit. I recognized quality,—judging from my best friend Cedric's wardrobe.

I felt my shoes sink into the carpet. The religion business must be good to him. At that point, I recognized him as nothing more than a hustler, preaching the word of God.

When I shook his hand, I couldn't help noticing how soft his hand felt against mine. I was pretty sure he didn't know the meaning of hard work. "I hope you don't mind if I ask you a few questions?"

Reverend Elders sat back with ease at his cherry wood desk. He looked as though he was ready to talk freely.

"Please pull up a seat, Mr. Love. Do you care for a drink?"

I was appalled. "A drink?"

"Yes," the Rev said laughing. "I'm human. There's no harm in drinking. Even the Bible says a little sherry every now and then is good for the soul. The trick is not to over indulge oneself." He got up, approached the entertainment center and extracted a bottle of dark wine and two glasses. He poured the Sherry generously. "This is my favorite wine, after I've had a long day in church." He sat back in his seat like a king. "How can I help you, Mr. Love?"

"I'm investigating the murder of Foster Owens. His daughter's charged with his murder, and I would like to find the real killer. Can you tell me anything about Foster's relationship in the church?"

"Brother Foster was a regular every Sunday. He even came out to our special events."

"Did the members like Foster?"

Reverend Elders chuckled to himself. "Everyone liked him— especially the women folks. He was a charmer." The reverend shook his head, showing no emotion, as if he were reflecting on past events.

"Did any of the women take a special interest in Foster?"

The Rev. sat up in his seat. His body became rigid. He glanced away from me as he spoke. "I don't get involved with gossip, Mr. Love." There was a quiver in his voice. "My business is to deliver the Word of God, not to involve myself in meaningless gossip."

"I didn't mean to offend you Reverend, but sometimes you can't help when you overhear things people say. Foster was a lady's man and I was wondering if he had any special interest in any of the women."

He leaned back in his chair. "I really can't answer that

question, because I don't get involved with folk's business. When Foster started fornicating in my church, I told him that I ain't gonna stand for no disruptions in my church, but things got out of hand and the women got to arguing and fighting. I was outraged. Foster wasn't allowed back in my church, unless he repented and gave his life to Christ." The reverend shook his head in disgust. "I thought Brother Foster had class when I first laid eyes on him."

"Are any of the women who were involved with Foster still members?"

"I don't know, Mr. Love. You're welcome to question any of my members."

"How did the men respond to him?"

"They didn't care much for him. Some felt he was full of himself and some were just plain jealous because the women were always in his face, laughing and grinning."

"Did you like him, Reverend?"

He picked up his wineglass, slowly sipping his sherry. "He was a soul worth savin'. I tried to get him to give his life to the lord, but he said he didn't wanna change one hundred percent, but that he'd try. If he gave his life to the lord, like I tole' him, he probably would be alive today." The Rev became nervous and tense, waiting for the next question.

I rose from my seat, leaning over his desk to shake his hand. "Thank you Reverend Elders for your time, I really appreciate it."

He leaned forward, stretching over to shake my hand. "Nice meeting you, Mr. Love, I'm here to help any way I can."

I thought it was a little odd the way he waited for me to get to the door before he came around his desk. I wanted to throw one more question, to catch him off guard. I turned around abruptly, almost kissing the Reverend's face. "One more question Rev. Think you can point any of the women who had a relationship with Foster?"

He stood in the doorway entrance, in a trance. I tapped him on the shoulder. I waited for a response. "Rev. Elders, are you okay?"

He forced a smile. "I'm okay, just a little exhausted from the funeral, that's all. What were you asking me?"

"Can you point out any of the women who had affairs with Foster?"

"One of the women left the church about a month ago to spare herself the embarrassment from her peers. I believe she moved out of town."

"What's her name?"

"I don't really know. She was a very private person."

I thought it odd that a Rev. didn't know his own member's names.

He gave me an abrupt goodbye, sending me into shock when he nearly took my nose off with the door. I got an uneasy feeling about the man. I needed to find out more about the mystery women. Their names had significance to the Rev, but why?

I walked down the hall, following the sound of voices. I opened a wooden door leading to the room where Foster's wake was being held. I looked at everyone laughing, and talking. I found it amazing how quickly the mourning crowd changed into a jovial bunch of folks. I stood in the corner away from the crowd. A woman walked toward me. She wore a tight black dress that exposed more than needed to be seen. Her walk emphasized the thrust of her hips. She was about five-feet six inches and very big-boned. She smiled at me.

"You look so distant; you don't look like you're from around here."

"I'm just here to pay my respects."

She stood there waiting for information. "I see. How did you know Foster?"

"From a mutual friend."

She moved in closer. "You don't give up much information, do you, big guy."

I extended my hand to give a proper greeting. "Name's Mosee Love."

"Oh, I'm sorry. I came over here invading your personal space, drilling you with questions," she said, looking flushed, "I didn't bother to introduce myself. My name's Everee.

I turned my head and continued to study the people, looking for anything peculiar.

"Excuse me, you look familiar. You sure you not from this area?"

"No."

"You don't like talking, huh?"

"Yeah, I'm just trying to concentrate on something."

"You know, Foster was a good man. I'm sorry that he's gone."

"Was he close to you?"

"Yes, he tried to get me a steady job, but I tells him I'm fine in my profession. It has it's up and downs, but the money is good."

"Where you from, Mosee?"

"New York City. I'm a Private Investigator, working on a murder case."

Her eyes became wide, as if she'd made a discovery. "I know now, I met you at The Holiday Inn, when I was working that night. I can't forget a name like Mosee Love."

I remembered the woman, but I'd tried to be as inconspicuous as possible. The less people I knew here the better.

"Yeah, I remember you. How can I forget a tall dark and handsome man? Now I remember you were trying to help some woman find her father," she said with excitement in her voice. "I bet Foster was her father. That's a shame, I mean to find someone you ain't seen in years, and they turn up dead. Life's a bitch, huh."

I began to feel myself perspire, when she stepped in closer. I moved back a few inches from the woman. Invading my personal space is a one way to tick me off. I needed space to think; I was right in the middle of an investigation.

"If you need my help, don't hesitate to call me." Everee opened her pocketbook and handed me a business card. "You can reach me anytime," she winked.

When she walked away, I must say I felt hardness in my loins, letting me know just what I was missing. I distracted easily by the smell of food. Behind a long rectangle table, there stood two matriarch no nonsense women. The food was lined up in aluminum trays. I grabbed a plate and waited for my turn. The line appeared to be getting longer, from everyone rushing back up for seconds.

One of the larger cooks with the wide hips gave a mean look to one of the men in line who jumped in front of me. "Excuse me, Joe," she said, "I know you ain't jumpin' in front of this man, here?" she said coming to my defense. "You done had your meal, now let other folks have their turn," she said, folding her arms across her chest.

The other women chimed in. "I swear, Joe, you act like you starvin'. Let this man have something," she smiled in my direction. "There's plenty to go round."

I smiled in gratitude at the two women. They filled my plate, covering every square inch. "Thank you ladies."

I moved out of line, heading toward the back. I was lucky to find a seat at the first available table. "Mind if I join you, ladies?" Just then I thought it was appropriate to question them about Foster's mystery women.

One of the younger women in her early twenties smiled at me, making me feel welcomed. "Sure have a seat," she said in a slight southern accent. "We like the company of a handsome man."

I took a seat, feeling all eyes upon me, as if I were on trial. "How you ladies doing?"

"We holdin' up. It's hard when you lose a church member."

"Foster was a regular here, huh?"

"The young woman had a bewildered look on her face. "I

wouldn't call him a member. He came most Sundays."

"Were you close to him?" I asked, watching each of the women's facial expressions.

It was the second woman, who looked to be in her thirties, that responded. "Some of us didn't know him that well, expect Ida here," she said pointing in her direction. Everyone had a little input, except her.

A woman, who looked to be in her mid forties, gave her a sharp look that told her to keep her mouth shut. Of course I jumped in on the perfect opportunity to reel her in. "Did you know Foster Ma'am?"

"Yeah, but I didn't know him that well," she said shrugging her shoulders.

One of the older women at the table gave her a wink. "Come on Ida stop pulling our legs."

Everyone was quiet. Tension filled the air.

"Well ladies, I hope everyone is fine." I finished the remaining piece of fried chicken and candied yams. I reached into my jacket pocket pulling out my ID. "Ladies, I'm a private investigator, looking into the murder of Foster Owens."

Everyone examined the ID, in awe.

"I don't believe this, here we are exposing our personal business in front of a stranger who happens to be a cop," the younger one said shaking her head.

"I told you to be careful of what you say around folks, you liable to get us in trouble," the dark-skinned one said, looking at me.

"Are we in trouble?"

"No. First of all I'm not a cop," I said putting my ID away. "I work for myself. I'm representing my client, Zoe Owens. She's the daughter of the deceased victim—Foster Owens."

Ida's mouth flung open. "He had a child?" Ida said, looking

wildly surprised. "You find out all kinds of dirt when folks die."

"Amen to that, sister."

I looked at Ida. "Do you mind if I ask you a couple of questions about Foster in private?"

Nervously, she agreed to a brief interview. "We can go in one of the meeting rooms."

We walked down a long hallway toward the end of the church where a brown door marked private was inscribed on the door in red letters.

"Please have a seat, Mr. Love."

"Thank you, Ida, this shouldn't take long. I'm sorry I have to question you under these circumstances."

"That's, okay, you have your job to do," she said nervously.

I took out my notebook. "Ida, how well did you know Foster?"

"I didn't know him that well. We spoke a few times, but nothing serious."

"You didn't know him on an intimate level, in any way?"

She turned away, looking at the picture of Jesus on the wall. I'll throw her a hard ball, I decided. A little white lie now and then, never hurt anybody. I'd tell her that Reverend Elders confided in me that she and Foster were more than friends. She had no way of knowing what the reverend did or did not tell me at that point.

"Rev Elders told me you were quite serious with him."

After what seemed like five minutes of silence, she spoke. "I was involved with him for about two months." She shot me a look, that could've killed me. I knew she had a little more to tell me than she wanted to admit.

"Why did you lie to me?"

She shrugged her shoulders, looking down at the table. "I don't know. I felt ashamed. I allowed myself to be seduced by him. I'm supposed to be a Christian woman and ..."

"Ida, we're all human. You have needs like anybody else. No one is perfect on this earth."

She bowed her head. "I was in love with him," she said. He

150

had a way of making me feel special. No one made me feel like that since my husband left," she said in a southern accent.

"Did he date someone else in the church, the same time he was dating you."

"And?" she said in an angry tone.

"How did that make you feel?"

"How do you think that makes anybody feel?"

"I don't know everyone responds differently to situations," I said, "What was your response?"

"I hated Foster for cheating on me. I even thought about.." She paused mid sentence, giving me a blank stare.

"Did you kill Foster?" I blurted out, jumping ahead of myself. It was a low blow, but I had to pull out all my tricks.

"No! I couldn't do anything like that, I'm a Christian woman." She said with indignation in her voice. "Thinking thoughts like that is a sin in Gods eyes." Her eyes kept shifting positions during the interview. This gave me the feeling that she was hiding something.

"You think that I'm glad the man is dead, well you're wrong. I wouldn't wish death on my worst enemy," she said taking a deep breath. "I'm Christian woman, Mr. Love; I try to forgive people for their faults."

I learned in my FBI training that you watch every movement and the reaction time it takes a person to answer a question. My training provided a solid foundation that I used in my investigation. I thought that most of my valuable skills had left me. Being an investigator is something that stays in your blood no matter how long you've been away from it.

"When you found out Foster was two timing you, how did that make you feel? Being that she's a sister to you in your own church?"

"I felt like a big fool, Mr. Love, wouldn't you?"

151

"You were so angry that you wanted to kill him?"

"Like I told you before, yes, I wanted to, but I'm a Christian."

I was tired of hearing people use religion as a shield. I had seen many people like her before, trying to justify their actions and use God to cover their mistakes. "Ida, what's the other woman's name who was also involved with Foster?"

She didn't answer right away. She turned away looking at the picture of Jesus on the wall. "Her name is Mavis, but she don't attend church here no more."

"Can you look up her address for me?"

"Yes. I can check the membership records and give you her address." She headed out the door. I'll be right back, Mr. Love."

A few minutes later, she came back into the room. "I'm sorry, Mr. Love, but we don't have her address on file," she said, taking a seat opposite from me.

"I would assume that you keep accurate records on all your church members."

"Yes, but unfortunately we don't have her address on file."

"Sometimes things get lost, Mr. Love."

I realized she was trying to get rid of me. "Thanks for your time," I said smiling.

Iris dropped me off at Zoe's mother's house. When I arrived Ms. Daniels was home as usual. She refused to dress or get out of bed, since her daughter's incarceration. She went around with a blank look on her face.

"Ms. Daniels", I said, "keeping yourself a prisoner in your own home isn't going to help Zoe. What you need to do is get out and get some fresh air."

"I don't need any fresh air, I'm fine," she said. "By the way how's your investigation going?"

I nodded. "It's coming along. I have a list of possible suspects. He's pissed so many people off; I haven't narrowed down any one person yet. Each person I spoke to has a motive, but there's no probable cause to justify if any of them killed him.

I made a phone call to Detective Burke to see if he found any information on the two potential suspects.

"Hello, Burke, this is Mosee Love calling you back. You find any thing on the two name's I gave you?"

"As a matter of fact, yeah, Agee Johnson has a prior for drug and weapons possession."

"Did he serve any time for the two charges?"

"He served five years of a ten year sentence and five years probation. Blake Reed's clean," he said in his southern accent. "You think Agee Johnson could have done it?"

"I don't know. Anything's possible in this business. He fits the criteria, but it's still questionable."

"I'll have one of my men go over there and shake him up a bit."

"Thanks Burke."

"Make this the last time you call me," he said slamming the phone in my ear.

17

A shot was fired. Iris felt a pulsating pain in her lower abdomen. She looked up for a split second at the figure holding a gun, hovering over her. Iris's vision became a blur. She could only make out a faint shadow. She glanced at the wound amazed of what her mind told her she was seeing. She blinked open and shut—another split second. Surely she would awaken and all this would be a dream.

She had a puzzled look on her face—why me? Her mouth was partially open. Trickles of blood crept from the sides of her mouth.

Her assailant moved quickly, looking behind to make sure there were no fingerprints left behind. It had been clean and easy. Now the others would be easy, too.

After I dropped off Iris, I wanted to map out my strategy for the next week. I dozed off in the bedroom, in the middle of writing notes. The following day, I realized that I had slept through the night. I was so exhausted that nothing could have awakened me. Excessive knocking on the door snapped me back into reality— Monday morning.

"Mr. Love, please wakeup, the police called here. They said it's urgent that they speak to you."

"What time is it?"

"It's eleven o'clock in the morning."

"I'll be there in a minute, Ms. Daniels." Before I returned Burke's call, I wanted to be alert and ready. I took a quick shower. There's nothing like getting into a shower and feeling the water massage every part of your body to wake you up. After that, I'm ready to take on any challenge.

I returned Detective Burke's call to inquire about the urgent message. I hoped that he found a break in the case: the murderer of Zoe's father was found. Now my client will be clear of all charges and she'll be a free woman. And I could head back home to familiar surroundings. If only my luck was good, like that.

"Hello, Burke, I got your message."

"Get your butt down here now, Love, I'm sending one of my men to pick you up."

"Pick me up? Why?"

"I'll explain later," he said ending the conversion.

Twenty minutes later, a black and white patrol car drove up in front of Ms. Daniel's house. I shouted from the front porch. "What's this matter about?" I courageously walked up to the officer to find out more information. Before I realized it, he had slapped a pair of handcuffs on my wrist.

"I was told by my superiors to pick you up." He proceeded to search me from head to toe. The officer pushed me head first, in the back of the patrol car. "What the hell is going on here?" I shouted, nearly causing my vocal cords to snap. "I'm bringing you in for questioning in a murder case."

"Murder!" I yelled "What the hell is going on here? I'm a former FBI agent and I'm a self-employed PI working for my client, Zoe Owens."

"I don't care nothin' 'bout what you did or what your plans are. I'm just doin' my job fella," he responded carelessly. He looked in his rearview mirror. "You'll know all the details soon," he said with a smirk on his face.

I had seen rednecks like him before throughout my career. Some white folks are sneaky about their hatred for blacks, while others speak their mind, and vice versa. Things haven't changed.

The ride to the police station seemed like an eternity. The officer opened his door, escorting me into the building. I was

lead to a basement. A few feet further down, I came upon a row of cells. A stench of decomposition emanated throughout the basement. I was lead to the last cell on the right. The closing of the bars sent a chill through my body.

There were two bunks against the wall. The sink was filled with brown crusty stains and a commode in the corner had brown stains around the rim of the toilet. I fell asleep on the bottom bunk bed, with my head pressed against the graffiti decorated walls.

I didn't know how long I had been asleep when a coarse voice in the background startled me. Suddenly I knew where I was.

"Hello, Mosee, so nice of you to join us. I hope you like our room accommodations here," I jumped up in a daze, half asleep, trying to get my thoughts together. "What the hell is going on here? I didn't kill anyone."

"I wanna ask you some questions about the murder of Iris Hall."

"Iris Hall!" I shouted, still not believing my ears. "She was killed? How can that be when I was just with her yesterday?"

I sat back down on the lower bunk bed, shaking my head in disbelief.

"I brought you in because I thought you might know something. Besides, we found your fingerprints in her house."

"What does that mean? That makes me a murderer? You got a weapon?"

"No. Can't find anything yet."

"You think I killed that girl?"

"We can talk more in my office," he said, unlocking the iron steel bars. "I have some more questions to ask you." I followed Burke down the hall and up a set of steps to his office. "Have a seat," he said pointing to the black vinyl chair in front of his desk.

"Why me, Burke?"

The detective sat down. "You were the first available suspect and your fingerprints were found in the victim's house. And that makes you the last person to see her alive."

"And that makes me a murderer because I was over her house? I hardly even knew her! I met the girl a few days ago."

He leaned over the desk, putting his elbows on the desk, "What were you doin' with her at Daddy O's?"

156

"I met her there to ask her some questions about Foster. What you people should be doin' is tracking down Foster's killer. Your problem is your men don't know anything about real investigation. The only problems you have in this small town are giving out parking tickets or breaking up barroom brawls."

Burke stood up glaring into my eyes. "Damn it," he said slamming his fist on top of the desk. I don't need you tellin' me how to do my job. Ever since you came in my office, you brought nothin' but trouble, with your slick city ways. Believe me I aim to keep a close eye on you. If I hear of another murder, that's connected to you, I'll haul you in myself."

I sat down, trying to calm to myself. I wanted to knock him to his knees, but confronting anger with anger in any confrontational situation only results in violence.

I gave Burke a cheesy smile. I'm a far cry from the FBI. In these parts I knew it would seriously behoove me to get some strong sense of strategy going. These Southern cops didn't take kindly to taking instructions from a dark colored city slicker like me.

"You're right, Burke, I need your expertise from your men. I can't do this alone," I said trying to appeal to his ego.

Burke leaned back in his chair with his chest expanding. "We do have some descent men on staff here," he said. "It's just that my men haven't gotten a real chance to prove themselves. Maybe they can make some sense out of this mess."

"Meantime, I'm clear to go?"

"Sure thing," he said. "By the way what kinda name is Mosee Love? You from America? I ain't never heard a ..."

I interrupted him. "You mean a Black man with a name like mine. Well welcome to America, Mr. Burke. I was born in America, same as you," I said. "I'm Afro-American. What do you call yourself?"

He paused for a moment. "I'm Irish," he shrugged. "I guess that makes me Irish American, huh?"

I just had to ask. "Detective Burke, what about Agee Johnson, you know the guy I told you who had a beef with Foster over his girlfriend."

"What? You wanna know his heritage, too?"

I stifled a laugh. "No, listen; he was also one of Foster's employees. And Blake Reed, he's the guy Foster cheated out of a business deal."

"I told you I'll have my men go pay them a visit to shake them up a bit."

"It's hard to believe that Iris Hall is dead. She was a pretty girl," I said. "How did she die?"

"We think she may have been killed by her former boyfriend. One of my men just told me before you were picked up, that she came in a couple of times to put a restraining order on her boyfriend for assault and battery."

"That doesn't make him guilty."

Burke shrugged his shoulders. "We can't find the son of a bitch either. He may have skipped town; My men were told to bring him in at first sight. No questions asked."

"It's really a shame to see women get beat up. It makes me angry as hell," he continued, looking at me.

"Do you think he was jealous of Foster? Maybe he killed Foster out of revenge."

Burke nodded. "Good point, Mosee," he said lighting up his cigar.

"What's the old boyfriend's name?"

"I can not tell you that information. Just stay off this case. We can handle our affairs. You concentrate on who killed Foster."

"When I get hauled into a police station for questioning in a murder case, I do make it my business," I said walking toward the door.

"Can you do me a favor, Burke," I continued, "bring in Agee

158

and Blake for questioning."

"I'll think about it."

"Is that all, I'm free to go now?"

"Yeah, but we'll be watchin' you, boy."

I slammed the door behind me, nearly shattering the glass. I went to the telephone booth to call Everee for a ride back to Ms. Daniels house.

My friend answered the phone in a hoarse tone. "Who's calling?"

"It's me Mosee Love."

"I know who you are," she said, "what's up?"

I hesitated. "I need you to come and pick me up at the Westfield county police station."

"What you doin' in the police station?"

"I was picked up for questioning in the murder case of Iris Hall. I don't have all the details, but the police think her former boyfriend could have killed her. They think it might be the jealous boyfriend syndrome."

"I'm sorry to hear that. Was she a friend of yours?"

"No. Not really, we had just met. Yesterday was my first time seeing her in person. We had a business meeting at Daddy O's. She was intimate with the deceased. She was helping me with contacts I need in my investigation."

I hung up the telephone and waited for Everee to arrive. I watched the second hand go around the clock on the wall. Forty-five minutes went by, before I decided to venture outside the building, I stood waiting at the side of the building.

A black Mercedes' SL 500 pulled up. "Hey big fella, it's me," she shouted.

Everee's car was one of those top-of-the-line Mercedes. At that point, it dawned on me that she made her living entertaining men. I walked up to the side of the car, admiring the elegance.

"Nice car you got there, Everee."

"Yeah, I worked hard for this, had to put in plenty of over time," she said laughing. "Get in, I don't bite. So what's up? You finally decided that you needed my help as your personal assistant?" Everee said giving me a wink.

"We can start by finding out who Iris Hall's ex-boyfriend is. Detective Burke wouldn't give me any information. Said I shouldn't stick my nose where it didn't belong."

"Fuck that cop. I have my own contacts on the street," she said. I know this ex-con who goes by the name of Willie T who can get information on just bout anybody."

I nodded. "What did he do time for?"

She shrugged her shoulders, glancing over at me. "I don't know. I think he was in for selling drugs and racketeering,. You might have to pay a little something for his services. And my services don't come free either."

My money was getting a little low, I had to count pennies or ask Ms. Daniels for a commission for my services.

"I was just joking about payin' me," Everee giggled. "I don't mind helpin' you out, besides I think you're kinda cute."

"How much will it cost me to pay your friend?"

"I can't answer that, you'll have to take that up with him yourself. I'll give you a brief lesson about Willie T. He appears to be mean, but that's so folks don't think he's a pushover, but once you get to know him, he's as gentle as a kitten."

"What type of work does he do?" I knew the answer to that question myself. I had seen enough men in my career to know that these men are usually repeat offenders. I know that most ex cons end up working minimum wage jobs. They travel in the same circles that got them in the penitentiary in the first place. It's a small world in the eyes of a criminal. Everyone knows each other. And if you need a favor on the street, you could always count on one of them giving you a hand.

"He works for Ira as a bails bondsman; his job is to rough

people up, and bring them back if they try to skip town." Everee took me to the bails bondman office to meet this Willie character. The office didn't leave much to the imagination, only the basics: a desk, telephone, computer, and a fax and copier machine.

A Black male who looked to be in his late forties was wearing a pale green shirt with cream color slacks and matching shoes. He wore a kangaroo white straw hat. He sat at the desk at the computer reading the newspaper. When the door made a squeaky noise, he turned to face it. His eyes brightened when he saw Everee enter the office.

"Hello, Everee, you lookin' good as usual," he said, walking from behind his desk to give Everee a hug. When he notices me, his eyes stayed focused, never leaving my sight.

"Okay, okay, that's enough, I'll have to charge you for the next hug. I have someone I want you to meet. This is Mosee Love, he's a good friend of mine who needs some help."

He looked at me, examining me thoroughly. "What business you in?" "I work for myself." He shook my hand. "Nice to meet you, name's Ira." Everee looked toward Ira. "How's business these days, still

Bailing crooks out of jail?" Ira took a seat behind his desk, facing Everee and Mosee. "You lookin' good as usual," he said again.

She smiled taking a seat. "Thanks, Ira; you know I have to keep up with my competition. Mosee Love is a private investigator from New York City."

Ira looked at me, trying to size me up. He bent forward, leaning across his desk. "So what is it you investigating?" he said in a southern accent. "I'm investigating the murder of Foster Owens. You know him?"

"Naw. Never heard of the man," he said leaning back in his chair.

Everee said. "He needs to see Willie T"

"What for?"

Everee spoke up. "Well, he needs to find a woman's ex-boyfriend, who might be connected in her murder."

"What's this got to do with this dead guy named Foster?" Ira asked, looking at me suspiciously.

I spoke up, filling in the gaps. "I have a hunch that these killing sprees might be connected in some way. It's my theory, but I'm trying to prove that my client, Zoe Owens, did not murder her father—Foster Owens." I need to locate Iris Hall's ex-boyfriend who might know something about the other murders."

Ira asked. "What does this woman, Iris Hall, and her ex-boyfriend have to do with this dead man named Foster?"

"Well," I said taking a deep breath. "Iris used to date Foster. I wanted to check out if Iris's ex-boyfriend had any hidden rage or jealousy over Iris dumping him for Foster."

"I see," Ira said shaking his head in agreement. "You ain't no undercover cop, is you? Cause if you are, my business is squeaky clean."

"No, Ira, I work for myself. My client's name is Zoe Owens. She's the daughter of the murder victim. She was charged in her father's death and I am tryin' to find the real killer in order to get her acquitted."

Ira said in a slow southern draw. "You think the ex-boyfriend killed this Foster?"

"I don't know, but if Willie T finds him, perhaps I can begin to put the missing pieces together."

"Ya'll wait here. Willie should be back in a few."

About ten minutes later, a short stocky black man with a shiny bald head came walking through the door. He looked to be in his mid-forties. His physique made him appear as though he'd spent most of his prison time pumping iron. He wore a colorful sweat suit in bright blue and teal green.

"Hey, Ira, I got the dude who tried to skip his bail. You know the pretty boy Jamaican fellow."

Ira turned around smiling. "Good work, Willie T"

Willie T stood hovering over Ira's desk. "I had to rough him up some." Willie T turned around and noticed Everee and me. He went immediately to Everee. "I ain't seen you in a ages!" he said, lifting her out of the chair.

"Well I've been busy, with business."

Willie T laughed. "You must have good customers, huh?"

"You can say I have a large clientele."

He put Everee down slowly.

"So what brings you here?"

She turned to introduce me. "I have someone I want you to meet," she said pointing in my direction. "His name is Mosee Love, he's a private investigator."

I was color struck by his jacket—teal green, and bright sky blue jacket with a hint of glitter and matching shoes. I looked over the peculiar character, assessing him. He wore rings on all four fingers on the right and left hand. He also had an earring in his left ear, with the initials W.T. In gold.

I came up with a character profile. He probably had a hat to match every outfit he owned. Willie T treasures two things in life: his Cadillac and clothes; these are the two things that give him pride.

You can see Willie T coming a mile away, even if you aren't looking for him, by his flashy dressing.

I stood up to shake Willie T's hand to show a friendly gesture. "How you doin', Willie T?"

"Fine. So what you want me for?" he asked, standing in the corner of the room with his arms folded, looking at me with suspicion written all over his face.

"I'm working for a woman by the name of Zoe Owens. She's been charged for the murder of her father." I returned to my seat and wondered if I was making a desperate move; getting involved with these crooks could only bring me more problems. Bails bondsmen are nothing but legitimate crooks. But because I didn't have any contacts in the area, I was forced to seek their help. "I'm tryin' to find out who killed my client's father. I wanna know if you can help me find her ex-boyfriend?"

Willie T asked. "You got the boyfriends name?"

"No."

"What's the woman's name who was killed?"

"Iris Hall."

Willie T shook his head. "How much you gonna pay me?"

I looked at Everee, and she shrugged her shoulders. "How's five hundred dollars sound?"

"How about five hundred more."

I had no choice at that point, but to pay the fee he was asking. "Willie T, it's a deal."

"How can I reach you?" I asked.

"I'll be in contact with you. I don't like folks knowin' where to track me down."

"No problem." I took out a piece of paper and wrote down Ms. Daniels' telephone number.

"Willie T, you can call me, too, in case you can't reach Mosee," Everee said.

"Girl, you sure look good," he said, showing his gold plated teeth.

"Thanks, Willie T"

"Willie should be calling us in a few days. He don't take long to find anybody. Where to now?"

"Home is fine; I have to check in with Burke to see if he came up with anything on Blake and Agee."

Everee reached into her glove compartment and took out a black cellular phone. "Here you go. Use this."

I reached into my wallet, looking for Burke's business card. Then I had an idea. "Everee you can start helping me by goin' to

Union Temple church where Foster attended. I need you to question some of the members about Ida and Mavis. They both had intimate relationships with Foster."

18

Everee pulled up in front of the church on the south side of Westfield County. The area was considered the uppity black folks section. The majority of people in the community work in government or municipal city jobs. A few have their own businesses; beauty shops, barber shops, and a few small clothing and corner stores.

She walked inside the church and saw a man down the hall, carrying a cane. He walked slowly, barely able to support himself. "Hello, there, sir, how are you?"

"Fine, young lady." The old man stood there reading the bulletin board. He continued to read, ignoring Everee, who attempted to get his attention.

"I need to ask you a few questions, sir, about two of your church members. Their names are Ida and Mavis. The name's ring a bell, pops?"

The old man had a puzzled look on his face. "They good church going folks. Why you askin'?" he said in a low shaky voice.

"My name's Everee and I'm an investigator." She felt proud to utter those words. Everee realized that it was the first time she had felt good about what she was doing, even though she wasn't an investigator. But playing the role boosted her self esteem. "I need to speak to you in private." Everee held the man by his arm and walked slowly down the hall. She went to the first available room she saw.

"What you want with me, fur'?"

Everee watched the man sit down on the sofa slowly. She took a seat next to him. Her heart began pounding. She sat there, trying to get the nerve up again to question the man. She pulled out her driver's license from her pocketbook and flashed it quickly in the mans face. She prayed that his eye sight didn't catch her false identification. He smiled, exposing his empty mouth. "Oh you a cop, huh?"

"You can say that. I need some info, pops, on the two women Foster was seeing in this church. That's why I'm here."

The old man smiled, shaking his head. "Oh, that's why you brought me back here. You have to excuse me, Miss, my memory ain't like it used to be. I'm eighty-five years old. I forgets sometimes."

Everee calculated her moves, now was the time. She inched closer to the old man, so close that the musty smell from the old man's clothing, engulfed her nostrils. She didn't know if that's a smell that old people carried with them or poor hygiene. "What's your name?"

"Larson, Joe Larson. I been comin' to Reverend Elders church for five years. I figure I ain't gettin' any younger, so I best find my place with the lord, while I still have a mind. What's your name again, Miss?"

"Everee," she said in an irritated tone. Everee was losing patience with the old man. She was in a hurry to get the information. She made her move kissing his outer right ear lobe. Everee was startled when the old man nearly jumped out of his skin.

He smiled, taking a handkerchief out of his pocket to wipe his forehead. She didn't wanna get him too excited because of his age. She moved away from him, giving him room to catch his breath. "Larson, you gonna tell me about the two women who were seeing Foster?"

He was breathing heavy, after his brief encounter. "I ain't have no feelings like this in a long time. A man my age can gets a heart attack from a pretty young thang like you. Foster was datin' sister Mavis, Reverend Elder's wife for a spell. No one ever suspect that the two of them of having an affair."

Everee looked at him with disbelief. "You mean to tell me the Reverend's wife and Foster were seeing each other?"

"Yeah. The rumor in the church was that the reverend came home late and catches his wife in bed with Foster. Lawdy ain't that something? I couldn't believe it. I thought people of God didn't do things like that, but we all gets weak at times," he smirked.

She kissed Larson's wrinkled forehead. "I can't believe it, ain't that some shit. Thanks Larson for everything."

He stood up. "Wait, where you goin'? You can't leave now, darlin'," he said walking slowly towards the door.

Everee arrived at Miss Daniels house shortly after her interview at the church. "I got your message. What's the news?" I asked feeling surprised. "You change your hair or something. Four hours ago, your hair was red and a bit longer."

"You know a girl gotta keep changing her looks. In this business competition is everything. Can I come in?"

I was in awe, looking at Everee's beauty." Sure come in. Excuse me, Everee; I'm full of stress and tension, since I took this case. Any luck in getting information about Zoe's case?"

Everee sat down on the couch, exposing her ripe breast wearing a white lace top. "I got the name for you, Mr. Mosee Love. Now you think I'm good enough to be your partner."

I laughed sitting on the opposite end of the couch. "I never got results that fast, unless I was holdin' a gun to somebody's head," I chuckled.

"Why you sittin' so far from me. You think I got Aids, sugar I don't bite," she said moving closer to me. She smiled. "Anyway, I got something you don't have—female charm. The old man at the church told me, Reverend Elder's wife, Mavis was havin' an affair with Foster."

"Reverend Elder's wife?" I repeated. "You sure, Everee?"

"That's what old man Larson told me."

"You think this Reverend could've killed Foster?"

"I don't know, Everee. Everything is just speculation, until we can get some concrete evidence. You got an address on Reverend Elder's wife.

"No. I got her name," she said with authority in her voice. "You the detective, can't you do the rest?"

Reverend Elders did not look too happy to see me at his place of worship a second time. The Reverend looked me over cautiously. "What brings you back here? Didn't I answer your questions during our last interview?" He stood by the window. "I don't like you comin' round here. It makes me look guilty, you know. You think you can come here unannounced anytime you like? Well next time you show your face, I better see a search warrant. I have a church to run and a reputation to uphold."

I took a seat on the couch across from Reverend Elder's desk. "I'm here to clarify a very important piece of information you failed to mention, during our last interview."

The man sat erect behind his desk. He started to breathe heavily. "Like what, Mr. Love?" he said. His tone grew irate. "Don't waste my time, unless you have something on me!" He rose from his chair. "I think this little interrogation is over, don't you?"

"Your wife was having an affair with Foster. Is that correct?"

Reverend Elders flopped back down in his chair, with a defeated look in his eyes. "How did 'cha you find out so quickly, Mr. Love?"

"That's what I get paid to do, Reverend Elders, find information."

He put his head down in shame, speaking in a low voice. "She was having an affair with Foster. It's hard to believe. We were married for twenty-five years. We were high school sweethearts, you know. I gave that woman everything and she repays me with a scandalous affair. I never cheated on her, god knows, I had lots of chances, but a man of my stature must uphold a certain amount of integrity."

"How long did you suspect your wife was having this affair?"

"I have no idea, Mr. Love, we're separated now."

"You found your wife in bed with Foster?"

The reverend inhaled and exhaled rapidly. He took a handkerchief from his suit jacket and wiped his forehead. "I tried to hide it, but you know how it is when women folks gossip. It's like the deadly plague spreading."

"I loved that woman. I kinda blame myself. She used to complain 'bout me being too busy for her. I guess I ignored the signs."

"What was your initial reaction when you found your wife in bed with Foster?"

He was silent for a moment. "Nothin' I ran out the house screamin' down the street, like a crazy man."

I carefully looked at his response time to each question. "You didn't try to kick Foster's ass. If I caught my woman in bed with a man, in my house, I'm sure gonna get physical. You mean to tell me you didn't do a thing but scream?"

I knew this guy was full of it, but I had to keep harassing him and eventually Elders was gonna break down.

"Mr. Love, I'm a man of God. The lord watches over his own. I could've easily lost my head, but the lord helped to control my temper."

"You're also human and we act on emotions first. I understand you're a religious man, but you have feelings, too."

The reverend was too good to be true. He started perspiring a little more when I questioned him on his reactions to his wife's infidelity. "Reverend, I think you better use a towel to wipe your forehead. Where's your wife now?"

"She's staying with her sister, Ellen, on 123 Murray Drive in Monroe, South Carolina. It's one hour from Westfield."

"You have your sister-in-law's telephone number?"

"Yes. It's 561-1244."

"Is there anything else, you care to mention?"

The Reverend Elders rose from his seat. "I believe this interview has ended, Mr. Love."

"Thank you for your time," I said, reaching to shake his hand. Before I went out the door, the reverend mumbled under his breath. "I ain't got nothin' to hide."

I turned around, standing in the doorway. "Really, now that's strange, why did you neglect to mention that your wife was sleeping with Foster, the first time I questioned you? Now I would say that's pertinent information, wouldn't you?"

He shrugged his shoulders. "I guess you can say that." "Can I ask you one more question, Rev? Why didn't you tell

me the first time I interviewed you?" "I didn't wanna get involved. I have a reputation to protect." "Just one more question before I go. Where were you on the

night of May 15, 1998, between the hours of 10pm and 12 midnight?"

"I thought this interview was over," he said sitting back in his chair. "I was here at the church doin' paper work with my secretary."

"That's late," I commented with a hint of disbelief in my

voice. "I keep myself busy, since Mavis and myself separated" "Thank you Reverend Elders, for your time."

19

The Weekend passed quickly with little progress. I wanted a jumpstart on my day. I believed in the old adage, "An early bird catches the worm." So I went to my first interviewee's home early Monday morning, at 11A.M. to be exact. I couldn't wait to revisit my dear friend, Agee Johnson. I parked my black Volvo in front of the condemned looking building for the second time.

The first thing I noticed, when I climbed out of my car, is the same group of kids I had seen on my initial visit here. Some wore baggy jeans with cut off white tee-shirts, hair in braids and shoelaces untied. They were a true reflection of urban hip hop culture.

Kids will be kids no matter where they live. Everyone wanted to belong to something or somebody, to give life meaning. The urban youth has its music and the hip hop culture to believe in. Dressing in the over-sized pants and untied shoelaces and listening to rap music, like Biggie Smalls and Puffy Combs, set the tone for America's Black youth. This gives them something to identify with. I hated seeing young kids hanging out on the streets. I believe kids need an outlet to keep them busy.

My heart pounded as I entered the dark apartment building. There was little lighting, so I used my sense of touch to make it through the dark hallway. I felt the sides of the walls, as I made my way to the third floor. When I reached the designated floor, I checked my gun holster, making sure my gun was accessible in case of an emergency. I didn't know what surprises awaited me. My 9"mm" is like my Bible, "never leave home without it."

I focused intently on the faded apt. numbers on each door, trying to decipher them, but the poor lighting in the hallway made it nearly impossible. Finally I made out the number three, which was turned upside down. Bits of paint chips fell from the pressure of my hand, knocking on the door. The only light came from the other end of the hallway from an open window. I heard a sound of a newborn baby crying at the opposite end of the hallway. Poor kid, don't even stand a chance living in an environment like this, I thought.

After the fifth knock on the door, I heard scuffling sounds from inside. I placed my eye up to the peep hole. I noticed a shadow moving in front.

A voice yelled. "Who is it?"

"Hello, Agee it's me, Mosee Love. I came to ask you a few more questions."

"What you want, man, I ain't done nothin', like I told you before. Same old shit."

"I know, but I need to speak to you again," I pleaded.

"The police done been here, harassing me, like I'm some criminal", he said in a southern drawl.

"I'm really sorry, but ..."

"Hold tight, man, I'll let you in."

The door opened slowly. I stood close to the entrance, trying to see inside. Before I had time to react, I knew I'd been hit. I heard the shattering sound of glass breaking. I felt a haze come over me. I did not have time to react. My first instinct told me to reach for my gun.

"Fuck you. I'm tried of answering questions for you cops."

Agee moved swift and easy, like a snake, gliding across the floor. I tried to zero in on his shadow, but the poor lightning made it difficult to see. All was quiet for a few seconds. Then "Boom", I was knocked down on all fours. Next thing I realized, I saw a shiny object coming toward my face. I held my right arm in the air, blocking whatever was coming towards me.

"Bang," I fired a shot from my 9"mm". First time I used my gun in five years. I thought I had lost my touch, but once you hold a gun you never forget how to use it. Agee was down. I prayed I hadn't killed the poor bastard.

I went over to Agee and heard him moaning in pain. I ran inside and dialed 911. After I made my call, I could hear the rhythm of my heart racing. The palms of my hands were clammy. I didn't know what my fate would be at this point if Agee died on me. After talking to the emergency operator, I went in to the bathroom, to see how badly I was hurt. I looked in the mirror and saw blood trickling down the right side of my arm and face; there was a big gash on my right forearm, where Agee had probably used a knife to cut me. And my head felt as though I was struck by an object of massive force. I reached up to feel my head. I moaned in pain. I looked at my hand and saw blood. I figure he struck me on the head.

I washed the blood and took a towel to wrap around my arm to slow down the bleeding.

I felt paranoid about calling Burke. I knew he would put me under surveillance and question me about shooting Agee. Self defense is my argument, I chose to use in my defense. That would explain the shooting, but Burke would question me, as to why I had gone over there a second time. I could feel my breath, as I inhaled and exhaled, watching my chest rise and fall. It took me ten minutes to get the nerve up to call Burke. If you're up their God, please help me. The last time I'd called on God was to bring my father back, when I was twelve. My prayers had never been answered and I learned to never rely on God's promises.

Burke's answering on the first ring threw me off balance. "Hello, Love, what's goin' on?"

"Well.. I..I came across a little trouble today." I tried to maintain self-control in my voice, but I knew Burke could detect trouble.

"What now, Love? Every time you call me, something tragic happens. I swear your like the black plague."

"I ... I . . came to visit Agee Johnson this morning, to question him again about Foster's murder. We got into a little confrontation.

He hit me on the head with a bottle and cut my arm up pretty bad, with a knife. It was dark in the hallway. I couldn't see him, except for the shadows."

"You better get yourself checked out, Love, I don't need another homicide folder sittin' on my desk," Burke said. "Any damages done to Agee?"

I could not answer him right away. I swallowed a chuck of my salvia. "I shot him in the stomach."

"Christ, Love, are you crazy? Or just plain dumb?"

"He's still alive, but he's barely holding on."

"I'll have someone come over and check things out."

I heard a click on the other end. I heard the sounds of sirens outside. Two white males in their early thirties came up the stairs, carrying a stretcher and a nap sack full of medical equipment. "What happened here?" the skinny one asked.

"I shot him in the abdomen. It was self-defensive." I blurted out.

"Why did you shoot him?" he asked, lifting Agee onto the stretcher. One of the EMTs placed an oxygen mask over Agee's face.

They pulled out a flashlight, looking over the wounded victim.

"You know this man?" one of them asked.

"Not really, I was just visiting him. His name's Agee Johnson, that's all I know."

One of the Medics looked at the towel wrapped around my arm. "You look like you better come and get yourself checked out. You want a ride to the hospital?"

"No thanks. I have to wait for the cops to get here. I'll go later on."

I stood by the stairwell, watching the two men carry Agee down the steps. I closed my eyes and said a Hail Mary and asked God would allow Agee to live. I trembled waiting for the police to arrive. A murder charge is not what I needed hanging over my head, especially down south. Being in prison is no place for a Black man down south.

Five minutes after the ambulance left, two uniformed police officers came up the steps. One of the cops was short and pudgy with a thin mustache. The other cop was slim and tall with a military crew cut. "What's happened here?" he asked walking over to me.

"I came over to visit Agee Johnson to question him about the murder of Foster Owens," I said with a lump in my throat. "Burke knows the whole story."

The short pudgy cop, looked bored, looking out the window. I knew these cops didn't care about Black on Black crime. I figured this is the most work they ever did, besides eating free breakfasts and donuts.

The tall cop with the military hair cut took out his note book. "Evans, get your tail over here, we are workin."

He walked over slowly, giving me a snarling look.

"Anyway, I knock on his door and he opens it slowly. I step close to the entrance, trying to look into the apartment. The next thing I knew I was hit over the head, with a sharp object. I fell to the ground and we started fighting."

"Did he have a gun?"

"No, but he did have a hunting knife. The hallway was too dark for me to see what kind of weapon he was using. I saw this shiny object come towards me, so I drew my gun and fired one shot. "Look at my arm—it's all cut up."

The short cop turned away, he said, "Are we done yet? I'm starving."

"You just ate, Evans."

"I had to defend myself. You understand being cops?"

"Yeah, you look pretty busted up," the tall one said. "He glanced over at his partner."

"You say you shot him, huh?" He continued to write down

every syllable. "We heard all about you from Detective Burke. You an investigator from up north?"

"Yes that's correct. I'm trying to get my client out of jail."

"Oh, yeah, the girl who killed her father. Shame ain't it."

"You already have her convicted. Well it's my job to find the real criminal, and that's what I aim to do."

I hated repeating myself. "That's what I said, right?"

"Evans, go and take a look inside the apartment and see if you can find anything."

The tall uniform said, "We'll take this information back to Detective Burke, he'll want you to come in and make an official statement."

"No problem, I have nothing to hide."

Two hours later I went to the medical center, where the doctor diagnosed me with a minor concussion. He recommended bed rest for one week. That translated into no work. I took my time driving to Ms. Daniel's house. I felt the beginning signs of a throbbing headache accompanied by dizziness.

The drive to Ms. Daniel's home felt like an eternity, sitting behind the wheel.

Ms. Daniels sat on the sofa, with a petrified look on her face. She jumped up when I opened the door. "Mosee, I heard someone was shot. The police been callin' here for the past two hours. They say, they wanna know about a fella you shot this afternoon," she said in a frantic voice. "What happened to you? Oh Lord have mercy."

I sat down on the couch, holding my head. "I was attacked by Agee. He hit me over the head with a glass bottle and cut my arm pretty bad, too. The doctor gave me orders to stay in bed for five to seven days. I need plenty of R&R. So I guess that means, I'll be out of work for one week. That really bothers me when I cannot do my job. Ms. Daniels, I am the kind of man who rarely gets sick and if I do, I always end up doing the opposite. But this time I better do what the doctor ordered and rest for a week. The pain in my head is unbearable. I have codeine to take and some other medication for the cut on my forearm."

Ms. Daniels went to the kitchen to fix some hot tea, with lemon and honey. She yelled from the kitchen, "Just rest and don't worry none, you got plenty of time to finish this case. Your health is more important, right now. You got plenty of time to find the man that put my baby behind bars."

Ms. Daniels came from the kitchen, carrying a tray with a cup of tea and cinnamon Danish. She placed it next to me.

"I think I'll lay down in the bedroom and rest for a while."

"You go on now, if you get hungry, just call me and I can fix you somethin'."

I rose slowly from the sofa retiring to my guest room. "Thanks, Ms Daniels, for everything."

Ms. Daniels yelled after me, "What should I tell the police if they call again? Detective Burke left a message saying you might be charged with Agee's murder. He wants you to come to the police station and make a statement."

"If Burke or Everee calls, you can wake me up." The pain in my head intensified, the more I thought about Agee. I couldn't sleep, until I found out his condition. It must be bad if Burke is talking about charging me with murder.

I asked Ms. Daniels what the nearest hospital in Westfield was. "I ain't sure but I can call the operator for you. We have two; one for the poor folks who ain't got insurance and one for those who can pay. The one you went to is for the poor folks, and that's probably where that fella went to."

I telephoned Westfield General Medical Center to inquire about Agee Johnson. I was told Agee's in critical condition and they will not know anything until his condition stabilizes. I sat on the couch with a troubled look on my face. There's nothing I could do, my fate was sealed. I might be joining my client soon.

Ms. Daniels asked, "How's he doin, Mosee?"

"It doesn't look good. I only hope he pulls through. The police might charge me for murder if he dies. I'm the one who had a gun and Agee had a knife and a glass vase." I bowed my head in shame. "I shouldn't have gone over there without informing Burke. He warned me stay away from the guy."

"You only tryin' to do your job, besides he tried to hurt you," Ms. Daniels said, looking confused. I don't understand the law. Someone attacks you and you protect yourself, and the police see that as a crime," she said shaking her head, "It just doesn't make sense."

I returned to my bedroom to sleep the pain and nausea away. It took me half an hour to finally drift off into a stupor, after taking my pain medication.

Just as I was about to relax, Ms. Daniels knocked on the door interrupting my sleep. "Mosee, telephone. It's that police officer callin' again. I hate to disturb you, but he said it was important," she said in a nervous voice.

I contemplated ignoring the telephone call, but I didn't wanna complicate things for myself. I got out of bed slowly, heading toward the door. Ms. Daniels stood there with a frantic look on her face.

"Mosee, please talk to police. They said if you don't come down and make a statement he'll charge you with aggravated assault."

I stood at the door motionless. Burke had me by the balls now; there's nothing I could do but humble myself. "Hello, Burke what's up?"

Burke screamed through the telephone. "What the hell you think, what's up? That boy you shot is in critical condition. I need you to come in here and make a statement. I'm charging you for his death, if he dies." I felt my stomach churn like spoiled butter. I felt myself get weaker at the thought of doing prison time. Who does he think he is asshole? Calling this house and making threats. I'll show him what real investigation work is all about.

"I'll be down there just as soon as I can. Give me a few minutes." "Can you drive with that concussion?" "No, not really. The doctor said for me to stay off my feet for five days." "Just get your tail here and make a statement. "My head is throbbing and I'm feeling faint at the moment." "Well excuse me, for wanting to save your Black ass! You're the most ungrateful person I ever met. They always say folks from the north are selfish."

I couldn't tell if Burke was serious or not. It's hard to tell if Burke had a human side. He was the type of guy, who spoke his mind freely. He had no consciousness of other people's feeling. One thing that I was certain, I knew where I stood with Burke.

"Well excuse the hell out of me, Love. If you didn't go see Agee, you wouldn't be in this mess. You should've left the work for my men. You better pray to God that he lives.

"Why did you go see Agee after I told you my men were going over there?" I wanted to tell Burke to go to hell, but I was powerless at that moment. My fate was dependent on Agee's living or dying. "I like doin' things myself, besides I'm used to working with, never mind." "Agee has an alibi: he was working until 12:30pm, so that puts him in the clear." "Now you tell me." I took a deep breath. "Alright I'll be in as soon as I can."

Before Burke hung up, his final words were. "Next time you'll do like I said." He spoke with an air of arrogance that I despised. Small town cops, the only thing they're used to is freeloading dinners and giving out tickets.

Ms. Daniels drove me to the Westfield Police Station on the other side of town. A police officer sat reading the newspaper. I walked down a long hallway through a set of double doors. I

walked past a row of desks. To the right a sign read Detective Burke's office.

I sat in front of Burke's desk. "Hello, Love, what's going on?"

"Nothing, except I have a deep cut on my arm and a concussion"

Burke leaned back in his chair and reached inside his drawer for a tape recorder. "You wanna tell me what happened?"

"I told you previously, that I went over to question Agee for the second time. I stepped closer to the front door, and bang! The next thing I knew I felt this pain on the top of my head. And the next thing I realize, he came after me with a knife. The only thing I could see in the dark is a shiny object, coming towards me; that's how I got this cut on my arm."

"I then proceeded to move far enough from Agee to draw my gun, in order to protect myself."

"I drew my gun from my holster and fired one shot at Agee. He falls to the ground and I called 911 and the police. That's it. There is nothing else to tell."

Burke shot me an I-think-you're-a-lying-ass look. "You better pray that he lives," Burke said, "How's your wounds?"

"My head's aching, and I'm sore as hell all over, but besides that I'm in perfect health. The doctor told me to stay off my feet. What are my options, now Burke?"

"First you can start by going home and getting some rest."

"I'm free to go now?" I said, rising from my chair. "I have one question, did you find Iris's boyfriend?"

"No, not yet."

"This means I'm free of any charges?"

"That's what I said, ain't it?"

20

Reverend Elders was too calm for a man who had just lost his wife to another man; he had too much at stake in his church. He was a leader in the Black community and well liked among his peers. This scandal was something he tried to sweep under the rug. I was convinced the Reverend had more to tell than what he was willing to admit.

It's been three days into my recovery. I needed to get back to work, so I opted to return to the field. My head felt groggy and my right arm ached from the twenty stitches, I received. Thank God I had the full use of my left arm.

I decided to put Reverend Elders under surveillance for a few days. I parked my black Volvo a few feet from the church. Sunday is a big feast in most Black churches. It looked more crowded than usual. There were well-dressed church goers in their fancy suits and dresses. The women wore big hats with flowery trimmings. The men walked proudly with their heads held high.

After everyone went inside, I entered the church and sat in the last pew. The church services started with a brief prayer from a young woman in her mid-twenties. Everyone stood up for a moment of silence, bowing their heads.

The choir sat in a balcony, just above the pulpit. They were dressed in black and white robes. Seventy percent were women and thirty percent men. They sang an upbeat verse of spiritual, "Jesus is a comin' home soon." The organ player and drummer used popular R&B lyrics in the church songs. The church members stomped their feet and clapped their hands in a joyous ceremony. I was caught up in the moment; I was energized after the music ended. I had forgotten what it felt like to be in a church.

The last time I attended church had been with my Aunt Josie who believed God was the answer for all man's problems. Being in church made me remember when my Aunt took me to be "Saved".

Vicious Karma

I was lead up front with other kids my age. The anointing was done by a preacher with a special oil that was put on our foreheads. The church members shouted "Amen!" and "Praise to Jesus!" After the ceremony, the preacher declared me saved. I stood there waiting for a bright light to shine upon me, but nothing happened. I felt the same as when I woke up that morning.

My Aunt Josie had streams of tears running down her face. She expressed her joy to me about what it meant to be "saved". No one took the time to explain what being "saved" meant. I didn't feel any different after the ceremony ended and now I'm thirty eight years old.

Reverend Elder's took his position at the pulpit. He was dressed in a white robe. He wore round wire frame glasses. The Rev is a medium build, about five-foot nine. Reverend Elders asked everyone to take their seats. He preached about the infidelities in marriage and the sacrifices men and women must make in a marriage. "Brothers and sisters many of us take our vows lightly."

"Amen," the woman said sitting next to me.

Reverend Elder's continued. "You Brothers need to take control over your emotions," he said waving his hands in the air. "We have some sisters out there who also need to check themselves."

Now I was getting bored with the theatrics. One thing I hate about Black churches, they never know when to stop talking; they'll keep you in church for hours. There were outbursts of laughter and hand clapping, each time the reverend raised the pitch in his voice.

When the services ended, the crowd disbursed. I went to the side entrance of the church, waiting for Reverend Elders to say his final good-byes to his members. It pained me to stand up for more than fifteen minutes, without getting a throbbing headache. Despite doctors orders, I chose to do the opposite.

His eyes bulged out like something out of a horror movie when he caught sight of me. "Well, Mr. Love, we meet again," he said with a sheepish grin, "What can I do for you?"

"You can start by telling me the truth, Rev."

He mumbled under his breath. "How dare you show your face in my church and on a Sunday of all days. I thought we concluded our interview last week."

The reverend was a cool guy. He certainly had me fooled.

"Well, I need to know the truth what really . . ."

He cut me off before I had a chance to finish my sentence. "You should have called first or made an appointment with my secretary. I don't like you showing your face here anytime you get the urge." He turned away from me, walking down the hall. "Follow me," he said quickening his pace.

I followed close behind, drilling him along the way. "You know what I'm talking about."

He turned around abruptly. "Hold your questions until we get to my office. I don't like discussing business in the hallway."

"Did you try to shoot, Foster?"

"No, Mr. Love, I'm a man of God," he said stopping in his tracks. "Do you respect God's house?"

"I don't think God has anything to do with you shooting at Foster."

I took a seat in front of the Rev's desk. He stood looking out the window with his back toward me.

"You're a man first, Reverend Elders. Catching your wife with Foster in your bedroom caused your adrenaline to rush; wouldn't that cause you to react, first?"

Rev. Elders continued to look out the window, as if something had his attention. A moment of silence went by, lasting for five minutes. "I was mad, but I would never try to hurt anyone."

"Being mad isn't appropriate words to describe your true feelings. Why don't you turn around when I'm talking to you. I don't like talking to a person's back."

Rev. Elders suddenly made an out burst, "Alright I did try to shoot the son of a bitch! Are you happy now?" He had a distorted look on his face, like a madman.

"That's what I wanted to hear: the truth."

"Thank God I'm a lousy shooter, Mr. Love, I would be sitting in jail for murder."

"I have a few more questions and then I'll leave you alone. I'll need your secretary's name and address to confirm your alibi on May the twenty-fifth."

"No problem," he answered, calming down. "Her name is Yvonne Thomas, and she lives at 221 Greenwood Place. She's twenty minutes from here."

I felt myself getting dizzy once again. I knew I was overdoing it. The doctor had ordered me to stay in bed for a week or I would end up in the hospital. I guess I'm somewhat of a hard head when it comes to following other people's advice. I need to swallow my pride and stay in bed in order to regain my strength and finish the case.

"You can speak to my lawyer next time you come around here, after today. I have nothing more to say to you, Mr. Love, have a nice day," he said holding the door open. Anything you have is pure speculation at this point. Sure I had a motive, and so did a lot of other folks."

The only thing on my mind was getting Zoe out of jail and seeing my daughters. I practically blew a whole summer with them.

On July fifteenth, I was sitting in my automobile speaking into the tape recorder reporting my findings on the Zoe case. It is hot as hell and I finished talking to Reverend Elders. He finally

confessed trying to shoot Foster. Now I'm down to two interviews and counting: the Rev's secretary, Yvonne and Iris's ex-boyfriend. That leads me to a dead end. I still have my suspicions about the Rev. There have been two deaths since I started this investigation.

Half way home to Ms. Daniels house, my beeper went off. I was filled with paranoia, when I looked down at my pager and saw Burke's number. My hunches told me Agee had probably died. I pulled my Volvo to the side of the road and hoped for the best. I reached into the glove compartment for my cellular phone.

"Hey, Mosee, we have a problem," he said, his tone dry.

Burke is the kind of man who wears an armor of steel. He was always straight up with you. That's one thing I admired about him. You always knew where you stood with him. I couldn't take any more tragic news from Burke. I took a deep breath and prayed that he wasn't calling me to report that Agee died.

"What's up, Burke?"

"We got ourselves another homicide, I'm afraid. Channel Peters is the third person shot to death."

I remained silent for a brief moment, collecting my thoughts. I'm convinced that the murdered victims and Foster's death are connected in some way, I thought. But proving my theory is the hard part.

"Love, you know she used to date Foster Owens."

"Tell me something I don't already know, Burke," I responded sarcastically. "I'm already five steps ahead of you."

"Meet me and my men at 123 Filbert Place."

I pulled over on the side of the road to gather my thoughts. I took a mental inventory of all the essentials an investigator needed; tape recorder, note pad, plastic gloves and gun.

I checked in with Ms. Daniels to let her know I might be a little late for dinner and about Channel Peters being found shot to death in her home. Ms. Daniels gasped when I told her the news of Channel's death.

"Poor woman, I don't know what's come over folks lately," she whined. "I'm havin' company over. My best friend Margo's comin' to join us for supper this evening. If you ain't back in time I'll leave your supper out."

Staying with Zoe's mother for the previous two months had made me realize what I had been missing. Since my divorce from Joyce, I had to learn to take care of myself. I felt like a newborn for the first time in ten years.

"Be careful, Mosee, I don't wanna see you get hurt."

"Thanks, Ms. Daniels. I'll be okay."

After thirty minutes of driving, I pulled in front of 123 Filbert Place, where police cars and a white medical examiner's van were parked out front. As I approached the door, neighbors were outside whispering to each other. I zeroed in on Detective Burke. He wasn't too hard to miss. He was dressed in beige Dockers and a white shirt with a blue tie. The sun reflected off the top of his greasy, bald head. I couldn't find a parking space, so I parked my car in the middle of the street, next to a police car. Just as I was about to approach the house, a uniform cop stopped me in my tracks. He shot me a condescending look.

"Sorry, fella, only police personnel are allowed here."

I walked past him flashing my ID badge in his face.

Burke yelled, "It's okay, Monroe, he's working on this case with us, let him through. I had already passed the arrogant son of bitch. I began taking on some of the burden of these murders. Channel's made the third person who was murdered in less than three months.

Detective Burke was standing with his three cronies "Hey, Love," Burke said waving his hand in the air. "You got here quickly."

"It wasn't as far as I thought."

"Love, you know anything about this woman?"

I interviewed her two weeks ago, in reference to Foster's murder. I had her down as a possible suspect because she was seeing Foster. Five months ago, Foster broke off their relationship. He left her for a younger woman named Iris Hall, who's also dead."

Burke had a snarl on his face, looking at me. "You know everything, don't you, Love?"

I refrained from responding to his negative comments, but I couldn't resist a challenge.

"If I had some decent help maybe you could solve these cases." I glanced over at the two uniform cops. His partner looked ten years his senior. He had a fresh and eager look about him. He reminded me of myself, when I first graduated from the FBI academy in Quantico, Virginia. I was ready to take on the world. The second cop looked more seasoned than his peer. The two cops with Burke didn't acknowledge my presence when I said hello. I became immune to rudeness, after working at the Bureau.

I walked behind Burke, closely registering everything. I gathered from the blood stains on the carpet that the murder took place here. "I was the last person to walk into the bed room; this is where the murder took place."

I took out my mini tape recorder to record everything I saw. "Nice house, she got here, huh? You people have made great strides, since Dr. Martin Luther King."

"We people have always made progress, it's people like your kind who hold others back." Everyone in the room remained silent looking at each other in amazement.

I spoke into the tape recorder, slowly. The medical examiners office carried Channel in a body bag. I've grown accustomed to seeing body bags; it comes with the territory in my profession.

The Crime Scene Technicians carefully collected all visible evidence.

The bed had a canopy and a cast iron frame, with a wooden stool used to step up onto the bed. Sheer curtains hung from the canopy bed frame surrounding the king-sized bed.

The body of Channel was found face up. Her blood covered

188

the top of the bedspread. She had a frightened look on her face at the time of her death. She looked somewhat surprised by whomever it was that came to kill her.

Burke reported his findings to me. "Someone shot her in the chest, probably died instantly from the first bullet that was fired."

He turned around, looking at his two assistants. "You two split up and search the house from top to bottom."

"What a pretty woman," Burke said, shaking his head in disgust. "It's a shame." I continued speaking into the tape recorder, Black female found shot to death in the upper right chest cavity. I walked around searching every inch of the bedroom, starting with the dresser drawers. The drawers are in disarray like some one was looking for something. I searched through the living room and kitchen. Everything was neat and tidy.

I checked the front and back doors—no signs of force entry. I thought it was strange that the bedroom is the only place that was searched by the killer. I returned to the bedroom where Burke was talking to the Medical Examiner.

Burke's two assistants came back into the bedroom half an hour later. "We couldn't find anything."

"Nothing!" Burke yelled. "You men wouldn't know hard detective work if it slapped you in the face." Burke focused his attention on me. "What do you think, Love, since you're the only one with brains around here?"

"It's hard to say, Burke. It looks like the killer knew Channel. Whoever killed Channel tried to make it look like a robbery."

The two uniform cops played a passive role in the investigation. The two men reentered the bedroom standing in close proximity to each other while Burke and I searched the bedroom a second time. I never saw such incompetent men in uniform in my whole life. These men weren't ready for the big leagues. Cops like that will always be comfortable in their small community. I wondered how anyone could be content as a cop in that kind of environment.

My next logical move would be to retrace my steps; this meant going to the beginning where everything took place. I had to tell Ms. Daniels to take extra precautions. As, I entered the door, of Ms. Daniels home, my nostrils were engulfed with the smell of southern cuisine coming from the kitchen when I opened the door. I imagined tasting the cinnamon, nutmeg and maple syrup, dripping from the side of my mouth, as I devoured the candied yams.

I knew where to find her—the kitchen. I needed to delve into Ms. Daniels personal life. I felt the timing was right for me to question her. She'd started to trust me. That gave me the perfect opportunity to get information from her.

I almost forgot what it felt like to be spoiled by a woman. Ms. Daniels did everything for me from cooking to cleaning. I might be looking in the wrong place for a companion. I heard people speak of southern hospitality and how good southern women can cook.

"Something smells good, Ms. Daniels, what'cha got cookin'?" "Meat loaf, yams and collard greens. My best friend Margo Watson is comin by for supper." Ms. Daniels continued talkin' from the kitchen. "We weren't always friends, you know." She sat next to me on the couch in her white apron. "You were enemies?" I asked her. "It's a long story, I ain't proud of," she said shaking her head. "We became close in the past fifteen years." I didn't want to push her, but this is her first time exposing herself to me on a personal level. "Let's just say we had our share of battles." "But you're close now, right?" She nodded. She seemed to get uncomfortable talking about Margo. "What time is she coming for dinner?" I asked. "Margo should be here shortly." Ms. Daniels walked toward the kitchen continuing her conversion. "Margo's been a big help to me, since Zoe's been in jail. Lawdy, every time I think about my baby being in that filthy place, it makes me sick. I haven't had a good night's sleep since you found her father. I knew trouble wasn't too far behind. When kids grow up, you can't tell them what to do no more. They have a mind of their own. You raise them the best you can and pray to God they don't get caught out in this sinful world."

I went to the kitchen to keep Ms. Daniels company. That gave me time to bond with her before Margo came to dinner. I sat at the kitchen table, while she finished preparing dinner.

"Why did you think something terrible was going to happen when I found Zoe's father?" I asked.

"You get that feeling when you think your child is in trouble. When you're a parent, it's something you know."

She continued with a fiery redness in her eyes. "When you found Foster, Mosee, I could've killed him myself. He caused me so much pain in the past and now thirty years later, he's buried six feet under and still causing me grief. The devil is always busy."

Changing the subject of Foster, I said, "That's nice you and Margo remained friends, it's hard to find a good friend that will stick in your corner."

Cedric and I had remained best friends for over twenty years. I knew what it meant to have a friend you can depend on. Someone who tells you when you're wrong, even when you don't what to hear the truth. I didn't know where I would be if it weren't for Cedric.

Cedric and I became friends at a crucial time in my life: when my mother died. He was the only person in whom I confided, especially growing up in a house full of women.

Ms. Daniels snapped me back to present day with her preachy sermons. "Amen, I count my blessings everyday. The church really helped me; they done raised two thousand dollars to help with Zoe's legal fees."

"Ms. Daniels, Zoe is good friends with my best friend Cedric, who's an attorney in New York. I've been corresponding with him since Zoe's incarceration. He's willing to come down here and help her."

She came over to hug me showing her gratitude. "Oh praise the Lawd, Mosee. I knew God would answer my prayers and send someone like you to help my daughter."

"Ms. Daniels, have you always been religious?"

"Yes, child I been religious as long as I can remember."

"I was just wondering why a good woman like yourself never settled down?"

"I had my share of men," she said in a southern drawl. "After Foster left me, I stayed to myself, until I met Buddy three years later in church."

I laughed. "Don't get shy on me now, Ms. Daniels.

"Child, some men, sure know how to give some good lovin'. After a couple of nights with Buddy, I thought I was in love," she said picking up a newspaper to fan herself. "He broke my heart when I discovered he was cheatin' on me. I was young and dumb, Mosee."

"How old were you?"

"I was about Twenty-five; I can remember that time just as clear."

"Was he your first love besides Foster.?"

Ms. Daniels bowed her head, speaking softly, "No, lord. Buddy was my second love. He was about thirty—three at the time."

"Can I ask you a few more questions about Foster?"

Her expression turned cold, avoiding eye contact. "I'd rather not talk about that. Let the past stay where it's supposed to."

"The past might be helpful with finding the person who murdered your daughter's father," I reminded her. "Why didn't you date other men after you broke up with Foster and Buddy?"

"I waited three years until I started dating again, but that was briefly. I wanted to raise my child by myself. It's been hard for me to bring men around my house. I was afraid somebody would have eyes on my Zoe. You'll understand what I mean when your daughters get up in age."

I sighed. "Yeah, I'm not looking forward to the teenage years. I have two daughters, so I'll be getting my gray hairs early."

"Ms. Daniels I was wondering if you knew Channel Peters? She was the latest murder victim."

"No, never heard of her."

"Do you know anybody who might have known her?"

"No, Mosee, I'm sorry I can't be more helpful to you.".

Ms. Daniels went back to the counter to finish preparing our meal and I went into the living room and sat on the couch, watching the evening news about the recent death of Channel Peters.

The police had found a suicide note next to Channel's body. I thought about the murders of the past two months. I didn't want to attend another funeral; this would make number three.

Since my mother's death, I hadn't attended a funeral until I came to Westfield. When my aunt died, my sisters cursed me for not attending her funeral.

Attending Iris Hall's funeral brought back vivid images of my mother's corpse, lying in the casket. I was in a daze, sitting in the pew. Streams of tears ran down my face, as if I had been living that moment over again.

During my mother's funeral, I showed no emotion. I sat frozen, as if I were dreaming. As a young boy, I didn't accept my mother's death. For half a year, I became a deaf mute, refusing to speak to anyone. Everyone assumed I was going through a breakdown, but this was my way of dealing with the pain. The school psychologist and my best friend couldn't get me to open up.

Finally, one day I broke down in my aunt's arms. I made a promise to myself never to attend another funeral; I kept my word, until Foster Owens was murdered. Putting myself in uncompromising situations was just part of the job.

Going to Channel Peter's funeral isn't going to be any easier, I thought. What did death mean? I didn't understand if it symbolized the end or the beginning of another life. I rationalized that death was the beginning of something better, at least I hoped. It seemed cruel to take a person away from this life when they haven't yet lived. Life is short for all human beings; it doesn't seem like there is enough time to accomplish all one's hopes and dreams.

I remembered my mother preaching about people dying and going to heaven if they lived a righteous life. I stopped believing in heaven and hell following my mother's death.

Ms. Daniels came from the kitchen breaking my thought process. "Lawdy boy, I heard something on the news about that woman you mentioned Channel committing suicide. You going to her funeral?"

"I'm afraid, Ms. Daniels, this makes the third funeral I've attended in three months. Can you do me a favor and find out the time and location of Channel Peter's services?"

"Sure, honey," she said patting my shoulders. "I'm a go back and finish supper 'fore Margo gets here."

I was still watching the local news when I heard the door bell ring.

Ms. Daniels yelled from the kitchen, breaking my concentration. "Can you get the door?"

"Hello Margo, you look lovely this evening," I greeted her.

"Thank you," she said stepping into the house. "I smell something good, Emma Jean Daniels. You always cookin' something good," Margo said sitting down in the brown reclining chair.

Ms. Daniels emerged from the kitchen wearing a floral print housecoat. "I'm cookin' meat loaf, butter nut squash, greens and biscuits, and Macaroni and Cheese.

"I haven't eaten a thing all day. I wanted to make sure I had plenty of room for your cookin." Emma Jean how you holdin' up?" Margo said, giving her a hug.

"I'm doin' a whole lot better, thanks to Mr. Love. He's been workin' round the clock to help Zoe." "That's good," she said looking over at me. "So, Mr. Love, how's your investigation comin' along?" "Well, besides people dying on me. Another name was added

to the list." "Who's that?" "Channel Peters. You know her, Margo?" "No, I try to stay to myself and keep out of folks' business." "You don't have anyone as a suspect?" "Not at this point. I have leads, but nothing concrete." "I hope you find the monster that killed Zoe's daddy." "Me too, Margo," I sighed. Ms. Daniels brought plates and silver ware from the kitchen,

placing them on the dining room table. "Supper will be ready just as soon as the sourdough biscuits and sweet potato pie are done."

"Margo," I asked, "how did you and Ms. Daniels meet?" Silence filled the room. I could feel the tension in the room. Finally, Margo spoke. "We go back a long ways. We haven't

always been friends," she said cutting her eyes at Ms. Daniels. I waited for Ms. Daniels to make a comment. She continued setting the table, bowing her head in silence. Margo went on, "We had our moments of not speaking for

a spell, but you know how friends are." She smiled. "Did you know Foster Owens, Margo?" "Am I on the witness stand? You askin' a lot of questions. I

saw him a few times at the dance hall. Everyone talked about how popular he was, especially among the women folks." "How did you know he was a ladies man?" I noticed Margo didn't keep her eyes focused on me, when I questioned her.

"Well, Mr. Love, a leopard don't change its spots overnight," she said with a smirk on her face. She yelled to Emma who was in the kitchen. "You need some help in there?"

195

I watched the two women place the food on the table. "I'm gonna get spoiled by you two."

I took my seat at the dining room table. "I'm thinking about finding a true southern woman to settle down with. "The warmth and friendliness of this state is beautiful. The city is getting too congested. I was born in Danville, Virginia and relocated to New York, after my mother's death. In New York, people don't acknowledge you half the time, it's like you're not even there."

Shaking her head, Margo said, "I wouldn't trade places with you for nothin'."

"I put on fifteen pounds, since I came here." I loosened my pants top button.

Ms Daniels burst out in laughter. "That's 'cause you finally gettin' some real food."

"Everything sure looks good, Ms. Daniels." I surveyed the food, patting my stomach. "See what you're doin' I'll have to go on a crash diet when I return home."

"Enjoy the food while it last."

"Let's say our grace; I'm ready to chow down, girl."

Everyone bowed their heads in silence, while Ms. Daniels led the prayer.

Then she started by passing the meat loaf and gravy to Margo, who sat across from her. Margo passed the dish to me. I'd long since gotten over any shyness when it came to eatin' I took three biscuits, macaroni and cheese and string beans. After I piled my plate, I sank my teeth into a piece of meat loaf smothered in brown gravy. "Hum . . . this is the best meat loaf I've tasted in a long time."

Ms. Daniels started blushing. "Thanks, I'm glad you like it, Mosee."

"Emma Jean could always cook up somethin," Margo said proudly. "They always said feed a man good and give him plenty of lovin, that keeps em' comin' back," Margo sank her teeth into a hot butter biscuit. The corners of her mouth were dripping with butter. "Girl, this here meal is gonna add on five pounds to my figure. I have to keep up with the young girls.

"You too old to be worried bout' some man," Emma Jean said, "You need to start actin' your age."

Margo rolled her eyes at Emma Jean. "Girl I' ain't dead yet. I don't wanna be like you, never going out, always cookin' for somebody."

I felt the tension between the two ladies. There was some hidden animosity between them.

I attempted to change the subject. "Ladies, being in the company of the two most beautiful women in Westfield has put me in the mood for a cold beer."

Ms. Daniels eyes widened, "Mosee, I don't allow drinking in my home."

"Sorry. I can relax just the same without it."

After we'd eaten almost all there was to eat, Margo started back in. "Now you act like you too good for the things you used to do. I knew you when you were shaking your butt in men folks' faces."

I stood up raising my hands to call a truce. "Okay ladies, how about clearing the table. Margo you go and relax in the living room, while I help Ms. Daniels in the kitchen. You two sound like you have some unfinished business to settle."

Margo walked away from the table, "we have our share of disagreements, like most people." She paused to pick up her handbag. "Emma, I'm leaving now, I'll call you later on." She went into the kitchen and kissed, Emma on the check and giving her a comforting hug.

"Thanks, Margo for everything."

I thought about Cedric and I having our disputes and feuds. There were times when we wouldn't speak to each other for weeks at a time. We still don't agree on some things, but we remained friends.

Margo walks out the kitchen, swaying her hips from side to side, trying to get my attention.

"Ms. Daniels, did Margo know Channel?"

"I can't remember if she knew. You can ask her yourself."

Ms. Daniels continued to wash the dishes in silence. "Didn't you say that she knew Channel?" I persisted.

"I can't remember one day from the next, Mr. Love. The only thing on my mind is my child."

Margo looks at me out of the corner of her eye. "See there, Mosee, friends have problems, too," she said heading out the front door.

"Ms. Daniels. What are your plans for tomorrow?"

"Why don't you go in the bedroom and rest some, I can finish up in here."

Ms. Daniels knocked on the door in a frantic state. I did not realize how long she was there; the codeine made it easy to sleep through anything. I responded in a groggy voice, "come in."

She peeped her head in the door. "Sorry to bother you, but a woman keeps callin' here every half hour. Says her name is Joyce."

"All right, I'll take the call."

I knew talking to Joyce would increase the headaches I still felt from Agee Johnson's glass vase. I slowly got out of bed and walked reluctantly to the kitchen.

Joyce answered in a pleasant tone that surprised me. I thought I was having a hallucination. "Hello, Mosee, I thought something happened to you. We haven't heard from you in two months. Summer's almost gone. We only have August left, before the girls go back to school."

"I'm still workin' on the case," I spoke slowly and calmly, trying not to get myself worked up.

"You don't sound good, Mosee."

You caught me in the middle of my sleep. And I got a

concussion from a fight, during an attempted interview."

"Are you okay? Nothin' broken I hope."

I could tell when Joyce was sincere. Speaking in her motherly concern voice was a rare moment when it came to my welfare.

"I'll live," pausing to catch my breath. "So what's up, Joyce?"

"I had to call Cedric to get your telephone number. I shouldn't have to call all over town to find out where you are. What if something happened to one of your daughters, and I couldn't reach you. I swear you act irresponsible at times."

"Sorry, Joyce. I got caught up in my work. How's the children doin'?"

"Fine, they keep asking for you."

I took a deep breath before speaking, "I know. I took on this case not realizing how long I would be in Westfield. But the case took a turn for the worse, when my client, Zoe Owens was charged with murdering her father. Not something I planned on. Now I'm obligated to help her outta this mess."

"How's the case coming along?"

"Slow, very slow. Two of my suspects have been murdered," I said moaning. "Now I'm down to one. One important factor to the case is two of the murder victims were intimately involved with the original murder victim."

"You think their deaths are related to the girl's father being killed?"

"I don't know, Joyce. Hopefully I can solve this case soon." I ended the conversation on a positive note with Joyce. "Kiss the girls for me and tell them I love them, too."

I returned to my room, where I continued to beat my head against the wall, trying to come up with a rationale behind these murders.

I pushed the record button, speaking slowly into the microphone on my mini compact tape recorder. Today is July 15th the questionable suicide of Channel Peters. Something I don't buy, but tell that to the police. She was one of the many former girlfriends of Foster Owens. This makes victim number three who died in less than three months. The local Westfield news gave Channel's suicide story, less than five minutes air time. When it comes to reporting the death of a white person, the media treats it like a ceremony.

The police treated Channel's death as a suicide, but I have my suspicions.

The second victim was Iris Hall, an Afro-American woman in her early thirties, shot to death in her home on July 15th.

Foster Owens was the first person murdered on May 25th. He was shot in the chest. The forensics reports his death as a homicide; he died from a single gun shot to the chest, and his only daughter, Zoe, is implicated in his death.

I thought I could close this case when Agee was one of my prime suspects who has a strong motive until I learned from Detective Burke that he was at The Cafeteria restaurant working until 12:30A.M.

The next suspect is Blake Reed, who was involved with a business deal with Foster that went sour. Blake's attitude was nonchalant, when he learned that Foster was killed.

I rewound the tape and hit the play button, listening attentively for any clues. My obsession with the case caused me to replay the tape for the fourth time; the one thing that stuck in my mind was the fifteenth of the month. Why does that date kept coming up in my mind? I asked myself, why? That was one answer I intended to find.

I played the tape over again and there was the date again— the fifteenth of the month.

The fifth time I replayed the tape it struck me like a bolt of lightning. Each person had died on the fifteenth of each month.

To reconfirm my findings, I pulled out old newspaper clippings on each murdered victim. I was amazed to see that each newspaper was dated on the fifteenth, starting from Iris Hall's death to Channel Peters.

"I can't believe it," I said softly to myself, each murder was committed on the 15th of each month."

My head started racing, and the blood rushed through my veins.

I jumped out of bed, forgetting about my injuries, running to the living room to tell Ms. Daniels. I burst into the kitchen, hugging her around the neck.

"What's that for?" she laughed.

"A few moments ago, I made an important link in these murders."

Ms. Daniels took a seat at the dining room table. "What you got to tell me that's so important?"

I took a seat across from her. "I strongly believe that when I can find the person responsible for killing Channel and Iris, I will have found the person responsible for Zoe's father's death."

"The police believe that Iris's ex-boyfriend killed her because of jealousy. And Channel committed suicide."

All the excitement caused me to have shooting pains in my head. I bowed my head down, speaking slowly. "Following the death of Foster Owens, there have been other victims who were murdered on the fifteenth of each month, Ms Daniels: Iris Hall died on June 15th and Channel died on July 15th. Looking confused she said, "So what's that mean?"

"It means that each person could have possibly been murdered by the same person; I'd bet my life on it," I said, pulling out the newspaper articles, pointing to the date on each. "I figure the killer probably has to rationalize why he has to kill on the fifteenth; this date is significant to the killer.

Ms. Daniels got up from the table. "You look awful, it's best that you get back in bed." She had a way of throwing her authority around. She made you feel like one of her children. She stood over me with her hands on her hips, giving me that, you better do what I say look. "You won't be any good to Zoe or yourself, if you don't get the proper rest," she said, sounding like an over protective mother.

"You're right, I need my rest. If anyone calls, tell them I'm outta town for the week."

"I'll do that for you," she smiled.

The last three days had given me claustrophobia. I knew just about every soap opera drama from whose man slept with whom and the latest talk show gossip. I also managed to read one novel and gain five pounds. Ms. Daniels took extra care of me, fixing me three square meals a day. Brunch is the heaviest meal down south, it was almost like eating dinner.

During my hiatus, the telephone rang in intervals. I was itching to return to work, but I had to be patient; these last three days felt like the longest days in my life.

When I got involved in a case, it became my life for that time period. Getting involved in Zoe's case made me realize how much I missed working in investigations.

I telephoned Big Rex at the Bureau. He's the only true friend I made during my ten years of employment. Leaving my job gave me doubts whether I would ever get involved with criminal investigations. Once I returned to New York, I knew, finally, what I wanted to do with my life—open a PI business. Once word of mouth spread about my business, I would have clients lined up at my door.

There are a few things I needed to make myself legitimate: getting my business registered, finding a location for my office, a computer, buying a fax machine, copier and a telephone. Because Real Estate prices are astronomical in New York, another option would be to share office space, which should help to keep cost down. I could tap into Cedric's contacts to help.

I waited be connected to Rex. Rex always managed to keep the same composure, since I first knew him. I questioned Rex about his professional opinion on my case findings.

"Mosee, any luck in your missing person's case?"

"Yes and no," I said. "Yes I found the girl's father and No, meaning, now he's dead. I got a call from my client's mother telling me her daughter's been charged with the murder of her father. And now two other people are dead, too."

"Sorry to hear that, Mosee. Don't hesitant to call me if you need my help."

"I'll keep that in mind, Rex, that's why I called you. I found out by coincidence that each victim died on the fifteenth of the month."

"That's interesting. I suggest you find out as much as possible about her father."

"He has a long list of enemies from people he cheated out of money to old girlfriends he spit on and even a disgruntled employee. This guy sure knew how to keep to friends."

"Call me if you find out anything."

Finally, my last telephone call was to my sister, Dee who was worried about her baby brother's investigation.

On the fifth day of my recuperation, I felt back to my old self. Thanks to my three mile run and weight training back at home, helped to speed up my recovery process. I wanted to start with questioning Zoe's mother about her relationship with Zoe's father. Digging in a persons past, sometimes helps to tie in with current events.

I became a little more anxious to question Zoe's mother about Foster again. Knowing about a person's past helps to bring things in the dark to light." Saturday morning, I went to the living room where Ms. Daniels was lounging, watching television. "How you doin' today Ms. Daniels?"

"Alright, I reckon' from all the problems I got."

I sat on the brown recliner, covered in clear plastic. "Mind if I ask you a few questions?"

She gave me a get-the-hell-out-of-my-face look, sitting on the couch with her arms folded tight, pressing against her chest. "I thought I done told you everything 'bout Foster," she said in an angry voice. "I don't have much to tell, considering I haven't laid eyes on the man in over forty years."

"Did the fifteenth have any significant meaning to Foster?"

Shaking her head she said, "Can't say that I remember anything 'bout that date." She looked at me, confused. "What does the fifteenth have to do with these murders?"

"The fifteenth represents a special day to the murderer. Perhaps it was an anniversary date. I'm just speculating right now, until I get something concrete to go on. I really don't have any other suggestions to give you, Ms. Daniels."

I asked her a second time, trying to separate my feelings from the interview. I had to drill Ms. Daniels no matter how frustrated she got. "You sure you have no idea what the fifteenth might have meant to Foster?"

Ms. Daniels became rigid and stiff during the brief interview. "I ain't got nothin' to hide from you."

I didn't want to push her anymore than I had to. I figured I'd get back to questioning her later. The next thing on my agenda was a phone call to Detective Burke, before I called it quits for the day. I had one more day of bed rest and then back on the streets.

I spoke in a cordial, non-threatening voice.

"What the hell you callin' now for, Love?"

I cringed every time I heard his voice.

"Love I don't know if someone else is dead or hurt. You seem to carry a trail of bad luck with you, huh."

I took a deep breath pausing to restrain myself from losing my temper with the man. "I'm calling to let you know I discovered something that could be an important link to the three murders."

"And?" Burke said.

I tried to refrain from cursing the redneck out, but deep down inside I knew I needed the man's help. "I found out that each person died on the fifteenth of the month. If you read your police reports, they'll prove it. I figure the three murders must connect in some way."

"I need more men like you, Love, on my team."

I was in awe to hear a compliment coming from Burke. He's the kind of man who never shows his emotions. Because of Burke's sardonic attitude, it's hard to tell if he likes you or not; you never know where you stand with a man like him. "I wanna come down and look at the police and forensics reports sometime next week, if that's okay with you."

"Sure, Love, you're welcome to come down anytime. I'm ashamed to say my men haven't had a solid lead since these killings started." There was a dead silence on the telephone. Burke continued. "My men haven't done real detective work. Some of them don't know their ass from their head."

I wasn't surprised to hear Burke admit that half his staff is incompetent. I'm almost fully recovered," I mumbled. I had the house to myself. Sundays is Ms. Daniels church day. I ate the breakfast she left and climbed back into bed for some real R&R. After all, it was the last day of my recuperation.

A group of political African-American big shots were on television discussing the solutions to poverty and crime in the black community. I was involved in the show when the sound of the telephone broke my concentration. Whoever was on the other end was persistent as hell. The telephone rang for three hours on and off.

I was determined to get my last day of rest without any interruption, but my curiosity got the best of me. A half hour later, when it started again, I picked it up, but didn't say a word. I could just make out the voice. It was the voice of an irritated woman.

"Mosee, what the hell's wrong with you? I've been callin' you all morning. I got some news for you."

"Slow down, Everee. The doctor put me on bed rest for one week. That meant no phone calls and no work."

"I'm sorry, about bothering you on a Sunday, but …"

"It's okay, Everee, what's up?"

"Willie T done found Iris's old man. He's fixin' to bring him to Ira's Bails Bond office today. What time can you be ready?"

"How did he find him so fast?"

"Let's just say Willie T is resourceful," she chuckled.

"What time will you be over to get me?"

"How does six sound?"

"That's fine Mosee I'll see you than."

21

Everee was outside at exactly 6P.M. blowing her horn. One thing I say about her, she's always prompt. She had a big smile on her face, waving to me as I approached the car.

The smoldering summer heat was at its warmest in the month of July. My tee shirt was getting wet, after being outside a few minutes. "Hey, sugar, how's your head and that arm of yours?"

"Fine. I'm one hundred percent better. I'm healthy as a Stallion."

"Willie T found Iris's old man for you. I'm not half bad for your assistant, huh. You think I can come to New York and work for you?"

"Everee, PI work can be a dangerous occupation. It's not all roses. Sometimes there's work and other times you might be hurtin' to get a pay check for weeks. You start to get uptight when you're hungry and your rent is due," I said, looking serious. "It's a fickle business to be in."

Ten minutes went by before either of us uttered a word.

"How did Willie T find Iris's old man?"

"I don't know. Ask him yourself." When the car pulled up to the building, the shades were drawn and a closed sign hung on the door.

I walked in first, turning the knob. I took out my pistol, in case there was any trouble. Everee walked close behind me. I could feel her breath on my back, as I steadied my gun with my right hand. "Ain't this exciting," she whispered.

I walked in slowly, looking at every corner of the office. I turned in a one hundred and eighty degree angle, making sure the place was secure.

Suddenly, the lights came on and Willie T sat in a swivel chair, behind a desk, holding a .45 magnum in his right hand. "There's the punk you wanted," he said pointing to the floor in the far corner of the room.

There he was, hunched over in the corner, with a black and blue swollen eye and busted lip. I hadn't expected any use of violence. I didn't realize how crazy Willie T was. I walked over to the man inspecting him carefully.

The man with the swollen lips said, "I ain't kill her, man."

"Shut the hell up, 'fore I kick your black ass again."

I sat in a chair in front Willie T, he was overly dressed, as usual, in a red and white suit and a wide brim big straw hat and black patent leather shoes. I knew one thing for sure. Willie T fit the stereotype of a true southern.

"You got my one grand you promised to deliver? I done brought you what you wanted, now where's my money?"

I felt uncomfortable with Willie T holding that gun so loosely. "I have your money right here." I placed the envelope on the desk. Willie T smiled showing his gold W.T. initials on his two front teeth.

"I like doin' business with you," he said picking up the manila envelope. "I made myself an easy one grand." He counted the money, as if he were in deep thought. "I can do this kind of work anytime."

Everee sat on the couch in the front office.

Iris's ex-boyfriend shouted from the corner, "Man, I'm innocent, I ain't kill Iris, I swear."

"Shut up 'fore I put a cap in your black ass," Willie T said pointing his gun at the man, who sat helplessly in the corner.

"What's his name?"

"Tell the man your name."

He sat in the corner holding his stomach. "Winston Harris," he said coughing. "I ain't killed Iris, but I should have killed the bitch for leaving me for a senior citizen."

"Where were you on July fifteenth between 10pm and 12

midnight?"

"I was at my sister's house chillin', man you can ask her yourself."

I took out my pocket-sized tape recorder, getting every detail of the conversation. "Where does your sister live, Winston?"

"Florine lives at 2104 Woodbine Terrace. Can I at least sit down?"

"I'm going to call Detective Burke of the Westfield Police Dept. We're working together on the Foster, Iris and Channel murders."

"If you do that, they gonna charge me with her murder. You know how it is for a Black man in the justice system. We ain't got no rights. They'll find anything to put on you."

I thought about the truth in what Winston said. There is no justice for a Black man. "If I need to get additional information from you, how can I reach you?"

"I'm staying at my sister Florine's house."

"How'd I know you won't skip town on me?" I said

Willie T walked over to Winston. "Make yourself accessible or they gonna find another murder in Westfield."

"I ain't goin' nowhere, man."

"If you do, I'll find your black ass with no problem. That's what I gets paid for, to find punks like you," he spat.

"Man, can a brother sit down?"

Willie T pointed to a chair in front of the desk, next to me. "Go on sit in that seat."

"Did you ever get physical with Iris?"

"Yeah, I pushed her around a few times cause she complained too much, always wantin' more than I could give her. She made me feel less than a man," he said coughing. "When a man is beaten down, especially a Black man, all he has is his pride. And once you strip him of his manhood, there ain't nothin' left. Beatin' her made me feel good."

I blurted out. "Beating on a woman is no excuse. I hate men who take their frustrations out on a woman."

Winston looked down in silence.

"How long were you dating Iris?"

"For 'bout three years."

"When she left you for Foster, you had a desire to kill her, didn't you?"

"I ain't never killed nobody."

I didn't know if he was lying or not. I watched his hand and eye movement for any sign of contradictions.

"You want me to finish this dude, for you?"

My mind went blank for a split second. I didn't intend on Winston getting killed. I didn't know how far Willie T was willing to go, and I did not want to find out either. I was here to do a legal job within the limits of the law.

"No Willie T that's okay. If I need you again, I'll call Everee."

Reluctantly, I made the call to Detective Burke, informing him that I had Iris's ex-boyfriend, Winston, at Ira's Bails Bond office on Tenth and Filbert Street.

"I'll send someone over to pick him up for questioning."

Everybody sat quietly waiting for Burke to arrive. I heard a woman's voice behind me. I had forgotten Everee was still there. "I don't know what we can do next, but we should go and pay Winston's sister a surprise visit."

I turned around in the chair, looking at Everee with a blank stare. "We'll discuss that later, not now Everee."

Everee folded her arms across her chest, looking like a scorned little girl. Willie T continued to run his mouth. My head started throbbing listening to Willie T talk.

"Mosee, if you needs me for anything, don't hesitant to call I always find my man," he said proudly, "Just ask old Ira, he'll tell you."

"I trust you're a man of your word, Willie."

Vicious Karma

"You damn right, man, in the joint, I was the man. I got big respect from everyone, even the guards, too. Folks still give me respect on the streets." Nodding his head. "You have to earn your respect on the streets."

I looked at this clown, dressed in a red suit with a black shirt and matching shoes. I knew guys like Willie wouldn't last in a big city like New York. Men like Willie T needed to feel superior and living in a small town made people take notice of him.

Detective Burke entered with one of his men. The uniformed cop was a tall lanky man who looked as if he'd trip over his own feet. He took an eternity to finish a sentence.

Burke said, "Hello, Love." He averted his eyes to Willie T

I stood up pointing to the far right corner of the room, where Winston sat hunched over in the corner, looking up with black and purple marks etched under his eyes.

"Man, I'm innocent until proven guilty," he said coughing.

Burke told Winston to get up. He put cuffs on him and escorted Winston out the front door. "I'll be in touch, Love" Burke said slamming the door.

"Let's go, Everee." I thanked Willie T for his help. "I'll be sure to use your services if I ever need them again." Willie shook his head smiling. Everee looked excited and full of energy. "I love doin' this

kind of work. It gives me a sense of pride. I ain't never done nothing in my whole life to be proud of. Helping you with this case made me realize it's a whole world out there."

"It's never too late to accomplish your dreams, Everee. Besides, you're young, single and no children. You have nothing but time. Everee sighed, "I was hustling on the streets since I was seventeen years old." I felt empathy for Everee. "Is there anything you always wanted to do?"

"I always wanted to work in the court, like a paralegal."

211

"People graduate as old as eighty years old, you know." Her eyes widened in amazement. "I ain't never heard of that

before. Someone graduating from college up in age." "Where does Winston's sister live?"

"I know where she lives, it's the projects. That can be a tough area, sometimes. I hate driving my car in that part of town. I might not have a car when I get back."

"You can wait in the car till I come back."

I knocked on the door at Woodbine Terrace. A dark-skinned woman answered the door with a scarf tied on her head. She inspected me like a piece of meat. "Hum you look good," she said smiling. Names Florine. I hope I got what you want."

I flashed my identification badge. My name's Mosee Love."

She looked at me carefully, before responding. "Private investigator, huh?" What kinda crime you investigating? What my brother do now?" She said shaking her head in disgust.

"I'm investigating the murder of your brother's ex-girlfriend, Iris Hall."

She gave me a blank look.

I could see her swallow a big lump in her throat.

"I hope Winston didn't kill her?"

I said, "I don't know if he killed her or not, but I would like to ask you a few questions, if I may."

When you first walk inside the apartment there's a kitchen table that's barely holding up on its own. The walls that once looked white are dingy gray.

I walked into the living room where three pieces of furniture stood: an off-white couch that had faded from years of deterioration, an end table with part of the a door missing in the front and a twelve inch television set that looked out of place sitting in the corner. The floors were bare and cold looking.

"You guys go outside and play, I got company," she yelled. "All you guys do is watch television. I just got off from work and I'm beat." She took a seat on the couch. "The hotel was busy today. Make yourself comfortable, Mosee." She bent over taking off her shoes. "My corns are killing me I have to soak these tired feet for an hour tonight. I swear I must have cleaned fifteen rooms today. I ain't never work that hard in months."

"Florine, I wanna ask you some questions about your brother, Winston."

"I hope that bum, didn't go out and get himself in trouble. I'm tryin' to give him a break and let him stay here until he gets his life together. I don't needs no trouble."

I interrupted her before, she told her life story. "How long did your brother date Iris Hall?"

"I guess about four years or so."

"Did he ever bring Iris over to visit?"

"Yeah. She was one uppity bitch who thought she was better than most folks. I told Winston she thinks she too good for him," she lit up a cigarette and headed toward the refrigerator, pulling out a can of Budweiser beer. Florine showed her hospitality, by offering me a can of beer. I graciously declined.

"Thanks, but I never drink on the job."

She flopped down on the couch, taking a gulp of beer. "This sure is relaxing after a hard day's work. I must have put in over eighty hours this week. My old man's been laid off at the factory. Thing's been tight around here. You sure is cute; you got a girlfriend?"

I didn't want to be here longer than I had to. The apartment made me feel depressed. "Florine, how did your brother and Iris get along?"

"Okay, I guess. Like any normal couple. Sometimes a man and woman gets physical."

"That means your brother did hit Iris?"

"Yeah. Once she threatened to leave him. She kept complaining 'bout she wanted more out of life. She wanted a man who could give her more, so he pushed her around a few times. It's like me and my old man. He gets physical ever now and then, but I goes toe to toe with him. I kicked his ass a few times," she stated proudly.

"Did your brother have a history of beating on women?"

"Not that I know of."

She paused for a moment, taking another drink of her beer. "Now that you mention it, Winston did hit on Wilma a few times. That was one of his old girlfriends. She ran her mouth too much. She always had somethin' to say. My brother got tired one day and punched her in the mouth. She called the cops and had Winston locked up for assault."

"Where was Winston on June, 15 1998?"

"He was here playing cards till 3 in the morning. I have card games once a month. I make fried fish, potato salad and fried chicken and we have plenty of liquor, too. She moved in closer to me, giving me the seductive eye. "You sure is cute, you got a girlfriend, sugar?"

"Yeah. She's out in car waiting on me."

She moved away from me, cutting her eyes. "All the good ones are taken. Is this interview almost over?"

I put a second tape in my pocket recorder. "Just a few more questions and I'll be done. How did your brother handle Iris leaving him for another man?"

"I thought he was gonna loose it."

"You mean he wanted to kill Foster?" I said.

"No. Don't be puttin' words in my mouth. You cops are good for twisting things around. My brother is a lot of things, but he ain't a murderer." She finished the last of the beer. "I can go for some fried chicken tonight. You wanna stay for supper?"

"No, thank you, Florine. I like to ask you a few more questions. Did your brother ever mention that he wanted to hurt Foster in any way?"

"No."

Vicious Karma

I stood up signaling the end of the interview. "Thanks, Florine for seeing me," I said. I took out my card and handed it to her. "If you come across anything give me a call, anytime."

She looked me over from head to toe, licking her lips. "You can call me anytime you wanna talk, Mr. Detective."

"Any luck in there?" Everee asked.

"No. Looks like there's not going to be enough evidence to hold Winston. I'm afraid he'll be free to go."

"Free to go!" she yells, "That's why men are always beatin' up on women. The system is, too easy on y'all."

"Everee, if there isn't any solid evidence to convict Winston, that makes him a free man. We don't know if he killed her."

Everee didn't utter a word on the way to Zoe's mother's house. I sure didn't have time to figure out her mood swings. She is one of the reasons I despised working with the opposite sex. Working with Everee made me remember when I was assigned to work with my first female agent at the Bureau. Her name was agent Michelle Dennis. She was always moody or complaining about something. Each day I dreaded working with her. That lesson taught me never to work with women as equals.

Everee barely gave me enough time to get one foot on the ground, before she pulled off spontaneously, causing me to nearly fall to the ground in front of Ms. Daniels' house. I dared not look back, giving her the satisfaction that she was getting under my skin. I would not be hearing from her in a while, at least not until her temper subsided.

I was exhausted. The only thing I wanted was a warm shower to relax my aching muscles and eat a hot meal. Everything was quiet in Ms. Daniels house. I went to the dining room table and noticed a note Ms. Daniels had left. "I went to visit Zoe; I'll be back after five," it said.

Ms. Daniels' Sunday dinners made me yearn for my family. I

especially missed the once a month gatherings at my sister Dee's house. When I return to New York, I anticipated, Dee would have an ear full for me. She kept up on everyone's business.

I was awakened by the sound of a tray, left by my bedside. "Ms. Daniels, you shouldn't have gone through the trouble."

"No problem, son. I just want you to get a hot meal."

I sat up in bed staring at the meal. "By the way, how is Zoe doing?"

"She's doin' okay, but I hate to see her in that filthy place. How can they hold her, she ain't never been in no trouble with the law," she said with streams of tears running down her face.

"I spoke to Detective Burke today. He informed me that there still isn't new evidence that points to another suspect. All the current evidence points to Zoe. He can't prove that the other murders are connected. Everything is based on circumstantial evidence on the other murders.

I got up and hugged her, "Everything's going to be okay. All you can do at this point is pray, Ms. Daniels."

"The church helped raise two thousand dollars to help with Zoe's expenses. I figure you can have half the money. They workin' on more fundraising. Seeing Zoe in that jail breaks my heart."

I moved in closer to Ms. Daniels and she placed her head on my chest and cried. "Every time I see her it takes more outta me."

"Everything's going be okay, don't worry, I'm working around the clock, if I have to."

"I know you doin' your best workin' by yourself."

"I have some help. You know the woman who came here a couple of times? Well she's been assisting me as needed and a friend of hers is helping me, too."

"My congregation has been a big help, especially, Margo. She even loaned me money."

"That's good when you have people to support you in a tragedy; it helps you get through the tough times."

216

"How do you know you'll find the real killer? You don't have a suspect yet and it's going on three months since my daughter's been in jail."

I took a deep breath, looking away from her. I knew she was right. Not one suspect. The case was getting more and more difficult to solve each day. I had to call Cedric and get him to come down to prepare for Zoe's defense. I didn't know how successful Cedric would be when all the evidence points to Zoe. The state was persistent in pursuing the first-degree murder charges.

22

First victim. Black male in his early sixties died from a single gun shot wound to the chest. The coroner estimated his death between the hours of 11:00pm and 12:00am on May 25th. Weapon used a .38 caliber handgun. The victim was found lying face down on his abdomen. Forensics reported the victim was dead approximately three hours. The Only suspect is Zoe Owens, the daughter of Foster Owens.

Second victim, Iris Hall, Black female, mid-twenties died in her home between the hours of 10pm and 12am. Cause of death, multiple gunshot wounds to the abdomen. The bullet casings found at the Foster and Iris Hall murder are not identical. Zoe is still held in her father's death. The only commonality of the two murders is the fifteenth of the month.

The recent victim, Channel Peters, Black female in her mid to late fifties.

Detective Burke entered the room where I was reading the police and forensic reports on the three murders. "Love, you find any new developments?"

"What's interesting is two of the victims are female and each was killed on the fifteenth of the month. I have a hunch that who ever killed Foster is responsible for the murders of Iris and Channel. Proving my theory will be more difficult than I anticipated."

Burke took a seat at the opposite end of the table, looking at me in amazement. "You do some good work, Love"

"Thanks. Anything happened to Winston?"

"No. He's clean, I'm afraid. I was hoping we could get something on the bastard. He has priors. He was charged in nineteen-eighty with assault and battery. The woman's name was Josie Adams. She ended up dropping the charges, so he walked on that one. In addition, in nineteen ninety-eight, he was charged with assault and battery on a woman named Joy Johnson. He served only six months and one year probation for that offense."

"Iris Hall ever press any charges on him?"

"A few times for domestic abuse, but she eventually dropped the charges, but the state pursued the case."

"I'm gonna keep a close eye on him, since he has a pattern of abusing women."

I thought about what Winston said about the police injustices against the Black man and how we're used as scapegoats for anything. I was kinda glad the police didn't find out anything current on Winston.

"Well, if he is innocent, let him go, no sense holding him, right?"

Burke took a deep breath lighting a smelly cigar." You're right, Love."

"You eat lunch, Burke?"

"Why?"

"I like to invite you to have lunch with me".

Burke and I were seated in the middle of the restaurant. The tables were covered in lime green vinyl tablecloths. And the walls had authentic paintings of Afro-American. The booths in the restaurant are lined up against the walls. A piano player sat, dressed in a black and white suit. Each of the tables had floral arrangement in pink vases.

I looked over the menu and decided to order my favorite: fried chicken, collard greens and baked macaroni and cheese. Burke looked confused as he looks over the menu.

Detective Burke constantly swifts in his seat, looking over his shoulders.

"You okay?"

"Yeah . . . I'm fine. It's just that I ain't never been around so many Black folks at one time, except for lockin' 'em in jail."

"We don't bite, I promise you that."

Burke nods his head, "Yeah I guess so," he said bowing his head.

"You ever live around white folks," he asked.

"No, but I have worked with you fellas for over ten years with the FBI. So the answer is yes I have been around your kind. Your problem is that you lived in a lily white town all your life."

Burke nodded.

"So what you gonna eat , Burke?"

"I don't know, I guess whatever you're having," Burke said looking over the menu.

"They make the best fried chicken I ever tasted. It's better than my mother's."

"Your mother's still living?" Burke asked.

I avoided eye contact with Burke. "No she died when I was thirteen."

"Love, I think, I'll have what you're ordering, plus a cold beer would be nice."

"Huh?"

Mosee had an angry look on his face. "For Christ sake, Love, I've been talkin' to you for the past five minutes."

"Yeah I'm fine, just reminiscing about old times. Here comes the waitress Burke."

The waitress wore a short black shirt that clung to her petite hips. Her hair was in a short natural curly style. Her skin was glowing like a radiant apple. "Hello fellas, how y'all doin' today?"

"Fine. Are you ready to order now, Burke?"

He nodded.

"We'll have the fried chicken platter with a side order of macaroni and cheese and string beans. And a Millers lite."

The waitress wrote the food orders on a small notebook tablet. "It'll be a few minutes, gentlemen. I'll bring your beers right over." She walked away putting a little emphasis on her walk. She looked back smiling at us.

Vicious Karma

"I think she likes me," Burke laughed.

"Like you? For one, you're too old by society standards."

"Oh a pretty young woman can't be attracted to me."

"Yeah, if you grow some hair and a couple of inches."

We both started laughing. I was finally breaking ground. The human side of Burke was emerging. For the first time, Burke was exposing his insecurities; he hid behind his police badge. Usually folks act differently when they're away from their work environment. My intention for inviting Burke to lunch was to get on his good side. I needed all the allies I could make down here. I learned early, if you feed your enemy, he's more likely to submit to you.

Burke was opening up more to me. His hard edge seemed to diminish after the third beer along with the combination of good food.

The waitress placed the beers on the table, along with two beer mugs. "Here you are, fellas," she said showing her pearly whites. "If there's anything you want, don't hesitant to ask," she kept her eyes on me the entire time. I liked the attention from pretty women, especially when they were half my age.

"By the way what's your name?"

"Tamika."

"That's a pretty name, for a pretty lady."

"Thanks." The waitress walked away to another table to take the customers' orders.

Burke opened his beer, drinking out the bottle. I poured my beer inside the tall beer mug. "Love, I admire your tenacity for coming down here. You really got balls coming to a place you never been to."

"Your alright yourself." I was feeling at ease and loose at the tongue, after my fourth beer. "You speak your mind and say whatever you feel to people. One thing I can say, people know where they stand with you. There is no pretending."

"That's right; I don't hold no punches back for anyone."

"Where do you think we're going with this case? Things are getting outta hand. I don't have any leads, except what you came up with. Everything is leading to a dead end."

Burke sat there sulking in frustration, gulping his beer down. He had that glassy look in his eyes, the way people look when they've had too much to drink. Burke was slurring his words. "I respect you, Love, you're one helluva a detective. I don't give out compliments, too often," he smirked.

"Thanks Burke," I said, shrugging my shoulders. "I was hoping your men had some answers."

"I forgot to mention that I interviewed Winston's sister.

"Oh really. Get any information on Winston?"

"Nothing. She said Winston was playing cards at her house till three in the morning, but she could be covering up for him."

"The only person I have left as a suspect is Blake and possibly Winston. I think surveillance on the two men would be a good idea."

"If you need any help, Love, I'll be glad to give you a hand. After all, we're on the same team. I hate seein' that gal in jail. I know she didn't kill her father. My hunches tell me she was set up."

I was relieved that Burke agreed to give me some assistance, even though we weren't on the same accord on the murders. "Thanks, Burke."

23

Willie T parked his white Cadillac a few blocks down the street from Blake's house. He drifted off into a semi-conscious sleep by the time Blake stepped out his front door. The house was a rancher style on five acres of land. It had a red brick exterior. The doors had large glass windows on the top. The circular driveway extended out to the street.

Willie T came to, and slumped down in his car trying not to look suspicious. Blake got into his black Durango, wearing a silk green tee-shirt and a beige pair of shorts.

Blake was a medium-built man in his late sixties. His hair had speckles of gray in the front. He's light-skinned complexion. He walked with his head high, arrogantly, with his chest protruding outward.

Once Blake pulled away in his car, Willie T started his engine and tailed him for most of the day. He didn't want to appear too anxious, so he waited until Blake was two blocks away.

The first stop was at Nations Union bank. Willie T figured he's probably retired, since he has so much free time in the middle of the day. He waited patiently for Blake to return. He put on a Stylistics tape. The soothing tunes put him in the mood to see his woman, Eartha. She was the kind of woman who was always there for Willie T. She made him forget about his problems.

Willie T recalled how devastated Eartha had been when he served time in jail for armed robbery. She waited patiently for Willie T to do his time in prison, making weekly Sunday visits. Eartha wasn't much to look at, but she could sure burn in the kitchen and she's a dedicated woman. Eartha would do just about anything for her man. He enjoyed her Sunday meals. She could make anything from scratch. Her specialty in cooking came from her being the oldest among three sisters and four brothers.

Besides cooking, Eartha was great in bed, too. When Willie T closed his eyes, Eartha was the most beautiful person in all of Westfield, South Carolina.

He was about to change the tape, when he looked up and saw Blake coming from the bank. Immediately he sat up in his car, starting the car engine.

Blake took I-15. He made a right off the bridge. Willie T followed him to an apartment complex. A woman who looked to be in her late forties greeted Blake with a hug. Shortly afterward, they disappeared into the building.

Willie waited patiently in the car for a sign of something out of the ordinary. He hated waiting around to catch his clients in the middle of an illegal act. He preferred bum-rushing his clients and catching them off guard.

But Ira had given him orders to ease up on his aggressive behavior. Fuck Ira, he thought. He don't know nothin' no how. I'm the one who take all the risk. I'm the one getting shot at and attacked. Ira has it easy. He sits behind a desk shuffling papers and giving me orders. Ira don't have to put his life on the line, not like me. Ira went out a few times to bring clients in, but I did all the nuts and bolts of the job.

But the fact of the matter was, Ira was the brains behind the operation. He took Ira's advice and waited for Blake to make his next move, instead of bum-rushing him.

I had asked Willie T to tail Blake for two days and record anything unusual about his activities.

About an hour later, Blake came out of the apartment. Willie T was itching to put his gun to Blake's head, in order to get a confession out of him. Willie hated wasting time on doing things by the book.

Willie T followed Blake, staying three cars behind.

Blake took Exit 36, driving through the downtown section of Westfield. He parked and proceeded to walk through town, passing

224

restaurants, and stores along the way.

Willie T parked his burgundy Lincoln Cadillac three blocks from where Blake parked his Dodge Durango. Blake went behind a restaurant and disappeared. Willie T quickened his pace before he lost sight of Blake. Willie T walked up to the front of the restaurant noticing that the place was closed. He saw yellow police tape draped across the door—do not trespass, criminal investigation, it said. All trespassers will be prosecuted.

He wondered why anyone would be interested in going to a closed restaurant. Willie T's curiosity heightened at the sight of the crime tape.

Why was Blake interested in a closed restaurant that's under police investigation? Somethin' came to him like a bolt of lightning. He remembered that Mosee informed him that Blake had been cheated out of some money by that dead dude—Foster Owens. At that point, everythin' started makin' sense to him.

Blake had come to get his share of the loot. He knew where the money was hidden. Jackpot. Today was payday for Willie T

Sometimes Willie T's brain was slow to register. Most people's reaction time might be twenty seconds, but Willie T might take up to half an hour to figure out the simplest things. He hated being called dumb, stupid, mash potato head. The names were clear as yesterday.

Willie T hadn't displayed the basic ABC"S of learning. His peers use to call him water bucket head. He'd hear voices inside his head telling him he wasn't dumb. Willie T was always behind his classmates. He never did comprehend subjects in school. Because Willie couldn't handle the humiliation from his peers' chastising him for being a little slow, he dropped out of the eight grade.

One thing is for sure, Willie knew how to use his fists. He took pride in his strength and being so big for his age. Like most kids,

Willie put all his energies into the one thing he was good at—fighting. Around the neighborhood, Willie T built himself a reputation for being tough. His size and strength were enough to intimidate most kids.

Willie T went to the back of the restaurant. Effortlessly, he slipped in and tiptoed through the kitchen, praying that he didn't trip over anything in the dark. The only light he could see was coming from the front. The place had a musty stale odor.

After five minutes, Willie T walked slowly behind the bar to scan the place. Another five minutes went by; he went to the back of the restaurant again. Willie saw a door cracked open. He peeped his eye between the cracks and saw Blake rummaging through the drawers. Willie T wanted to bum-rush this guy, but he counted to ten and took a deep breath.

Blake looked up quickly, glancing toward the door. Willie darted away from the door, before he had been seen.

Blake pulled a picture down from the wall. Behind the picture was a safe combination. Willie watched Blake trying for twenty minutes to break into the safe. No luck.

Willie's interest in the safe intensified. He began thinking about calling his friends Buckets and Al, who are both career prisoners. Their specialty is robbery. They each had a rap sheet that could fill up Yankee Stadium. Willie T tried to make a clean life for himself on the outside, but sometimes temptation hit you square in the face.

No one wanted to be to be labeled an ex-con, no matter how much rehabilitation or training you got inside the joint; life was still a bitch sometimes. It gets hard when a man tries to go straight; society don't give a damn 'bout us, he thought. That's why a lot of us end up making a living back on the streets. You gotta eat and put a roof over your head. A woman don't wanna hear you can't find a job. Hell no. They wanna get cash in their pockets. No woman wants a broke ass man. No sir.

Just as Blake moved toward the door, Willie T jumped up and

blocked his way. He rushed through, pointing his magnum at the man.

Willie T grabbed Blake by the collar hoisting him against the wall. He ordered Blake to turn around slowly, put his hands on top of his head, and walk out the door. Willie T felt his adrenaline flowing as he forced Blake out of the office. This was the best part of the job; he told himself, is roughing up the clients.

Willie instructed Blake to get on his knees.

"Hey, man," Blake yelled, "what the hell is this all about?"

Willie answered with a left clip to the jaw. "You got a smart ass mouth for somebody who don't know nothin." He pressed his gun into Blake's head, forcing him to the floor.

Blake lifted his head up, understandably dismayed. "What the hell is going on here?"

Willie gave Blake his widest grin and introduced himself. "I'm Willie T, you son of a bitch. I'm here to keep an eye on your ass." He enjoyed this part of the job—intimidating folks. Willie T felt his blood race through his veins in the mist of confrontation.

"Why are you here, following me?"

"Same reason you're here," Willie T said.

Blake voice started cracking. "Look, man, I don't know what it is you want, but if you want money," Blake said taking his hand from behind his head, reaching into his back pocket. "I have some cash on me, it ain't much ..."

'I don't need your money, "I wanna know why you snooping 'round this restaurant for."

"I came to see about some personal business here." Blake closed his eyes and prayed this mad man didn't kill him.

Willie shouted, looking down at Blake. "Personal business? What can be so important 'bout a restaurant, when the place's been closed for months?"

Blake hesitated before answering. He didn't know what

relationship this guy had with Foster.

"Put your hands back on top of you head!" Willie T shouted.

"It's a debt that Foster has owed me for quite some time." Blake tried to hide the nervousness in his voice. The only thing he prayed for was getting out alive. He didn't know why he had been followed. His head kept spinning, making him feel nauseous from the pain in his right jaw. Blake never hurt anybody in his life. He knew he wasn't perfect, but he never cheated anyone out of money. Blake thought maybe he did something to someone in his past that he couldn't remember; and things were catching up to him.

Willie T pushed the barrel of the gun into the right side of Blake's jaw. "Man don't be lyin' to me, I don't have time for wise asses. I'm gonna ax you again," he said bending over, whispering into his hear, "What is it you come here fore?"

Blake inhaled. It felt as though his lungs were closing up on him. He closed his eyes and prayed again that the crazy man wouldn't shoot him.

"I'm a ax you again. What is you doin' in here?"

Blake slowly moved his hands from the top of his head.

"Put your hands where I can see them!"

Blake placed his hands on top of his head, following his orders. "Alright, man, I'm here to see if Foster has any money around here. He owes me money."

Willie T looks at him frowning. "You come here to do a cover up?"

"No." The only thing he could think of was going home climbing into bed and waking up in his warm bed, relieved that this was only a dream.

"By the way, what's your name?"

"Willie T"

"What is it that you do?"

"I goes out and finds people and bring em' back."

"Find people for what?"

228

"Man you ax too many questions. I'm here to find out 'bout you. I find whoever they tell me to find," Willie T said "Look I'm here axin' the questions, man."

Blake's voice started to quiver, when he tried to explain to Willie T "I came here lookin' for money that Foster owes me. I never killed the guy, but I do know he kept a list of enemies, so anybody could have killed him."

"How much we talkin' ?"

"About twenty grand."

"Twenty grand?" Willie T repeated excitedly. "Shit. That's a lot of cash you talkin.'

Willie T's wheels started spinning. His face was bright, like a Christmas tree. "I tell you what. If you find that money, we can split it and I'll let you go. How's that?"

He walked away from Blake and stood by the bar, leaning on the front. "Well, what you gonna do, man? Where's the loot?"

"I don't know. I just took a chance and figured it might be here."

"So you tellin' me you don't know where the fuckin' money is?"

"No. I just came here, like I told, you to see if the money was hidden. The truth is, I probably won't never see that money, now that Foster's dead."

He walked behind the bar putting the overhead light on. He kept his gun aimed at Blake in case he tried to get away or make a move toward him.

Willie sat at the bar keeping a close eye on Blake who was on his knees, with his hands behind his head. "My knees are hurting, Willie T I have arthritis in my knees and legs. Mind if I sit down for a spell?"

"Stays where you are! I don't care nothin' 'bout your pains," Willie T said in a cold voice.

Asa Allen-Showell

When I called back, Willie told me he had a surprise waiting for me at Foster's restaurant.

Thirty minutes later, I enter through the back door. My mouth dropped open, when I saw Blake in the middle of the floor, with his hands on top of his head. I hoped I wasn't getting in over my head, with an ex-convict and a prostitute working with me. I was now an accessory to kidnapping, if Blake went to the police. Willie T had crossed the line. He was the kind of man who doesn't know how to play by the rules; he makes them up as he goes along.

"What's going on, Willie?" I asked, taking a seat next to him at the bar.

"I was tailing Blake most of the day, when he stopped at Foster's restaurant. I followed him inside, until he made his move. That's when I comes inside and lay it on him heavy. I pulls my gun. He cooperates with no trouble. He fessed up to why he came here—to collect twenty-grand that Foster owes him."

"I'm impressed, Willie T I couldn't have done it without you." Willie T smiled, showing his gold initials

I walked toward the back of the restaurant. My nostrils were engulfed by the mildew smell of the place. The back of the restaurant had three doors painted in black. The third door to the far right had a sign hanging in the front, that read Manager's office.—Do not enter. There is a dark oak rectangular desk that took up most of the office space. There were papers scattered over the top desk. Perhaps Blake had created that mess looking for his money. There was a picture of an Afro-American ballet dancer on the wall, hanging askewed. I got closer to examine the picture and to my surprise I saw a safe behind the picture. I wondered what the contents were in the safe—legal papers, money. I sat behind the desk on the brown cloth swivel chair contemplating the reasons Blake had come to the restaurant of a dead man. 1. He came to cover up his tracks in Foster's murder or 2. Foster really did owe him money and he had come to collect.

I tired to put together all the possible scenarios that could fit the crime. Maybe Blake was an angry man who was apparently cheated out of some money. Twenty grand, is enough to make anyone want to seek revenge, I thought to myself.

Blake had been at the top of my list for possible suspects. If Blake did kill Foster, then who killed Iris and Channel? I could not come up with a valid reason why Blake would want to kill Iris and Channel. Without a motive, I had nothing to work with.

Motive equals Blake, I said under my breath.

Each time I thought I was one step closer, I kept running into dead ends. The pain in my head got sharper the more I concentrated on solving the murders.

I was getting nowhere searching Foster's office, so I returned to the front of the restaurant. Willie T sat in the same position, with his gun pointed and ready to fire at any moment, with his chest out, gloating over his progress. His impulsive behavior scared me at times; I had to remember that I was in charge of this investigation.

Being in a power position reminded Willie T of his early teen years. "Now you boys know whose boss," he must have been thinking. Nobody's gonna mess with Willie again, he would snarl, holding one of the kids in a head lock. He was a boy again in Macon, Georgia. The name calling and taunting became clearer—stupid, clumsy, bus head. His mother, Eve, hadn't helped, he later learned. She would call him those names herself whenever he did something wrong. "Boy you, fool, you as dumb as they come," she shouted.

Willie T used the one asset he had—strength. In Willie T's later years, he was known as the neighborhood bully. That's how he earned his respect from his peers. He wore his gun like a badge of honor.

"Mosee, you find anything, in there?" I took a seat next to Willie T at the bar.

231

"So what we gonna do with Blake?"

"Nothing Willie," I whispered.

Willie T's eyes looked like they were going to burst out of his head when I made that statement.

He raised his voice in a high southern pitch. "What you mean we ain't gonna do nothin'?" he said. "After all the work I did, tailing this dude all day."

"Willie T, we have nothing to hold him on. Haven't you heard? 'A man is innocent until proven guilty.'"

"Yeah," Willie T said with an edge. "That means we let him walk." He sighed. "All that hard work for nothin'."

"You can go now, Blake," I said apologizing for his misfortune.

Blake attempted to stand up, but his knees started to wobble and he fell to the floor, losing his balance. "My knees," he yelled. "I told y'all I have arthritis.

I got up from the bar, to help the old man off the ground.

"Thanks," he said, breathing heavy, "you could have caused me to have a heart attack. I hope I won't be seeing you two again," he said walking toward the back door. "I have a mind to press charges on you two."

Willie and I sat in silence, watching Blake walk toward the back of the restaurant.

"I think he's guilty as hell, if you ax me."

"We can put more pressure on him in a few days." He's scared, but he may talk later. There's nothing else to do but wait."

Willie T looked at me with contempt and disgust, repeating my statement. Alright, Mosee, Give him a chance to think about all this. He's scared now, but you're right, he may talk later."

Willie stood up from the bar, putting his gun in his suit jacket. "Any more work?"

"Not now, I'll call you if I need your help, Willie T Thanks for your help." I knew that using a man like Willie T was nothing but trouble.

Vicious Karma

I stood up and extended my hand to give Willie a handshake. "I thank you for your help, Willie."

We said our good byes. My eyes stayed focused on Willie T until he was no longer in view. I wiped the perspiration from my forehead with the palm of my hand. I was relieved that the ordeal had ended peacefully. I didn't need another strike against me and Blake was the last person I wanted to hear from.

I sat in the far corner of the restaurant, contemplating my next move it's only been five years, since I did any real investigation work. One thing about an investigator is that you must never lose your edge.

I wanted nothing more than to return home to New York and be with my daughters, but my love for a challenge had brought me to Westfield, South Carolina. Then, tragedy after tragedy had begun to make me feel beaten down these previous few weeks. I had my fill of funerals. I hoped Channel Peter's would be the last one I attended. Human life isn't valued anymore; people will take a life away without having a conscious thought for their actions.

I made up my mind not to let this case get the best of me. I had an obligation to Zoe and her mother to find her father's killer. Each time I envisioned Zoe's pretty face sitting behind those iron bars, I became more determined to find the person who murdered her father.

I was grateful that Johnson hadn't died from the gun shot wound. I sure didn't need a murder hanging over my head. I had a few friends left at the Bureau who would help me out if ever I got in a jam, especially Rex, who is a long time friend.

I didn't think I could ever have a white male as a good friend, but Rex had proved me wrong. My first two years at the Bureau had been mentally and physically draining. I was the second black male on the training crew at the academy in Quantico, Virginia. I didn't have many friends; I kept to himself mostly. Racism was prevalent during my formative years, but I refused to be driven away due to the ignorance of a few. I carried myself with an air of authority, demanding respect. Because of my size, I was able to gain respect from fear. And then, of course, there were some who didn't care about my size.

Rex, a senior agent with the Bureau, had befriended me. He had helped me through some of the toughest times. Finally, after eight months I let my guard down and accepted Rex's friendship, without any prejudices. Our friendship had endured for over ten years.

I felt one hundred percent better than I had five days before. I understood fully when it came to giving orders, but when it came to taking my own advice, I was my own worst nightmare. My sisters, Shelby and Dee, thought I should be a psychologist because I was good at listening to people's problems and instructing them on what to do with their lives.

Before I became burned out, I decided to leave the Bureau after ten years of service. Listening to tons of motivation tapes, Les Brown, Anthony Robins and many others, helped to speed up my decision. I gave my two weeks notice and called it a day.

24

I was relieved to see the familiar beige rancher, with the rickety fence, barely holding up. I returned to Ms. Daniels house before the sun started setting. The view of the sun is breath taking overlooking the mountains. Being in the country made me realize what I'd been missing. Hearing the crickets and the sound of birds making their calls, made me yearn for a change of scenery.

Living in the city, I couldn't have gained an appreciation for the country. City living can be hard on the mind and body. The crowds of people always rushing. People never seem to relax and slow down. People are not friendly in the North as compared to the South.

I lived only a short time in Danville, Virginia. My sisters and I never knew what true Southern living really was. Being on a murder case for three months gave me a taste of what I had been missing in my life. I turned my key quietly into the key hole, sneaking into the house like a little kid, who was about to be scolded.

I heard the sound of the television set, when I stepped into the house. I could smell the mouth-watering aroma of something wonderful filling the air. I tiptoed to my room, before she realized I had not been there.

I managed to change my clothes and climb into bed. Twenty minutes later, I heard a female's voice trying to gain access into my room.

"Come on in," I said, sitting up in bed.

Ms. Daniels came in carrying a tray of food: Corn beef and cabbage. She placed the tray of food beside my bed.

I smiled. "Everything smells so good, as usual."

"Thanks, I try."

"It must come natural to you. One thing for sure, I'm gonna miss your cookin', after the investigation ends."

"You plan on leaving soon?" she said with panic in her voice.

"I'm committed to seeing this case solved to the end."

Ms. Daniels sat at the edge of the bed, relieved. "How's it going?"

"Slow, but it's coming," I said taking a bite of the corn beef and cabbage, capturing the savoring flavor in my mouth.

"You got any suspects?"

I chewed my food, before I responded to her question. "Blake is one and Iris's ex-boyfriend and Reverend Elders. Each has a strong motive for killing Foster, but I don't have any solid evidence." I paused to take another mouthful. "I'm gonna see if Detective Burke can issue a search warrant for Blake and Winston."

"What 'bout those two girls getting killed? Seems mighty strange how they died."

"Yeah, I'm not sure who could've murdered Iris and Channel. Pieces to this puzzle just don't seem to fit."

Ms. Daniels walked toward the door. "I'm gonna leave you alone to finish your meal."

After I finished my meal, I looked forward to catching a good night of sleep. I hadn't done that since I had taken on Zoe's case. Being confined to bed rest the previous week, made me realize how exhausted I was.

I lay in bed, thinking about my agenda for the up coming weeks. I was interrupted by the sound of light tapping on the door.

"Mosee, I got the information about Channel's funeral."

"Come in," I responded.

Ms. Daniels handed me a section of the obituaries in the Sunday newspaper. "The funeral is gonna be held on Wednesday at 11:00 in the morning and the viewing is at 10:00."

Vicious Karma

25

The body of Channel lay in a white marble casket with an interior that matched a fire truck. She was dressed in a white lace dress. Her hands were folded as if she were in a deep slumber. She didn't look half-bad for a dead woman, I thought, viewing the body.

Bright floral arrangements and grave wreaths surrounded her casket, in a variety of colors and styles.

Everee stayed behind, sitting in last pew. She didn't care much for funerals; she felt they were opportunities to waste time so folks could cry over dead bodies. Her philosophy was live life to the fullest. The dead leave to go to a better place, anyway. She felt life wasn't easy for most of us; maybe there's something better beyond life on earth. She hoped that God would forgive her, when judgment came. She didn't exactly live a perfect life. Everee didn't know what happened to you when you die; she could only wonder, like me. She wanted to give up her job and retire and join a church. She believed that would give her enough time to start over and make it into heaven.

She wasn't keen on getting close to people. She had never shed a tear that she could remember. Her exterior was like a crab's protective shell, never allowing any one to get too close.

Everee's family consisted of a mother, whom she hadn't spoken to since the start of her promiscuous behavior at the age of sixteen, and a brother whom Everee hadn't seen or spoken to in over fifteen years.

Above the casket, a choir sat, waiting their cue. They were dressed in black robes trimmed in gold. The choir started singing "Home Coming," at exactly eleven-thirty.

I returned to my seat in the last pew next to Everee. An elderly woman in her sixties wore a white lace head piece, matching her dress, which resembled a nurse's uniform. The white color made a striking contrast against her dark skin. She handed Everee and I programs of the funeral services. Nearly every seat in the church was filled.

I watched the mourners come through the doors. My mouth fell open when I saw Detective Burke in the group. I nodded at him, acknowledging his presence. A hostess escorted him to a seat in the middle aisle.

A man stood up in front of the choir dressed in a black suit. He raised his hands in slow motion, signaling to the choir to stand up and begin a second hymn. When the choir started singing, people in the church started singing and clapping their hands. Everee looked at me in awe. I knew she was wondering how a funeral could be a joyous occasion. But she felt the sprit and joined in. I kept my eyes focused on the people.

When the choir stopped, Everee bent over to whisper in my ear. "Sure feels good. I ain't been inside a church, since I was a young girl."

I smiled. "I haven't been inside a church since I met you."

Everee began to think about the innocent times she and her younger brother attended church with their mother Sunday mornings. The feeling of nostalgia made her yearn for her family.

The preacher stepped up on the black and white marble tile. He spoke about "Sister Channel." He described her as a giving person, willing to help others. "God bless Sister Channel, I know God's gonna' have a special place in his kingdom for Sister Channel," he said raising his hands.

He bowed his head. "Amen, please let us pray."

As I went through the agonizing rituals at the funeral, I didn't notice anything out the ordinary or unusual, but I kept my eyes focused on everything that didn't move.

The preacher took up another thirty minutes, preaching his sermons. About thirty minutes later, the final viewing took place.

Each person went according to rows, starting from the last row in the back of the church.

Finally came our turn to view the body. I felt queasy in the pit of my stomach, the closer I got to the casket. Everee held my arm, squeezing tightly. When I approached the front pew where the family was seated, I gave a handshake, giving my condolences. Standing in front of Channel's body made me envision the time I saw my mother's body lying in her floral rose dress.

Everee nudged me whispering in my ear. "C'mon, now we have to keep the line moving.

"Sorry, Everee, I must'va been daydreaming."

"Do you always get depressed at funerals?"

"I was thinking about my mother, Everee," I whispered.

Everee looked at me with sympathetic eyes. "I'm sorry, Mo, I ..."

"It's okay, Everee, how are you supposed to know."

We returned to our seats in the back row, waiting for the preacher to put the final touches on his sermon. He said a final farewell to the deceased, and the people joined in a prayer.

The family stood up to view the body for the last time. I saw a light-skinned woman sobbing uncontrollably and a tall dark-skinned man trying to comfort her.

I made a mental note of each person who had attended the funeral. Still nothing appeared out of the ordinary. When the family took their seats the preacher concluded the services with another prayer. After the prayers ended, the hostesses came to the back rows, signaling for everyone to rise to exit the church two rows at a time.

Twenty minutes later, three men came up front to help take the casket. The preacher asked if anyone else would like to give their assistance as a pallbearer. I walked forward to the front of the church, making my presence known, in order to get close to the family. I grabbed the back of the casket following the three men. One of the men was middle-aged in his late fifties and the other two men looked to be in about thirty something. Just as we exited the church, the people departed one row at a time, starting with the family.

It was a thirty-five minute ride to the burial ground. I wanted this scene to end as quickly as possible. I prayed it would be my last funeral. Everee managed to find a space next to the Hearst. I went immediately to assist with carrying Channel's casket to the burial plot.

We placed the casket on top of a metal frame that was located above the ground where the casket was to be lowered into the ground. I took my place beside the family. An older woman with salt and pepper hair sat in a fold up chair. I looked around to see if Burke was anywhere around. He stood next to a tree, away from the crowd smoking a cigar. Everee stood by the car smoking a cigarette, nonchalantly, checking out the faces in the crowd. When the casket was lowered into the ground I walked over to check on Everee. She looked up at the crisp blue skies. She wondered what that better place really was like. She wondered if she should get saved or continue living as she has been. She reflected on her father, who had been missing in action, since she was ten years old.

"Can we get outta this depressing environment, now? I ain't in the mood for this shit."

I placed my hands on her shoulder. "What's eaten' you Everee? You've been fidgeting since we got here."

"I ain't a fan of funerals. I can think of better places to be," she said climbing into the driver's seat. "I hope we're done here, Mosee, cause you costin' me money. I already turned down five clients, since I been helpin' you."

I tried to humor her. "Everee, I appreciate everything you've done. I don't know what I would have done without your help."

She smiled. "I just wanna feel appreciated for my services."

"When this is all over, I promise there's something in it for you."

Everee followed blue Maxima for twenty minutes. She said, "Maybe I can get some clients at this wake."

"You ever get tried of what you're doing, Everee?"

"I've been doing this business for so long. I don't think I could do anything else. I can't imagine going to a nine to five everyday," she said twisting her face in a knot. "It makes my stomach turn. Even if I do start over, I ain't gonna make the kind of money I'm used to."

"What other things have you thought about doing? Everybody has dreams and goals, Everee."

She was silent for a moment. Well I … I thought about medicine. I used to watch Quincy, the Medical Examiner on television. And my favorite subject in school was Biology. What about you, Mosee, you ever thought about doing anything besides investigation work?"

"I always loved investigation and solving criminal cases. I really can't think of any thing else I'd rather be doing. I like to run my own PI business and work for myself," I shrugged my shoulders. "That's about it."

Everee said with excitement in her voice. "I have my own business. I'm managing my own clients; I answer to no one and I'm independent, too."

I nodded my head in agreement. "Yes, that's true."

After following the blue Nissan Maxima for twenty minutes, we pulled up in front of a two-story brick row house.

The house was filled with people, covering every inch of the house. People filled the living room, kitchen and dining room area. There were people standing along the sides of the hallways. I scanned the three rooms, trying to select my prey for questioning.

There was a woman sitting in the far corner in the dining room with her eyes filled with tears, sobbing quietly. I thought it would be a good idea to comfort her before pumping her for information; I needed to learn about Channel Peter's life as much as possible.

242

Everee made friends with a dark-skinned man in his late twenties. She sat by him, whispering in his ear. It looked as if Everee found herself a customer.

I walked over to the woman, handing her a tissue to dry her eyes. "Hello, I think you can use this."

She looked up forcing a smile on her face. "Thank you, for your concern," she said.

I extended my hand to introduce myself. "My names is Mosee Love, I'm a private investigator, working on the Foster, Iris and Channel murders.

Her mouth hung open, looking at me as if I was speaking a foreign language.

"May I join you?"

"Sure, there's a fold up chair over there," she said pointing to the closet. "My name's Rose Johnson. I'm Channel's youngest sister. We're five years apart. I can't understand how folks can come into my house drink and party like nothings happened. They don't realize we came from a funeral two hours ago," she sobbed.

"Can you tell me a little about your sister, if you feel up to it? I won't push you, if you don't feel like talking."

"No problem, Mr. Love. My sister was a loving woman. She never bothered anyone. She was very active in church, giving her life to the lord."

I held my breath until Rose finished giving her "goody two shoes" speech. We all have skeletons in the closet, some have more than others; nevertheless, no one's prefect. When she finished describing Channel Peters, there wasn't a scar or blemish left behind.

I didn't like the direction the interview was going; I decided to take charge by asking more direct questions. "Did you know Foster Owens, Rose?"

She sighed heavily. Yes. I know that he and my sister dated."

"How was your sister's relationship with Foster?"

"I don't know," she said fidgeting in her seat. Each time I mentioned Foster's name, she moved a little more than usual in her seat and she folded her arms tightly across her chest. Her non-verbal actions, gave me an indication that she was very nervous and uptight about answering questions about Foster.

"Can we change the subject? I don't wish to discuss my sister anymore." She rose from her seat. "Well talk some other time. This is just bad timing. You can understand I just buried my sister."

"I'm sorry, Rose, I understand."

I knew she was hiding something. I got up and decided to get a bite to eat. There was a spread of different assortments of southern food on the table: pig's feet, roast pork, black-eyed peas, fried chicken, yams, and collard greens and so on. On the other table were desserts, cakes, sweet potato pie, and chocolate cake. You name it. They had it.

Standing in line gave me a tremendous amount of guilt, because I hadn't exercised since I took this assignment. I grabbed a plate and awaited my turn in line to sample the food. When it was my turn, I covered every inch of my plate.

Then I found a seat in the corner next to an older man who looked to be his seventies. He was very thin with a bald head and mustache. I smiled at the man. "Mind if I join you?"

"No, son, help yourself."

I wanted to immediately question the old man about Channel, instead I took another approach and tried small talk. "Channel, certainly has a lot of people who loved her, huh?"

"Yeah, she did. She's my sister's child."

"Did she have any children?"

"No sir. She never wanted no children."

"Was she married?"

"No! She had a funny lifestyle. I took a spoonful black eye peas and rice. "I believes she was one of them women who likes women."

"I heard she and another man who died named, Foster Owens, were dating before her death." The old man shrugs his shoulders. "I know my niece was dating Mr. Owens, but I know she liked women folks, too."

I was shocked to hear this new information on Channel. So far I had received nothing but lies from these people. Channel's sister failed to mention Channel's alternative lifestyle, if in fact, that was the truth.

"You know this woman who was dating Channel?"

"You a cop or something? You sure askin' an awful lot of questions. I seen you talkin' to folks round' here. I don't miss nothin'. I may be old, but I got ears like a microphone and eyes like a magnifying glass."

I savored the juices in my mouth from the baked ham before speaking.

"No. I'm not a cop. I work for myself; I'm a private investigator." I reached into my wallet, handing over my identification badge.

"I'm here to find out who killed your niece. There were two other murders that might be connected to your niece's death."

The old man nods his head. "Ain't that something."

I was a little dumfounded over the news that Channel could have possibly been a lesbian. How could a beautiful and elegant woman like Channel be involved in such an indecent act? I didn't want to judge Channel's lifestyle until I had all the facts; that's one thing I learned being in the investigation field, never take anything for granted.

The man, who claimed to be Channel's uncle, rambled on about his niece's behavior. I wanted to get back to questioning him, before I had any interruptions.

"Wasn't she involved in the church? I don't see how the

church could have allowed her to join as a member if she was involved with women."

"She kept that quiet. I know she and Foster were sleeping with each other. Son, I can't tell you much, I can only tell you what I know." I gave the old man, a card and asked him to call me if he came across any pertinent information.

Just as I was about to walk away, I heard the old man yell across the room, "Frank, you know who Channel's lover was?"

"I only saw her once or twice," his friend responded, shaking his head. "I believe I saw her at the funeral today."

The old man looked around the room. "I think that's her there going out the front door.

I turned around abruptly, nearly knocking an old lady down, pushing through the crowd. I stepped onto the front porch, and saw a black BMW pulling off. I caught a glimpse of the license plate. I quickly pulled out a notepad and jotted down the last four letters, before—STARYD4.

I returned to the house, hoping to see Channel's sister again to question her about her refusing to answer any more questions. I walked over to Everee to see how she was doing on her end of the investigation. To my surprise, she was sitting in the dining room, the same place I had left her before.

It infuriated me to see that Everee wasn't attempting to help me out. My six foot frame towered over her, like the empire state building.

"Oh, hello, Mosee, what's up?" she said avoiding my eye contact.

"I wanna see you right now!" I snapped.

"Everee, I'll call you later," the man said getting up from his seat in a hurry.

"Look you done scared him away. I'm tryin' to make some money here!" she shouted.

I sat next to Everee, trying not to make a scene, but people in the dining room had their eyes and ears open. "Keep your voice down, Everee; we're here for business not for your pleasure."

Everee stood up and placed her hands on her hips. "I'm workin' for myself. You think I punch a time clock? Remember, I'm doin' you the favor," she said moving her head from side to side.

There's no sense arguing with a black woman. They never let you have the last word. It's a cultural "thang," with the black female the head movement and the hands on the hips.

I hated to admit that she was instrumental to me with these murder cases. I didn't want to push her over the edge and cause her to leave the case. "I'm sorry, Everee. I get carried away sometimes. I guess I've been overworked, lately. I barley sleep at nights since this mess started."

"Can you do me a favor and get any information you can?"

"That's what I've been tryin' to tell you. This guy I've been talkin' to, Tony told me a lot of information. A woman can use her charm on a man and get whatever she wants. That's my greatest asset, you know."

"I thought he was another one of your customers."

"Give me some credit. I've slowed down my activity, since I met you. I'm even thinking about retiring from my business. I put money away in mutual funds and IRA'S. I have a nice nest egg saved," she said proudly.

"I'm just a little jealous, cause I'm not getting the attention," I said. We both laughed.

She moved her chair in closer to me, bending in my ear. "Sugar all you got to do is ask and you shall receive."

I was mesmerized for a brief moment by Everee's beauty. I forgot how attractive she was. My loins started swelling up on me. It had been a while since I was intimate with a woman, three months to be exact.

"I think, I'm gonna take him home," she winked. I'll have all the info for you in a few."

I nodded my head, taking out a tissue to wipe the sweat from my brow. "All right, we wrap things up in about half an hour."

I spent the remaining half hour walking through the rooms, scouting out prey. I zeroed in on a woman in her late forties standing by the bar, nursing a drink. Her eyes were glassy and her

Lips were dry and cracked. She appeared to be holding up the bar by shear luck and a prayer.

"Hello, may I join you?" I said putting on my charm.

"Sure ... sure go on honey, I can use some male company. You good lookin," she said licking her lips. "What side of the family is you on? I don't wanna flirt with one of my cousins; I ain't into the incest thing. You know Channel's family can be a bitch. That stuck up heffa, I never could stand her. She's my first cousin, you know. We never did get along as kids. Her family thought they was always better than us. Just cause they high yellow, she thought that made her special. She was nothin' but a woman lover," she said taking a sip of her drink. What's your name, anyway?"

"Mosee Love, I'm an acquaintance of Channel."

"My name's Thelma, please to meet you," she said licking her lips. "You ain't from round here is you?"

"No. Actually I'm from New York City."

Her eyes widened with surprise. "Oh, you come a long ways sugar."

"I'm down here on business. I'm investigating the deaths of your cousin, Iris Hall and Foster Owens."

"I hope you find who done killed my cousin. Even though I couldn't stand the sight of her, I still loved her."

"That's sentimental of you, Thelma."

She stepped in closer to me; I could feel her breath on my neck. "You sure is fine," she said. "You married?"

"No. I'm divorced."

"That's too bad," she smiled.

"You ever meet Channel's boy friend, Foster Owens.?"

"No. I heard he was the owner of a big time restaurant."

I knew this line of questioning was getting me no where. This woman named Thelma was only interested in one thing. I gave her my card and asked her to give me a call if she should remember anything.

"I'll be glad to give you what ever your heart desires," she said winking at me.

"Thank your for your time," I said ending our conversation. I was getting a little tired of questioning people. I wanted to make an early night of it.

26

I wanted nothing more than to get on with my life and solve Zoe's case and get her out of jail, before her trial date, which was about two weeks from August 15th, the anniversary of the third murder victim. That didn't leave me much time. I prayed for a witness to emerge to put an end to this madness.

I felt powerless, sitting by while Zoe rotted away in jail. She had a hard exterior, but deep down inside, she was a softy. I knew Zoe couldn't survive in jail and that scared me more than anything. I was happy Cedric would be in town in three days to prepare for Zoe's defense.

I was the first to break the silence in the car. "Everee, you find any information, yet?"

"No. Nothing."

"What about that guy you met, get any information from him?"

"He wanted me to take him to my place for a little hanky panky in exchange for the information. Here I'm tryin' to conduct business and he thinks I'm an easy pick up. I told him no thanks, I don't roll like that."

"Mind if I comment?"

"Sure," she responded abruptly.

"When you're with me, you need to be professional and tone down your dress. Most people judge you on how you carry yourself and by the clothes you wear. If you dress like a . . ."

Everee cut me off in the middle of my thoughts. "Go on say it, I ain't ashamed. I'm a hooker! That's what you wanna say."

"I didn't want to offend you in any way."

"Mosee, I know who and what I am. I don't try to hide the fact that I make my living by fucking men." She turned her lips up at me. "I'll try to tone down my dress, but it's hard when I've been dressing like this since I was sixteen-- force of habit."

"When you're conducting business on the streets and you want people to take you seriously, you have to take yourself seriously."

"I get your point."

Neither of us uttered a sound for the rest of the drive back to Ms. Daniels house.

I got out of the car, giving Everee a nonchalant goodbye. She avoided eye contact with me, driving off in a hurry.

Ms. Daniels and Margo were sitting in the dinning room, having Danish and coffee. "Hello, Mosee, you remember Margo, don't you?"

"Yes. How are you, Margo?"

"Fine and you?"

"I just came from Channel Peters funeral today. It was exhausting, but I managed to get some new information that may help Zoe's case."

Ms. Daniels's face sparkled with joy. At that moment, she looked more vibrant and full of life since Zoe's incarceration.

"Praise the Lord," she said clapping her hands. "I pray every night that my daughter will be outta that jail soon enough."

"What did you find, Mosee?"

"We'll discuss it later. I have a call to make now." I phoned Detective Burke's office to ask him for a favor.

"Hello, Mosee, how you doin'? You find out anything at that funeral today?"

Burke was in a good mood for a change, or maybe I was getting used to his temperament. I noticed a sudden change in his mannerism, since we had lunch together. We started talking to each other more like human beings, but there were still moments, when Burke was in rare form. "As a matter of fact, I found out that Channel may have been bisexual. I got a license plate and the model of her alleged lover's car."

"Ain't that a bitch. As pretty as that gal was and she turns out

251

to like women."

"Nothing surprises me anymore in this business. I've seen and heard just about everything you can imagine."

"What's the license plate number?"

"STAR YD4 and the model of the car is a black four door, BMW."

"I'll have one of my men run a check on the car for you, Love."

"Thanks, Burke."

After I got off the telephone with Burke, I stretched out on the bed, contemplating my destiny and Zoe's trial. I sure hoped I could collect enough evidence for her defense.

Burke said he'd called back to give me the owner's name and address of the BMW. I was relieved that I finally had an ally in the police department. I remember the difficulty I had when I started my investigation into Foster's death. I had no help with the Westfield, South Carolina Police Department. I felt a lot of resistance. The cops hated the fact that an outsider knew their job better than they did. Cedric had to be picked up at twelve forty five Saturday at the Westfield International airport. I'm glad to have a familiar face join me.

One hour later, I got a bizarre call from Burke; ordering me to stop my investigation into the murder cases. Direct orders from his superiors.

My mind went blank for a split second. I closed my eyes and opened them to get my equilibrium in balance. "Who the hell do they think they are, anyway? After all the leads I gave you. I'm the one who did all the fucking ...."

"Don't raise your voice at me, boy, who the hell you think your talking to? I'm not your enemy. I'm just following orders. You should understand how the legal system works."

"I'm a grown man, Burke, in case you forgotten."

Burke spoke in a soothing tone, trying to calm me. "I'm sorry, Mosee, I got a lot of pressure on me coming down from my boss.

They think my men are slouching off."

"Well, maybe they have," I said sardonically.

"Mosee I know you're a good cop, but ...."

"Look, Burke, I appreciate your support, but I'm licensed in most states to practice."

"Not in South Carolina, you ain't."

I remained quiet. He had me there. There was nothing I could do. Of the few states I hadn't been licensed in, South Carolina was one.

I knew where he was heading. Burke was trying to use that fact to get me to back off. Burke probably had someone check into my background. Bastard, I thought.

"Originally, I took the case in New York."

"Yes, this is true, but that doesn't give you authorization to practice in this state, Love."

"Oh, we're getting technical now! You weren't technical when I was out there bustin' my ass to help your Department look good!"

I wasn't getting through to Burke, so I slammed the telephone in the middle of the conversation. I was infuriated with the man, for tossing me to the side like garbage. I'm not the type of guy to let things go on without a fight. I was more determined to find the person or persons who killed Zoe's father.

It took me nearly forty-five minutes to calm down. I made up my mind to pay Channel's lover with the black BMW a surprise visit, by the end of the week. I didn't care what the DAs office or Burke's superiors had ordered I would simply have to suffer the consequences later. I had a job to do and that meant taking on risks. This gave me stamina to see this case solved to the end. Cedric could advise me on my rights later.

I had some catching up to do before Cedric arrived on Saturday. My agenda included: visiting Blake and Star on Friday.

Asa Allen-Showell

Visiting Blake would be an opportune time to pump him for more information. I knew that Blake's encounter with Willie T probably still had him shaken up. In addition, I needed to question some of the neighbors of the murder victims to see if they saw or heard anything suspicious. I knew that every neighborhood had its busy bodies; they devoted every spare second to keeping up on other people's business.

I pulled out my laptop, entering all the new information I gathered up to that point. I made some updates on Zoe's case—number #208 missing persons/murder case.

I sat in bed, replaying the tape recorder, listening to the interviews, and reading data and newspaper articles on the three victims. I must've replayed the tape recorder, about five times, looking for patterns in this madness. So far my only conclusion was someone took revenge, but why? I felt strongly that the killings were done by the same person.

I currently had nothing concrete to help Zoe, at this point. I used my contact at the Bureau to get an address on the mystery woman behind the BMW. In an hour Rex returned my call with the name and address of the woman. Her name is Star Reynolds. Rex gave me additional background information about her education and any recent information that may be of importance. I was "off and running to the races," once again. I never let any obstacles stand in my way. I take everything as a challenge and move forward.

27

Everee showed up at Ms. Daniels house on Thursday evening, unexpectedly, to treat me to a night on the town. She thought I need a little entertainment to loosen me up. Me? I didn't think I needed anything but a trip back to New York City.

We jumped into her Mercedes SL convertible. As we drove on I-130, I felt the summer breeze blowing throughout my body. The beauty of the sunset resembled the Caribbean on a warm summer night. Everee's hair blew with the wind, along with the smell of her perfume engulfing my nostrils, causing me to have feelings I'd buried since going to South Carolina.

She drove seventy miles an hour on the highway. I felt a little out of place having a woman chauffeur me around.

"Mosee, what's bothering you? You always full of talk."

"I got some news from Burke today; he told me to stop my investigation on the three murders, said he got orders from his superiors."

Everee was incredulous. "After all the work you done, is he crazy?"

Closing my eyes, I took a deep breath. "I won't let this problem stop me. I take it as a challenge."

I never learned how to relax. I was always busy with my career. I remember telling myself, I'd take a vacation and get away, but something always came up at the Bureau. Perhaps working for myself would give me the flexibility to use my time more wisely.

Fifteen minutes later, we pulled up in front of the Blue Filbert Jazz Cabaret. The inside had three levels. The first level had round tables that overlooked center stage. The main bar was located against the back wall, beside the exist doors. The lights were dimmed to reflect the mirrors on the ceiling.

Everee and I squeezed through the crowd, taking a seat near the front. The band played John Coltrane and a mixture of contemporary jazz sounds. The waitress came over to take our order. I ordered a Fuzzy Navel and Everee ordered her usual Berginer's white wine.

"How you feeling tonight, Mosee?"

"Fine now, really needed this outing."

"You got to learn to relax and have some fun."

"You're right. This case has gotten me so wound up. I feel like I have exhausted every possible angle."

Everee looked into my eyes, taking a sip of her wine. "Don't worry—something will break soon. You have to keep attacking the problem head on."

"I know, but Zoe's trial is two weeks away and I still have nothing concrete."

"What'cha plan on doing now?"

"We can interview some of Channel's neighbors; maybe someone has seen or heard something out of the ordinary."

I tried to block my mind from anything pertaining to the case. I let myself flow with the soothing sounds that the jazz band played. The second drink heightened my awareness of Everee. For the first time, I noticed her caramel skin glowing against the soft lights and her breasts, protruding from under her black lace top. The hip huggers she wore outlined her hour glass figure.

I felt my temperature rise, watching Everee across the table. I saw how beautiful she was for the first time. I thought my mind was playing tricks on me—or did I actual feel some sort of physical attraction toward her?

Everee talked freely about herself and her family. The combination of the alcohol and the music helped us both to relax. "Me and my brother grew up in single family household. My daddy left us when I was ten years old. I haven't seen or heard from him since. My mother put me outta the house cause I refused to obey her rules, when I turned sixteen. I haven't spoken to her since I left home over twenty years ago."

"Have you thought about trying to contact your family?"

"Sometimes I wanna call my mother, but I . . . I don't know, maybe one day, after I quit this business. She'll be glad that I gave it up. You think you outgrow wanting your parents affection, but you never do," she said bowing her head.

In a way, Everee and I were both hurt children, crying out. I felt her pain, too. I had a father whom I wanted to reach out too, but my anger and pride had gotten in the way. I wanted to grab Everee and hold her tight in my arms.

"What about you? You ever think about seeing your father?"

"Sometimes I do. I'm still trying to deal with my mother's death. You can hire me to find your father, Everee. Tracking a person down today is much easier than it was ten years ago."

Everee's face twisted up. "No thank you I don't wanna end up in no jail, like your client."

"I'm one of the best detectives in the business."

"I believe you," she said taking a drink of the white wine. "I thought about finding him, one day."

"What about your mother, you ever talk to her?"

"No. I told you we haven't talked since I started ...."

I placed my hand gently on Everee's lips. "You don't have to say another word, Everee."

I listened attentively to her stories. She opened up for the first time; I felt connected to her because I shared a common pain and hurt from my past.

After Everee confided in me about her family problems, I began to express myself more freely. I told Everee about my problems with my divorce and my two daughters and the reasons I hate my father.

"Mosee you should give your father a call, you have to learn to forgive and forget."

As the band got louder, I leaned over the table, close to Everee, and talked into her ear. "I'll never forget, Everee the past is too painful for me. I understand everybody makes mistakes, but some mistakes are unforgettable." I leaned back in my chair, taking a sip of my Fuzzy Navel. I wanted to call my father and forgive him like my sisters did, but each time I tried to pick up the telephone, visions of my mother's nervous breakdown creep into my mind as if it happened yesterday.

I wondered if I could bond with a stranger, who called himself my father, after twenty-five years of absence. I knew it would be awkward, but making the first step would be the hardest thing to do.

"Family is so important, Mosee, trust me. I don't have one. I have a mother who doesn't want to speak to me and a gay brother who ran off somewhere. You're lucky and don't even know it."

I sighed heavily. "I know, but I still have my problems."

The band took a break, after the first set. The waitress brought a fourth round of drinks. My third drink and counting started to have an effect on me; now I was ready to express my deepest thoughts. The thought of reuniting with my father became a little more appealing. After each drink I consumed, I pondered over what my options were. Maybe I would give him a call when I got back to New York. My sisters Dee and Shelby would be ecstatic to hear I was considering calling our father. I was the only one who had refused to forgive the old man. I had an obligation to my mother's memory to keep my father out of my life, but I have two daughters, Jewell and Tiffany, who have a right to know who their grandfather is. I owed them that courtesy. I hated bringing my children into the middle of a family feud.

I felt that being together with Everee, in a relaxing atmosphere, had made me see her in a different light. I started having feelings that I had tried to suppress since I met her.

Vicious Karma

I had my share of relationships every now and then, but nothing of substance and quality. I had a hard time meeting women who have something to offer. It seemed that everybody was out for themselves. Nobody took the time to know each other. I hated short-term relationships. Work and my children were the only therapy for the resulting loneliness. I'm the kind of man who believes in commitment. Having pressing issues on my mind made me vulnerable to women.

We talked until the band played its last set. The owner had to throw us out. We finally made our way toward the front door. Everee looked at me with glassy eyes, trying to maintain her composure. I grabbed her waist, tightly pressing against her body. I felt myself melt in her arms. Then, thinking better of it, I pulled away from Everee's embrace. "I think its best that we go home now."

"Fine, Mosee, you're really gentlemen. I haven't met anyone quite like you in a long time."

I climbed into the car, remaining my code of silence on the drive to Ms. Daniels's house. "Everee, can I ask you a favor?"

"Sure anything for you," she said smiling.

"I need you to visit Star Reynolds."

"Who is Star Reynolds?" she asked.

"At the funeral, Channel's uncle told me that his niece was a bisexual."

Everee's eyes bulged from her head. She shouted, "Are you nuts? I ain't gonna see no lesbian! I'll do anything, else, but that's asking a bit much too much, Mosee, come on now."

"If I go, she'll resist me, cause I'm a man. This situation is very touchy. If Channel did leave Star for Foster, that means, she has a stronger hatred for men."

Everee rolled her eyes, looking straight ahead at the road. "I'll go for you, Mosee, but just this one time. I don't need a lesbian

Asa Allen-Showell

looking down my throat.

28

Everee drove to the townhouse, condominium complex on Roosevelt Blvd., located in a middle class neighborhood. She drove through the development, searching for 616 Meadow Court. The development has three sections divided into different courts.

Finally, after fifteen minutes of driving, Everee stumbled across Meadow Court accidentally. She parked her car next to the black BMW. She checked herself over thoroughly, before getting out of the car.

She had dressed in a pair of white linen pants and cotton black Donna Karen jacket with a silk tee-shirt.

She took a note pad and pen in case she needed to write anything down that was important.

At the door, she waited for five minutes. Everee saw a shadow walk in the house through the curtains. A stocky woman with a male hair cut came to the door, in cut-off jean shorts and a white tee shirt. Everee could tell from the outline of the upper body and legs that she visited the gym on a regular basis. Her clear complexion radiated a healthy glow. She wore little makeup. Everee could tell Star was an attractive woman who tried to hide behind her lesbian male role. Her face had a softness to it that was feminine.

"Hello, my name is Everee Johnson; I'm here to ask you some questions about Channel Peters."

Star Reynolds mouth hung open for a few minutes. She had a dazed look in her eyes.

"Ms. Star, are you alright?"

"Yeah, I'm just a little shaken up when you mentioned Channel's name. It's just been two days since she was buried. Who are you, anyway?" she frowned.

"I'm Everee Johnson. I work for Mr. Mosee Love. He's a private investigator from New York who's working on the murder cases of Foster Owens, Iris Hall and Channel Peters." she said standing outside the door. "He believes the three murders are connected in some way."

"The police have already been here to question me about Channel, I'm not up to rehashing the same questions over again," Star said moving to close the door.

Everee blocked Star from closing the door. "Wait a minute," she cried, taking Mosee's ID from her pocketbook. "Here's proof of what I just said," she said handing her the photo ID.

Star took a couple of minutes to examine the ID. "Where's your ID? This says Investigator Mosee Love, not Everee Johnson. You think I'm some kind of an idiot?"

"I don't have my identification card; I was hired recently and ...."

"Alright I'll take your word, Ms. Johnson. Come on in honey," Star smiled. Everee followed Star into the townhouse. The cathedral ceiling had a sunroof at the top. The sunken living room was a few feet from the front door. The house was immaculate.

"You have a nice place here, Ms. Reynolds."

"Please call me Star."

Everee wanted to keep it professional, but she remembered Mosee told her a trick to investigation. You have to make the person feel like you're on the same level. Be a friend to them, that's how you get information. She smiled, "Star, please call me Everee."

"Please have a seat," Star said pointing to the love seat in the corner of the room.

The living room was filled with all kinds of exotic plants. It gave the room a fresh look.

Everee felt herself shaking uncontrollably. She couldn't figure out if Star's smile was sincere or if she had eyes for her. She felt a lump in her throat and her skin was getting clammy. She pulled off her Donna Karen jacket and placed it on the chair. Her stomach tightened in a ball. She prayed that this would be a quick interview.

Star smiled. "What questions can I answer for you, Everee?" You wanna know if I killed Foster and Channel, which one is it?" she asked insincerely. "That's why you're here, right?"

"Part of the reason, but I need to know about your relationship with Channel."

"I loved her and she broke my heart, 'cause of that bastard Foster she left me for," she sneered. "Now she's dead." Star lowered her head. "I told Channel that the man is wicked and evil. He was nothing but a womanizer. He treated women like a piece of his personal property. If she hadn't broken off our relationship, Channel would be alive today."

Everee tired to remember the questions Mosee had gone over with her the night before. "I wanna ask you another question." Everee wasn't good at this interview stuff, it made her feel awkward, and this one was her first live interview. "What are your feelings about Foster?"

"I hated the son of a bitch if that's what you wanna know. If I could have killed him and gotten away with it, I would have no problems. He broke up my relationship with the woman I loved."

Everee wanted to vomit when she heard those words.

"Okay, Star," she said, taking a deep breath. "You wanted to kill Foster, right?"

"Yeah. That's right," Star said with a cocky attitude. "Haven't you ever wanted to kill some one in your mind?"

Mosee told her to rephrase any questions that made the interviewee defensive and to watch out for role reversal. In addition, don't let them put you on the spot.

"Sure, Star, everybody has those thoughts at one time, but that's what separates those who do commit a crime and those

Who just think about it." She spoke in a confident tone, with her posture at attention; she spoke with clear diction. She felt sure of herself for once.

Everee had always doubted her abilities. Working with Mosee Love had given her a new perspective on life. When Mosee had first called her for her assistance with the case, she had been unsure of her abilities. She felt like she wanted to take on the world now.

"Yes, but that doesn't make me a murderer." "When Channel left you for Foster, how did that make you feel?"

"I was angry and hurt. I wanted to kill his Black ass, but I'm not a violent person." The ceiling light reflected the dark circles around her eyes. Everee thought they probably came as a result of getting little sleep and too many tears from Channel's tragic death.

"Did you and Channel always get along?" "We had our share of ups and downs. If you wanna know if we argued; the answer is yes." "Did the two of you ever get violent with each other?" Stars eyes darted across the room, avoiding eye contact with

Everee. Mosee's words of advice popped into her head. "Remember, Everee watch the persons body movement and gestures." When Channel left you for Foster, did you argue or get into any kind of altercation?"

"I'm not going to lie. Yes, we did have a heated battle that went on for two weeks before we broke up." "Didn't that make you want to seek revenge on either Foster or Channel?" Everee noticed Star squirming in her seat. "I thought about getting revenge, but I knew that wouldn't help solve anything." Star sat slouching on the sofa. "Anything else you wanna know?" "Did Channel have any enemies?"

"Enemies, hum. I don't know about any enemies she might have had."

have had."

"Slow down a little Star, I'm tryin' to take down all the information down." Everee felt like a piece of meat, with Star's eyes watching. She took a deep breath and exhaled. "Just a few more questions Star. Where were you on May 25th between the hours of ten and twelve midnight?"

"I was working late that night."

"Where do you work?"

"I work for IBM."

"Really? What do you do there?" Everee asked.

"I'm a Systems Analyst. I was working on a project that night; I must've stayed until eleven-thirty."

Everee nodded her head. "I'll be going now, Star thanks for your time," she said rising from her seat.

"Would you like to stay for dinner?"

Everee felt a knot in her stomach. She tried to force a fake smile on her face. "No, thank you I have a ton of work waiting for me at the office."

Star escorted Everee out the front door. As she walked to her car, Everee felt eyes watching her the entire time. After leaving Star Reynolds's house, the only thing on her mind was a good shower to wash off the filth.

It was Friday evening on a mild summer evening. I was glad I had listened to my conscious and wore a pair of black Dockers and a pull over cotton beige shirt. I didn't want to dress in a suit because this wasn't my first time meeting Blake. When he opened the door and saw my face he tried to slam the door. I blocked it. "Hey, Blake, wait! I need to ask you a few more questions."

"I've already answered enough of your questions, you can draw your own conclusions from my little meeting with that character Willie T," Blake said in a nasty tone. "I have my rights, you know."

"I tried to think of something to pacify him, by appealing to his ego. "I understand your rights, but I'm trying to save the life of a young Black woman, who's been falsely accused of killing her father, and I need your help, Blake," I begged.

Those words must've hit a soft spot in Blake. His whole demeanor changed when I asked him to help me. One thing I learned from working with the Bureau is how to appeal to a persons emotions to get them to respond to what you want.

"Sure come on in, Mr. Love, I'll try to help you if I can."

I stepped into the house, thinking about how I was going to phrase my questions.

"I'm not going to jail just to save somebody. I believe in doing what I can. All you had to do was ask for my help, you didn't need that gold-toothed nigger treating me like some animal."

"I apologize for his behavior. I didn't know how far he would go. I take full blame, Mr. Reed."

"I'm a church going man, so I'll forgive and forget this time."

I followed Blake to the far back of the house. "I had no idea Willie was going to do those things to you." The back room looked like an added extension of the house. It was a large room, and contained a wide screen television set and a stereo set that looked like it cost his two month's teacher salary.

I sat on the country style sofa, feeling my skin stick to the plastic seat covers. It wasn't too extravagant There was a book collection that covered the entire length of the back wall.

"Well, what questions do you care to ask me, I already haven't answered?"

"You said Foster owed you a large sum of money."

"That's right, he did."

"I don't understand why you didn't take him to court."

"I didn't feel like being bothered with the legal system, besides I had nothing on paper to prove I gave him money. All we had was a verbal agreement."

"Did you have any plans for revenge?"

Blake paused for a moment, before answering my question. "You ain't gonna use this information against me, is you?"

"No, Blake, you have my word." "The thought did cross my mind," he said shrugging his shoulders," "You ever think about carrying your plans out?" "I went over ways to get him back, but killing him never entered my mind."

I watched Blake become fidgety in his seat. I watched the sweat drip from his forehead. I rephrased the question a second time. "You ever have plans on murdering Foster?"

"Ah … sort kinda, but …." "Blake, answer the question please." Blake inhaled, as if he was on the witness stand. "Yes . . . kinda, but I didn't kill him, I swear. The only thing I tried was hiring somebody to scare him a little, but that was one time." "What happened when you hired this person and when did it take place?"

"Last October." I took out my note writing down Blake's statement.

"You have an alibi on the date of the murder—May 25th between the hours of 11:00 and 12:30 midnight?" Blake was quiet for a few seconds. As if he was carefully considering his answer. "I was home, by myself on that night." "Did you make any telephone calls between those hours?" "Yeah . . . I think I did. Oh, now I remember I did make a phone call to a friend of mine, in Augusta Georgia. We talked at least two hours," he said with a sign of relief on his face.

"You have any copies of your telephone bill dated that day?" "I'll go check in my back bedroom." Blake rose from his

seat heading to the back bedroom. Find anything, Blake?" "No. I'm afraid I can't find nothin'," he said shaking. "You

gonna bring me in as a suspect?"

"No, Blake, but you are listed in my book as one because you can't prove your whereabouts on May 25th and you have a strong motive."

Blake sat down in the chair, looking flustered, with his shoulders slouched over. He bowed his head in shame. "I didn't kill Foster and you can't prove nothin'!" he shouted raising his voice. "I want you out of my house!" He got up from his chair. He stood by the door, holding it open, waiting for me to walk out the door.

I rose slowly, walking toward the door. Blake slammed the door behind me.

Blake yelled out the living room window, "I'm gonna get me a lawyer, you hear. You can't put nothin' on me!"

29

After Everee completed her investigation with Star Reynolds, she drove to the Marriott lounge to meet me for dinner. She arrived twenty minutes early. She ordered a glass of white wine and waited.

She was nursing her second drink, when she looked up and saw me. Her soft brown eyes and caramel skin glowed with a radiant shine. "What took you so long, Mosee? I was beginning to think you stood me up."

"No, I'm fine. My interview took longer than I expected. Blake tried to give me a hard time, about letting me speak to him. I convinced him after ten minutes of negotiation to let me interview him again. How did your interview go?" I asked.

"Good. I really surprised myself. I handled the interview well," she beamed. "I can really get use to this kind of work, you know. I think its fun."

"It's not a game, Everee. Investigation work can be dangerous at times, especially when folks start shooting at you. Look at what happened to me, Johnson tried to kill me. Instead he gave me a concussion. It's times like this I wish I could choose another career."

The waitress came over to the table to take our dinner orders. "Are you ready to order now?"

"No, but I'll take a vodka and cranberry cocktail, before we order." The waitress headed to the bar, picking up our drinks, returning to the table.

"I'll take the Fried Shrimp platter with a side order of French fries," Everee said.

"And I'll take the Prime Rib with a baked potato and a salad." I said, "My treat tonight, Everee."

"Thanks, that's mighty kind of you."

I took a sip of my Vodka and cranberry drink. "Tell me all about your interview."

"Star told me she was working at IBM on a project the night Channel was murdered. She also told me she ain't kill Channel or Foster, but the thought of killing Foster did enter her mind.

"You did a good job, Everee; I told you could do anything if you put your mind to it."

Everee smiled, "You're right, I haven't felt this good about anything in a long time. Anyway how did your interview go with Blake?"

"He denied everything again, as usual. He didn't have an alibi on the night Foster's was murdered. He claimed to be talking to a friend long distance. He couldn't produce a telephone bill to prove he was home either." I took another sip of my drink. "I'm gonna keep an eye on him."

The waitress brought over a tray of food.

"I'm famished, Everee, I haven't eaten a thing since lunch time."

"Here you are, I hope you enjoy your meals," the waitress said placing the food on the table. "Is there anything else I can get you?"

"No, we're fine. Thank you."

"Hum, the Fried Shrimp is nice and tender. How's your Prime Rib?" Everee's head was submerged in her plate. She looked up with a look of contentment written all over her face. "This is the best food I've tasted. The portions are just right. You think Zoe's gonna be convicted?"

I had a blank look on my face. "Everee I can't really say. I haven't made a dent in this investigation since I started. I thought this was going to be an easy case. I find her father and they live happily ever after and I return to New York. But unfortunately the real world doesn't work like that. One thing about this business, nothing is black and white. You don't get instruction manuals when your plans go haywire. You have to "go with the punches".

"What about The Rev and his wife?"

"She was home with her sister."

"People lie, Mosee. You can't believe what she tells you."

"I have to put pressure on them. It seems like people break under stress."

"I hope she's gettin' outta jail soon. That ain't no place for nobody; believe me I had to do some time for prostitution. They put me in jail for one month. I thought I was gonna lose my mind in that place. It does something to you, being locked up. I've seen the nicest people go in for misdemeanors come out the worst people. I don't wanna scare you, but Zoe's at great risk if she's not out soon," she said shaking her head. "It's a shame, the girl wanted to see her father after twenty something years. She finds him and he ends up dead three days later. Ain't that something for luck?"

Everee looked at me in silence. "How many suspects you got now?"

"Blake, the Rev. and Star could possibly be a suspect, but it depends on if she was actually at work on May 25th."

At the end of our meal, a man dressed in a gray business suit walked up to the table. "Hello, Everee, how are you," he said bending over to kiss her cheek.

Everee had a surprised look on her face. "Malcolm, how you doing? I ..."

"Where you been woman? I have been calling you for the past month you never return my calls."

"I been busy with my new job," Everee said holding her head up proudly. "This here is my friend and boss, Mosee Love. He's a private detective from New York City."

Malcolm looked at me with contempt. He reached out to shake my hand. "It's a pleasure to meet you." He looked back at Everee continuing his conversation. "You have someone new now.

I see you don't need me. You found yourself a better stud, he said walking away."

"That arrogant son of a bitch. , swear I wanted to beat the shit out of him for disrespecting you. He didn't know if I was your man or what," I said, steaming.

"It's alright, Mosee, he's one of my regular clients. He's a little full of himself sometimes."

"You want dessert?"

"No. I'm stuffed. Can't eat or drink another thing," she said holding her head. "I feel light headed now."

"I'm feeling those four drinks, myself. I hope I can make it home tonight."

We sat by the pool side in lounge chairs. I felt myself sweating, looking at Everee's beauty under the moonlight.

"Mosee, you never said why you left the FBI."

"I had some bad experiences. They started one incident at a time, but I let things go because of my ego. One thing that made me upset about being a Federal employee for the FBI was being transferred from one city to another. The second reason is I never got the promotions I deserved. Disguised racism is prevalent.

"My final decision to resign occurred when I was given an assignment with another agent and myself. We infiltrated this Black organization called the Black United Front. We were told they had guns and weapons to destroy the government."

Everee moved in closer placing her hand on my shoulders. "You don't have to talk about it no more."

"I'm fine, Everee. It's an image that never leaves you." I continued my story, talking slowly. "My partner and I joined the Black United Front in order to collect evidence for prosecution. The Government planted false evidence to destroy the organization. We were used as suckers. It turned out the BUF wasn't planning a conspiracy; in fact, they were helping the Black community in many ways, by doing job training and other programs to help empower Black people. They were so successful

Vicious Karma

that there were other branches of the BUF opening in other cities.

Eventually, pressure came down on the leader and he committed suicide. I let my pride get in the way of my judgment."

Everee hugged me, pressing her head into my chest. "I'm sorry, Mosee. You okay, honey?"

I snapped out of the brief depression when Everee asked me to take a dip in the pool. "We don't have swim suits."

"You heard of skinny dipping?"

"Naked? People might see us."

"Mosee I don't think I can make it home tonight, my head is spinning. I had one too many drinks this evening," she said leaning on my shoulder. "I was hoping you could do the driving."

"I feel exhausted and too drunk to drive myself. We might as well get a room here tonight. It's best that we play it safe tonight."

30

We talked by the poolside for about an hour, before we checked in at the front desk.

Everee fell on the bed, looking up at the ceiling, while I was immobilized, lying next to her. Being alone with her for the first time made me feel inadequate.

"I wouldn't mind goin' skinny dippin,'" Everee said, slurring her words.

"You still talking about that nonsense, huh?"

"Yeah. I think it's a good idea and it's daring. That's the problem with you, you need to loosen up and have some fun."

"Next time when I'm not so drunk, I might reconsider."

My eyes were fixed on Everee when she started taking off her clothes, without any thought or hesitation about my presence in the same room. She had no inhabitation showing her body. Everee had legs that looked like they belonged to a graceful dancer and her stomach was flat, as a wash board. I wanted to feel myself inside her. One of her favorite recreational sports was roller balding. She told me she skates at least three times a week. Along with exercise, she adheres to a strict diet; she believes that staying in shape helps her to keep up with the competition.

"Everee, please put on a towel or something," I said slurring my words.

I closed my eyes for a brief second. My concentration was broken, when Everee climbed on top of me, unbuttoning my shirt. I didn't try to fight back the feeling or what was happening between us. I let myself enjoy the moment while it lasted. I helped Everee along, by pulling off my pants. I kissed the back of her neck, down to her lower spine.

I lifted her on top of me, caressing her gently, kissing her nipples. I felt myself move inside her, our rhythms in complete harmony. We both were exhausted toward the early a.m.

31

I woke up at ten in the morning, the following day. I looked over at Everee, watching her sleep peacefully. I noticed how beautiful she was, even in her sleep.

Before taking a shower, I ordered breakfast for two from room service. I wondered if it was a good idea sleeping with Everee last night. I hated leading women on; I believed in honesty. One thing I could say, my conscious never haunted me about treating women badly. Growing up in a house full of women taught me to respect women.

My first attempt at disrespect occurred when I tried to string two girls along at the same time. I was on the telephone, when my Aunt over heard me talking to one of my girlfriends and Shawnee came over to visit me unannounced. I wanted to get rid of her anyway. My aunt let her in for soda and cake. They talked briefly. The next thing I knew, my aunt busted into my room standing in the middle of the floor with her arms folded, giving me a stern look. My aunt had a way of intimidating you with her looks. I glanced over at her and continued talking to my number one girlfriend.

"Mo, you have company downstairs, you gonna come down here!"

"Yeah, in a minute." I didn't wanna ask who was downstairs, when I already knew. "Tell her I'm not home, please." Why did I tell my aunt to lie for me. Her face contorted in all kinds of shapes. She snatched the telephone away and gave me one of her lectures.

She sat down next to me on the bed. "Look, you getting to be a man now, and sometimes your hormones are getting a little crazy, but that's what we all have to deal with growing up, son," she said placing her hand on my shoulder. One thing I don't believe in is lying to people. Now I watch everything, even when you think I'm sleeping. I know you seeing two girls and that's normal for boys and girls to have more than one boyfriend and girlfriend, but you have to be honest about what you say to people, especially women. I raised you better than that. If you don't wanna see Shawnee no more, you march down stairs and tell her, instead of hiding up here in the bedroom." At that moment, I knew I only had one option.

Shawnee was seated in the kitchen, waiting patiently for me. She gave me a big hug. My stomach got tighter standing there, trying to search for the words to tell this girl to get lost, scram. I knew I had to be a gentleman and tell her the truth, or I had consequences to face. The only image I had on my mind was my aunt wipin' my ass, cause I refused to be honest with Shawnee. I learned about being a man the hard way. Being the only male in a house full of women left me to learn the ropes myself. My aunt was up stairs, listening to my conversation, holding a thick leather black belt in her right hand. I sat down and took a deep breath, looking Shawnee in the face.

"Shawnee, I have something to tell you."

"Tell me what?"

I closed my eyes, trying to concentrate. "I don't wanna see you no more." I said taking a deep breath. "I'm dating someone else now." I sat there for a minute feeling numb and stupid. I was waiting for her to hit me with a frying pan or some thing.

"Mosee, are you okay? You look a little red."

"I'm fine. What about you?"

"I'm okay, I'm a little hurt that you don't wanna see me no more, but at least you're honest," she said with a half smile on her face. "Can we still be friends? I like coming over and talking to your aunt."

"Sure you can come over anytime, Shawnee. We still cool."

We talked for about forty-five minutes. After Shawnee left, I felt good about telling her the truth. I learned a lot from my aunt about being honest to women.

Whenever I find it hard to be honest in a relationship that I'm in, I always remember the incident I had with Shawnee. I wandered if it was a good idea sleeping with Everee the night before. I didn't wanna lead her on in anyway. I feared what she might read into this brief encounter. I would talk things over with her when she woke up.

Being on the case for three months and not having a steady woman had made me weak. I had to separate reality from fantasy. Being with a woman like Everee for a life time was not something I had considered. For one, she was a professional hooker, and two, she had too much emotional baggage. One thing I didn't have time for at this point in my life was trying to mend somebody's life together. I had my own set of problems to deal with.

Room service knocked on the door, and I was still dripping wet.

"One minute, please," I called, grabbing a towel. I opened the door and let the young man in. After I took the tray of food, the room service guy stood next to the door, looking silly. I realized I hadn't given him his tip; I retrieved a five dollar bill from my pants pocket that laid over the arm chair. I handed it to the boy.

"Thank you, sir."

I smiled. I felt generous after the night before. It had been a true tension releaser. Now I was ready to take Zoe's case on full force.

Good sex always made me feel like I could take on any challenge. I thought about all the things I could accomplish if I had a woman living with me.

"Sleeping beauty finally wakes up."

"How long you been up?"

"Since ten this morning, I'm an early riser."

"I'll say. My head's still throbbing from last night," she said rubbing her head. "Can you get me a couple of aspirins from my purse?"

I rolled the tray of food by the round table next to the window. "Here's something that should help your headache."

She smiled. "What did I do to deserve to get breakfast in bed?"

I gave her a sheepish grin. "You're a deserving person." I served Everee her food in bed and I sat at the oval table by the window. "I hope you like what I ordered. I figure you can't go wrong with pancakes, eggs and beef sausages and a side order of toast and coffee."

"That's fine."

I didn't want to be the first to bring up what had happened the previous night. I ate my food in silence trying to anticipate what she was going to say. Maybe it's best to let things go unsaid. "Everee, I have to meet Cedric at the airport today at 12:45P.M."

"That's fine. I can catch up with you later," she said, sipping her coffee.

32

Cedric stepped off the plane wearing a brown linen suit, carrying an attaché case and an Yves Saint-Laurent carry on luggage. Whenever you looked at Cedric, you could tell he was a man of distinction. He believed that appearance is important in how you feel about yourself.

As we gave each other a friendly hug, people had questioning looks in their eyes, probably wondering if we were gay. But Cedric and I go back to so far, we're not afraid to express our affection openly with each other.

After giving Cedric a hug, I smiled. "Thanks, it's good to see a familiar face. I feel isolated sometimes. I have no one here I know except Zoe's mother, Everee, and a character named Willie T"

"I haven't seen you for three months, since you took Zoe's case. You don't know how to call anybody? Dee's been calling my house every week. She thought you were having a breakdown or something. She nearly drove me insane trying to figure out what you were up to. I don't know how you stomach her sometimes."

"I know I've been a little depressed lately about money and Joyce, but I'm not suicidal. She means well, but she over reacts. Dee thinks she has an obligation to look after my best interests, because she's older than me." I laughed. "You know me better than that. I get a little depressed sometimes but nothing I can't handle."

We talked briefly about Zoe's upcoming trial on the way to baggage claims. "Cedric I don't know if we can win this case," I said shaking my head. "I don't have a solid shred of evidence for her defense."

Cedric pats my shoulder. "That's why we lawyers are hired, to create doubt in the jurors' minds. I can take it from here."

"You're too cocky, Cedric."

"We have to think positive about winning this case."

I looked at Cedric with the word doubt written all over my face. In my heart, I believed that Zoe was going to be convicted of murdering her father. All hope had left me during these past three months. I began thinking my investigating abilities were becoming stale. It had been over five years since I did any real crime solving. There was a time I remembered being on top of my career. I was long overdue for being recognized for my outstanding service with the FBI. I was one of the top men in the field of investigations, but that was past tense.

I had a gut feeling that the murderer was closer than I thought, watching and waiting for me to make my next move.

"Here's my luggage." Cedric grabbed two of his bags. "You can help a brother, if you like. I know physical work is not your style." We both laughed. "I'm trying to help take your mind off this case, Mosee."

"My car's parked on the third level parking lot G."

"You drove that piece of car to Westfield? How'cha make it?"

"What are you trying to say?"

Well, that's a long drive, and I know you've been having car trouble, lately."

"This car is dependable. Besides, I used some of the deposit money Zoe gave me to give my car a make over. I had this car for over ten years. Yes, she gives me problems sometimes, but it beats having a car payment and high insurance premiums. I don't have money to spend, like you.

"I don't always have money, like you think. I have bills, too."

"You have any hotels in mind you would like to stay?"

Cedric shook his head. "No not really. I trust your judgment."

"There's a major strip, not too far from here, that has hotels rated in the top ten percent."

"I prefer to be centrally located in the city. That'll give me easy access to everything I need. You been to any hotspots down here?"

"Yeah, a few. There's one place called The Oasis Jazz Café. It reminds you of something outta the village in New York. The people dress in Afro centric clothing. It's like a hip hop jazz/poetry club.

Cedric nodded, "Sounds good to me, didn't think a place like Westfield, South Carolina, had any real entertainment. You meet any women since you been here?"

"I met a few women."

"You haven't had a woman since you left home?"

"That's all you think about, that's your problem, man."

"Please don't play that sanctimonious bullshit with me. You're a man and so am I. We both have needs, so spare me the preachin'. I like beautiful women and so do you. So what's happening with Zoe's case, so far? Can you handle that question?" he said chiding.

"I have suspects, like I told you. Star Reynolds who was a former lover of Channel Peters. It turns out Channel was bisexual. And Blake Reed to whom Foster was indebted; Foster owed Blake twenty grand. And a fella named Agee Johnson whose woman was taken by Foster. Shortly, thereafter, he was fired. These are my best and only possible suspects right now."

"What the hell you been doin' the past three months?"

'I've been workin' my ass off. Don't venture into territory you know nothing about. Criminal investigation takes time. You should stick to the law."

"I was just asking you a question. I don't know what's eating you."

"I have things on my mind."

"Like what, Mosee?"

"We'll talk later on. I'll be there to take you where you need to go," I said opening the trunk of my car. I placed Cedric's bags in the back seat.

"I know, but you might be busy. I need to depend on myself, in case I have some research to do."

I drove about thirty-five minutes to the city to check Cedric into the Holiday Inn in the downtown business district of Westfield, South, Carolina.

The business district wasn't much, but a fifty block radius of small barbershop, beauty saloons and a library and a one stop shop of your government offices, welfare assistant and a court house and all the conveniences of modern home, not to mention your local restaurants and a few bars.

33

After Cedric checked into the Holiday Inn, we stopped in the hotel restaurant to have lunch and discuss Zoe's upcoming trial. Cedric came prepared carrying his leather folder and gold felt writing pen.

The hostess sat us in a booth on the south side of the restaurant. She handed us two menus.

Cedric drilled me about the details of my investigation. "Mosee, let's start with the suspects you have so far."

"There's Blake Reed, and Agee Johnson. Reed and Johnson have air-tight alibis, but I don't trust their alibis.

"That doesn't mean nothing, people lie for each other. I can always find gaps and holes in peoples stories," Cedric said writing down the information.

Cedric sounded angry. "That's it? That's all you have from three months of investigation? What'cha been doing, sleep walking?"

"Oh, I forgot to mention Star Reynolds, she was Channel's lover, before she left Star for Foster."

"Tell me about each suspect's motive and how it relates to Foster's murder."

"Blake is a middle-aged retired business man, who loaned Foster twenty grand; he never saw a dime of his money. Johnson is a former employee of Foster. Foster took his girlfriend and fired the man. Star Reynolds was Channel's lover. She might have a jealous motive. You know the scorn lover with the broken heart. And Reverend Elder's wife, Emma Jean Elders, had an affair with Foster in the church. His marriage was ruined by her illicit affair. He probably blames Foster for destroying his marriage."

"Now we're talking, Mosee, I was afraid you lost your touch for a second

"When Rev Elders caught Foster and his wife in bed together in his house, he pulled a gun out on Foster and his wife. He claimed he was working with his secretary at the church the night Foster was killed."

Cedric took notes carefully, asking the same questions over again, but in a different ways. He also had his tape recorder, to pick up anything he might miss. "Your saying the Rev, has a strong motive?"

I shook my head. "One thing disturbed me about Rev Elders; he seemed too calm for a man who recently caught his wife in bed with another man. He doesn't seem to have any emotions at all. The Rev told me he's over his wife, but I have my doubts."

"I find it strange that a man who catches his wife cheatin, in their bedroom, shows no pain. If that was me, it would've been some bloodshed. When I interviewed Rev Elders, he appeared oblivious to what had happened.

"How long were they married?"

"I say about twenty to thirty years."

Cedric put his head down continuing to write on his tablet. "A man doesn't get over his wife over night, fifteen years of marriage invested. Plus, his reputation is on the line as a preacher in his church. Folks will start to look at him differently. They might think that a man who can't keep his home life together can't keep his church in order. It's sounds hypocritical, but people are judgmental about everything, especially church folks. They'll condemn you in a minute."

I shook my head in agreement. "I didn't look at it that way."

The waitress came over with the food, placing it on the table. I ordered a corn beef special, and Cedric ordered a turkey club with a side order of fries.

"Thank you," Cedric said, smiling at the waitress.

The waitress couldn't take her eyes off Cedric. She probably thought Cedric had money. He dressed in the best of clothes, and he's good looking. Cedric had no problem attracting women of all kinds. In high school, Cedric had so many girls; he occasionally tried to pass some of his girls on to me. Cedric always saw himself as a ladies man, a trait he adopted from being raised in a single parent male household.

"She hasn't taken her eyes off you since we came in here. You always get the women. They're drawn to you like a magnet," I said somewhat envious.

"You're not jealous are you?"

"No. Of course not," I said taking a bite of my Corn beef Special.

"Okay, now there is four possible suspect who have strong motives based on jealously and financial debt. "All hope is not lost," he smiled.

Cedric pushed his notebook and tape recorder to the side, to start eating his meal. "You have any evidence on these four people?"

"No. I already told you that."

"What about any witnesses?"

"None."

Cedric continued to eat his Turkey Club sandwich, in-between taking notes.

"You have any of the police reports?"

"No. Detective Burke ordered me to stop my investigation by his superiors."

We talked in detail, going over everything a second time. "Mosee, I need to visit Zoe sometime tomorrow around twelve noon. I like to hear her version the night of her father's murder."

"Sunday is no problem; I don't have anything planned on my agenda. My job has no set schedule. I work anytime of the day or night."

"Okay, pick me up around eleven in the morning. I like to start early."

Cedric went back to his hotel room to unpack and get himself organized. I returned to Ms. Daniels' house, around 3P.M. I had time on my hands, something I wasn't used to. My mind raced in a million directions contemplating my next move. I found it hard to relax whenever I had a pressuring case ahead of me. I sometimes equate having too much time on my hands with not doing my job."

When I got back to Ms. Daniels' I'd let myself relax until tomorrow. I hated wasting time, so I used my free time to catch up on old family business. My family worried about me, they haven't heard from me in over three weeks. It was going on three months since I had seen or spoken to my daughters and sisters. I was long over due for my sister Dee's once a month Sunday dinners. I hoped Zoe would have an expedient trial and that she would be found not guilty, and everyone would live happily ever after. I knew that wasn't reality.

34

I received two telephone calls that day, one from Detective Burke, and the other from Everee. I refused to call Detective Burke back. I wasn't in the mood for any more depressing news. Instead, I called my sister Dee who was overdue for a phone call and my children, Tiffany and Jewell.

My sister Dee rambled on for over an hour, giving me the latest update drama on everyone's life. "Mo, you'll never guess what great transformation took place while you were gone. Shelby, your baby sister, found a man. I had them over for dinner. I can't believe she picked someone who's the complete opposite of her. He's funny, down to earth and pleasant. And to top it off, he's the owner and operator of a plumbing business," she said excitedly." Can you imagine that, Shelby and a dirty hands man," Dee said laughing.

"Maybe that's what she's missing. I'm glad she found somebody. Shelby can be one evil woman, always on the defensive about everything. I was beginning to wonder if she had an interest in men at all."

"Okay, I told you about everybody, so what's happening with you and your investigation? You've been in Westfield for three months, now don't you think it's time to call it quits?"

"Dee, I can't leave now, I'm in way too deep. The case has gotten more complicated since I last spoke to you."

"How's that possible, Mo? You found the girl's father, right? You did your job."

"Yes. That's true, but her father's dead now and she's been charged for his murder. Now there's two other murders in two months that might be connected to her father's death. If I find

out the killers of the other two murders, then I can find the person who killed Zoe's father."

"Your problem is you don't know when to say 'no.' your job was to help her find her father: dead or alive, right?"

I hate it when Dee gets too preachy. She still carried that older sibling syndrome. Dee occasionally forgets that I am a grown man who can make my own decisions. "Mo, technically your job is done down there. You can come home anytime, but no, no, you have to always take on more than you can handle."

I knew Dee was right, even though, I hated to admit it. I knew after I found Zoe's father I was done with the case. I thought I had made myself an easy ten grand, but things got a little out of hand. For one, I felt responsible for what had happened to Zoe.

"Why do you think the other two killings are connected?"

"I discovered each murder took place on the fifteenth of each month."

"And?" Dee said with an attitude.

"That means that the fifteenth has a special meaning for the killer. It's like an anniversary date or something."

"That's interesting, Mo, you always could come up with the strangest things. How's the girl doin'?"

"Zoe's still in jail, awaiting trial. Cedric is going to represent her."

"You been down there for three months and you still ain't solved nothing. Let the police do their work."

"I'm getting closer each day, Dee. Some murder cases go unsolved for years. I miss you, Dee, kiss the girls for me."

I was overcome by feelings of nostalgia when I ended my conversion with Dee. I longed to be in familiar surroundings with my family and friends. I made one final call to Joyce; dialing her number made my fingers cramp. I hoped she wasn't in a confrontational mood.

"Hello, Joyce, it's me, Mo."

"Oh, hello, Mosee, I thought you changed your identity and started a new life."

Vicious Karma

For some reason my ex and I couldn't have a decent conversation for five minutes, without one of us getting sarcastic."

I took a deep breath and inhaled, counting to ten. "Joyce, I'm still here." I was going to remain pleasant to my ex-wife even if it killed me. "How're my daughters, doin' Joyce?"

"You mean our daughters. They're fine, Mo. They'll be starting school in a few more weeks. I am going to need extra money to cover additional expenses.

"Joyce, I recently gave you four thousand dollars for child support and any other expenses that might come up. Remember I'm paid up in child support, in case you've forgotten.

You couldn't have spent the money I gave you that quickly.

"Didn't you get paid for the last case you took?" she asked.

"Joyce, I'm down to my last dollar."

"You never have no damn money. Didn't you get an advance from that case?"

"I did, but I spent most of if on my expenses. My client is in jail and she hasn't paid me any additional monies, Can I please speak to them?" After I asked that question, there was silence on the other end. I waited patiently for her response. "Joyce, say something, will you."

"Hold on I'll get them in a second." Joyce was still the same money sucking leach since I met her. During our first encounter, she talked about what she needed in a man. She was selfish and self-centered. I bought her everything during our time we were married; she was never satisfied, the more I gave, the more she complained.

I talked to my daughters about their events and trips this summer. "We'll see you soon, Daddy," Tiffany, the oldest, said. "Mama said you left us and moved away."

"I'll never leave you and your sister. I took some work to make a few extra dollars, but my work took me to Westfield for a few months. I'll be home as soon as I complete my work. That shouldn't be too long. I promise Daddy will be home soon."

I hung up the telephone feeling more depressed about the investigation. I couldn't see any light at the end of the tunnel. Proving Zoe's innocence was something that haunted me. The final decision wasn't up to me, but to the court of law. I hated to see Zoe convicted of a crime she didn't commit. I laid on the bed, pondering Zoe's case.

I questioned what really happened the night of Foster's death. I had no way of knowing if she was the killer; I didn't know if I could accept her confession as being true. There was always that shadow of doubt that warns us about a person or place. I thought maybe she did kill Foster and she was looking for a scapegoat. Or maybe she hired someone to kill her father out of revenge, for deserting her for all those years.

I remember very clearly, when I spoke to Zoe, after she had reunited with her father. Two days later, she called me in anger, stating how she hated her father and that she wished I had never found him.

I thought about my built up hatred for my father over the preceding twenty years. I still carry the pain from my mother's death. I didn't know how I would respond if I saw my father for more than ten minutes. I wondered if I could possibly kill my own father. That was a question I dared not answer.

After I ended my telephone conversations, I went to the living room to relax with Ms. Daniels. She's certainly a talker. She found everything to talk about. She knew how to turn a simple topic like the weather into an enlightening conversion.

"You gonna eat somethin', Mosee?"

"No thank you, Ms. Daniels. I had a hearty lunch that's still sitting on my stomach. I'll pass until tomorrow."

Ms. Daniels was certainly an interesting woman. I was too tired to exchange much dialogue. My response was head movements and one syllable words. Being a good listener is one of my strong qualities.

Around nine at night I fought to keep my eyes open. I excused myself and retired for the evening. I had a long day ahead of me. Sleep is what I needed.

I lay in my bed oblivious to the world. I couldn't have been wakened if the sound of fire engines came into the bedroom.

35

A tall lanky man answered the door, dressed in a white tee-shirt and a pair of faded jeans. His hair was braided in cornrows on the top and a close faded hair cut on the sides. When he smiled, you could count the spaces in between his teeth.

"Who is you?" he greeted me.

"I'm looking for Isaiah Jones. My name's Mosee Love," I said handing him my Private Investigators badge. The man who answered the door examined the badge carefully for a few seconds, before he responded. He stood with his arms folded across his chest and his back erect. He looked at me suspiciously.

I spoke up to break the silence. "I'm looking into the murder of Foster Owens. I know you're Isaiah Jones and you were a cook at Foster's restaurant, is that right?"

He looked at me in amazement, with his mouth hanging open. "How'cha know my name?"

"I get paid to get information on people, Mr. Jones."

"Alright, man, come on in, but make it quick."

I followed Isaiah inside the apartment. The living room was very small and well kept. There wasn't a lot of furniture in the apartment, only a black sofa and a recliner chair.

"It's a shame, ain't it. Some body had it in for Foster."

"You have any idea who could have wanted him dead?" I spoke in a voice of authority

"Man, he was always pissing somebody off, especially the men. He flirted with anybody's woman; he ain't give a damn who she was. He was one arrogant son of a bitch. It didn't matter, married, single; he had balls for a senior citizen." Isaiah said chuckling out loud.

"Did you ever hear Zoe make a direct threat against her father in the restaurant?"

"No, but I heard them arguing a lot. I heard her say she hated him."

"Brandy, your waitress for the afternoon heard Zoe threaten Foster in the restaurant, earlier in the day."

His eyes bulged out of his head. He made all sorts of faces, trying to maintain his composure. "Me and Brandy were the only ones in the kitchen when they was fussing. Zoe said she hated him, but she never said she wished he was dead. Brandy and Zoe never got along from the start."

"You think Brandy had any reason to lie about Zoe's statement to the police?"

"You said it, I didn't."

"Did any of his employees have a vendetta against him or Zoe?"

Isaiah frowned, looking at me. "What's a vin ... What ever you said?" Isaiah had dropped out of school at the seventh grade. He could barely read and write. The one skill he had picked up from his mother was her southern cooking. He was cooking since the age of ten. Isaiah knew how to prepare anything from scratch. And baking was one of his specialties.

"It's when someone tries to get even at somebody, because they don't like them, or they did something against the person to hurt them. The person who was hurt tries to get even by being malicious."

"Oh," he said with a grin. "It's when folks try to set you up. They wanna see you fall flat on your face. I may not be book smart, but I know people. I can read a person's mind by their body language.

"Agee had it in for Foster. Foster and Agee got into a bad fight one night. Agee came back with a gun to shoot Foster, abut I talked him out of it. Instead, he used his hands to beat Foster.

Foster kicked his ass. Foster was a big strong man for his age. He believed in exercise, jogging and lifting weights. Him and I worked out together a few times. He was strong as a workhorse for an old man."

"Yeah, Agee had it in for him," he smiled. "Foster took Agee's girl away and fired him. Agee kept coming around after he was fired, hanging around and making threats against Foster."

"One thang for sure, his daughter clashed with just about everybody, the first time she came to the restaurant. That gal had a little attitude, like she thought she was better than us."

"You think Brandy had any reason to lie, to get even with Zoe?"

Isaiah shrugged his shoulders. "I don't know, I just went to work and did my time, man. I ain't had no time for no nonsense. That's women folks gossip. Like I said, I was in the kitchen with Brandy when Zoe and her father were fussing. I ain't never hear her say she wished Foster was dead."

I sat there for a few minutes, taking a minute to make sense out of all the madness.

"Is that all?"

"Thanks for your time, Isaiah."

"Any time, man."

I took out one of my cards and handed it to Isaiah. "You can call me day or night if you come across any information. I shook hands and that was the last time I saw Isaiah. I heard he left town and moved north.

The forty-five minute drive from Tremont back to Ms. Daniels' house gave me time to think about my relationship with Everee. I wanted to find the right words to explain to her that there was nothing between us. I hoped Everee didn't get misled from our brief encounter. I believe in the old adage "keep business and pleasure separate."

Once Zoe's case was solved, I did not want any bad feelings between us. It made me nervous, when Everee talked about changing careers and moving to New York. In my heart I knew I could never consider having a serious relationship with her. The thoughts of all the men she's been with would always be in the back of my mind.

The walls were closing in on me. Suddenly, I felt claustrophobic. There are three suspects I had on my list: Blake, Agee, and Reverenced Elders.

I entered Ms. Daniels house thirty minutes late. There Cedric was, sitting on the sofa on time, prompt as usual, dressed in a linen and silk beige short sleeve shirt and a pair of Bermuda white shorts.

It was five o'clock and I was half an hour late for our meeting. Cedric made himself at home; he was in the kitchen talking to Ms. Daniels while she prepared her special dinner for us.

The table was set with cream linen and matching china in a set of four. There was an assortment of rhododendrons in the center of the table.

Margo was in the kitchen with Ms. Daniels, putting the finishing touches on the meal. I kissed Ms. Daniels and Margo on the cheek.

"Hello ladies, in the kitchen as usual, "I hope you ladies have plenty of food for us growing men."

I gestured to Cedric to come into the living room where we could talk in private. I hated discussing private business in front of a stranger. I knew that Ms. Daniels considered Margo like one the family, but I had my own code of ethics to follow. Ms. Daniels confided in Margo too much, I felt. She was one of those friends that made it her business to pry into ever aspect of your life.

I had spent every waking moment absorbed in Zoe's case. And since her trial was set in a week, things intensified even more.

Cedric sat on sofa next to me with his utensils in his hand like he was about to perform surgery. "Mosee we need to go over everything in detail about each suspect."

"No problem," I responded. Margo and Ms. Daniels came out

carrying food on dishes and serving trays, just as we were about to discuss Zoe's case. "C'mon you guys, dinners ready," Margo said, placing the food on the table. I was overwhelmed, thinking about the smell of good food; I felt like a kid at a candy store waiting to sample the goodies.

I sat in the middle of the rectangular table across from Cedric. Ms. Daniels led the prayer at the dinner table. Ms. Daniels gave thanks to God for the food and all the support she was getting from her friends and church members. She also said a brief prayer for her daughter, Zoe.

"Now, we can all eat. Just help yourselves, I made plenty for everybody."

My eyes shifted from dish to dish. "Boy I don't know where to begin. Everything looks so good. You outdone yourself again this time Ms. Daniels."

"I enjoy cooking and I love to see people eat. I had help from a special friend," Ms. Daniels said shifting her eyes to Margo.

Ms. Daniels smiled proudly. "I hope you boys enjoy the food. I believe in feeding people. No one should have to starve in this country. It's a sin that some folks don't have food to eat."

"I agree," Margo said fixing her plate. "So, Cedric I hear you

A big time lawyer in New York City," Cedric blushed, "I do alright." "What type of lawyer are you?" "I'm an Entertainment lawyer. I handle cases for celebrities,

sports figures. Some are in the music and movie business."

"Boy that must be exciting, huh? You get to meet all kinds of

famous people. I would love to meet folks like that." "They're just like you and I."

"You came all the way from New York just to help Zoe? She

must be mighty special to you."

"Zoe and I have always been friends for a longtime. Coming down to assist Zoe is something I have to do for her. I don't wanna see her suffer for something she didn't do."

I finished my food in twenty minutes. Cedric said laughing, "Man I can't believe you cleaned your plate so quickly."

"This investigation has me running nonstop. You have it easy; you do your research and sit behind a desk all day. I'm risking my life each time I step outside that door." I pointed to my head. "That's how I got this concussion, from that crazy fool, Agee, who tried to kill me. He hit me on the head and sent me to the hospital."

Cedric chewed his food before speaking. "I know you work hard, Mosee. You always justify your work. We all know your job is difficult, but you're not the only one working hard on Zoe's case."

"Ladies, I must get back to work, I have a ton of things to do on Zoe's case. Everything was delicious. I'll see you soon, Margo."

Cedric followed me into the living room to discuss the suspects I had found so far. We went over all the details for two hours, rehashing my steps. After two hours of intense briefing, Cedric sat down with Margo and Ms. Daniels to discuss Zoe's character.

I asked Ms. Daniels if there were any people who could testify in Zoe's trial the following week as character witnesses.

"Well, there're folks from my church who be happy to help out."

Cedric nodded his head.

"I don't mind testifying," Margo said.

"That's fine, Margo. The more people we have the better. I want to prove to the jury that Zoe's a good person, who was searching for her father. I have to show that she would never have the personality to kill anyone."

Frowning, Margo said, "How you gonna do that? It seems so hard, since you ain't got no evidence."

Ms. Daniels looked at Cedric blankly, waiting for a reply to Margo's question.

"I have to use the law to the best of my ability. Nothing is black and white when it comes to the law. When you think you know the law, something creeps up and takes you by surprise. Other parameters govern the outcome of a case; one is money; sometimes the person with the bigger pocketbook wins and the guy with nickels in his pocket loses. And there are the public defenders that can't find a decent job as a real lawyer, so they opted to work for the local government. These lawyers I wouldn't trust to defend my dog in court

"It's a shame Black folks can't get an honest break. You think the law is fair," Margo said shaking her head, "The laws in this country are written for White folks, if you ask me."

"I have faith the lord is gonna free Zoe, but if it's God's will for her to be in jail, then I'm gonna trust in the Word of God," Ms. Daniels said in a humble voice.

I sat on the sofa watching the end of the season playoffs for basketball. I was tired of people waiting for the Lord to help solve their problems. People have to get off their butts and make things happen.

"Trust in God? Please, Emma you act like nothin' bothers you, that's your problem. You act, too good, like you perfect and all.

"Margo, I'm not perfect. I have to put my faith in God." Ms. Daniels had lines of stress on her face and dark circles under her eyes that made her age ten years. She walked with her back hunched over. When I first met Zoe's mother she looked like a fighter, but the stress of her daughter's being in jail had mentally and physically torn her apart.

Monday, at eleven in the morning, Everee came to pick me up at Ms. Daniels house, dressed professionally in a two-piece white business suit. The suit was nice for a change from what I was used to seeing. The suit was a little too short and she wore a lace top underneath that exposed her round bosom. I felt my loins getting swollen, just from watching her walk toward me. "Hello, Mosee, how you like my new business suit? I wanted to dress professional for you today."

"Its nice, Everee," I said with my eyes nearly popping out the sockets. I did not want to discourage her for trying, but if Everee was working for a company, she would be written up and sent home for inappropriate dress.

I got into Everee's car, trying not to show how I felt. I had forgotten, for a moment that she was a prostitute. "What a waste of human potential," I mumbled. I found myself becoming attracted to her vulnerable side; she wasn't afraid to express herself.

"We're almost there boss," she said laughing. "You awake, Mosee? You been awful quiet since I picked you up." "Yeah, I'm just resting my eyes."

After forty-five minutes, we came to a multi-level office complex. The IBM building was divided into five sections. There looked to be twenty acres of land surrounding the building. The parking lot was divided into two sections visitor and employee parking.

"Everee, don't say a word, just follow me and keep your mouth shut," I ordered, stepping out of the car. "I don't have a search warrant, so I have to rely on my old FBI badge to get us in. White folks respect the word FBI. It's like using a nuclear weapon."

Everee walked beside me. "Isn't that badge old?" replied Everee. "People are gonna notice the picture is ten years old. You don't look nothin' like your picture."

"Let's hope in my case, it's later."

We walked up to the building where a guard sat behind a desk reading a newspaper. He interrogated us asking a million questions: who we were and who we wanted to see. One thing about corporate buildings, they're heavily secured. They don't allow you in the building unless you have a valid reason and if you want to visit someone, the guard usually telephones the person to inform them they have a visitor. The security guard's concentration stayed fixed on Everee. I hoped she could distract him long enough for me to flash my FBI badge, without the guard wanting to examine the ID. Everee walked closer to the guard, showing her bare essentials. I took out my badge and held it in the guards face long enough for him to see the FBI symbols.

"Hello, sir, we're with the Federal Bureau of Investigation. I put my ID back inside my jacket. "We're here to get an employee print-out of all your employees who worked on the night of May 25th. We're investigating a murder that happened on that night. We think one of your employees might be involved in a murder."

The guard's eyes widened with surprise. He stood up at

attention. "Sir, I'd be glad to help y'all folks," he said stepping from behind the desk. "I have all the information right back here. Everything is highly secured in this building," he said proudly. I've been employed here fifteen years, and we never had no trouble."

The guard was in late fifties. He had a head full of dark hair, with a hint of gray in the front. He had one of those beer bellies and his pants sagged in the butt. That's something that every male gets when he approaches middle age.

Everee and I followed the guard down a narrow hall, third door on the right, marked private, in capital letters. The room was filled with high technical state-of-the-art computer surveillance equipment.

"Y'all can see we don't have too many problems with all this computer equipment. We can scan every floor and see whose where. And we can see the front, back and sides of every inch of the buildings.

"Each employee has a sledge card to enter the building. We know who comes in and out, at what time, and with whom. The guard pushed a few buttons and watched the computer print out a list of names. "We got over four thousand folks workin' here. I know most of their names most times. I do remember faces, though."

The guard looked at Everee and smiled, "I hate seein' people get away with a crime."

"Thanks, a lot."

"Thanks a lot," I repeated.

"If you need anything else, don't hesitant to see me 'bout anything," he waved.

I reclined backwards in the passengers' seat as Everee pulled out of the lot. "Good work, Everee, I don't know if I could have pulled this off without you."

301

She smiled deeply. "Thanks. I got myself a good teacher. Did you see the way the guard kept looking at me? If he had some money, I could have signed him on as my client. I don't need clients with low paying jobs, its waste of my time."

I wasn't in the mood to hear prostitution stories. I closed my eyes and let Everee continue driving.

I pulled out the two hundred-page computerized report. "I can use this time to start looking for Star Reynolds's name on the list."

"You wanna come over to my place and do your searchin'? You got more privacy over my place. You don't have to worry 'bout nobody nosing in your business."

"Who are you referring to anyway?"

"I don't trust that friend of Zoe's mom. She's always askin' questions. My mama always said 'watch out for a busy body.'"

"You mean, Margo? She's a close friend of the family for over thirty years. She's harmless," I said.

"Whatever you say boss man, but last time I was over there, she gave me all kinds of dirty looks."

Now I realized why I hated working with women. They get too emotional and worry about the stupidest things. Maybe that's why women and men are from different planets. I thought about reading that book when I got back home, "Women are from Venus and Men are from Mars."

"Everee, she's not important. She and Ms. Daniels are best friends."

Everee huffed and buffed like a spoiled child. "Alright I won't make a fuss," she said giving in. "I can help you go over those names; it'll be faster if the two of us work together."

I knew what Everee was pushing for. I had to stand my ground and take control.

37

When I arrived at Everee's house, we spent an hour going through the computerized data sheets, looking for Star's name. My concentration was broken when Everee emerged from upstairs, dressed in a white silk lounging outfit. The two-piece pants set had a low-cut front. She smelled like peaches and whipped cream. I did not want Everee to know she had my attention. I was one step ahead of her game by ignoring her and continuing my research. That's how you get control over women; don't let them know they have your full attention. "You wanna grab a couple of sheets," I said placing a pile on the couch.

"No, thank you, I need to relax for a spell." She hovered over me rubbing my shoulders. I continued looking over the computer sheets.

"You work, too much. You need to relax. Your back and shoulders are tight from stress. She walked over to the leather lounge chair and stretched out. "I ordered us some Chinese food for dinner and I have a bottle of Perrier-Jouet I've been savin' for a special occasion."

"You call this a special occasion?"

"Well . . . I guess so," she said, stuttering. She walked over to me and tossed my paper work to the floor. "Leave that alone for a change; you don't know how to relax."

I hated to admit it, but she was right. I worked too hard on the case; I was consumed in Zoe's case day and night. Sometimes I got four to five hours sleep a night. "Everee, Zoe's trial is less than one week away and I haven't made a dent in this investigation. It's hard when you're working alone."

Everee twisted her lips. "What am I, chop liver?"

"I'm sorry Everee, you've been a big help since I met you, but it's only so much you can do when you're not trained properly."

Everee went to the kitchen mumbling to herself. She returned with two floral dishes and two wine goblets. The table in the dining area was set up in a separate part of the house. The table had matching table cloths and seat pads. The black lacquer table had white chairs trimmed in gold. Everee's house was immaculate and color coordinated.

"Our food should be comin' shortly. After you drink some wine and relax a bit, then you can go back to your work."

I felt a little uptight being in Everee's house. I started regretting sleeping with her. I did not want her to get mixed emotions about me. I understood the female psyche; sleeping with a man meant that you're in love. I didn't let my guard down around Everee, not even for a few minutes. She was trying every trick in the book to seduce me. Women are the sneakiest creatures. I decided I'd used this opportunity to drill Everee about her private life.

"Everee, I was wondering why a pretty lady like yourself don't have a man."

"Why you askin'?" she said smiling. "You want first choice?"

"I was just wondering why you never got married."

She shifted her eyes downward looking at the floor. "I'm kinda afraid of commitment. In my profession, not many men will accept me. Besides no man is gonna accept the truth about how I make my living, I never hear from them again," she said shrugging her shoulders. She finally gave me eye contact.

In the middle of our conversion, someone knocked on the door.

"It's the Chinese food from the Golden Pond," Everee said jumping out of her seat. She rushed to the door, like an excited kid, waiting for her goodies. "Hello there," Everee smiled, taking the packages. "Here, Mosee, you can put the food on the table. C'mon in, I have to get the money." Everee went to the kitchen and came back with a twenty-dollar bill. "Here you are," she said handing him the money.

The Asian man handed Everee back six seventy in change.

"No, you keep the change, please," she said refusing the money.

The man smiled and nodded his head. "Thank you very much, you're kind woman."

Everee sat down at the table across from me. "I think he likes you."

"Well, I'm not attractive to those kind of men."

I started opening the bags of food. "Everything smells good. I might clean you out."

"Help yourself, please, I'm treatin' tonight," she smiled sheepishly, looking at me with seductive eyes.

I took in a mouthful of Chicken Lo Mien. "Your place looks like you don't live here."

"I hate a cluttered house. I usually do my spring cleaning every four months," Everee said pouring the Champagne into the glasses. She lifted her wine glass in the air. "Mosee this toast is for us. I hope Zoe gets out of jail and may we become closer friends. To a man who helped make a difference in my life."

I lifted my glass and tapped Everee's wine glass. I looked at Everee trying to steer the conversion into a serious mood. "Everee what are your plans, after this case is solved?"

"I don't know. I thought about this investigation stuff. That's the only thing that's been on my mind. I need a change in careers. I ain't gettin' any younger; I needs something to fall back on for security. I got me a good nest egg saved up. Maybe I can come to New York and we can work together!" she said excitedly.

"Wouldn't that be wonderful, working as a team? I think that could work. We could hire a couple of people like, Willie T."

I finished my second glass of champagne. I could feel the bubbles working on me; I felt a little more talkative than usually.

"Willie T? He doesn't know anything except how to commit robbery and threaten people for a living."

"What about yourself, Mosee, what are your plans after this case ends," Everee said sipping her drink.

"I plan on opening a Private Investigation firm and teach criminal justice courses at the college."

Everee fixed herself a third glass of Champagne. "What about me working for you?"

I almost choked on the champagne when Everee made that comment. She just wouldn't let go of the subject. "Work for me? That's a generous offer, but that's a little off the wall, wouldn't you think?"

Everee sat erect in her chair, slamming the wine glass on the table. "What the hell do you think I'm doin' with you now! I'm good enough to work with you in this hick town, but I ain't good enough to work with in a big city, like New York, huh?"

I took a deep breath, before responding to her statement. "Everee, I didn't mean it like that, but working in this field requires specialized training, a license, and a permit to carry a gun."

"Yeah, but my Black ass is good enough to work with in Westfield, South Carolina, ain't it?"

She had a valid point. I had to come back with something. I grabbed her hands and squeezed tightly, looking her in the eyes. "Working in a big city can be a lot more dangerous than working in a small town. If you were on a case, I would be worried to death about you," I said trying to sound convincing. "Everee you've been a big help to me, I would not have come this far without you. If business is booming after a year, I'll hire you as my Administrative Assistant."

"Oh! That sounds like a big title, I'd like that."

"We're friends again, no yelling and fussing, right?"

She nodded, pouring me a third glass.

I blocked her hand. I don't need any more alcohol; "I'm a little light headed from the bubbles."

I walked over to the couch kicking off my shoes, and stretching on the sofa. "That's some good stuff you got there. I haven't gotten a buzz this quick with anything I drank before."

Everee walked over to me, gently rubbing my shoulders. She sat in close proximity to me, leaning on my broad shoulders. We sat on the couch talking about our personal lives. Everee gave me a little more detail about herself.

She spoke about why she never had a steady man in her life. She told me she was afraid they would leave. "I never had a stable home environment, so I thought it was normal to have different men. My mother wasn't a shining example for me either. She became attractive each time she exposed more of her personal life to me. I looked down and felt a tingling sensation in my pants.

"Mosee, why haven't you made contact with your daddy? You know you only got one chance on this earth, so make the best of it."

"I've been thinking about making contact with my father since, Zoe's father was murdered. I figured I didn't have nothing to loose."

Everee bent over stroking her tongue in my inner and outer ear. I closed my eyes letting myself float through ecstasy. She thrust her tongue into my mouth as I lifted her on top of my lap, kissing her neck and breasts. Everee's a woman who isn't afraid to let a man know what she wants. A woman making advances first it rare. She took me by the hand, leading me to the master bedroom. She whispered in my ear, "How's this for relaxing, huh?"

I smiled. "Not bad, not bad."

In the bedroom, assortments of candles lite up the room. The bedroom décor was done in soft pastels of pink and white with matching comforter and curtains. The bedroom had a fire place in the middle of the room. Everee's bed is a king-size dark

307

oak canopy bed with sheer curtains hanging from the frame. I looked around in awe at the beautiful fixtures in the room. There were Afro-American paintings on the wall. A sliding glass door led to a patio. I stepped on a wooden stool that was used to climb onto the bed. I lay on the fluffy bed spread; it felt as if I were floating on air. The fluffy pillows gave the bed an added touch.

Everee jumped on top of me caressing my chest and upper body parts. I took off my pants and shirt and tossed them to the floor. We made love off and on all night. The sweat from our bodies created a powerful sweet odor. Everee was in rare form, we were nonstop for three hours. It didn't take me long to fall asleep. Everee tried to wake me one last time, but I was in La La land, snoring away.

38

Insomnia was written all over my face. For four days, I was worried about Zoe's impending trial, scheduled for Wednesday, August 24, eight days from today. I looked over at sleeping beauty, kissing her gently on the forehead. I slipped quietly out of bed and went to the living room to continue searching through IBM's employee list.

I was consumed in my work when I looked up and saw the early sun's rays shinning through the curtains. After endless hours of searching, I realized that Star Reynolds' name wasn't listed as one of the employees working on the night of May twenty-fifth. I couldn't figure out why Star had lied to me about her whereabouts, but she was another potential suspect in the Foster murder case.

My adrenaline was racing now, I felt alive and full of vigor. I remembered getting that feeling whenever I came close to solving a case. It was almost as good as making love. Star made my murder suspect list increase from two to three.

Still, I had one hurdle to jump, finding concrete evidence on one of the suspects. Everything on the suspects is based on motive and opportunity. I still needed concrete evidence to prove Zoe's innocence. Half the battle was won.

I returned to the bedroom trying to come up with a valid reason why Star would make up a bogus alibi. One thing I was certain that Cedric could create a reasonable doubt in the jurors' mind that was good enough to get a verdict of not guilty.

Asa Allen-Showell

All the information gathered from Foster's crime scene pointed to Zoe: The fingerprints on the gun, soiled blood stains from Foster found on Zoe's clothes and the statement from Foster's employee who claimed she heard Zoe threaten her father's life five to six hours before his death.

39

I went back to bed for another hour of sleep. Before long I could hear Everee stirring, and I reached over giving her a kiss on the lips. "Good morning, honey, how you doin?"

"Besides having a hangover, I'm fine."

I sat up in bed, slowly, holding my head. "Everee, just for bein' hospitable to me, I'm gonna fix you the best breakfast you ever had."

Everee smiled, "Sounds good to me. What's up for today? You need me for anything."

"No. I'm going solo today. I plan to visit Star to question her alibi on May 25th. You know the strange thing is I couldn't find her name anywhere on the employees' printout list."

Everee sat up in bed abruptly, looking at me. "What? You got to be kidding! She told me she was working late that night, between 11:30 and 12 midnight. Ain't that somethin'? The lyin' bitch is trying to hide something.

"You can go without me; I ain't fit to go nowhere today."

"That's okay; you can stay behind and rest."

"If you need me for anything, just call or beep me," she said winking at me.

I went to the kitchen to use the telephone in private. "Hey Cedric, I didn't wake you, did I?"

"Yes," he grunted in an inaudible tone. "I've been up all night working on Zoe's defense."

"I discovered that Star's been lyin' about where she was the night Foster was murdered."

"And? What does his death have to do with this woman named, Star?"

I proceeded to explain to Cedric that Channel and Star were

lovers. "Channel dumped Star for Foster. The case of the scorned lover could be used in Zoe's defense. You know, lover breaks off relationship, the case of a lover's revenge. Star takes out her revenge by killing Foster and possibly Channel."

"It's becoming clear. We use her motive as part of Zoe's case. She makes a strong suspect."

"I'm gonna pay her a surprise visit to find out where she was the night Foster was murdered."

"Where were you? I was beeping you last night."

"Over a friend's house," I whispered.

"Any other time you answer your pager. Who is she?"

"It's a long story, man. I met her at the Holiday Inn on my first night here." I put the telephone closer to my mouth. "We'll talk later."

"Alright I get the message; she's nearby. I'll check you out later."

I hung up the telephone and proceeded to make breakfast for myself and Everee. I cooked eggs, beef sausage, pancakes and home fries.

After thirty-minutes the meal was complete and fit for a king. I searched the kitchen and found two serving trays, made of Mahogany. I placed the food on each tray and carried one at a time to the bedroom. I placed the tray beside Everee's bed. "Boy this looks good; I got me a hearty appetite this morning. This food should relieve my hangover."

Sitting with Everee had made me realize she wanted more from the relationship than I was willing to give. Why is it that all women I have a fling with want to settle down, I asked myself.

Everee wanted the romance to go one step further, but she knew there wasn't a descent man who would want her. With the money Everee invested in IRA"S and mutual funds, she thought about starting a new life. She wanted to make a major move, but she was a little scared to start over. After all, she was at a pivotal age when most employers don't want to hire you based on age.

Vicious Karma

She'd be considered "over the hill" in the eyes of America.

Starting over has its complications. For one, she didn't have any skills to support herself. Moving to a big city like New York is a big step. Everee knew that she was only lying to herself, starting over would be a stressful thing. Besides, she wasn't in the mood to start school at this late date. She felt stuck in her world. Still, she daydreamed of hitching up with a decent man and settling down to have a family. She had good looks and people skills. She surveyed her options, but she kept hitting a brick wall.

"What would you say if I came to New York?" she blurted out.

My mouth hung open, looking at her in disbelief.

"Calm down, Mosee I was just making a suggestion. I ain't gonna come to New York cause of you. I' m a big girl now; I know how to take care of myself. I been in Westfield, South Carolina, all my life, and I think it's time for a change."

My words became tangled. "Well, If ... If, that's your prerogative, but living in New York is completely foreign from living in a small southern town. You'll be swallowed up."

"I'm a big girl, Mosee. I don't need a lecture on survival tips."

I wanted to tactfully tell Everee not to pursue the goose chase, but who was I to talk someone out of their dreams? I didn't know if she was serious about moving because of me or if she actually wanted to start over. The last thing I need is a woman following behind me. I'm getting used to freedom, after ten years of marriage, I thought. I'm not about to give my freedom up to any woman, at least not now.

Everee got out of bed, after finishing her breakfast, and walked over to the window overlooking the outside deck. She lit a cigarette. "I know what you're thinking, don't flatter yourself. You think I wanna come to New York 'cause of you." She puffed away. "I have enough money saved to take care of myself; I ain't stupid, I can get some kinda job."

I didn't want to hurt her feelings, but she didn't have a work history, at least not on paper. And who would want to hire an ex prostitute?

"Everee, be realistic, what type of job can you get? You haven't exactly had a legitimate job."

Everee's eyes were fire engine red. She stood there for a moment taking everything in. "I can start a business," she responded.

"Business? I blurted out. "What kind of business, Everee? You have one in mind?"

"Yeah, I have an idea."

"Turn around, please. I'm tried of talking to your back."

"Just drop it, Mosee. This is America and I can move any damn where I please. New York is big enough for the two of us."

She moved in closer to me, smiling. "What about me being your assistant?"

I took a deep breath. "You have no idea what investigation is all about."

"I'm helpin' you out now, so what's the difference?"

"Everee you have to get a license in the state of New York."

Everee waved her hand in the air. "Okay, okay, just forget the whole thing." She sat in bed pouting like a spoiled child.

I wanted to tap dance, having convinced Everee to change her mind. I prayed that she wasn't falling for me. The last thing I needed was a serious relationship. I wanted a steady companion to help ease the lonely nights, but I had too many issues to deal with in my life. Besides, I was enjoying the single life. Suddenly I understood why Cedric had never settled down with one woman.

I grabbed Everee and gently laid her down, thrusting my tongue in her mouth. She wrapped her legs around my waist. "We still friends now?"

She smiled nodding her head. She didn't talk much after that.

40

I interviewed one of Star's neighbors. I was hopeful that someone might have heard or seen something on the night of May 25th. It was a long shot, but what did I have to loose?

The long drive to Star's house gave me time to sort things out in my head. My problems with Everee were another headache I did not wanna face. I thought the best thing to do about Everee was sit her down and discuss our feelings for each other. There was no doubt in my mind that I liked her, but that's as far as I would take it. The thought of her being a prostitute put a sour taste in my mouth. I tried to rationalize about seeing Everee; maybe things would not be so bad if she came to New York to live. At least no one knew her past there. I could lie to my family, tell them I met her in Westfield, South Carolina, and we dated a few times, or maybe I could fabricate a story that she was an ex-cop in Westfield, and I met her during my investigation.

My sister, Dee, would be one hurdle to jump. She had an uncanny intuition. She can read between the lines and decipher the truth. There was no getting over on Dee. She knew whenever I was deceiving her.

The first time I tried to deceive my sister, Dee, was my first sexual experience with one of my high school girlfriends. I remember coming home from a late date with my girl. The following day, I was cocky with an attitude. My sister Dee jumped in my face.

"Boy I'm in charge here, not you," she informed me. "Just cause' you got your little pecker waxed, don't you think you can come in here and take charge!"

I didn't realize my strength, until I pushed her to the floor. Dee was a big girl for her age.

"I ain't having any sex," I shouted. "You think you know everything!" Of course I denied everything, but Dee kept blabbing out around the house that I wasn't a virgin no more. I had become tired of Dee's meddling, so I made my confession. I knew I could not hide my feelings from Dee. She's like a leach, always out for blood. I always thought Dee missed her calling as a talk show host.

I took a deep breath to clear my mind for a moment. The scenic view with its mountains and hills looked peaceful, with the vast green open areas. I was in awe, looking at the scenery. I wondered why Everee would want to come to a smog-ridden, congested city and give up all this. Some people don't know how lucky they are, I thought, shaking my head.

I knew I needed to talk to Cedric about my recent involvement with Everee. Having a close friend like Cedric enabled me to open up. I never pulled any punches when it came to being honest with my best friend, Cedric.

41

I stopped at the next gas station on Rt. 50 to get directions. The sun was beaming down on my forehead, as I stepped out of the car. I unbuttoned my shirt and took off my tie, just until I reached my destination. The temperature was a mixture of cool in some areas and hot in others because of the surrounding mountains. I walked up to the window and asked for directions to the Windyham condominium complex.

The gas attendant's skin was darker than a newly paved road. His processed Jeri curl gave him a back woods look. The Jeri curl style went out of fashion in the early eighties. The attendant wore a yellowish tee shirt and a pair of Jean shorts. He had a distinctive scar on the left side of his face, below his left eye, and down to his jaw line. I concluded that a jealous woman had cut him or he had been in a barroom brawl with some drunken fellow. The attendant stepped out of the comforts of the air conditioned booth, chewing gum like a cow.

"Howdy, there fella, how can I helps you? We self-service in these parts," he said, looking at my license plate.

"I don't need gas," I said concentrating on the man's scar. "I need directions to the Windyham condominium complex."

The attendant felt my gaze on his scar. He took his hand out of his pants pocket and put his hand over the scar. "Well, you ain't that far from the place. You just keep driving about five miles. Once you past the five mile mark you'll see a rest stop on your right. Then you got 'bout one more mile and take a right turn and you gonna see a hill. You go up the hill and that's the place you lookin' 'fore." He concentrated on my car tag. "You from New York, huh?"

"Yes. That's correct."

"I bet that city is a crazy place to live?"

"Sometimes, but I love the craziness." I felt that southern people gave me a sense of respect. Detective Burke had hidden respect for me that he refused to admit.

"Thanks for your time," I said driving off.

Whenever I felt sluggish, I played my favorite, "Share my World," Mary J. Blige CD.

I drove up the hill and made a sharp right, driving through the entrance to the condominium complex. I drove my Volvo through the development for fifteen minutes before coming across 123 Sycamore drive. I parked my car in one of the empty parking spots in front of Star's house. I decided to start with questioning one of Star's neighbors.

I knock on the door for ten minutes. Just as I was about to call it quits, an elderly woman came to the door. "Hello there," she said. "Who is you?" She looked at me over wire-frame bifocals. The old woman had wrinkles on her face and stood about five feet tall in a floral print housecoat. Her gray hair was matted down to her head.

"Hello, Ma'am my name is Mosee Love," I shouted, showing my identification badge.

"I ain't deaf, fool, just old, that's all. I can hear plenty."

"I'm sorry, Ma'am, I didn't mean to offend you." I smiled trying to clean up my act.

"I'm here to ask you some questions about your neighbor, Star Reynolds. I'm looking into a murder case."

"Murder, huh? Oh heaven, praise God!" she said looking up at the sky. "Don't tell me that gal is involved in killing somebody. What is this world comin' to? Folks need to go to church."

"No, no. I didn't say that. Her best friend's been murdered. And there are two other murders that might be connected."

"These young folks are living in sin without Jesus. All the killings wouldn't happen if they just accept the lord as they personal savior." She gave me a stern look. "Young man you

318

saved? Cause I don't let just anybody in my home that ain't a Christian."

I had to choose my words carefully, before answering the question. "Yes. As a matter of fact I did get saved some years ago in my Aunt's church in New York."

She looked me up and down, before giving her answer. "All right, come on in then. My name's Ms. Essie. I can't let sinners in my home, you know," she said walking with the aid of a wooden cane. "Have a sit, young man and make yourself at home. I'm gonna make me some tea. I'll be out in a spell."

A couple of minutes later, she called from the kitchen. "You hungry young man?"

"No. I'm fine. Thank you."

I was at a loss for words, sitting quietly, waiting for the old woman to come back to the living room. I hoped this interview wouldn't take all day, senior citizens can be long-winded. A few minutes later, she emerged from the kitchen, carrying tea and donuts. She sat at the opposite end of the couch. "I live here with my daughter. She's single and ain't got no children. She's waiting to get married, you know." She got up in the middle of her conversion to retrieve a photo of her daughter from the red brick fire place mantle. The fireplace sat in the middle of the living room. It gave the place a modern look. There was a picture of a blue eyed Jesus hanging over the mantle. The living room had a huge cathedral ceiling. I noticed a sunken room off to the right.

"Here's the picture," she said, handing me the photo.

"Oh, she's really pretty. I see where she gets her looks from."

The old woman had a sharp preaching streak in her. She reminded me of my aunt. I remembered my aunt preaching to me about the do's and don'ts of living right. One particular event at the church that went for a week was Revival Week. That was a long religious ceremony to save the souls of the world. I would sit in church until the early morning falling asleep during the second half of the services. My aunt explained the importance of being saved. That's what Jesus died for, to save us from our sins. Saved—saved from what? I thought to myself.

I remember telling my aunt, "How can I be saved, if I live on earth?" Her pastor tried to explain to me what being saved meant.

In any case, I realized I would have to take charge of the interview, before the old woman continued to ramble on about her daughter.

"How well do you know Star Reynolds?" I asked.

"I talk to her some. I know that gal was strange. She never had no man, as far as I can remember. Some woman was always comin' to visit Ms. Reynolds. She's goin' to hell for that," the old woman said coughing.

I showed Ms. Essie a recent photo of Channel. "You ever see a woman who looked like this going to visit Star?"

She put the picture close to her eyes. She bent over to examine the photo, twisting her face like a pretzel. "I seen her before," Essie said shaking her head. "She was always over there, sometimes she'd be over that gal's house for weeks at a time."

"Did you see this woman over at Star's house on the night of May 25th?"

"The old woman shook her head in disgust. "I saw her over there around 5P.M. I hears them fools over there arguing. They was so loud I started to call the police. I hates to hears when people are breaking the law. Who wants to hear all that noise?"

"Do you remember hearing them having any disagreements?"

"Yes, sir, that Star's like a man. She was always bossin' that poor woman around."

"You mentioned that you heard them arguing on May 25th, is that right? Do you recall what time you heard them fussing?"

The old woman sat back down in her chair rocking back and forth, peering over her wire spectacles. "I say I heard those two fussing bout' nine o'clock. I knows that cause Law and Order comes on that time. Yes sir, Mr. Love. What kind of a name is that, Mosee Love? I know your mamma ain't from down south."

Mosee took control over the conversion. "You were telling me about the night Star and her friend Channel were having their disagreement."

"Oh, I'm sorry, honey, I do get carried away sometimes. I watch my show, Law and Order, every Wednesday, unless my daughter has plans to take me out to dinner, shopping or a church function. I stays busy all the time. A woman my age has to stay busy. I hates sittin' round here," she said looking over her wire frame glasses.

"Ms. Essie, you mentioned that you heard them arguing at home between nine and ten o'clock on Wednesday May 25th."

"That's right, Mr. Love."

"Did you hear any particular words that were said?"

"Naw can't say that I did, but I did see Star slap that gal in the face. Sat here and watched the whole thing." Ms. Essie said pointing to the window." Ms. Essie started her preaching up again. "Young folks need religion. I tell you this world would be half bad, but this world is gone crazy. The men are going with the men and the women folks are gonna to their own kind," Ms. Essie said, folding her hands over her chest, like the matriarch mother of mankind.

"Are you sure you heard them argue?'

"Yes, Mr. Love, I may be old, but I ain't senile. I knows what's goin' on."

"Were you able to hear what they were arguing about?"

"They stood outside by the car fussing. I heard somebody say, 'I'll kill Foster, if you leave me for him. I'm the one who helped you; I'm the one who loves you, not him."

Essie stopped talking to get up and walk to the window. "I stood right here and heard them. I opened the window a little, so I could hear better."

"Ms. Essie, I thank you for talking to me," I said, standing up, walking to the window, where Essie stood.

"You married, cause I got a daughter."

"No, thank you, I'm not looking for a wife."

"I just ax cause you a handsome fella."

I smiled. "I'll be leaving now, Ms. Essie," I shook her hand. "Oh Ms. Essie could I use your telephone?"

"Sure, honey, it's in the kitchen hanging on the wall."

I telephoned Cedric in the middle of a meeting at the DA's office. They were trying to get Cedric to accept a plea bargain of guilty and a ten to fifteen-year sentence for third degree murder. Cedric wasn't about to give up that easily for his client. Cedric excused himself to take my call.

"Cedric, I'm over Essie May Johnson's house. She lives next door to Channel's ex-lover, Star. She made a statement just a few minutes ago, that she heard Star and Channel arguing outside. Ms. Essie also heard Star threaten to kill Foster if Channel left her for him. Man, I'm really pumped up. I can't believe how lucky I got."

Cedric spoke in a low voice. "That's good, Mo, I can't say too much here, we can talk later. I'm at the DA's. I've been here since 10 am. I don't want anyone to hear my conversation. lawyers are the scum of the earth. They'll use anything to win a case. I'll submit the subpoenas papers for Star and Essie. You're doing one hell of a job."

I felt that finally I was making progress. I returned to Ms. Essie.

"Boy, I'm getting' a neck ache, from looking up at you. You ever play basketball?"

"In college, but I never was good enough to make the pros."

42

The lines were filled with traveling motorists passing through on vacation to fill their empty stomachs. Children were full of mischief in the line waiting for their food. Watching the families made me realize how much I missed New York and being with my family. I especially missed my sister Dee's once a month Sunday dinner gatherings at her house in the Bronx.

The moment I got back to New York City, I had a list of people to visit: my two daughters and being reacquainted with my sister Shelby and possibly being reunited with my father. I could finally lay the lesbian suspicions about Shelby to rest, since she had found a man. Being in Westfield on Zoe's case, made me think about my father and how short life is. Maybe I should forgive and forget.

There was a twenty-minute wait for the food. The sound of my stomach rumbling made me feel embarrassed that others might have heard it, too. Finally, I was the next one in line to grab a tray. My height made it possible for me to look over the customers' heads and see the assortment of food that lay in the hot trays.

The girl stood behind the counter, looking up at me smiling. "Howdy, sir, welcome to The Cafeteria, today."

"Thank you. Yes, I'll take some of everything: Fried chicken, crab cakes, macaroni and cheese, string beans and candied sweets and a side order of meatloaf."

The waitress helped me bring my second tray of food to the table.

I sat for one hour savoring ever last morsel of food. I ate until I could hardly move. After I finished my double-layer chocolate cake, all I wanted to do was sleep. One of the reasons I never indulged in heavy meals while working on a case, was because it always made me sluggish and lazy.

I drove north, back to Wyndingham condominium complex. I drove pass the section, where Star lived and parked on the opposite end of the street.

I feel asleep, waiting for Star to get off work. I could not believe I had slept through the alarm I set on my watch. Good food always does that to me. I should have known better. I ducked down to keep from being seen.

43

Star's black BMW was parked out front. She walked by my driver's door, glancing down at me, with a look of serenity on her face. I was already caught.

"You're awful tall, there," she chuckled, making fun of how I was crouching down.

"Yeah. I have trouble with door ways, too lately." I smiled extending my hand to Star. "Actually, I dropped my pen and I was sure it was down here. I guess I'll have to use my spare." I couldn't tell if she was buying it. I extended my hand, "Please to meet you Star, I..."

"How did you know my name? I don't know you," she frowned.

"Let me introduce myself. My name's Mosee Love, I'm a Private investigator from the city of New York. My associate Ms. Everee came here to interview you yesterday," I said handing her my identification badge to examine.

She handed me back my ID, looking me over carefully. "What brings you here, Mr. Love?" She asked in an uppity tone.

"I'm investigating the murder of your friend, Channel Peters, and her boyfriend, Foster Owens."

Star stood there with her mouth gapped opened. "Come on in, since I don't have a choice. I don't have anything new to tell you, Mr. Love. I told everything to your assistant, Ms. Everee.

I followed her into the house. "I know, but I'd like to ask you a few more questions, if I may?" I said trying not to sound threatening.

We sat at a rectangular oak table, in the dinning area. On the wall was a matching china cabinet. The cabinet was filled up with expensive china and vases. Star sat in the chair with her legs and arms crossed defensively.

"Get on with your business, please, Mr. Love, I don't have all day. I'm tired from working ten hours today, and I don't care to spend my evening with you, answering questions I've already answered."

"Okay, I'll get down to business. You told my assistant, on the night of May 25th between the hours of 9:30 and 11:30P.M. You were at work that night working on a project. Is that right?"

Star looked away from me. "Yes ... yes I... was working on a project at work."

I pulled out the computerized data sheet from IBM, spreading it on top of the table. Star's eyes darted from the sheets of paper that lay on the table back to me for at least five times. "What do you want from me?"

"The truth what happened that night; There are no record of you working that night."

Star looked down at the table. "I didn't kill Channel or Foster!" she said, raising her voice.

"I understand that, but I'd like to know why you lied about being at work. The print-out shows you never went to work that day. Employees in big companies like IBM use sledge cards to monitor who enters and leaves the building."

"I didn't want no trouble from the police. Channel and I had a bad fight on the night of Foster's death. We ended up taking our fight outside in the front of my house. I know my nosy neighbor, Ms. Essie told you everything. I swear that woman has nothing better to do with her time than to pry her nose in other peoples business."

"What were you and Channel fighting about?"

"Why she left me for Foster in the first place. I begged her to come back to me, but she said Foster made her realize she needs a man in her life." Star bowed her head in shame. "I slapped her in the face, but I wouldn't never kill her or Foster."

"Did you think about seeking revenge against Foster when he

was alive?"

"I told Channel that I was gonna have Foster killed if she left me for him. I was just trying to scare her into coming back to me."

"When did you tell Channel you were gonna kill him?"

Star started breathing heavy. "I don't know. I don't keep track of when I tell somebody something." She scratched her hair, getting a little nervous. "I only said it 'cause I was angry."

"I did question some of your neighbors about your many fights with Channel. One neighbor told me that she heard you two arguing outside on May 15th. That's ten days before Foster was murdered. That gives you ten days to plot his death." I wanted to evoke some emotion out of her now. Sometimes that's the best way to get someone to admit to something—out of anger. People don't realize when they have slipped up and given the wrong information that can incriminate them. It's one of the oldest tactics used, but it still works.

Star jumped out of her seat. "I ain't a killer and I didn't kill Foster or Channel. That scum bag deserved to die. He had a list of enemies a mile long. I wish I did kill Foster first!" Star had maintained her cool as long as possible. "You aren't a real cop. You don't even have a search warrant. You can't prove a damn thing, Mr. Love, so just leave my house!" She walked from the table escorting me to the door.

I didn't argue. She had given me enough ammunition.

44

A note on the dining room table read: "Help yourself to dinner on top of the stove. Hope you like what I fixed. See you when I get back, Ms. Daniels"

I was glad Ms. Daniels had left me something to eat. After all the work I did that day, I didn't have the strength to fix myself dinner. I guess you can say Ms. Daniels had me spoiled. I made myself a meat loaf sandwich with all the trimmings. Afterwards, I telephoned Cedric at the Hyatt Regency. He answered in a good mood for a change.

"Hey, Mo, I thought you were coming over tonight."

"Not tonight, man, I'm, too exhausted."

"All right, so what's new?"

"I have Star on tape making a threat on Foster's life, and I have a witness who heard her and Channel fighting outside her apartment. The neighbors name is Ms. Essie Johnson. She told me she heard Star threaten to kill Foster back in June."

"Just how old is this neighbor?"

"I say about eightyish. Why?"

"Mosee, we can use her, but be aware that the DA's office is gonna have a field day with her. For one, they'll say that she's too old to hear anything, and they'll use her age, too."

"That's silly."

"I know all the tricks lawyers pull, remember I'm one, too. The one thing, I can do to make a credible witness, is to bring in a hearing expert to testify that she has good hearing. One more thing before I hang up how's her sight?"

"She wears glasses, why?"

"I have to cover all angles, that's why. Mosee, tomorrow I need you to bring over the employee print-out on May 25th from Star Reynolds employer."

"All right, Cedric." I was attempting to get off the telephone, in hurry, before he brought up any questions about Everee.

"Wait don't hang up, I thought you were gonna tell me about your friend you met."

I was not in the mood for one of Cedric's lectures. The best way to deal with my best friend is to put him off. "I'll tell you all about her tomorrow when I stop by."

"What time you comin'?"

"Around eleven."

I hung up the telephone, and stretched out on the recliner, watching a little television. The telephone rang five times nonstop I hesitated to answer, but I didn't know if it was an emergency. A million and one scenarios went through my head, as I listened to the telephone ring off the hook. Maybe one of my daughters or sisters were hurt. My nagging thoughts caused me to answer the next time it rang. My conscience would eat me up later, if someone was really dead or hurt.

The telephone started up again fifteen minutes later. Before I could say hello, Burke was on the other end in his usual pleasant mood. "Hello, Love, this is Burke, in case you forgotten, who I am. "How can I forget."

"I met your slick lawyer friend. I hear he's gonna represent her in the trial, huh?"

I hated humoring this man. Kissing up to someone is not something I'm used to. "That's right, and?"

"Oh, just call to check up on you. If I hear you still doin' your investigation, I'll bring you up on charges."

"Burke, I'm layin low, now. I'm officially off the case," I snickered under my breath. "So what's up? Anything new on Zoe's case?"

"Nothing. Love, you're lucky I like you. It looks like all state evidence points to your girl. This trial should last no more than one week. It's an open and shut case."

"We'll see, Burke. One problem you have is those sorry ass men you have working for you." They don't know their ass from their head. The only thing your men are good at is passing out parking tickets. Maybe if you had some decent men working for you, this case would have been solved a long time ago."

The conversation ended abruptly, with Burke slamming the telephone in my ear. I hung up, feeling elated.

I decided to end the night early. I was not accepting any more phone calls. I stretched back on the recliner chair and watched a little television.

An hour later the telephone started up again. Whoever was on the other end was determined to get through. My curiosity made me answer the phone on the third ring. Being an investigator puts you on edge. I picked up the phone, breathing heavy. "Hello, who's calling?"

"Me, fool, Everee, I ain't hear from you all day. So how did the interview go with Star?"

"She admitted to everything. She said she told Channel she was going to kill Foster, as a scare tactic, to keep Channel from leaving her. And she admitted not being at work on May 25th. I also interviewed one of her neighbors, Ms. Essie. She was more than helpful. I call her the neighborhood busy body."

"What!" she shouted. "I can't believe that bitch. She sat there and lied to me. You're good, Mr. Investigator. What's on your agenda for tonight?"

"Nothing. I'm going to stay here and relax tonight."

"I guess that means I shouldn't ask you to come over tonight, huh?"

After, I talked to Everee I fell asleep on the recliner chair. The sound of voices awakened me. I woke up sneezing uncontrollably, which meant Margo was not too far behind. I sneezed again. "Hello ladies," I said in between sneezes. Margo walked over to me, giving me a hug. 'Hi, you doin' sugar?"

I sneezed another five times, as Margo stood hovering over

me. "What's wrong, sugar, you catching' a summer cold?"

"No, I have bad allergies sometimes. It's strange, cause I haven't had any problems all summer. It's one of those things that can flare up at any time."

Margo sat on the sofa, crossing her legs. She was one of those older ladies who had never had any children, single, never married. She traveled a lot and enjoyed her freedom. I could tell she preferred younger men. Her gaze met mine, as if she were giving me an invitation. Older women weren't at the top of my list. Nothing about her looked her age.

Unlike Ms. Daniels, who looked like a grandmother whose attire consisted of house coats ninety-nine percent of the time. And she loved to stay in the kitchen and attend church functions. Ms. Daniels never changed her hair style; she wore her hair pushed back in a bun or one straight French braid in the back of her hair. Looking at a person's house and the way it's decorated tells you a lot about that person's personality. Ms. Daniels still had her original furniture from some twenty years ago with the same plastic covering. She even had an antiquated picture of Jesus hanging over her mantle.

My sneezing slowed down when Margo moved away from me. "What type of perfume you wearing, Margo?"

She smiled. "Why, you like it? It's new, I brought it yesterday--Gardena Roses."

"Your perfume might be making me sneeze. I'm allergic to certain flowers and scents."

"I'm sorry, Mosee, I won't wear this fragrance when I come over.

I got up from my seat. "Margo, please excuse me." I went into the back room.

"I'm really sorry," she repeated, "next time I know not to wear this scent around you."

331

"That's okay, Margo. I'm tired anyway. I have an early day ahead of me."

"By the way, how's the investigation goin' ? They find anything on the people who killed them other folks, yet?"

"No. Not a clue. The killer is good. Not one trace of evidence found. I think a serial killer is in the making. I have to take one day at a time, that's all."

"I hope somebody finds out who killed Foster, so Zoe can get outta that jail. She's a good kid, never hurt a fly."

"I don't wanna see her in jail, either. Cedric and I are working hard on her case."

"How's your friend, the lawyer?"

"He's fine."

"Is he married?"

I wanted to laugh, Margo and Cedric. I knew he would not hear of dating Margo.

"I think he's cute, that's all," she said innocently.

"I'm gonna to bed now. Ms. Daniels I'll see you later," I yelled.

She came from the kitchen, carrying two cinnamon buns on a white saucer, placing them on the coffee table. "Good night, Mosee. See you tomorrow."

45

My pager went off five times on the way back to Ms. Daniels house, Friday evening. The familiar black Mercedes was parked out front of Ms. Daniels house. I was trying to avoid Everee, but she wouldn't give me the opportunity. Parts of me wanted to drive to Cedric's hotel room and hide out, and the other half of me said be a man and face the music. My conscience got the best of me, so I decided to go inside.

My hand started shaking, as I opened the door slowly. There she was, sitting on the sofa in a white lace slip top and a short skirt that outlined her curves. Everee looked at me with those big brown eyes that sucked me in like a magnet the moment I saw her, but I had to maintain control.

"Hello, ladies how are you two doing? It must be my lucky day, when a man comes home to two beautiful women." "You always say the sweetest things, Mosee," Ms. Daniels said. Everee smiled. "I been beeping you all day. Where you been?" I sat on the opposite end of the couch, away from Everee.

"Working, Everee, in case you forgotten, I am a private investigator down here on assignment, remember?" Everee rolled her eyes at me. Good my sarcasm was working on her. Maybe she wouldn't want to see me tonight, I thought. "I wanted to spend some time with you. Don't you take two days off from work, like most people?" "My job is not like most people, Everee. Whenever I get a lead or a phone call, I have to be ready to go at anytime." Ms. Daniels got up and went into her bedroom, excusing herself. "I m gonna leave you two alone. Nice seeing you, Everee."

"I'm glad you're a dedicated man," Everee said, inching closer to me. "I love a man who loves his work."

I moved away from Everee's clutches. She was like a cat in

heat calculating her next move.

"You tryin' to avoid me, Mr. Love!" she said raising her voice.

"Be quiet, Ms. Daniels can hear you."

Everee folded her arms across her chest, sucking her teeth. "If you don't wanna see me no more, then be a man and speak your damn mind; I ain't got time for no games!"

She was right I had to be a man and face the music and stop being a coward.

"Everee, please lower your voice. Ms. Daniels is a Christian woman. She doesn't like cursing in her home." I put my arms around Everee to pacify her. "I haven't been avoiding you, I'm tried and under a lot of stress. I needed time to be alone."

She remained quiet, soaking everything in. Everee studied my face for a few seconds, as if she were searching for something. She inched closer to me, rubbing against my thighs. "You wanna come home with me tonight and release some of that tension?"

I felt a lump in my throat. I couldn't hold back my male instincts; my hormones began to take over. Trickles of sweat dripped from my brow.

I finally, conceded and gave into my urges.

"You don't need me no more in your investigation, huh?"

"Everee, things are getting a little hairy now. Three people have already been murdered. I don't want anything to happen to you, I like you a lot."

Everee leaned in closer, kissing me on the cheek. "Thank you for caring."

We talked for two hours. I felt really relaxed being in her presence. Nobody made me feel special, like Everee. If she were in another profession, like a teacher, waitress, or even a housekeeper would satisfy me. I could not justify to my family that Everee is a prostitute. I could not take all the abuse and humiliation I would have to endure.

"Let's go to my house, Mosee, we can have more privacy there."

"It's getting late, Everee, and I have an early day ahead of me."

"Late? It's only 9P.M. We can stop for a few drinks on the way home."

46

I resisted Everee's female clutches; instead I spent Saturday evening with Cedric, at the hotel lounge for a nightcap. Anticipation of Zoe's final days in court gave me insomnia. Doubts plagued my mind about Cedric winning the case. I knew Cedric had his doubts too, but he hid his insecurities well; he continued to display the highest level of confidence. His confidence was so convincing, you couldn't tell if Cedric had insecurities about the trial.

I spotted Cedric sitting at a round table. He had the word stress written all over his face. "Hey, Mosee, what's up?"

"Nothing, man."

"I can tell when something is bothering you. I've known your black ass for over twenty years. You can't fool me, no matter how smooth you pretend to be."

Cedric gave me a dumbfounded look. "I ... I . . . know I can't fool you. I'm worried about Zoe's trial. I'm not ready for it. I have nothing concrete for her defense."

"Let's take a seat in the back, it's more private."

We sat at the table in the far corner, in silence. "Cedric you're a damn good lawyer so stop feeling sorry for yourself. All you can do is your best."

Cedric put his head down. "I know Mosee. Thanks for the words of encouragement."

"Your problem is that you had it too easy. Every case you took on you always won. That should tell you something."

The waitress took our orders.

"I need all the details of your investigation, so far," Cedric said.

"My notes and cassette tapes are in the envelope."

"I'll look at everything tonight. We need to pray on this one, Mo."

Vicious Karma

I had of hint of hope in my voice. "You think we can win this case for Zoe?"

"I really don't have an answer for you, Mo. I wish I could lie to you, but I can't. This case is going to be difficult for us to prove Zoe's innocence, especially when all the evidence points to her. For one, her fingerprints were found all over the gun. Cedric looked as if he were in deep thought.

The waitress returned toting drinks on a small tray.

Cedric shook his head, picking up his wine glass. "What about the suspects you found?" he asked.

"They're all dead, but I do have four more, which might live through this ordeal. Cedric I strongly believe that all these murders were committed by the same person."

Cedric was an intelligent lawyer and very articulate. Even though his specialty was entertainment law, he still has an in-depth knowledge of the criminal court system. He's a person who always set goals for himself and ninety-nine percent of the time, he achieves eighty percent of what he sets out to do. Since I can remember, Cedric has never failed at anything.

The waitress comes back. "You fellas sure you don't want anything to eat?"

She looked in my direction. "I'll have the Buffalo wings appetizer."

She turned toward Cedric smiling. "And, you, sir?"

"Yes, I'll take the chicken finger platter."

The waitress walked away.

"Tell me your impressions of Foster."

"He was an arrogant man. Not too friendly," I said shrugging my shoulders. "I didn't get the chance to spend too much time with him. I met with him about one hour during my investigation."

"Can you elaborate on your one-hour meeting with Foster?"

"How did he react when you told him he had a daughter, who

had hired you to find him?"

"He thought someone was playing a cruel joke on him. After twenty minutes of hard persuading, I finally convinced him, that I was legitimate. After the initial shock wore off, he seemed genuinely happy."

"What about the people who worked for him. Did they get along with him? Didn't that fella Agee have it in for Foster?"

"I already checked out his story with the police. He has an air-tight alibi. He was working late that night." I finished the remainder of my drink, trying to drown out the reality of the trail. "Blake is another person we can use. Foster owed Blake about twenty grand from a business deal.

"And the Reverend Elders is a prime suspect. His wife was having an affair with Foster."

"I like to use the Rev as a prime suspect in theory along with the others, to prove that there are other people out there who had a strong motive for killing Foster, as well. I'm trying to create doubt in the jurors' minds; that Foster had a list of enemies in line, waiting to kill him.

Cedric picked up his wine and drank the last drop. The waitress returned with our food. The aroma from the food filled the air. I looked like an elated child when his mother comes home from the super market.

After we got our food, I could not think about anything but Zoe's trial.

"Mo, you barely touched your food."

"I haven't been able to eat for the past two days. The only thing I can think about, is Zoe's trial on Monday."

"I'll tell you what, let's visit Zoe Sunday. We can give her moral support, Cedric said. "How's her mother doing?"

"She's holding up; she's one strong woman. She's always going out of her way to help people."

I wanted to close my eyes and pretend that the whole ordeal was a nightmare.

Vicious Karma

"Cedric, I can pick you up around eleven in the morning."
"That's fine, the sooner the better. I have a ton of work to
  do before the trial."

The same gatekeeper was sitting in the booth, when we arrived. The guard smiled and handed us our visitor's passes without question. "I see old red head remembers us," Cedric said. I wasn't in the mood for any interruptions today.

"My aren't we testy, today. Mr. Cool is finally losing it, huh?"

"I break sometimes, too, under pressure. You act like I keep things under control all the time," Cedric said.

"I rarely see you snap, Cedric. You're always Mr. Cool."

I try to maintain a certain amount of self control, but we all break sometimes.

We waited for Zoe inside a closet-size gray room. When she entered the room, she looked pale and drained. Her hair was neatly done for Monday's trial. She sat down with her head bowed down.

Cedric tried to sound positive and confident. "Zoe, everything looks good. I think we stand a good chance of winning this case."

She spoke in a low voice, keeping her eyes focused on a coffee stain on the table. "That's good; I'm not getting my hopes, too high. I take one day at a time in this place."

I spoke up, putting my two cents in. "Your hair looks nice, Zoe." She tried to force a fake smile on her face.

"Thanks, Mosee."

Cedric pulled out his leather briefcase, pulling out papers to prepare Zoe for the witness stand. "I need you to go over these papers. I may have to put you on the witness stand. Some of the questions I'll ask you, for example, are why did you want to seek out your father after thirty years had passed? Tell me what your natural response is going to be."

"I had this curiosity, since I was a teenager, to know who my father was. I only saw him once when I was seven years old."

"Was your mother supportive in your search?"

"No. In fact, she wanted nothing to do with this whole thing."

"Did she try to discourage you?"

Zoe shook her head, slowly. "Yes."

"Zoe when you're on the stand try to answer either yes or no, unless it's an open question. Zoe how did you feel when you found your father? I'm asking that to see your initial reaction. It's important to let all your emotions out. I need the real you. If you feel like crying, do so. Don't hold back anything. Jurors like to see real emotion."

"I was elated. I felt like the happiest person alive."

"Now I need to know what your activities were up until the time your father was murdered."

Zoe lifted her head and took a deep breath. "I really don't feel up to anymore questions today."

"I know, but this is important. I need to go over everything in detail, for my rebuttals for the prosecutor."

Zoe explained everything in detail. From the time she woke up to the time up until the last day she saw her father alive. She started crying toward the end of the story. "Excuse me, Cedric and Mosee; I didn't want you to see me like this."

The officer entered the room. He wore a black and white cap with the words Yardsville Correctional Facility written across the top of it. His face was round and plump. "Y'all finished in here? Her time is just about up, folks," he said smiling.

"Give us five more minutes," Cedric said.

"Sure. I hope everything is gonna work for her. Zoe's been a sweet gal. I hate to see her in this place. Prison can change your whole personality. I been here for over twenty years. I've seen them come and go. Some come in here the nicest women who got caught for something stupid. They never leave the same person. It's like a metamorphosis."

Cedric smiled, trying to remain friendly. "Mr. Love and I are working hard to keep Ms. Owens from going to jail." The guard

341

walked out of the door and closed the door behind him.

"Zoe, I left you a cream-color suit and a pair of matching shoes, your mother picked out for you, to wear on the first day of your trail."

"Remember when the prosecutor asks you about your argument with your father; try not to show any anger. That's what they're going to use against you. Remember, they're going to try and raise any anger or hatred that you may have felt for your father. Don't be fooled by them."

"I'll remember, Cedric. Thanks for everything." She stood up giving us hugs. "It really means a lot to me that I have such good friends like the two of you."

We embraced Zoe and said our good-byes.

48

One of the reporters was a redhead, with freckles to match, pushing through the crowd. He wore baggy tan pants and a white short-sleeved shirt. I wanted to push the reporter, as he stood there shoving the microphone in my face, but I looked closer and saw that the reporter was a female dressed in men's clothing. She looked like a leftover from Gloria Stein's generation.

I looked through the crowd, trying to find Cedric and Ms. Daniels, but they had already made it through the crowd and entered through the front doors. The male-looking reporter stood tiptoed trying to push the mike closer to my face.

"Mr. Love, do you believe Zoe Owens killed her father?"

I shrugged my shoulders. "I don't know you'll have to ask her yourself." I tried to quicken my pace, trying to reach the top of the steps. The redhead was trailing fast behind me. For every one step, she stayed two steps behind. She attempted to question me a second time.

I felt myself get nauseous, suddenly realizing that I forgot to mention a small detail of information to Cedric.

I spotted Cedric and Zoe sitting at the rectangular table up front. I went up to Cedric, whispering in his ear. "Cedric I forgot to mention something that's important to the case."

Cedric's eyes widened with a surprise look in his eyes. "What?"

I bent over closer, leaning into his ear. "I'm not licensed in this state to practice PI work."

Cedric stood up with rage in his eyes. He grabbed my arm pulling me closer into his body. "What the hell do you mean, keeping this information from me until today!"

We walked outside the courtroom, standing in the far corner of the hallway. "Mosee, are you an idiot?" That information is vital to the case," Cedric said pacing the floor.

"Relax will you. Rex is my friend and former coworker at the FBI. I asked him to call Detective Burke to vouch for my creditability. After Detective Burke received the call, from Rex, I was treated like gold, afterwards. I had no trouble from the Westfield police. I had to use my last trump card." I became a little cocky. I chuckled to myself. Seeing Burke squirm was pleasing to me.

I stayed behind watching Cedric go back inside the courtroom. I sat beside Zoe's mother and Margo in the courtroom. Ms. Daniels barely uttered a word. I knew that was hard for her, especially when she's such a talkative person.

The courtroom was filled with women and a few friends of Foster Owens. I kept an eye on anyone who might be out of place.

Cedric sat at a long rectangular table with Zoe. Zoe was dressed in a cream color suit. Her hair was cut shot in a conservative bob hair style. The hair in the front hung just below her eyebrow.

The DA's team sat opposite of Cedric and Zoe. The prosecutor's team consisted of a two males and one female. The woman dressed in a tailor navy and white suit. The woman's hair was pulled back in a bun giving her a conservative look. The fine lines around her eyes showed her age. She had a flawless complexion and smooth skin.

One of the males that made up part of the prosecutor's team, looked to be in his mid twenties. He looked like he just graduated from law school, taking this job as his first. The other male looked to be in his late forties. He carried himself with an air of authority, when he made his opening statement to the jury. Their statement emphasized Zoe's distraught emotional state that she was in, when she found her father. The Prosecution stated that she had a built up animosity over the years for her father abandoning her as a child. The D.A.'s opening statement focused on Zoe's anger that she had carried toward her father over the years for abandoning her. In my opinion, she could have built up animosity for her father. I never got a chance to talk to Zoe about her true feelings about finding her father.

The female DA paraded across the floor. The woman described Zoe as a "time bomb, waiting to explode." She charged that Zoe had carried a vendetta for her father over the years; that she wanted to locate her father in order to carry out the hatred she had felt for him.

Cedric had a tough lead to follow, after the DA's' made their opening statement. He spoke about Zoe's character. Cedric mentioned in his statement that Zoe wanted nothing but love from her father and how she would never hurt her father. Cedric tried to appeal to the emotional side of the jurors. His statement lasted for twenty minutes. I watched my best friend in the courtroom for the first time. I was flabbergasted to see how articulate and detailed Cedric was. He gave a comparison of Zoe's personality as a young girl and as an adult. He was trying to show similarities between Zoe's personal feelings as an adult and as a young girl. She was still the same young girl yearning for her father's love.

Objectively as I could, I listened to each side's remarks. Both the DA and Cedric had valid points and both were very persuasive. The determining factor came to who had enough evidence to substantiate their claim. I felt that Cedric had some valid points. Who would kill their own father in cold blood, after spending large sums of money to find him?

I began to examine my feelings for my father, whom like Zoe's father, had not seen his offspring in over twenty plus years. I knew my hatred for my father was something that was real. Maybe it was possible to kill someone whom you had hated all your life. Having hatred could lead you to doing anything.

I sank in my chair, when the DA's office presented the

evidence from the crime scene: "38" Snub nose Revolver and the bloodstain clothing. Ms. Daniels tried to maintain her composure, but she broke down. I placed my arms around her.

"It'll be okay, just have faith," I told her.

She was silent throughout the rest of the day and Margo spent most of her time outside the building, smoking cigarettes.

Cedric had subpoenaed his witnesses: Blake Reed and Rev Elders. The court gave Cedric a hard time about getting subpoenas for them, but I had made some phone calls to Rex my friend at the bureau. I convinced backward Burke at the police station to put things through. Rex informed him that this case is part of the FBI's case files. Rex informed Burke that the Bureau is working closely with me on the three murder cases.

The Reverend fought up until the last moment to be excused from trial. He didn't want to put his reputation on the line for the case. He had an obligation to his church members and the community. I thought, fuck his image. An innocent girl is on trail for murder and Rev Elder's is worrying about his reputation.

Cedric put Reverend Elder's on the stand first, since he had the strongest motive for killing Foster. The man caught his wife in his bed with the deceased. And he took a gun and shot at Foster, nearly killing him. Now who wouldn't believe that story? The Rev had too much at stake in his personal life—his church. and his reputation. Now if that isn't a strong motive, then what else is? After Cedric had finishing tearing The Rev to shreds, he studied the faces of the jurors, who looked shocked. They each had doubt written all over their faces. I smiled and thought to himself that perhaps we can win this case. Cedric is right about showing the jurors that there are others on Foster's list that had good reasons for killing him.

The jury was made up of sixty percent white and forty percent black, which included five white males and three women, three black women and one black male, ages from twenty-six to sixty-five.

Vicious Karma

Next, Cedric presented Blake Reed, a former business associate and friend of Foster Owens. Cedric drilled Blake on his relationship with Foster and the large sum of money in the amount of twenty grand, that Blake lent Foster to be a business partner in the restaurant that Foster was opening. Because Cedric didn't have any concrete evidence, he wanted to show the court that Foster had a list of enemies, each of which could have killed Foster. Even though, Cedric didn't have anything to back up his theory, he still believed that he could create reasonable doubt in the juror minds.

Blake finally conceded to Cedric's badgering and confessed that he wanted to kill Foster. "That bastard, I helped him get on his feet. I was supposed to be a business partner and he cut me out!" Blake became emotional on the stand. That's what Cedric wanted; to bring out those emotions. Cedric smiled after he ended his questioning with Blake.

The court took an hour recess for lunch. I heard my stomach make unusual sounds. I looked around and wondered if anyone heard.

Cedric and I walked to a nearby deli. He looked around to make sure no one from court was nearby. Cedric stood outside for fifteen minutes. He didn't want any ears around when he discussed Zoe's case to me. Wisely, he didn't trust anyone during court proceedings. He didn't want anyone to take any of his words out of content and use it in the trial against Zoe.

We took a booth in the back of the restaurant, away from the crowd. I ordered a turkey club, with a side order of French fries and salad.

"Cedric, I can't wait until this whole ordeal's over. I'm tried! I can't wait until Zoe can be reunited with her mother."

Cedric raised his glass. "Amen, to that brother." He looked up and noticed Margo and Ms. Daniels waving as they approached the table.

"You fellas mind if we two old ladies join you?" Ms. Daniels asked.

"Sure. Have a seat. There's plenty of room for the two of you," Cedric smiled.

"I'm plum tired. I don't know how much more I can stand. Thank God I have the lord and Margo," Ms. Daniels said, hugging her best friend.

Margo smiled. "I don't mind being here. I'm gonna see this through to the end."

I commented. "You're one lucky woman to have a friend like Margo. She's been a good friend through all this."

Ms. Daniels sighed heavily, with trickles of tears rolling down her cheeks. "I really wanna thank Mosee and your friend Cedric for going through all this work for my daughter. I don't know what I would've done without you two."

"Ms. Daniels, Zoe is my good friend; there's nothing I wouldn't do for her," Cedric said.

"I wish I had some money to pay you and Mosee."

"I'm not worried about money, Ms. Daniels, I'm here as a friend," Cedric said.

I looked up and saw Everee standing at the restaurant entrance. She walked over to our table smiling. She wore a cream color linen suit. She wasn't dressed in her usual hooker attire, thank God. "Hello, Everee come and join us," I said.

"Hello everyone," Everee said, sitting down.

"This is Everee, she's my assistant. She's been a great asset to my investigation."

"Hello, everyone," she said taking her seat next to me.

Ms. Daniels said, "You and Mr. Love have been doin' a great job. I want to thank you, Ms. Everee, Cedric and Mr. Love," she said teary eyed.

Cedric commented. "No problem, Ms. Daniels, I enjoy helping others. I have confidence in myself and Mosee. Your daughter will be free to walk at the end of the trial," he said with an air of confidence.

I prayed that Everee didn't over talk and accidentally slip at the tongue about our casual relationship.

Everee smiled. "Maybe I'll be starting a new business. I'm considering going to New York City."

I sometimes get a mental block when it came to choosing women. I tried to search for reasons why I'm so unlucky when it came to choosing women. Maybe I was suffering from a delayed reaction from my mother's death. You would think I would be emotionally recovered from my mother's death after twenty years, but some wounds take time to heal. I guess I'm a slow healer. Perhaps Cedric was right, maybe my mother's sudden death still had an affect on me as an adult.

Everee gazed at me with her big brown eyes. I tried to keep my mind preoccupied. I quickly turned to Cedric, starting up a conversation. I could feel my best friend had a million and one questions about who Everee really was. He'd been hounding me for info on Everee since he came to Westfield and I kept evading his questions.

49

Court commenced that afternoon during which time Cedric and the DAs spoke for two hours. I shut my eyes the remaining half hour of the trial, after lunch.

Cedric was brilliant in his performance. He tried to persuade the jurors that Foster was not a likeable man. He had a list of enemies who wanted him dead.

Foster Owens was a man who spit on people most of his life. He did not care how he treated others. Now his past has come back to haunt him resulting in—"Karma's. "Whoever murdered Zoe's father is someone he mistreated in his past. But who is a good question.

Now it became clear to me. "What goes around comes around;" treating others badly comes back to you in misfortunate and bad luck. I began to think about my father losing both his legs. Could that be" Karma" he had to pay for abandoning his family?

The trial lasted for nearly three hours. I was glad the first ordeal was over. I went back to Cedric's hotel room since it was centrally located downtown. I stretched out on the bed trying to think pleasant thoughts.

"How did you manage to get an assistant down here?" Did you go to a temp agency?" And why did you choose a woman of all things? Not that I'm being a male chauvinist, but ..."

Cedric continue to drill me, like I was on the witness stand. I wanted to conceal the truth, but unloading my secret would lighten a load off me. I confessed. "I met her at a lounge at the Holiday Inn, on my first night here. She's been a great help to me. I wouldn't have gotten this far if it weren't for her."

I sat up on the twin bed feeling depressed. "I slept with her a few times. It's nothing serious, Cedric, just physical."

"Not the way she kept looking at you at lunch today. I'd say she had that committing look in her eyes. I've seen it plenty of times in women I've dated." Cedric took off his suit and changed into a pair of shorts and a tee shirt.

"Well, I didn't lead her on. We're grown adults."

Cedric yelled from the bathroom. "Well, I suggest you better talk to her again." He came from the bathroom looking very relaxed in his denim shorts.

"What's her occupation, anyway?" Cedric toyed with me. He already knew the answer. Cedric sat on the other twin bed.

"I asked you a question, Mo. Are you trying to hide something? I know when something is troubling you." I inhaled and took a deep breath, looking up at the ceiling. "She was tryin' to pick me up at the Holiday Inn lounge on my first night here," I said in a low voice. There I said it. Boy was I glad that question and answer period was over. He had a blank stare, looking as if he seen a ghost. "What, are you nuts?" You've been going out with a prostitute, c'mon, Mo, I knew things in the romance department were getting a little bad, but . . . don't you have respect for yourself?"

I avoided eye contact with him. I concentrated on the ceiling. "The first call I made to her was strictly business. I was getting desperate, so I needed her help. She's a native of Westfield and knows her way around. She also gave me a contact person named Willie T"

"That ex-con you told me about earlier?"

"Yeah, that's right."

"Man, what can a prostitute do to help you in murder a investigation? I think you been reading too many detective mysteries."

"She and Willie T did help me," I said trying to sound convincing. "I don't have to explain nothin' to you. I don't tell you how to do your job and you don't tell me how to do mine. I think that's fair, don't you?"

351

Cedric continued to look at me in disbelief.

I continued to explain to Cedric my reasoning behind dating Everee. "I called her for help. I was alone down here with no contacts, how do you expect me to get anywhere on this case? She helped me out and one thing led to another."

"Women allow their feelings to get mixed up. When it comes to sex, women think their in love when it's really lust. We men know how to keep our feeling separate," Cedric said sounding like a preacher giving his worldly advice to the congregation on Sunday services.

I felt a lump in my throat again. "You're right; I'll talk to her again." Distance between myself and Everee was the only way of solving the problem. I knew the real reason for seeing Everee. Part of the reason was stress I was experiencing from Zoe's case; I needed to release my tension in some way. Everee had been at the right place at the right time.

After eating dinner with Cedric in his hotel room, I made a stop to retrace my steps. I felt that I missed something during my initial investigation. They always said the best way to find clues was to retrace your steps where the crime took place.

50

I sat in my car, in front of Foster's restaurant. I couldn't explain what had brought me here, but I had a gnawing feeling that something was lurking in all those murders. Maybe it could be pure coincidence that two women died who had intimate relationships with Foster. Why?

The yellow tape was still draped across the front entrance. I went to the back door of the restaurant where I had left the door unlocked, in case I had a need to venture back inside.

I reached for the light switch, but I forgot that the electric was turned off. I took my 9'MM semi automatic out of my holster, preparing myself for unexpected surprises.

My heavy-duty flashlight could light up a whole room. Everything was still in its place: cook ware, cooking utensils, knives, forks and various other kitchen apparatus. The bathroom was cleaned and well kept. The office is a place where everything could be found. There were still papers scattered on Foster's desk. I searched underneath the desk—Nothing. I went back to the restaurant section searching the place over once more. I wasn't able to find anything concrete. The mystery of June 15th was still haunting me.

I pulled out my cellular phone to call Rex, at the Bureau. Rex had been transferred to the Forensics Department. I stayed on the line, until the operator transferred my call.

"Hello, Mosee, how's the investigation coming along?"

"Slow as hell. I haven't gotten a solid lead, since I last spoke to you. I keep running in circles. And my client, Zoe is facing murder charges, for her father's death. Today is the second day of the trail."

"Have patience. You know how long it takes to solve a murder case."

"True. I know all the reasons, but I've been on this case since May25th."

"Did you find anything in common with the other murders?"

"All the victim's were involved with Foster in some way."

"Hum, that's interesting. You don't have any clues, at all?"

"Nada."

"Think, Mosee, I know you can do better than that."

"This case is the work of a serial killer, if you ask me. Every case like this has its similarities, no matter what the evidence is."

I need a favor from you Rex. Can you get your hands on the evidence found at the crime scenes of all the people who've been murdered? I need a Forensics investigation report. Detective Burke is in charge of the murder investigations in Westfield. You can tell him the FBI has an investigation on the random killings. The names of the deceased are Foster Owens, Iris Hall and Channel Peters. He's a small town cop who thinks he knows everything."

"I'll try, but that might be out of my jurisdiction. I'll do what I can, Mosee. If get a chance to do a crime lab analysis on the evidence, you can beep me and I'll call you back with the fax number to send the information to me."

"I really appreciate your help, Rex."

51

It was the last Friday in August. The temperature was mild and sunny. It was too nice to be in a courtroom all day, I thought. You can peel the tension off your skin. I squeezed Ms. Daniels hand, while the DA made their closing argument; once again they put emphasis on Zoe's emotional state at the time she found her father.

Next the defense team, which consisted of Cedric himself, presented his argument to the twelve jurors. He worked up a convincing argument that created reasonable doubt, by bringing up other people that Foster has wronged in some way. He cheated on his girlfriends and stole money from his business partner and treated people unfairly. Cedric brought up the fact that Foster had "KARMA"S to pay for all the wrongs he did to people in his life. There was a list of names that could have pointed to anyone murdering Foster. Also Cedric used Zoe's testimony. "How could a woman murder her father after she went threw all the trouble of hiring a private investigator." When Zoe took the stand, my heart went out to her. She maintained control for a brief time, but then she started sobbing uncontrollably, explaining that she only wanted to reunite with her father and connect with her past.

Eleven o'clock marked the time both sides were finished with their closing arguments. The judge gave his instructions and ordered the jury to deliberate in the back room. We waited patiently for the jurors to come back with their verdict. It felt like hours sitting in the courtroom. I looked down at my watch and noticed it was twelve-thirty. All twelve jurors emerged from the backroom. Everyone took their seats and waited for the final verdict to be announced. I was shivering in my pants. I closed my eyes and said a silent pray. I never asked God for anything. I figured maybe my prayers would be answered.

Asa Allen-Showell

A man in his late sixties came out and handed a piece of paper to the sheriff standing by the judge's podium. The judge opened the paper and read the message. He then handed the paper back to the sheriff, who proceeded with reading the verdict.

Everyone was quiet in the courtroom, anticipating the outcome. I squeezed Ms. Daniels hand closing my eyes. Then a voice spoke. "We the commonwealth of Westfield South Carolina, find the defendant Zoe Owens, guilty of First Degree murder.

There were immediate outbursts in the courtroom. Ms. Daniels yelled and cried out hysterically. "Not my baby, she ain't killed no body. Oh lord help, me!"

I grabbed her to try to calm her down.

Margo yelled, "There ain't no justice for Black folks!"

The church members and long time friends of Zoe started shouting and crying out.

The judge banged his gavel; "order in the courtroom, before unless everyone would like to do jail time!"

Another guard came inside to calm everybody down. Zoe sat motionless at the large rectangular table. She had no expression on her face. Cedric leaned over, whispering in Zoe's ear.

"Don't worry, I'm not gonna give up the fight for your freedom." Zoe sat still, she didn't respond to Cedric's statement.

When I exited the building, there were cameras and press people outside waiting for interviews.

"Sir, excuse me. I hear the verdict is guilty," the round short man said, pushing the microphone in my face.

"No comment, sir," I blurted out. I pushed the reporter down the steps. Sometimes I didn't realize my strength. I grabbed Ms. Daniels by the hand pushing our way through the crowd. I looked up and saw Margo driving up. I grabbed Ms. Daniels hand running to the car.

On the way home no one uttered a sound. Everyone was still in shock over the verdict. I could not believe that Zoe was going to spend twenty-five years in prison. I felt such pain for Zoe's mother. Her only daughter was in jail. She had no other relatives that she ever spoke of. Ms. Daniels continued to sob uncontrollably.

"I can't believe my baby's going to jail. I ain't never gonna see her again."

I grabbed her in my arms like a baby. "Ms. Daniels, Zoe is eligible for parole in fifteen years. Be thankful she doesn't have any previous record," I said trying to sound reassuring. "With good behavior she may be released even sooner than twenty-five years."

"That don't mean nothin'. Can't you do something?"

I paused for a moment before speaking. I didn't know how to respond to Ms. Daniels. She was in a volatile state. I knew there were no words that I could possibly say to ease her pain. "I don't know Ms. Daniels; I've exhausted all my leads. There's nothing to prove Zoe's innocence. Her fingerprints were all over the gun."

"I know you done your best. I really appreciate all you done."

I tried to force a smile on my face. Twenty-five years will be over in no time," I said trying to sound comforting.

When we reached Ms. Daniels house, no one spoke a word. Entering the house, Ms Daniels retired to her room for the rest of the day. Margo and I sat on the sofa discussing the case. Margo was the first to break the silence.

"I cannot believe Zoe's going to prison."

"I know she ain't kill her daddy."

"It's a travesty to find someone who's been out of your life for years and you find them and they end up dead. And then you get blamed for it! That has to be devastating."

The telephone kept ringing for two hours. I wasn't in the mood to speak to anyone, but my curiosity got the best of me. I didn't know if it was Cedric trying to reach me, Detective Burke

or Everee. He was the last person I wanted to speak to. Everee was another person I was trying to avoid. I wanted to cut all ties with her before things got out of hand. I wished Ms. Daniels had Caller ID, or at least an answering machine. That would make things a lot easier to screen calls.

After ten minutes of debating with myself, I decided to answer the phone. "Hello, Ms. Daniels residence, how can I help you?" I said trying to disguise my voice.

"Mosee, I been trying to reach you for two hours, what's going on there? How's Ms. Daniels doing?" It was Cedric.

"Not good. She's been in her room since we came back from court."

"How's Zoe's doing?"

"She hasn't spoken a word since we left court. I think she's still in shock. It'll take a while for everything to sink in."

"I said in a low voice. "How long you plan on being in South Carolina, Cedric?"

"I'll be leaving Monday afternoon at three forty-five in the afternoon. What about you?"

"I'm staying here for a week or two to make sure Ms. Daniels is settled. I feel obligated to Zoe and her mother."

Cedric was irritated. "Mo, we all tried our best. Don't be hard on yourself."

"I know, Cedric, but this case has a place in my heart."

"What can you do, Mo? Nothing. Let it go." Cedric was getting tired of what he considered my pompous attitude. He thought I was under the impression I could save the world.

I wanted to tell him to get off my back. I wasn't in the mood for any preaching. Cedric knew me better than most people. "You're right, Cedric, I'll let the case go. I've gotten too personal with Zoe's case. I have to learn to separate my personal feelings from business."

"I'm glad you're making sense now. That's the old Mo I used to know. I thought you were getting weak on me, man."

I ended my conversation and sat beside Margo on the sofa. She looked at me with a seductive look, the first time I met her at the

Holiday Inn. I thought it was odd how she found me on my first day here, but stranger things have happened.

"Should I stay here for a couple of days?" she asked.

"That'll be fine, Margo, she sure could use all the support she can get, right now. I'll be leaving in a week or two."

"You don't have to stay that long, I'll be here as long as she needs me. I'd do anything for her." Margo suddenly went off on a tangent. "I'm glad that Foster is dead. I truly believe when folks do bad things to others, it has a way of creeping back in your life. He ended up paying for all the evil things he done did to folks. Foster hurt too many people, if you ax me."

"Margo you sound a little personal, like he hurt you in some way."

She avoided eye contact. "No, I just don't like anybody taking advantage of me, especially no men folks."

The telephone continued ringing again. I unplugged the telephone to keep my sanity.

"Margo, I'm gonna go in the back to lay down for a while, I'm sorry I can't keep you company, but I had one exhausting week." I went over to Margo, kissing her on the cheek. She turned her face around, aiming at my lips. I pulled away just in time.

Margo wanted me desperately since the day I met her at the hotel. Although she looked good for an older woman, I wasn't into having a woman who was old enough to be my mamma. That thought made me want to vomit.

I took a deep breath. "Margo, you been a great deal of help to Zoe and her mother. I just wanna say thanks for everything."

Margo smiled. "Well I hope to see you before you leave. Maybe we can have dinner, huh?'

"Sure why not."

"I'll give you my address, incase you wanna come by and visit for a spell. I live an hour away from here, over on Terrace place. I

Asa Allen-Showell

live on a dead end street 142 Terrace place."

52

I managed to get myself out of the house around three-thirty. Slowly I opened Ms. Daniels door to peep in on her; she was still asleep. Next I walked down the hall, standing over Margo, smiling at her as she slept on the sofa. What a dedicated friend, I thought. It sure is hard to find someone like Margo. I felt lucky myself, because I, too, had a best friend that sticks in my corner through all the difficult and good times.

When I arrived at Cedric's hotel room, I got a serious shock. The room looked as if a strong gust of wind had ripped through. Papers were spread over the table and the twin bed. He had clothes spread out on top of the dresser. A half-eaten dinner plate was on a tray in the corner of the room.

"Make yourself at home, Mo!" he yelled through the bathroom door.

"Sure, if I can find a place to sit. I never saw such a mess in my life." I pushed the piles of papers to the side and sat on the edge of the twin bed. I looked around the room and saw empty Corona beer bottles sitting on the table and the floor. "I see you did a little drinking last night?"

"Yeah, I needed to unwind. He grabbed a pair of shorts and a tee-shirt from his suitcase.

Feelings of nostalgia took over me. "Well, Cedric, this is it. I'm going to miss this southern living, especially the food," I said patting my stomach. I must've gained at least twenty pounds since I came down here. I need a crash diet and plenty of hard exercise.

"Don't tell me your thinking about staying here?"

"No. I'm a home grown city boy. I'd never leave New York. Besides my family's there, too."

"I'm going to treat for lunch today. And afterwards we can

visit Zoe one last time," Cedric said. He quickly cleaned up his room. He noticed I had my head down. "Don't look so depressed, Mo, your job is done and the investigation is over. You did your best."

I spoke in a low voice. "Yeah, I know I tried, but I hate leaving things incomplete." I still felt that I hadn't given it one hundred percent.

Cedric packed his legal papers in his black coach brief case. "I forgot the maid comes around straightening up, but I don't want my important papers loose when the cleaning woman comes through this room.

"I cannot believe Zoe's going to jail. I still feel like I'm dreaming. I should've taken the DA's plea bargain and opted for a guilty plea, which carried a lighter sentence," Cedric said in a low voice.

"Man, you did what you thought was best for her at the time, don't blame yourself."

Cedric sighed heavily. "I know you're right."

Emma Daniels lay in her bed wearing the beige dress she bought to wear for her daughter's homecoming celebration. She felt that she was living a nightmare. Ms. Daniels prayed all night asking the lord to help her. She had waited all night hoping for an answer. Maybe God didn't answer her prayers because he had a reason for having her baby in jail. Being a Christian woman Emma understood that God has his reasons for doing things. Emma accepted the fate of her daughter; she figured it was best left in the Lord's hands.

A knock on the bedroom door broke Emma's concentration.

"It's me, Margo. I made you some breakfast," she said standing on the outside of the door holding a tray.

"Come on in, Margo, the doors unlocked," Ms. Daniels called weakly."

Margo placed the food beside the bed on the night stand. She opened the curtains in the bedroom and sat on the edge of the bed.

"I was worried about you." Margo bent over, kissing Emma on the forehead. "I'll be here as long as you need me."

Emma smiled. "Thanks, a lot, I'm not hungry now, I'll eat later. I need to get some sleep."

Margo left quietly and ate her portion of the breakfast in the kitchen.

During lunch, my pager kept going off. When I recognized Everee's telephone number, I turned my pager off, in order to avoid contact with her. I wasn't in the mood for her theatrics. She never gave up. She wanted to spend more time with me. I had to talk to her one last time—tonight to end the romance. I knew Everee was falling in love; that's the last thing I needed. My head was clogged with the outcome of Zoe's murder trial.

"Mosee, your pager is going off, you gonna answer it?"

"Later, not now!" I snapped.

"Alright, alright, No need to get touchy. It must be that woman, huh? What's her name ...?"

I had guilt written all over my face. One thing about Cedric, he knew how to push my last button. Shit! I wasn't giving into Cedric's game.

The waitress came over to the table and took our orders. She smiled extra hard at Cedric, standing in front of him for a few extra seconds. "That's all for now, thank you."

She snapped outta her blank stare. "Oh ... That's all gentlemen? I'll be right back."

"I wasn't prying into your personal life, but I suggest you squash this so-called relationship," Cedric said.

I took a deep breath to maintain my composure. "I know how to handle my personal life. Thank you. At least I know how to have a stable relationship with a woman."

Cedric yelled. "You sayin I don't ?"

"Hush, lower your voice, people are looking at us," I said.

He picked up his soda and took a big gulp, slamming the glass on the table. Cedric carried on like a child who was denied a piece of candy, whenever I exposed his character flaws.

"You're always going out with different women every week and you don't have any children. If you ask me, I think you're scared of commitment," I said, leaning in Cedric's face. I looked up and saw the waitress approaching us.

She placed the food on the table. "I hope you enjoy the meal."

I was the first to chow down on my cheese steak sandwich. "You gonna eat. If not, I'll finish your food."

Cedric sat motionless, staring at me. Cedric felt a tightening in his throat and he could feel his chest rising and falling. "What the hell does a child have to do with my relationships?"

"You're afraid of commitment," I said. 'That's why you haven't settled down with one woman." I paused for a moment swallowing my food. "I think it has to do with your mother leaving you and your father."

Cedric took a bite of his grilled chicken. He took his sweet time before responding to me. "I'm not carrying around baggage from my mother's past." Cedric said raising his voice.

"Hush, people are staring again. Can you have a conversation without getting all emotional about your mother? You're always quick to preach to me about seeing my father."

"At least you know where your father is."

I took the last bite of my cheese steak. "You're forgetting what I do for a living."

"Drop the subject, Mo."

53

After having my late lunch with Cedric, I returned to Ms. Daniels house. I was thrown off balance and confused to see police cars parked out front. One thing that caught my eye was the blue van with the words, Medical Examiner written on the side. I've seen those familiar vans more than I cared to remember in my days as an agent. When the Medical Examiner van comes to a crime scene—it means death. I drove slowly parking the car in the middle of the street.

There was the familiar yellow and black tape draped across the entrance of the house. My mind went blank, but my instinct told me something had gone terribly wrong. I hoped it wasn't what I suspected. Was Ms. Daniels or Margo dead? Maybe the killer found the two of them and murdered them both. Or maybe Ms. Daniels killed the suspect? My mind raced in a million directions.

I rushed from my Volvo making an attempt to run up to the house, but a tall man, with a long black pony tail wearing a white dress shirt and beige Dockers stepped up and blocked my path.

"Excuse me, sir, but only Police personnel are allowed in," he said in a snarl.

"Wait. I . . . I'm staying here," I stuttered. The uniform stepped up closer giving me the Don't-fuck-with-me look.

"Who are you?"

My body temperature was elevating in the ninety-degree heat; I was overcome with dizziness standing in the heat. "My name's Mosee Love. I was assisting Ms. Daniels and her daughter in the investigation of Zoe's father. I ..."

The uniform cop puts his hand in my face. "Slow down, will you? I heard all about you. You the uppity one from up north."

I felt a numbness go through my body. I tried to maintain

control, but my head felt like a bolt of lightning went through my skull. I had to realize I was a stranger in Westfield, South Carolina. I took out my investigator's license and handed it to him. He studied it with intensity.

"Wait here a minute," he said mumbling under his breath.

I studied the movements of the two men. I tried to make out their lip movement. The man dressed in the suit, was shaking his head back and forth. They talked for a few minutes, looking back at me. The man in the suit approached me, introducing himself.

"Hello, I'm Sergeant Williams, the chief investigating homicide detective."

I extended my hand to the Sergeant, who looked at my hand, ignoring my friendly gesture. I was surprised I didn't snap under the circumstances. These cops would love to have a reason to take me to jail. "So you were staying with the victim huh?"

"That's right. I'm the one investigating the murder of her daughter's father." I was growing impatient with these back woods cops. "Please, tell me what happened in there, is she alright?

The sergeant grabbed me by the arms. "Come with me, we wanna ask you a few questions at headquarters."

I snatched my arm away. "You're not taking me in as a suspect!" I yelled.

"Calm down. You're the only witness, who might have some information." The sergeant signaled the uniform to bring around the car.

"Hey wait, you still didn't answer my question, about Ms. Daniels."

"How'cha know she was dead, anyway, Mr. Love?"

"You're forgetting I'm a PI. I also have over ten years of experience working with the FBI. The Medical Examiners van parked out front usually means death. And there isn't an ambulance in sight. I know how to pick up clues, Sergeant Williams," I responded scornfully. "I want some answers."

"You'll get all the information you need in a few minutes."

Vicious Karma

I sat in a small dingy room, with a light bulb that flickered on and off. I sat in the middle of the table with two uniform wolves hovering over my shoulder, whispering to each other. One of the uniforms was a big stocky man, a bit taller than myself. The other was short and pudgy, with a crew cut. One of the uniforms slammed the chair against the wall. The second uniform grabbed a chair and sat directly in front of me. I could feel his breath on my face. I knew what they were doing; I was one step ahead of them. I sat motionless, watching the two men make asses of themselves.

The short pudgy cop shouted. "You kill Ms. Daniels? He said leaning closer in my face.

"No! If I did commit the crime, would I be that stupid to return to the crime scene? I have to be an ass to do something like that, wouldn't you think?"

The other uniform stood behind me, bending over in my ear. "Ms. Daniels was murdered three hours ago. We found your bags and some papers in one of the spare bedrooms."

"I told you I'm a private investigator from New York hired by Zoe and her mother."

The tall cop stood over me with his arms folded.

"Where were you between the hours of three and six this evening?"

"I was out having lunch with a friend of mine, named Cedric Hollis. We ate lunch at the Holiday Inn restaurant. You can ask him yourself." I was getting a little annoyed with these two cops. "Can I please have my things? I need to pick them up."

I could not believe the nightmare I was living. I remembered seeing Ms. Daniels asleep in her bed before I left and Margo was asleep on the sofa. I wondered what time Margo had left. She was the only person left in the house.

The police found her in the kitchen shot in the chest with a "38" There was no witness, just like the others.

"Hey, buddy," the tall uniform said, standing over me. "You know Ms. Daniels very well?"

"Yes, well, no—"

The short pudgy cop got red in the face. He leaned over the table, almost touching my face with his lips. "Which is it? Don't make me mad!" He spat. I wiped my face with the palm of my hand. I felt the after effect of the detective words all over my face.

"I only knew her for three and a half months. She allowed me to stay with her while I conducted the murder investigation of her daughter's father." I kept thinking about poor Ms. Daniels. She was a sweet woman who would do anything for you. How could anyone kill a woman like her?

"What about Margo, you question her, to see if she may have seen or heard anything? She stayed there too, after the trial."

"Boy, don't tell us how to do our job!" the short uniform said spitting the words on my face.

Shit! These bastards don't know who they fuckin' with. My hand felt a bit jumpy. They wanted to see me break under pressure, say something that might incriminate me. I knew better. Cops will go to any extent to push you over the edge. "Look, fellas," I smiled humbly, "I need to look around the house for a few minutes."

The two uniforms walked outta the interrogation room and a third one came in place of the two men. His features were a bit softer. He looked humble and reserved. He was medium height very thin. He sat down at the end of the table.

I thought this cop was more approachable.

"Hello, Mr. Love, I'm Officer James Cox. I'm gonna take you back to get your things out of the house. Ain't that a shame how that poor woman was killed." I was glad this officer was taking me back instead of the other two assholes.

"You kin to that woman who was murdered?"

"No. I was helping her daughter find the person who murdered her father. Mind if I take a look around the house. All this is a shock to me. I can't believe she's dead."

The uniform smiled. "I'm sorry, Mr. Love, but I'm just a flunky in this department. They think I'm too dumb to handle the tougher jobs. If I could help you believe me, I would."

"I appreciate it, Officer Cox."

I had so many things to do: call Cedric and Zoe about the news about Ms. Daniels. Oh, yes that was going to be the most difficult thing to do. How do you tell a woman who has been falsely convicted of killing her father that her mother is lying in the morgue? I didn't know how much more bad news she could take. This might push Zoe over the edge.

I'll take you up front where you can wait outside. I have to go around back for the patrol car." I followed him down a narrow hallway, and through a double set of wooden doors. Everything looked clean and fresh about the place. I could tell the police station was not broken in. There was no noise in the department that made it appear alive. I'm used to people shouting, computers buzzing, and copiers in motion. I would be brain dead working in quite atmosphere like this. No thanks, I thought. "You people don't get much action here, huh?"

"Well … Not really. We may have an occasional domestic violence call or a drunk driver, but other than that it's quiet. This homicide is the first time this towns been shaken up in a long time."

"I would go crazy working in a small town like this. You ought to try workin' in a big city like New York."

James the uniform shook his head. "No thanks," he said in a southern voice. "Most of us wouldn't know where to begin in a big city like that. I kinda like the country myself. I'm too old for that confusion, only if I was twenty years younger."

I waited outside on a bench in front of the police station wondering how cops could work in an environment like this. I liked excitement and action. I enjoyed the country, but my Private

Investigation business would not thrive in a place like Westfield, South Carolina.

I got in the back seat of the police car. I was in deep thought over the tragedy. I wanted to put the case behind me, but Ms. Daniels death changed the perspective of things. I could not leave Westfield now. I needed to know what had happened to Zoe's mother, it was the least I owed to Ms. Daniels memory.

James looked back in his rearview mirror. "You mighty quite, there."

"I'm just thinking about Ms. Daniels and her daughter."

"It's a shame ain't it. All those women dying like that. I hear you used to work for the FBI. That must've kept you busy, huh?

"We had too many cases to solve; there are a lot of crimes that you don't hear about."

"It must've been pretty exciting workin' for them. I wish I had the courage to work for the FBI. I always got bored workin in this town. Sometimes we get something exciting, like these women folks getting killed, but that's rare."

"You could have worked for the FBI, James. They train and groom you so you wouldn't have any trouble. They get people from all over the country. That's what makes it so unique. You get a blend of different personalities, like a melting pot.

54

I felt nauseous as the police car drove in front of Ms. Daniels house. I could picture the vivid images in my mind of Ms. Daniels laying dead. I got out of the police car and walked slowly behind James. I stood at the entrance of the house for a few minutes, closing my eyes taking a deep breath at the same time.

"Come on in, Mr. Love, its okay," the uniform said, standing in the middle of the living room.

"Just give me a few more minutes, please." I walked a few more feet, trying to pace myself. I needed to get my emotions in check. I had to separate my feelings from my professional side. I stood in the middle of the living room scanning it over quickly. Everything was still in place. I went to the kitchen which was adjacent to the living room. The kitchen was very neat. There were two coffee cups in the sink. I went back to the living room, noticing the sofa was sunken in two places. What time did Margo leave the house? I estimated that the suspect waited for Margo to leave the house to make his move.

"You find anything, Mr. Love?'

"No, James. Nothing."

He followed me from room to room, watching me closely. I went to the back door checking for any signs of forced entry. Nothing, Shit! I said under my breath

"She had a neat house, huh?" James said.

I looked at the dining room table, where Ms. Daniels and I had sat having our many meals together. I recalled the warmth she showed me when I first arrived here. "I'm going to the backroom where my bags are." James did not let me out of his sight. I walked toward the backroom where I had once slept.

"Mind if I go in the kitchen and take a look around?"

"Yeah, but make it quick. I have to get going. I don't want anyone snooping up on me. I'm supposed to be back by now."

I felt as though I were violating her private space. The kitchen was Ms. Daniels place of sanctuary. She found peace in cooking and preparing meals for others to eat. In the kitchen the visible signs of white chalk outlined where Ms. Daniels body had been found. The smell of death filled my nostrils. The faint smell of blood filled the air. I scanned the bedroom quickly. "Come on now, we best get goin'," Officer James said.

"Okay, I'm ready. My car is parked down the street. I'll grab my bags." I took one last look around the house quickly, feeling pain and anguish. I wondered what Ms. Daniels last thoughts was when she looked death in the eyes. Living with Zoe's mother for the past three months had given me an understanding of how she lived. Ms. Daniels believed at the time of her death she would be going up to meet her Maker; the savior of man kind—Jesus Christ. Church people have a sense of peace when they're faced with death. They feel as though they made their peace with God. I just hoped she didn't suffer. I thought about her daughter and how she was going to take the news of her mother's sudden death. I stood by the kitchen trying to think of something to convince Officer James to get him out of my sight. "James you better go back to Ms. Daniels bedroom. I think I found something in her closet you better check it out."

"Thanks, Love. You stay here, I'll be right back." I watched him disappear down the hallway. Once he was completely out of my view, I scurried towards the kitchen door, quickly unlocking the door that leads to a small yard.

I managed to finish just in time, before Officer James returned. "Love, what did you see in the closet? I ain't see nothin,' but shoes and women folks clothing."

"I thought I saw something. My fault. I guess I'm tired from all the tragic events that took place."

"Thank you for your time." I extended my hand to Officer

James. "I really appreciate your help."

"Sure anytime. I know how some of these jerks can be. I like helpin' when I can."

I stood by my car waving to him as he drove away. When Officer James was no longer in sight, I got inside my car and threw the bags in the back seat. It was cluttered with McDonald's bags and crumbs. I reached inside my glove compartment and took out a pair of gloves I kept for emergencies. I had to make one final search of Ms. Daniels house for myself. I had to move quickly; I didn't know if any of the cops would be coming back to check on me. I ran to the back of the house and opened the door. Sweat dripped from my forehead, my hands started shaking uncontrollably, as I entered the house a second time. I didn't know what I was hoping to find, that the police hadn't already found. I prayed for a miracle of evidence to surface.

I went back to the bedroom searching the dresser draws. The top draw had hairpins and an assortment of hair products. The second and third drawers had her undergarments and housecoats, neatly folded. The other drawers had sweaters and blouses folded in rows by color. Next the closet had dresses and suits lined up by color. Ms. Daniels's closets were lined with shoes, neatly in a row. I searched the other rooms in the house---Nothing.

I telephoned Cedric at the hotel. I let the phone ring five times. I slammed the telephone down in anger, when no one answered. I locked the back door as I had found it.

I jumped into my car and drove like a manic down the highway. My head was still in a fog; I still could not comprehend that Ms. Daniels was dead. I did not know how I got myself to the Hyatt Regency. I did not remember driving at all. My mind was a blank. I could not feel my legs or hands. Everything was numb on my body.

I parked the car in a zigzag pattern in front of the hotel. I jumped out of the car, barely closing the driver's door. When I arrived at the hotel, I shoved my way through the revolving doors, almost smashing people between the glass doors. I broke out in a sweat, running to the front desk. My words came out in jagged edges, like a worn-out sword.

The front desk receptionist looked at me, baffled. "I'm sorry, sir, can you please speak slowly?"

"Yes. Yes, I'm Love, Mosee. I mean Mosee Love. I need to see my friend—he's staying here."

"What is your friend's name, Mr. Love?" I stood there with a blank look on my face.

"Oh, I'm sorry his name is Cedric Hollis."

She telephoned his room. No answer. "I'm sorry, Mr. Love, but there is no answer."

Just tell him to meet me in the lounge when he comes in." I took a seat in the far corner of the lounge, away from the giggling and happy crowd. I tried to fathom why someone would want to kill Ms. Daniels.

I was asleep in the lounge when I felt the impact of hands on my shoulders. "Hello, Mo, I got your message, what's up?"

I looked at Cedric with glassy eyes.

"What's wrong, Mo, why the sad look. Did your girlfriend break up with you?"

I closed my eyes, speaking slowly. "Ms. Daniels is dead."

"What!" Cedric yelled. "She's dead? How? Why?"

I spoke slowly in a low voice. "Someone shot her in her home. She was found dead on the kitchen floor. "I should've told her to be more careful. I should have seen the signs coming."

Cedric hugged me tightly. I put my head in Cedric's chest. People stared at the two of us in awe.

"You can't blame yourself for this, Mo; you had no way of knowing she was going to be killed today."

"I could have kept closer tabs on her."

"Stop feeling sorry for yourself. We all did our best."

I pulled away from Cedric's embrace. "All right, man, you're right. One thing for sure, there was no sign of forced entry and no struggle on her part. Everything in her house is still neat.

There was not anything moved out of place. So that tells me she probably knew the killer."

Cedric asked. "Did you tell Zoe the news?"

"No I figure, you can break the news to her, since you knew her longer."

"Sure, put the burden on me."

What a mess this whole thing turned out to be Cedric thought, with unspoken words written on his face. He never had a murder trial in his life. He wondered if Zoe should have gotten herself a criminal attorney, instead. After all, his specialty was entertainment law. It is a long cry from criminal law.

"I feel for Zoe," I said. "She's facing a long sentence and now her mother is dead. Ain't that a bitch?" I tried to make sense out of all this. "Maybe it wasn't meant for me to find Zoe's father. Some thing's are better left in the past." That's how I felt about my father.

"Any suspects?"

"Nada. I think the cops in this town sleep, man. Four people are dead and there isn't one suspect. When black folks are dying, the police seem to drag their feet, but if white women were dying instead of black women the cops would have somebody in custody as we speak."

Cedric looked at me with disbelief written all over his face.

I went over everything in detail from the very beginning for Cedric.

"When you searched the house, did you find anything?"

"No. I——."

"Come on upstairs and get some sleep, I know you're exhausted." My body felt limp and lifeless, as if I were dreaming.

"Cedric, can we visit Zoe in two hours? I need to get some sleep. I hate carrying around this burden. I don't want her to get the news from anyone else. Someone might tell her in prison. You know how fast news travels."

After I negotiated with Cedric over who was going to tell Zoe, we went upstairs to his hotel room. I headed straight for one of the twin beds, extending my limp body in a horizontal position. I felt like I gained an extra forty pounds from the stress of Ms. Daniels sudden tragic death.

Cedric agreed to tell Zoe the news about her mother's death. Two hours later, I woke up with a splitting headache.

"I have this throbbing pain in my head."

"I have a couple of pain killers I can give you for that headache."

Cedric went into the bathroom and handed me three Tylenol and a glass of water. I sat up slowly, holding my head. "Here, these should help you."

'Thanks, man, I really need this." Cedric sat on the opposite twin bed. "I was wondering what kind of animal could have done this."

I swallowed the pills. "I believe that the same animal that killed Iris and Channel is responsible for Foster's death. "I've been banging my head against the wall, tryin' to come up with a theory to explain all this, but I kept coming up blank. I even kept extensive notes on the details of each murdered victim."

We drove forty-five minutes to the Yardsville Detention Center.

55

The warden gave us the okay to meet with Zoe in a room that gave us more privacy. Fortunately, the warden thought Zoe was a model prisoner. That certainly worked for us.

She was escorted in the room, wearing a tan jumpsuit. Her hair was still neatly trimmed in a bob from the trial. When she saw Cedric and me sitting at the table like two sick puppies with long faces, she didn't know what to expect. One thing for sure, Zoe didn't need more bad news. She hoped her mother wasn't sick in the hospital, after the outcome of the trail. She hoped we had come to tell her it was a mistrial or that the real murderer had been found and that she was free to go home. I did not want her to jump to conclusions.

She entered the room, smiling. "Hello, fellas, I hope you have good news for me."

I turned my gaze away from Zoe. Cedric looked down at the table.

"What's with the long faces? Did somebody die?"

I jumped outta my seat and hugged Zoe tightly.

"Mosee what's wrong? Talk to me, please. I hate silence."

Cedric got up and sat beside Zoe, putting his arms around her.

"What's wrong?" she asked. "Don't tell me I got more time in jail."

Cedric looked at me to start the conversation off.

"Zoe, something terrible happened today, that's why were here." I looked at Cedric to signal for him to continue.

"Look, tell, me what happened. I can take anything, after being in this hell hole."

Cedric said in a low voice, almost barley audible. "Your mother was murdered today, Zoe."

I looked at Zoe anticipating her response. "Zoe didn't you hear what Cedric just told you?"

"My mother isn't dead, I saw her today in the courthouse. That's ridiculous," she said pushing Cedric's hand away. She started laughing hysterically. "You got proof?"

"Zoe, Cedric and I would not lie about something this serious."

"I arrived at your mom's house this afternoon after I had visited with Cedric. I saw police cars and a Medical Examiners van parked out front. They questioned me extensively about your mother's death." Cedric grabbed Zoe by the shoulders. "Please, Zoe we wouldn't come here to lie to you," he pleaded.

Ten seconds later, Zoe buried her head in Cedric's chest, yelling at the top of her lungs. The guard was standing outside the door, busted into the room. "Is everything okay in here?"

"Yeah, she's fine. Thank you." The guard returned to his post outside the door.

Zoe had streams of tears running down her face. My ... mo. Mother, is dead, How? Why? I don't understand. I saw her today. Please Cedric this cannot be. She's my only family!" Zoe put her head down on the table, crying hysterically.

I went over and sat on the opposite side of her, trying to comfort her, rubbing her back. "We're here with you Zoe. Anything you need, we'll be here for you."

"I have nothing left to live for now," she whispered. Zoe's face looked as if she had aged twenty years, after hearing about her mother's murder. She sat in a comatose state.

I touched her gently on the right shoulder repeatedly, but she did not respond. I jumped outta my seat, grabbing her by the shoulder blades. I turned to Cedric in distress. "I think she could be going into shock."

Cedric hurried outta his seat and went to Zoe's left side, hugging her tightly. She finally spoke in a monotone voice. "I'll be okay, Cedric really, I'm gonna survive."

"Zoe, I don't know why she died, but I promise you I'll find the person who did this. I'll remain here until I find your mother's killer." I could not believe what I had just said. That meant that I would have to stay in Westfield, for who knows how long, with very little money. I would have to hit Cedric up for a loan.

"When is her funeral going to be? Did you tell Rev Reed? He can make all the arrangements. And my Aunt Margo, too," she said in a low voice.

The guard entered the room. "Sorry, but her time is up," he said standing there with his hands folded, across his chest.

"Zoe, call me collect anytime day or night, if you need me."

We both got up at the same time to hug Zoe before she left.

"Thank you. The two of you are really special to me." The cast iron door slammed hard, causing a ringing in my ear. "I feel so sorry for her. First she loses her father, who she only knew for a short time and now her mother is dead. In addition, she's being sentenced for murdering her father. "Life's a bitch," huh?" Cedric shook his head. "We'll go by the church and tell Rev Reed what happened. Cedric said. "I can't handle anymore bad news, right now."

Rev Reed was an average man, about five nine. We sat on a black and beige sofa. Cedric explained to Rev Reed that Zoe's mother had been found dead.

The Reverend bowed his head, covering his face, with his hands. He put his head up slowly, "Dead? Oh, my God, what happened?" The pastor's mouth continued to move, but no words came out. Murdered … My God who could have done such a terrible thing? Sister Daniels never has done nothin' to hurt nobody. She was a sweet woman, always willing to lend a hand.

Rev Reed shook his head in disgust. "Was it a robbery or somethin'?"

"We don't know if it was a robbery. There was no sign of forced entry. My hunches tell me she knew the assailant."

Cedric shifted his eyes toward me, clearing his throat. "She died from a single gun shot to the chest. There are no witnesses or suspects."

Cedric said. "We came here to ask you to plan her funeral."

"Sure. No problem. I'm in shock over this. Sister Daniels was a devoted member here. I'm gonna miss her," Rev Reed said. "I appreciate you coming over here telling me in person."

"Zoe and her mother are our good friends." Cedric stood up and extended his hand to Rev Reed.

I shook the Pastor's hand. "Thank you for helping out."

"Where can I reach you two, when the arrangements are completed?"

"I handed the Reverend one of my business cards. "My pager is on the back; you can reach me day or night. Cedric and I are staying at the Hyatt Regency."

"What's your last name, son?"

"Hollis, Cedric Hollis."

"Her services gonna be held here at the church. I will make everything very special for Sister Daniels. How's Zoe doin?"

"She's holding up best she can. It's hard for her," Cedric said.

"Yeah. I'll keep her in my prayers," the pastor said nodding his head. "Please give Zoe the church's condolences and tell her she'll be in our prayers here."

My mind raced in a million directions about where I was going with Ms. Daniels case? There were no leads no murder weapon and no suspects and witness.

"Why did you tell Zoe, you're gonna find her mother's killer? Come on, Mosee, you've been down here for over three months. Let the police here do their job. You need to go back home and see your family; I know they miss you and what about your daughters?

You should not stay any longer than you have to. Things are getting out of control, Mo."

I knew he was right. The fact was, and I hated to admit it, but I felt that nobody could do a job like me.

I telephoned Burke from my cellular telephone to get some information on Ms. Daniels murder. Hopefully, Burke was in a good mood. Burke answered the telephone cheerfully. "Hello, Love, how's it goin'?"

"Fine, Burke."

"I was expectin' your call, Love," he said.

"Burke, I need to see the police and forensic reports on Ms.Daniels."

"You lucky I like you. Come on down here. Love, I wish you were on my team," Burke said. You're one helluva of man," he said hanging up the telephone.

I dropped Cedric off at the hotel, and I continued on to the police station to check out the forensics report. Burke was buried in paper work, in a room full of stale cigar smoke sitting in the same position when I first met him. He looked up as I stood at the door way entrance. "Love, I'm kinda sorry that gal, Zoe didn't get cleared of those murder charges. It's a shame that her mother is dead," he said shaking his head. "Life can be cruel. This is one tough business. I try to detach myself from my cases; if you don't it'll eat you alive." He leaned back in his chair coughing before taking a few more puffs. "I used to be just like you—too caring. I developed ulcers and crap. No more. I'll be retiring soon, can't wait." He walked around from his desk, opening the door. Follow me, Love. Make this the last time I see you down here. Leave this investigation to us and return to "The Big Apple."

We walked down a flight of steps that lead to a basement. The same gate keeper sat at the desk reading a hunting magazine. He was so engrossed in his reading that he failed to acknowledge us.

Burke cleared his throat to get the officer's attention. "Hello, there Detective Burke, what can I do for you?"

"I need the evidence collected at the Daniels murder. Anything ready?"

"Sure I got something here." Burke turned around looking at me. "Love, the forensics report won't be ready for five days."

We past a dozen rooms, before he stopped. We went to the end of the hallway.

Burke unlocked the box and pushed the contents in my direction. My stomach muscles tightened up, as I proceeded to open the gray metal box. Burke handed me plastic gloves. There were blood stained clothing she wore; a floral housecoat and a hair bow. There were bullet casings found at the crime scene. I swallowed my spit and took my gloves off, placing them in a black metal trash can in the corner. Burke looked at me with intensity, waiting for me to comment. "Burke, I don't see anything here, but after forensics takes a look at the evidence there should be more concrete finding that may help to track down the killer." I took a deep breath, before continuing. "Burke, I'll be leaving here in a few days. I like for you to keep me posted on any up coming news.

56

I felt a lump in my throat and trickles of perspiration dripped from my forehead, as I entered the church with Cedric. It was bad enough funerals are depressing, without wearing dark colors.

In my mind I was obligated and I was determined that I would stay in Westfield a few more days until Ms. Daniels killer was brought to justice. When I decided to take Zoe's case to find her missing father, I hoped the case would be an easy one to solve. But it had gotten so involved.

We grabbed the only available seats in the last pew of the church. I spotted Zoe in the first aisle shackled in handcuffs, sitting beside a sheriff, before I took my seat.

The choir started singing a spiritual hymn. In my head, I counted how many funerals I had attended since my arrival in Westfield. Ms. Daniels made the fourth one in four months. Seeing people die was becoming commonplace for me now.

After the choir ended their song, Reverend Reed made a grand entrance through a back door located behind the choir. He sported a black and gold robe, carrying a gold colored Bible in his right hand. He put the "s" in smooth. He reminded me of a television preacher—very dramatic.

He stood at the pulpit and placed his Bible on the podium. He raised his hands in the air and bowed his head, gesturing everyone to pray. "Please bow your heads and pray in silence for Sister Emma Daniels homecoming," he said changing the pitch in his voice, emphasizing certain words.

Cedric and I bowed our heads. I could not concentrate on the funeral; I was too busy watching everyone in the church. The term homecoming reminded me of my aunt. She had often used the term homecoming whenever someone died and gave their soul to the

Lord. I thought it sounded like God was giving parties for all the dead folks who were saved. I pictured everyone singing, dancing, and eating plenty of fried chicken and buttermilk biscuits with gravy. Reverend Reed raised his head and hands simultaneously in the air.

"Please take your seats, bothers and sisters. This here is a special gathering to give thanks to Sister Emma. "Can I get an Amen?"

"Amen," everyone repeated.

"Amen." A big woman in front of us yelled, nodding her head.

Revered Reed raised his voice with inflections. "Sister Emma has a special place with the lord! Yes, sir. You got to have reservations made in advance!"

"Amen, rev, preach," someone shouted.

"Sister Emma made her reservations ahead of time. I hope some of you made yours already!" he shouted, raising his hands in the air. "You don't know when your time is coming. You can step outside these church doors and get hit by a car and die. So you better make your reservations to get a place beside the lord, yes sir."

"I hear you brother; I made my reservations a long time ago," a man yelled in the choir.

"Sister Emma was a dedicated mother and Christian woman. The lord had bigger plans for her." He pointed to the ceiling as if he was expectin' something.

"Yes, Lord," a woman shouted.

Rev Reed opened his Bible to read scriptures. The service lasted approximately an hour and a half.

Each row at a time got up and proceeded up the aisle to view the body of Ms. Daniels for the final time. That marked the end of the services. Cedric and I were the last one to view the body. Once we reached the front of the church, I gave Zoe a hug, Cedric stood in the background, waiting his turn to give Zoe his condolences. She stood up crying hysterically at the top of her

Lungs. I pulled away from Zoe's embrace to look at Ms. Daniels one last time. Cedric hugged Zoe and told her how sorry he was to have this happen to her.

Margo was sitting next to Zoe, giving her comfort. Margo's eyes were blood shot and puffy. I bend over and hugged her tightly. I whispered in her hear. "I'm sorry, Margo, I'll be around to find the monster that killed your best friend." She closed her eyes, sobbing out loud.

Viewing Ms. Daniels body, lying in a coffin, made me think about my mother's funeral. I could clearly see her face smiling up at me, telling me to be a good boy and listen to my aunt and older sisters.

Cedric tried to break my trance, by tapping me on the shoulder to get my attention. "You okay?"

"I'm fine. I was just remembering my mother's funeral." We returned to our seats in the back of the church. Everyone waited for the reverend to make his final speech. He made an announcement that the church had prepared a little gathering after the burial in memory of Sister Emma Daniels. "Please, y'all come on back here. We got plenty of food."

Cedric gave me an I-don't-wanna-come-back look. Cedric wasn't in the mood to socialize with anyone. He wanted to go back to his hotel room and relax.

I responded to Cedric's nonverbal cues. "We don't have to come back here. I get your message." We've been friends for so long, we could tell what the other one was thinking, before either of us spoke. I bend close to Cedric's ear. "I have something to do, anyway"

Cedric cut his eyes giving me a cold stare. "I hope you're not contemplating about going on with this investigation? "It's done and over with," he said.

I took a deep breath. "I know its over, but I ..." I discontinued my sentence in mid-thought. I did not want to argue with Cedric or raise suspicion about my plans to return to Foster's house that day. "Ok Cedric you're right, but I have to see Everee to say my good-byes to her. So I might not be coming back tonight," I winked.

Cedric laughed. "Yeah I hear you, go and finish your goodbyes to her even if it takes all night."

Cedric and I stood near the church exit, as the choir sang an uplifting song. "I'm not thinking about this case. I know it's closed and there is nothing that you or I can do. I'll let it go," I said trying to sound convincing.

We watched Zoe climb into back seat of the sheriff's car, while Margo stood beside the car, waving goodbye. I told Margo to call me at the Hyatt. I informed her I'll I needed to make arrangements to stay here a few extra days, until I found Zoe's mother's murderer.

After the last car in the funeral procession was out of sight, Cedric and I headed back to the hotel.

Cedric said. "You gonna stop up for a while?"

I did not feel like getting in a heated debate with Cedric. I had one last stop to make before I could officially call off my investigation. I had to retrace my steps, where everything took place. And that was Foster Owens's house. I didn't know what I hoped to gain by going there, but a voice in my head kept telling me to stop there one final time.

"No," I answered. "I'm gonna go on."

Cedric waved goodbye to me. "If I don't see you before I leave town, call me when you get to New York. Don't do anything stupid. You have that hungry look in your eyes."

"I'm not stupid, man, the only thing I wanna do is sleep and get some lovin'."

"Well I'm sure you shouldn't have any trouble with that. Not the way I saw her looking at you. The woman wants you bad."

"Cedric, I'll call you before your plane leaves."

57

I drove up to the ranch style home. They always said if you wanna find the origin of something, start from the roots of where it all began—Foster Owens's house.

I quickly tried the locks on the front and back doors. No luck. I returned to my car and opened the trunk. I reached inside and scrambled for an object that would allow me to break a lock. Underneath the spare tire there was a crow bar and a pair of black leather gloves. I slipped on a pair of gloves, making sure I didn't leave any fingerprints behind. I did not want to give the police an excuse to bring me in. I sat in my car and waited a few minutes for the next door neighbor to go inside the house.

I grabbed the crowbar concealing it in a Macys's shopping bag. I struggled with the lock for twenty minutes, and then finally, the lock broke leading to the kitchen area. I went through the cabinets and refrigerator. I almost fell to my knees upon opening the refrigerator door. There was food left in the refrigerator before Foster's death back in May. The cabinets were lined with an assortment of goods.

The dining room table was made of beige lacquer and black. A ceiling fan hung over the table. And the living room had an olive green Italian leather sofa and a matching chaise lounge chair. I knew Foster had expensive taste. Also there was a black and gray glass metal wall unit. The wall unit contained a variety of women's pictures. I looked over the pictures carefully, nothing registered.

I spotted a hand painted pink and gray chest in the middle of the floor, which served as an end table. I opened the chest and found four photo albums inside. There were old photographs of Foster and his friends in the army.

There was a picture of a short man, standing beside Foster with his arms around his neck. I recognized Ellis Worthington in one of pictures. Ellis still looked the same, just a little more gray and twenty pound heavier and Foster looked the same. Both men aged gracefully. There were pictures of an old Juke joint with Foster and his swinging friends.

I recognized Ms. Daniels in the photo; she was hugged up with Foster in a picture. Ms. Daniels had been one beautiful woman. It was remarkable how Ms. Daniels has aged. Compared to the picture she was a good hundred and eighty pounds and much more conservative, too. Some of the photos were faded from years of deterioration. I figured some of the photos had to be over thirty years old.

There were a few pictures of Zoe, sitting on her father's lap when she was a child. Zoe had to be five or six years old. She looked like a happy child. I remembered times when my father would plan special events for the two of us. The moments were some of the happiest times in my life. I took the picture and stuck it inside my suit jacket, thinking about Zoe. I was dripping with perspiration, from the heat. All the windows were boarded up. Perhaps Zoe would like to have that photo, I thought. I couldn't recognize half of the photos in the album. I was on the third album, when I recognized pictures of Iris and Channel and many other women that Foster dated. Foster was truly a ladies man. It was then that I saw another woman I recognized. My mouth dropped nearly to the floor. It was Margo!

Or was it? The picture was faded and torn. I examined the picture closely, putting the picture in my pocket to examine later.

Next, the bathroom was neat and tidy. The bathroom was done in dark and baby blue colors. The white oval tub was so large it could fit two comfortably.

Inside the master bedroom is a king-sized waterbed, with mirrors above the bed. I looked over at the nightstand and noticed a picture of Channel and Foster. The first top drawers were lined up neatly with underwear and socks in a row. The other drawers

..d sweaters and pants.

The walk-in closet had suits lined up by color. Slacks and shirts were separated on the opposite side. On the floor, shoes were lined up in the back of the closet. There must have been over fifty pairs of shoes of every color. I looked up and saw a shoebox on top of the shelf. There were letters in the box. I sat on the edge of the waterbed and skimmed through a few letters. There were love letters from Iris and Channel. I couldn't believe an old man like Foster could still pull young women.

I looked further inside the shoebox and stumbled across a letter dated in the 1950's. In the letter, the woman wrote she wanted Foster to come back and be with her, promising to do almost anything to get him back. "I can be everything to you, just give me a chance." My eyes popped outta my head, when I saw whose signature was at the bottom—Margo Watson. The letter indicated she was obviously hurt over Foster. My conclusion was that Foster must've left her for another woman, but who was the other woman?

I started drawing my own conclusions. Maybe Ms. Daniels and Margo were intimately involved with Foster at the same time. A million questions raced through my mind. I wondered if Zoe's mother was involved with Foster first or Margo. Did the two women have a rift between them some years before?

I had exhausted all the possible scenarios in my head. I tried to fit the missing pieces together. There were still too many questions that needed to be answered. I sat on the floor, stumped. There were no other women in Foster's past to question. Everyone was turning up dead. The only remaining former girlfriend left was Margo. A light went off in my head.

I looked at the foot of the bed and saw a wooden chest, I tried to open it, but it was locked. I continued to search the room for something to break the lock on the trunk. Nothing. I ran back in the living room, breaking out in a cold sweat. I grabbed my crow bar from the living room floor and ran back to the master bedroom. With little effort, I broke the lock on the trunk on the first try. Inside the trunk were books and mementos of Foster's army days, pictures of his mother and father and a little girl, who probably was his sister. I kept digging further until I came across a notebook of some kind. The notebook was a three hundred-page diary of Foster's life. I sat on the floor and started reading some of the diary entries. Each entry was written by date. I started reading an entry that touched on Foster's experiences boot legging liquor and running numbers with Shep Anderson. Foster kept a detail account of his life in the army and his life as a young kid.

"Damn, pops, drunk again. I swear if he puts his hand on my sister and mama and me, I swear I'm gonna kill the bastard. I don't know what went wrong, but we usd'a have a happy family until pops started hanging out and drinkin that corn liquor. I'm gonna join the army and get away from this place. My little sister wants to go to college and study nursing and get outta this hell hole."

I skipped from the year 1950 to 1960. The current entries might lead me to a clue. Foster wrote about his experiences with fatherhood and his love for Zoe and her mother.

"I know I loves me some women, but I'm sorry for my weakness, I can't helps it. Hopefully one day I can calm myself and grow out of this obsession for women."

I glanced at my watch, not realizing I had been in Foster's house for two hours. I skipped a couple of pages, to the year 1955.

I'm sorry foe' sleeping with Emma, but she came on to me so strong. She had those big pretty brown eyes. She looked so innocent looking. Her hair was pulled back in a long pony tail and she wore dressers down past her knees. Emma always went to church. I swear I thought girls like her didn't do things like us worldly people did. She comes to see me when Margo went to work. She stayed for two hours talkin' bout' the lord and all. She spoke about the sins of man and what we must do to get into ven. I swear that gal was so intelligent. I told her about my childhood and my pops kicking our asses. I ain't never poured my heart out to no woman, before. Margo and me just had sex and went dancing most of the time, but Emma was special. Yes sir.

She came over Thursday when Margo went to work. Margo knew she was comin'. Margo trusted her best friend to keep an eye on me and make sure I wasn't runnin' with no women's. This one particular day Emma came over dressed in her long skirt and short sleeve shirt. We sat on sofa and talked about everything. Well she did most of the talkin', I just listened. Emma moved in closer and started feeling my arm and lookin' in my eyes, like women folks do when they want you. I sat still, not knowing what to do. Emma moved in closer and kissed me on my big brown lips. Lord help me. I thought I died and went to heaven. I kissed her back gently rubbing her shoulders with ease. Emma was a sensitive girl, not fast like Margo. I took her in the back room and we made love. Emma laid there like a zombie. She started crying softly. She said she didn't know what to do. Well I climb on top of her and tell her to relax and let me do all the work. I lick my tongue in her ears and down her stomach to her belly button. She made crazy sounds, I never heard coming from a woman. I turned her over and licked her back down to her toes. Now I figure she was ready for me to do my man thang. I got on top of her thrusting my penis, slowly inside her. She complained bout' how much it hurt, so I stopped and tells her she can come over next week and try again. She got dressed in hurry and ran out the door.

I didn't see Emma for four weeks. I thought bout' her all the time. She was special, not like the other fast women's around here. No sir, Emma was one of a kind. I started gettin' worried when I didn't see her. I ask Margo want happened to Emma.

Said Emma was busy, but she'd be by next week. My heart fluttered, finally, I gonna see my Emma again.

Asa Allen-Showell

After her visit last week, she came over twice a week when Margo went to work. We made love passionately for hours at a time.

Word started spreadin' round that me and Emma was seeing each other. Margo came home early and found us naked as a jaybird in bed. I didn't know what to do. I jumps up and runs butt naked after Margo, but she ran out the front door. She ran too fast. I goes back to the bedroom and tells, Emma to get dress and leave. Margo has a bad temper, she liable to do anything. She might even get a gun and shoot me and Emma. Margo cut me with a butcher knife last month. She gave me twenty stitches on my arm. I tell you the woman is crazy.

I must confess Margo made my life a living hell. I'm sorry I slept with Emma. That was the worst mistake in my life. I had to leave Margo after that. She was always threatening to kill me. She even came after me with a gun, too. When I moved to my own place, she usd'a sit on my porch for hours waitin' on me. Sometimes she had that daze look in her eyes, like she didn't see nothin.' I swear Margo wasn't right since the day she saw me and her best friend in bed.

I had to move out of the area, so I went to stay with my old army buddy, Ellis Worthington, who lived in Denver. He had his own construction business. So I figures I can go work for him and start over. I told Emma about' me leaving town. She cried like a baby. She wanted us to be together. I found I was gonna be a daddy. I told her I can't come back until things cool down there a bit.

I left for four years and came back to be with my daughter Zoe and her mother. Things were going good for the first year. I worked hard and came home every night. No drinking and hangin out in juke joints. I went out one night with my friend, Jr. from work. He took me to juke joint. The pretty women had my appetite goin' again. After that I started sneaking round' with

different women and comin' home late. Emma was patient for

a spell, but she got tried of me and threw me outta the house. She said I can't ever see Zoe, unless I change my ways and get into church. "The lord is the only one who can save you from your sins, Foster.'"

I left Emma and started over again. I Moved out of town for twenty years. I came back to Westfield South Carolina found me a business partner, and started my own restaurant. I felt like I was finally making some progress in my life.

I felt my adrenaline flowing and my heart started racing. I collected my things and ran out the back door to my car and called Cedric at the hotel.

"Hello, Cedric, guess where I'm at? Foster's house." I said answering my own questions. "I came over here to give it one last try. You know me, I can't let things rest, until I give it one final attempt. It makes me feel like I've tried."

"Hold it, are you nuts going into that house. What could have possible find there. The cops already confiscated most of the evidence."

"I had to give it one final try to put my mind at ease. Anyway, stop complaining and listen. I found a trunk with all kinds of shit: pictures letters, and a diary."

"Slow down, Mo, what are you talking about, you found something?"

"I found Foster's diary and pictures of him and Margo and Ms. Daniels," I said continuing to talk at a rapid speed.

"Please I can't make out what you're saying!" Cedric shouted. "All I heard was pictures and diary."

"I found out that Ms. Daniels slept with Margo's man, who was Foster at the time. And Margo was extremely jealous. She carried hatred for Foster after all these years. Foster wrote that he feared Margo."

'So?' That was over thirty years ago. People don't go around carrying vendettas for people that length of time."

"Margo found out that Emma was sleeping with her man, Foster Owens." I shouted. "Are you listening to me? That's your problem. You think your right all the time."

"Where did you get that information from?" he asked.

"I told you, in his dairy. After I dropped you off at the hotel after the funeral, I went straight to Foster's house. I been here for two hours, looking through his things."

Cedric got nervous and anxious now. "I can't believe what I'm hearing, Mo. It was Margo committing the murders, all along, huh?"

"There is no evidence that Margo could have killed the others, but anything is possible. Can you believe Margo killed her own best friend?"

Cedric said. "You need to give that information over to the police."

"Police? Are you nuts? The police might try to suppress the information. I'm going over there myself to confront Margo in person."

"Be careful and remember she's a psycho. I'll call Burke and have him go to Margo's house to back you up."

"Cedric she's the one who killed Ms. Daniels and Foster. I don't know about the others. I took the dairy and a few pictures to prove my theory."

"All right, I believe you, now. I'll call myself a taxi and meet you over her house," Cedric said.

"I remember Margo giving me her address to invite me over to dinner. I think its 142 Terrace Place. I'll find her house. See you there, Cedric."

58

It took me longer than expected to reach Margo's house. I had to stop for directions three times, before reaching her house. I prayed I didn't get a ticket for speeding. If I got stopped, I figured I'd just flash the old federal badge and hope for the best.

Finally, I reached the street where Margo lived. I drove down the long block, which made up ten city blocks.

I tried to remember the description of Margo's house, when she'd first described it, but nothing looked familiar. One thing that stood out in my mind was a swinging chair on the front porch that she described to me.

I drove toward the other end of the block, along the dirt road, until I spotted her burgundy Lincoln Town Car parked in a drive way. My heart almost leaped out of my shirt.

Margo's house was positioned on a dead end street, along with one other house that sat directly across the street. The white rancher had a mini garden in the front of the house. I knew I was at the right house, because I noticed a swinging chair big enough for two. She had a perfect house for the cover of House and Garden.

My shirt stuck to my skin. I felt clammy all over and my palms were sticking to the steering wheel of the car. Parts of my body would go through a reaction, whenever I came close to solving a criminal case.

I prayed that the apprehension of Margo would be quick and easy. I didn't know what kind of psychopath I was dealing with.

The majority of serial killers try to rationalize why they had to kill in the first place. They feel it is their obligation to kill their victims. And they never feel any remorse or emotions for their crimes.

It still didn't register in my brain at the time, why Margo was the main suspect. Whenever I had seen Margo at Ms. Daniels house, she was always calm and laid-back. I sat in my car making sure my gun was loaded and ready. Perfect. I grabbed a box of shells and stuffed them into my pocket. I loathed using guns, only in extreme emergencies.

At that point, I remembered Everee's comment about not trusting Margo. She picked up on negative vibes from the first time they met.

In my ten years as an FBI agent, I had never killed anyone. Sweat poured down my face, as I knocked on the door. No answer. I saw the Lincoln parked in the driveway. I put my ear to the door and heard the television set. I waited five minutes, but no one came to the door. Trying the door, I found that luckily, it was unlocked. Before I entered the house, I had to think of something quick to say to Margo, to eliminate any suspensions, she might have.

I walked into the house shouting, "Hello, Margo! It's me, Mosee. I came by to see how you're feeling. I know it's been kinda hard losing your best friend."

No answer.

I took out my gun and held it in front of me, in case Margo had a surprise bullet, with my name on it. I didn't like surprises; they make me nervous.

I went through the rooms, and still no Margo. I noticed the bathroom faucet was running. I went to the living room and noticed the pillows were sunken in. My instincts told me she was lurking somewhere in the house, but where?

I went to the kitchen and noticed the back door was wide open. I went outside into the yard, where I thought I saw one of the bushes move.

I jumped out of the way just in time. Two shots rang out.

I shouted, "Margo, give yourself up! I don't wanna hurt you. We can make this easier for both of us."

"Fuck you, Mosee. I know you went to Foster's house after Emma's funeral. I been keeping close tabs on you and your investigation."

"Your time is up, Margo."

She fired two shots. "I ain't gonna go to no jail, sweetheart," Margo shouted.

I darted quickly for cover, diving head first behind a red storage bin. Two more shots whizzed by me from Margo's gun.

I leaned against the bin on my knees in the dirt. And then I crawled against a tree. I heard two fire crackers in the air.

"That, bitch stole my man!" Margo screamed out. She was losing it. "I was gonna marry Foster but miss goody two shoes ruined everything. He's was the only man that I loved. I had to kill Emma and the others. It was the only way, the only way."

"But why, kill Iris and Channel?" I asked.

"Cause they were in the way. When I tried to forgive him I told him to come back with me. He laughed in my face, said I was too old. He wanted somethin' younger. So I had to kill cause I was angry. Revenge is the proper word, Mr. Love," she said with bitterness in her voice.

Everything was quiet. I thought, what a perfect opportunity to make my move. I stayed low to the ground, crawling on my knees. I heard a clip sound that told me she was reloading her gun. I saw a tree ahead of me about four feet away. Just as I was about to plot my move toward Margo, another shot fired. I took a chance to leap in Margo's direction, while she rambled on about her broken heart.

"Margo if you turn yourself in and cooperate with the police, they might go easy on you."

"Fuck you," she shouted. "You should've taken your black ass back to New York, after Zoe's trial, but no you had to spoil my plans, didn't you?"

"I was only trying to help Zoe get out of jail."

"Well I ain't gonna to nobody's jail."

I tried to keep Margo talking by stirring up her emotions, in order to keep her distracted. "Margo why kill Emma, I thought she was your best friend?"

"When I heard Zoe hired herself a detective to find Foster that stirred up all the painful memories from the past. So I thought I'd stick around to see if Foster was dead or alive."

I continued to talk to her. "But that's no excuse to kill your best friend."

When I thought I had clearance, I stood up and made an attempt to leap in Margo's direction. Just as I was close enough to grab Margo, I felt a burning sensation in my stomach. I tumbled on top of Margo, wrestling her to the ground. I managed to hold her down, but felt myself getting dizzier by the minute. Margo managed to get on top of me. I screamed out loud, feeling an agonizing pain, like someone was cutting into my stomach with a sharp knife. I closed my eyes and prayed that the police would come soon. Where was Cedric? Did he call the police like he said he would? Was Detective Burke being an ass and refusing to assist me?

I caught the color of crimson dripping from my shirt out of the corner of my eye. I tried to hold Margo down, but I felt myself get weaker from the pain. I tried to open my eyes, but I was blinded from the glare of the sun. I looked up to see the shadow of Margo standing over me, pointing her gun in my face.

She had a crazed look in her eyes. "You had to go and stick your nose in other people's business"

I tried to form words to express myself, but no words came out. I felt myself get weaker. I knew that I would surly die if help didn't come soon.

I could barley hear what Margo was saying. I felt myself

starting to slip out of consciousness. "Margo, please turn yourself in," I mumbled.

Flashbacks of my ex-wife and kids raced trough my mind. I was sorry I wouldn't be around to make my daughters' weddings or their college graduations. I thought about the relationship I could have established with my father, if I hadn't been so bullheaded. As the pain intensified, I thought about all the things I was going to miss in my life.

"Just turn yourself in," I mumbled.

Before I could complete my sentence, Margo yelled, "You crazy fool. I ain't gonna to no jail. I loved Foster, but that damn, Emma had to take my man. She's always actin' like she some goody two shoes. I knows she ain't nothin' but a snake!" Margo shouted with tears rolling down her cheek. "I didn't mean to kill the other two women, but they one of the reasons my man didn't come back to me."

Margo bowed her head in silence, pointing the gun away from me.

Burke yelled. "Put the gun down Margo and come with us. I know it was you doin' all those killings," he said breaking her trance.

"Fuck you cops!" she yelled resuming her aim at me. I tried to focus on Margo, but she was becoming a haze.

Burke signaled for his men to go around the house, while he tried to distract her. He started talking about Emma and Foster and her relationship. Margo felt tense and confused. She proceeded to talk about herself and Foster and their former life together. She talked on getting emotional. Burke seized the opportunity, and shot Margo in the shoulder blade. She dropped the gun and one of Burke's men ran and tackled Margo to the ground.

Burke came over to check on me. "You okay, Love? Just hold on, an ambulance is coming soon."

I was slurring badly. "I'm . . . I'm fi...fine, it's just a flesh wound."

Burke bent over, holding my hand. "You gonna be fine once you go to the hospital," he said in a reassuring voice.

I felt myself unable to speak. I looked up and thought I saw Cedric standing over me, but everything looked unreal to me. Cedric got on his knees, bending over me. "Hey, Mo, you, okay? You're a big man; I know you'll be fine. You're a fighter." The tall uniform put cuffs on Margo and escorted her to the parole car. Cedric said. "You did good, Mo. I had a feeling you were still workin' on Zoe's case." "No, I'm ..." I couldn't form my words. "Shush, save your strength."